The Off-Chance of Me and You

The Reyes Siblings
Book 1

Anj Miranda

ISBN: 978-621-06-1037-6

Edited by Jennia D'Lima
Cover art by Aya Zafe

Published by Anj Miranda
Quezon City, Philippines
anjmirandawrites@gmail.com

www.anjmiranda.com

Contents

For my family,
who gave me the courage to dream
and the support to turn my dream into reality.

Prologue

tagpuan – (n) meeting place

SEVEN YEARS AGO

Tala

Even the trees looked different here.

They reminded me of the palm trees we had in the Philippines, only they weren't as tall. The trunks spanned wider across, their leaves shorter and broader. Similar, but not the same.

Drawn to that semblance of home, I crossed the street and wandered to the clearing between the not-quite-palm trees and an old two-story building. A small garden was nestled beyond it. I checked for a fence or a sign, any hint that it was private property. Nothing. I walked in, needing the silence and solitude it offered.

Wild vines creeped all the way up one wall, while windows covered the other, their glass dark and wavy. I followed the brick path to the center of the square space where an antique fountain stood, its three tiers half-filled with murky green-brown water. The farther I walked, the fainter the sound of passing cars grew, replaced by the gentle rustling of leaves.

Here, I could finally breathe. No eyes judged me. No laughter made me wonder if I was the punchline of someone else's joke. I could just be. I could dance like no one was watching—because no one was.

It was the best feeling in the world.

Dumping my bag on the lone chair, I pulled out my phone and put on some music.

I didn't know how long I danced. I was free to keep going as long as I wanted. But then a figure on the reflective window-panes caught my eye.

My breath lodged in my throat. I spun around and stared at the boy striding toward me from the garden path. As he neared, I realized he was at least a foot taller than me, with short dark blond hair and broad shoulders that stretched the material of his shirt. He had that muscled build that screamed *athlete*. Add in his clean-shaven face and high-bridged nose, and he probably had all the girls looking twice.

If only he wasn't scowling.

"What are you doing here?" he demanded, narrowing his light-colored eyes on me.

I shifted my feet. "Ah, I was just...dancing?"

Spotting the phone that I left on top of my bag, he reached out and stopped the music without bothering to ask my permission. "How'd you find this place?"

I winced. "I was exploring the campus and ended up here."

"This isn't part of campus."

"I know—"

"You shouldn't be here," he said in a louder voice.

Pressing my lips together, I swallowed. Nodded. "I'm sorry. I'll go."

My backpack felt heavier in my hand as I picked it up and

swung it onto my shoulder. The disdain on the boy's face weighed me down.

No way would I beg to stay where I wasn't welcome. Maybe I should have argued, but he looked like he could over-power me without breaking a sweat. I knew what could happen to a girl alone with a boy in an isolated place—and here, I had no one at all to call for help.

So, I dropped my eyes and walked away.

"Wait," he called out.

My shoulders grew tenser. I turned to face him, but my legs were prepared to run.

He approached me and held out a familiar metallic rectangle. "You forgot your phone."

"Oh." A breath whooshed out of me. I took the phone, care-fully avoiding any physical contact. "Thanks."

As I turned to leave again, he said, "Are you always polite to assholes?"

I did a double take. "I wasn't—I mean, you're not..."

Shrugging, he gave me a half smile. Was I imagining it or did he look a bit...sheepish? "You were, and I was," he admitted. "I'm sorry. I promise I'm not usually an ass. I was just surprised to find you here. It's kind of my getaway and I never see anyone else come around."

I was too busy processing his words to answer.

"What's your name?" he asked abruptly.

Should I tell him the truth? Or was it better to just leave? He didn't seem like a threat, but wasn't that what made serial killers so effective?

I scoffed at my paranoia. "Tala," I said. "My name is Tala."

He repeated it. With his accent, my name came out as *tuh-luh* instead of *ta-la*. "I'm Jason."

I tried to stay still and keep my nerves from showing even

3

though my heart was racing. "What sport do you play?" I blurted out without thinking.

Immediately, my cheeks burned.

Why did I ask that? I didn't even know this guy.

The corner of his mouth twitched. "What makes you think I play one?"

Up close, I could tell that his eyes were blue. They twinkled as if daring me to tell him how ridiculously fit his body was.

Keep your eyes on his face, Tala.

"You look..." Against my better judgment, my gaze drifted across his strong chest to his flat stomach.

He chuckled, and my eyes flew up to meet his.

"Fit," I almost shouted. Then I groaned out loud.

His laughter sounded musical.

"Please forget this happened. I'm going now." Mortified, I turned to leave.

He caught my wrist in a gentle yet firm hold, then let me go as soon as I faced him again. "C'mon, stay. This space is big enough for the two of us. I'll even tell you what sport keeps me so...fit."

"Is it basketball?"

The smile that broke across his face made my breath hitch. "How'd you guess?"

"You're tall. And you have big hands." My eyes widened. I did not just say that. Would someone please beam me straight back to Manila right now?

Laughing, he said, "You know what, dance girl? I like you."

Despite my mortification, I thought I liked him too.

1

Ate – (n) older sister

Tala

"Yes, yes!"

I fought back a groan as my younger sister Luna shouted at the television for what felt like the thousandth time.

"Get that ball, Miles!" Luna yelled.

Fighting the urge to look at the TV, I kept my eyes fixed on my laptop, where a digital version of myself stumbled in the middle of a dance routine. Another clip to add to my bloopers video. As embarrassing as it was to post myself tripping over my own two feet, those clips brought in better engagement. It showed my audience a more personal side of me. Made me more relatable—or so Luna said.

"Yeah, Jason!"

My head snapped up at the name, just in time to watch number sixteen sink in a three-pointer.

Luna jumped and threw her fist in the air. "Tie!" she sang out. "Need to pee!"

The commentator announced a time-out, and Luna dashed to the bathroom, her long black hair swaying behind her. With her gone, I could shamelessly stare at the players trailing into the sidelines.

Well. One player in particular—Jason Meyer, point guard of the Bay Area's Santa Mila Barons.

Basketball fans knew Jason as the NBA's golden boy. I knew him as science guy.

In his blue and yellow jersey, he sat wiping his face. He stared ahead, like he wasn't hearing the noise around him. His eyes held no emotion, and it was such a marked change from how he used to be.

We had only been friends for less than a school year, and really only after class hours. When I was done with my shift at the library and he with his training, we'd find ourselves in that abandoned garden. There, I wasn't the weird foreign student whom other girls mocked for wearing baggy clothes and rolling her r's. And he wasn't the star basketball player. We were just two people doing what we loved.

For me, it was dancing. For him, it was reading up on the environment.

At the end of the year, he graduated and moved on to the NBA without looking back. And me? I was still in Sterling, South Carolina. Still dancing on the side while trying to get by.

The bedroom door slammed shut as Luna dashed back inside the living room. She plopped on the sofa that had doubled as my bed since she moved in with me a year ago.

"We're about to win the championship! Come watch, Ate," she said, pronouncing it as *ah-teh*.

The Filipino term felt like a cage, like my identity was tied to being the older sister—and the responsibilities that went with it. But it was the traditional way of showing respect. Luna had called me Ate since she learned how to talk.

I got up from the dining chair and sat next to her. Despite my feigned reluctance, I was grateful for the excuse to watch.

It wasn't that I didn't like basketball, which happened to be our national sport. On the contrary, I'd watched more games than Luna could ever guess.

It was that, even after six years, I still felt a pinch in my chest whenever I saw Jason.

"Here we go," Luna said. A second later, she was on her feet again as Jason stole the ball from a member of the opposing team and dribbled it across the court. One of his opponents blocked him, making a grab for the ball.

Seven seconds on the shot clock.

My heart raced as Jason took a step back. He feinted to the right, leapt to the left. And passed the ball forward—straight into the hands of his teammate Miles Gomez.

Without missing a beat, Miles whirled to face the basket and shot the ball high.

The buzzer sounded right as the ball sank into the hoop.

Shrieking at the top of her lungs, Luna jumped up and down. She pulled me up and squeezed the air out of me with a massive hug. "We won!"

I barely blinked as she let go of me to dance around the room. My gaze was locked on the players piling one on top of the other. Jason and Miles stood in the center, their arms wrapped around each other as they laughed.

"And there you have it, folks. Your NBA Champions, the Santa Mila Barons," the announcer droned while the camera panned to fans in the crowd cheering, dancing, and crying.

"I knew it! I knew it," Luna crowed. Bending over the coffee table, she grabbed her phone and began tapping on it.

I sank back into the sofa. Contradictory emotions warred within me.

Elation. Sadness. Excitement. Regret.

"Ate, we need to celebrate!"

"Sure. What do you want—" I stopped mid-sentence as my smartwatch buzzed.

Jose calling.

Sighing to myself, I said, "Sorry, I need to take this call. Be right back."

Luna's face fell.

This happened often enough that we both knew the drill. We'd been trained for it even before we were teens. Unplanned phone calls meant bad news or abrupt goodbyes. Rarely did they signal anything happy.

Resigned to what was coming, I ducked into what used to be my bedroom and answered the call on my cell phone. A few minutes later, I was in my scrubs, apologizing to Luna as I refilled my water bottle. "I'm so sorry, Lu. They need me to sub for the night shift."

"Right, I understand," she replied, all excitement gone. "Go do your thing."

"Why don't you go out with Kriz? I'll give you some cash—"

"It's fine. I'm tired, anyway. Too much adrenaline. I'll talk to Lonzo for a bit, then go to bed," she said, referring to our younger brother.

Slinging my bag onto my shoulder, I hesitated. Then I dug out my wallet. "I'll leave money in case you get a craving for something." I pulled out two ten-dollar bills and placed them in the catchall tray on the dining table.

Her smile didn't reach her eyes. "Alright. Thanks."

I walked over to her and gave her a quick side hug. "I promise we'll celebrate. This weekend?"

"Sure. Take care." Luna squeezed me back and let go. "I'll lock up after you."

Guilt weighed on my shoulders as I walked to the elevator. Interrupted plans were nothing new, but they sucked all the same. Like I did every time it happened, I reminded myself that emergency shifts meant extra money.

Our family needed it. Thankfully, I had the opportunity to help. My salary wasn't anything grand, but with the dollar-to-peso exchange rate, any money I sent home made a difference. And since Luna only had a partial scholarship, I needed to earn enough to support two people...and then some.

This wasn't exactly the life I'd pictured when my parents convinced me I'd have a better future outside the Philippines. America was the land of opportunities, they'd said. A place where dreams came true.

Jason's face flashed in my mind again. He'd made it big—just like I always knew he would.

I was happy for him. I only wished he hadn't completely cut me out of his life. Clearly, our friendship had mattered more to me than it had to him.

But the past was past, and I had bigger concerns to focus on in the present.

2

ubos – (adj) depleted

Jason

"Jason, how does it feel to win your first championship?"

"Looking great, Elena!"

"Jason, Elena! Can we get a smile over here?"

Elena tugged on my arm, stopping me midway to the car. Over the fourteen months we had been dating, I'd learned that was her way of prompting me to pose for the camera.

Out of habit, I stepped to her left—never the right, because that was her favorite angle to have photographed—and wrapped an arm around her waist. She draped her arms around me in a show of affection. Truth was, it emphasized the line of her jaw and the curve of her ass, which was barely hidden by her skintight dress.

As a model, Elena knew all the tricks to highlight her best assets. She worked them every time, using me like a prop.

Not that I could complain. I'd always known why she was with me—for my fame and my body. Our careers meant we didn't see each other often, but when our schedules matched, she'd catch my game for the guaranteed photo ops, then we'd hit the party scene before holing up in her hotel. In the beginning, that was fine. But lately, it felt superficial. Cold.

After posing and smiling through questions I'd heard a million times before, I called out, "As great as this has been, we're running late. Have a good night, guys." I gave the reporters my signature two-finger salute and ignored the jumble of words they tossed at me.

Elena tensed but I nudged her toward the car with my arm around her back. Ahead of us, her bodyguard cleared a path as best he could.

I should have hired one too. Between my team winning the championship and Elena posting our date on her socials, the paps were hungrier than usual.

Growing up with an NBA player for a dad meant I was used to reporters, but my patience had run thin over the past weeks. My smile felt more forced, and my temper was quicker to spike.

I never let it show. That wasn't the Meyer way. Instead, I gave them what they wanted...as long as it suited me.

And now, it suited me to be in my car and on our way.

Elena's bodyguard opened the back door for us, and I helped her in. The hem of her dress rose as she sat, exposing the length of her bare legs. In the past, that would have been enough to stir my cock. Now, I only wondered if she ever wore jeans outside of ad campaigns. If she did, I had yet to see it happen.

I rounded the car and entered through the opposite side. I preferred to drive, but it felt strange to have a bodyguard in the backseat. Also, Elena hated to sit in front. So whenever I was with her, I gave up the car keys to have her next to me.

Only right now, she wasn't beside me. She straddled my

thighs, the movement lifting her dress high enough to reveal her lack of underwear.

"I like it when you take charge," she said in a breathy voice as she ground against me.

Old me would have pulled down the straps of her dress and cupped her breasts as she rode me to a finish. Present me stilled her hips and glanced at the rearview mirror, noting how her bodyguard kept his gaze on the road.

"Don't worry about him." Undeterred, she reached for my belt. "He's used to it. If you want, I'll get him to join in later."

Her words made me stiffen, and not in the way she wanted. Her bodyguard might be used to her sexcapades, but I didn't want to get used to any of this. Not the sleazy encounters and definitely not this numbness in my chest. Elena was supposed to be my girlfriend, and what did I feel for her? Nothing but a distant sense of weariness.

She unbuckled my belt and traced a finger down my zipper. "What do you say we give people something big to talk about? Maybe get me a diamond ring?"

Like winning the most important game in the basketball world wasn't big enough? Also, when did we ever put marriage on the table? It wasn't even on the menu.

I stopped her hands before they undid my zipper. "We need to talk."

———

"THERE HE IS." Miles bounded toward me, a huge grin stretching across his face. With a height of seven feet and shoulders as wide as a standard door, no one could miss him.

His annual end-of-season party was big every year, but this was one for the books. Neon lights transformed his formal living room into something reminiscent of a club with multiple bars set up along the perimeter. Uniformed waiters milled about carrying liquor bottles and platters of finger food. A deejay spun music on a dais in the center, and behind him a huge LED screen spelled out 'Home of the Champions.'

It was the Barons' first championship in thirteen years. In addition to that, Miles had been voted MVP, a first in our team's history. From the looks of it, everyone who was anyone was here to celebrate.

I nodded at the people I passed, slapping high-fives and patting shoulders here and there. A couple of my teammates had their arms around their girlfriends, others their hookups for the night. Most of the women went heavy on the makeup and low on the skin coverage. I ignored the inviting looks they threw my way, evading the more forward ones who attempted to graze parts of my body.

I smiled at them but didn't stop walking. Not until my best friend—and his two hundred and twenty-five pounds of pure muscle—knocked right into me. I let out a grunt.

"J-man!" Miles shouted as he thumped my back. "What the fuck took you so long?"

"Elena," I said, matching his volume so he could hear me over the crowd.

He nodded. "Gave you a good time, did she?"

"Not exactly."

More like she gave me an earful. She said I'd never given her any hints that I wasn't happy with our arrangement and accused me of wanting to trade up now that I'd won a championship ring. I told her I wasn't interested in anyone else.

Truth was, I was just generally disinterested. I didn't know what bothered her more—that I was the one to instigate the breakup or that I had done it days after our team took the gold.

Probably the latter. Neither of us had strong feelings for the other, but we shared something in common: our pride. Hers might have taken a hit with my rejection, but mine couldn't accept the idea of being with someone whose interest in me only ran skin-deep.

"Ahh." Miles clapped a hand on my shoulder. "Another one bites the dust. Well, there are plenty of women here, and you're a fucking champ."

I forced a smirk. "Not tonight."

He studied me with narrowed eyes. Then he jerked his head to the right. "C'mon."

Without waiting for a response, he took off in the direction of the private wing that only a handful had access to. I didn't just have access—I had my own room.

He opened a door off the hallway that led to the basement.

Out in the living room, people partied hard. Downstairs, it was quiet and still, the dim, warm glow of wall sconces giving the space a cozy atmosphere. Going straight for the wine racks along one brick wall, Miles pulled out a bottle and showed it to me.

My brow rose as I took in the label. "Bringing out the big guns?"

"We're champions, man. Not that anyone can tell by your face."

I huffed out a breath and grabbed two wide-rimmed wine glasses from a cabinet. I placed the glasses on the marble countertop as Miles unscrewed the cork. The bottle opened with a pop.

He sighed. "No better sound in the world."

"I feel sorry for your ladies." I snickered.

Unfazed, he poured wine into both glasses. "You don't need to. Trust me."

We clinked our glasses together. I sniffed, swirled, and sipped, letting the notes dance in my mouth.

"Perfect," Miles declared.

Raising my glass to him, I said, "Here's to the MVP."

"Sit your ass down and tell me what's got you so broody." He plopped onto an armchair and stared at me expectantly.

The guy was hosting a party, yet there he was, waiting for me to talk like he had all the time in the world. Miles was the real deal—my brother by another mother. I took the seat next to him.

"Is this about Elena?"

The mention of her made me jerk. "What? No. Of course not."

"Didn't think so, but I had to ask. Is it me getting the award?"

I almost spat out my mouthful of wine. "The fuck? No. What the hell are you talking about?"

Shrugging, Miles said, "You aren't giving me anything to go by, man. Making me do all the work, as usual." He chuckled at his own joke, one we'd thrown at each other countless times throughout our six years of playing together.

He might be our top player, but both of us knew individual talent wouldn't cut it without great teamwork. Every time we stepped on that court, we backed each other up and gave the game our all.

Only somewhere along the way, I'd gotten stuck on empty. Nothing else to draw from.

Staring at my wine, I asked, "How'd you feel when the buzzer sounded and you realized we won?"

"I knew we were gonna win. There was no other option." Miles spoke like a championship was something he could guarantee. If anyone could, it would be him.

"Yeah, but when it was for real. What did you feel?"

"Buzzed. Like I was literally high. You know."

"That's the thing. I don't know."

Frowning, he sipped his wine. "How did *you* feel?"

"Honestly?" I lifted a shoulder. "Fucking tired."

A dark eyebrow winged up. "Well, we've been playing for months. It's normal to feel tired."

"Were you?"

"No," he admitted. "I felt like I could climb Mount Everest."

I tipped my glass at him in a silent *there you go*.

Truth was, I hadn't just felt tired—I'd felt exhausted. Part of me still was. When the announcer called out the final score, I'd looked at my teammates and seen the elation on their faces. They had whooped and cried, jumping over each other.

Me? The first thing I'd thought was, *Finally, the off-season*.

Of course, I hadn't said it out loud. I'd plastered a grin on my face, hugged a shit ton of people, answered interview questions, posed for photos. Elena was supposed to be there, but she was called to a shoot in Milan, which I only learned about that morning. My lack of disappointment should have told me then that our relationship had run its course.

After having dinner with my mom and stepdad, I drove myself to my apartment. Empty, as usual. I wondered if that was all there was to my life.

Then I questioned what the hell was wrong with me. That championship signaled the biggest highlight of my career. But it felt like I was just crossing an item off my checklist.

Miles slapped his palm against his thigh. "I got it," he announced. "You need a break."

"Don't we all?" That was what the off-season was for. Between back-to-back games, traveling to different cities, and endless workouts and practice, every member of our team needed a break.

"Yeah, but it sounds to me like you're burned out. You need a reset. Someplace different."

"I'm sick of traveling." I'd barely stayed in the same place longer than two days—not to mention that my carbon footprint had blown up from all the private flights we'd taken.

"Pick a place and stay there. Drive if you don't want to fly," Miles said, as if anticipating my argument. "You and I know next season will be brutal. So make the most of these three months."

The more I considered it, the more it made sense. Santa Mila was a beautiful city with its vineyards and bay views, but people here recognized me. Reporters followed me.

Not like in Sterling.

Images of palmetto trees and candy-colored Colonial-style houses flashed in my memory, followed by a montage of hiking trips, boating excursions, and garden hangouts. Two people stood out, their faces anchoring me to some of my happiest experiences.

"Maybe you're right," I murmured.

"Damn right, I am. Now that's settled, we gotta celebrate before you motor." Miles jumped to his feet and grabbed the wine bottle, along with his glass. "Move your ass, bro. My fans are waiting."

Shaking my head, I stood and trailed him back to the party. The music pumped loud and people kept sidling up to me. Women tried to get me to dance.

But my mind wasn't there. It was fixed on the last place I'd felt normal. Alive. And as I began planning my trip, I felt something I hadn't felt in a while.

Excitement.

3

OFW – (n) Overseas Filipino Worker

Tala

The staff room wasn't the best place to take an unofficial work call. But when half the nurses were on break and the rest were attending to patients? It almost served as a private meeting room. I only hoped we would finish early enough so I could eat lunch before it was time for my afternoon rounds.

"Thanks again for slotting me in." Nat Petrova, my longest running PR partner, smiled at me through my phone screen. "I wanted to chat with you because I have a big campaign coming up. Does the name Nike ring a bell?"

My eyes widened. "No way!"

She laughed. "I thought that would get you excited."

I heard something in her tone that made me pause. "There's a catch," I guessed.

"The campaign involves a week-long lineup of events with other content creators and fitness influencers. Press launch, workshops, interviews..." Nat paused. "In Los Angeles."

My heart sank. California was on the opposite side of the country.

"Good news is it's not until November, so you have time to make the necessary arrangements. The flights and accommodations will be sponsored, of course."

"That sounds wonderful."

She arched an eyebrow, like she knew there was a *but* coming.

As much as I hated it, I couldn't commit to a project I wasn't sure I could fulfill. "Unfortunately, I don't think that's possible for me right now."

"You can't tell me you don't get time off."

Of course I did, but it came with a healthy dose of guilt from my boss, coworkers, and myself. More than that, I worried about not having enough paid time off for when I really needed it, especially if I had to go home. I'd already missed one family emergency. I wouldn't be able to forgive myself if I missed another.

At the end of the day, that trumped everything else.

"It's complicated," was all I said. I avoided declining opportunities whenever possible, not wanting to risk being ruled out of future projects. Plus, I considered Nat a friend, and I hated letting my friends and family down.

Maybe I could rearrange my schedule so I wouldn't need to take time off. Talk my colleagues into swapping shifts, call in some favors. It could work. Projects like this didn't come every day.

"Tell you what. I'll email the details and let you review them. Think about it and give me your answer by Monday. Does that sound good?" Nat asked as if she picked up on my hesitation.

"Yes. That would be great," I replied. "Thanks, Nat. I

really appreciate you thinking of me. If things were different, I wouldn't even hesitate."

"I hope you can work things out. You're perfect for this. You have the vibe they're looking for, and it would help you expand your audience too."

"I'll do my best."

"Are you sure you can't quit your day job yet? You know you'd make more money if you did this full time," Nat said.

I glanced at the door, checking that no one could overhear our conversation. It wasn't the first time she brought up the idea of me resigning. As always, I told her, "I would if I didn't need a work visa to stay here."

"Or you could marry and get a green card." She grinned at me mischievously. "Are you dating anyone now?"

I blinked at the sudden change in topic. "Where would I find the time?"

Between my nursing job, content creation, and Luna, I barely had a second for myself, let alone a man. I would take more hours of sleep and downtime over the stress of dating, thank you very much.

"You just need to find the right person. Then you'll want to make time for them. Or so I've been told." Nat laughed.

"I'm guessing you're not dating, either?"

"Eh." She wrinkled her nose. "I tried here and there, but I don't have the patience for boys who can't handle me. Not when I have an empire to build."

"Hell, yes."

Smart, efficient, and unstoppable, Nat was the ultimate girl boss. I wanted to be like her one day, so sure of herself and her capabilities.

"That said, whenever you're ready to date, let me know. I have the perfect person in mind."

Her smile was so smug, I had to laugh. "I'll remember that."

I appreciated the offer, but no way could I add dating to my schedule. Maybe one day when I didn't need to keep my foot on the pedal, I could indulge in flirting and the mess of emotions that came with being attached to someone.

For now, I'd be more than content with booking that partnership. I just had to find a way to do it.

We spent a few more minutes chatting about a campaign she had wrapped up for a skincare brand. When we ended the call, I grabbed my lunch bag and headed to the break room. Only a handful of people remained, and they were already gathering their dishes. Giving them a nod, I snagged an empty table and unwrapped my food.

Halfway through my sandwich, my phone vibrated, notifying me that Lonzo had posted a new photo. It showed him and our mom smiling with huge bowls of *adobo* and garlic rice in front of them. I recognized the restaurant they were eating in. It was one of my favorites.

Just like that, I missed home—missed our big family meals with flavorful dishes and massive pots of rice. Thankfully, Luna being here meant I didn't have to eat alone. It wasn't the same as being home, but at least she could recreate Lola's recipes. To me, our grandmother set the standard of what Filipino food should taste like.

I should ask Luna to cook *adobo* sometime. Maybe that would help with my homesickness.

I was about to get up when I saw a post from a news account that I followed.

Jason Meyer spotted in Santa Mila airport after break-up with Elena Carson. Is he flying into the arms of a new woman?

Groaning under my breath, I locked my phone and shoved

it in my pocket. Ever since the Barons won, Jason's name had been popping up more often. Haunting me. Taunting me with thoughts of what could have been.

Although Jason had signed with a team on the opposite side of the country, his fame ensured I could never forget him. I doubted he could say the same about me. In the years since he'd moved to California, he had been linked to models, actresses, and socialites. From light to dark skinned, lean to full-figured—he didn't discriminate, so long as they were beautiful, charismatic, and at the top of their game. Just like he was.

If only I could say the same about myself.

———

Jason

Whispers and stares followed me to the VIP lounge, as did the lens of more than one camera. Reporters had accosted me as soon as I stepped out of my car, asking questions, including,

"Jason, what do you think about your ex-girlfriend moving on with Draymond Pike?"

"Is it true that Elena broke up with you because you slept with a groupie in New York?"

"Are you visiting the woman you allegedly knocked up in Dallas?"

If I had a dollar for every time they accused me of getting a woman pregnant, I'd be a multimillionaire. Not that I wasn't one already. But at that moment, I would have given up a healthy chunk of my bank account to be left alone.

Thus, the trip to Sterling.

I would have escaped Santa Mila sooner if not for the press events and charity engagements my agent Sam signed me up for. Did I feel like a self-righteous ass trying to get publicity from my good works? Without a doubt. But it was part of the job. The promotions didn't negate the fact that I was able to help people who needed it. Or so I reassured myself.

It was the press commitments I could have gone without. Unfortunately, that too was part of the job.

As of this morning, though, I was officially on break. Only a couple of hours to go and I'd be back in the place where I had been just another cocky student with big dreams. I only hoped the town was still as low-key as I remembered it.

I took a glass of orange juice and sat in the far corner of the lounge. To keep myself busy, I cleared out my messages, scanning work-related texts before I moved on to one from my childhood friend, Stassy.

> STASSY
>
> Have a safe flight and enjoy. Let me know if you bump into any familiar faces. ;)

If there was one person who knew why Sterling meant so much to me, it was her. I'd shared bits and pieces with Miles when we bonded as rookies, but Stassy was the only one who knew the entire story.

I typed out *Thanks, Stassy. Talk soon.*

My phone vibrated with an incoming call from my mom.

"Hey, Mom," I answered.

"Jason. How are you?" She spoke in a perfectly modulated voice that carried a hint of her natural British accent.

I leaned back in the chair. "I'm good. Waiting for my flight."

"I still can't believe you're going back to Sterling," she said.

"You go every other month."

"Only because of Bernadette. If it weren't for her living there, I wouldn't go back at all."

Bernadette, whom everyone but my mom called Berna, was

23

my grandmother's best friend from her university years in California. When Mom moved to the US to marry Dad, Berna had been there to help her acclimatize. She'd been like a second mother to Mom, especially after Grandmother passed away. More so when Dad followed.

"Well, I haven't visited since graduation. Besides, I thought you'd be happy to have me nearby."

"If you wanted to be near me, you'd go to Florida," Mom snapped.

I had already explained my reasons for traveling to Sterling, and she still didn't get it. Wasn't that how she had always been? If something didn't fit her liking, she would maneuver or outright shove her way forward. I had learned early on to choose when to stand my ground and when to give in. She was the only family I had left, and Dad would have wanted me to keep the peace.

But this was one of the things worth standing my ground for.

"You know Sterling is important to me," I said.

"Your decision to study there baffles me to this day. You had better universities to choose from. Ivy League. Sterling didn't even have a winning team before you came along."

"Dad loved it there. We used to go every year for my birthday. Don't you remember?"

I'd lucked out by being born in the off-season. After months of Dad playing nonstop, we would drive up to South Carolina and just soak in the outdoors. Hiking, boating, camping—we did it all. Mom passed up on our adventures, not wanting to go anywhere that didn't have her modern comforts. I didn't mind. It gave me and Dad time to ourselves away from basketball.

"Of course," she murmured. "You boys would go out and come back filthy as ever."

"It's not so different from the locker room after a game."

From the corner of my eye, I caught a woman looking at me with recognition. I shifted, giving her my back. Hopefully that would dissuade her from coming over.

"Well, since you're determined to go, I moved my trip up. I've scheduled a visit with Bernadette tomorrow morning. We can do lunch after."

No asking if I had my own plans. Lucky for her, I didn't, though I wanted to spend time reacquainting myself with the town.

"Sounds good," I said. "Listen, we're boarding in a few. Send me the name of your hotel so I can pick you up tomorrow. I'll see you then."

"Alright. You take care, Jason."

"I will. See you, Mom."

I had just ended the call when an unfamiliar female voice came from my right.

"So it's true. Jason Meyer is a mama's boy."

The woman who had been eyeing me stood next to the coffee table, her hip cocked to one side like she was posing for a photo. It reminded me of Elena.

Irritated by the disturbance, I forced a light tone. "The best men are."

"That you are," she purred. Her lips curved in what I guessed was meant to be a seductive smile.

All it did was cement the fact that I had to get out of the city pronto.

The PA system crackled to life, announcing the boarding call for first class passengers on my flight. Right on time.

I stood and picked up my duffel. "That's my cue. Safe travels, ma'am." I nodded at her and walked away, fighting a laugh at the dismay on her face upon hearing me call her ma'am.

Adjusting my cap, I ducked as I walked to the boarding gate. Still, heads turned in my direction and phones rose to take my photo. I boarded quickly and went straight to my cabin, settling in with my headphones and e-reader.

My mind was already in the place—and the memories—I'd left behind.

During interviews, reporters sometimes asked if I had any regrets. I always said I had no room for them. Unlike what they assumed, it wasn't because I didn't have any. The two regrets I lived with took up more space than I could spare. I'd trained myself not to think about them. Conditioned myself much like I did every day when I went to the gym.

Wasn't it ironic that I was flying nearly three thousand miles to confront them now?

4

pamilya – (n) family

Tala

"Happy birthday, Alonzo. Happy birthday to you," Luna and I sang in front of the monitor placed on our dining table. Our voices were so off-tune, they created a weird kind of melody.

The looks of amusement and horror on Mama's and Lonzo's respective faces told me that not even the poor internet connection could mask the dissonance of our voices.

"Make it stop." Lonzo covered his ears with his hands. "Is this a greeting or punishment for being alive?"

"If that's how you feel, I'm taking back my gift," I threatened.

Just as I expected, he jerked upright, his eyes wide. "You can't take it back. I already used part of it to book a hostel in La Union."

I frowned.

"You're going to LU?" Luna screeched. "I'm so jealous."

"Yep," he said. "Next month."

27

La Union, or LU as we called it, was a beach town six hours away from our home in Manila. I had only been there once, during Papa's last visit before I flew out to the US. He and Mama knew it was the last time we'd all be together for a while, so even though money was tight, they splurged on a vacation. The town held bittersweet memories for me.

But that wasn't the reason I was annoyed.

"You're spending it on a beach trip? I was thinking you could save it for your law school fund," I told Lonzo.

The rolling of his eyes spoke volumes. "That's boring. It's a birthday gift. It should be used for something fun."

"But law school is expensive. Even if you get a full scholarship, you need to have money saved up," I insisted. That was the very reason I gave up a chunk of my Manila trip fund for his present.

"It's alright, Tala," Mama chimed in. "Let him enjoy himself. He worked hard the past school year, and he kept his honors standing."

My mouth tightened with the effort to hold back what I really wanted to say. If I didn't stop myself, I'd tell them exactly how hard *I'd* worked the past seven years. I'd worked my butt off in college so I could keep my own scholarship.

Vacations? Nonexistent. I'd spent summers working two part-time jobs while struggling to build my social media following. The cash that didn't go toward my living expenses or my content creation gig went straight to a money transfer service for my family.

"Don't worry, Ate. I got extra shifts at the coffee shop this summer. That's why I won't be able to travel right away," Lonzo said, like he could feel my mounting indignation.

I forced a smile. "That's great, Lonzo. Mama's right—you should enjoy your break too."

Luna snapped her fingers. "You should go to that cafe

where we tried horchata for the first time. You remember Lola's reaction when she tasted it?"

My chest squeezed. It always did when I thought of our grandmother. She had been the heart of our family. When she was diagnosed with breast cancer twelve years ago, she laughed it off and said it would take more than a tumor to bring her down. Two months after, when Papa announced he had signed up for a job in the Middle East, Lola had held Mama's hand and assured them she would help look after us.

Only later did I learn that our family's business had gone bankrupt. With Lola's hospital bills and our tuition fees piling up, we needed money. Papa worked overseas while Mama began taking on night shifts as an ER nurse. That left Lola at home to take care of us. As her condition deteriorated, the responsibility shifted to me.

I didn't mind. I loved Lola and would do whatever I could for her. It broke my heart that I hadn't been able to see her one last time before she passed away.

Luna's shoulder bumped into mine. "Ate, you're spacing out."

"Sorry." I shoved the memories back into the vault where they belonged. "What did I miss?"

"I'm planning to take surfing lessons. I really wanted diving lessons, but they're too expensive. I'll save up for that next time," Lonzo said.

Mama put an arm around him. "I don't know why you're so fixated on diving. What if you drown?"

"That's what the lessons are for," he told her. "The ocean is such an amazing place, and we only see the surface of it."

"Are you planning to be a lawyer or Aquaman?" Luna teased him.

"Maybe I want to be both."

If anyone could do it, it would be Lonzo. He had been

accelerated in school, putting him at the same grade level as Luna despite her being a year older. Unlike us, he'd stayed in the Philippines for college, saying that he wanted to look after Mama.

Did I resent that I'd never had a real choice but to leave? Yes. Sometimes the bitterness grew so thick, it choked me.

"If you want to be both, do it," Mama said. "Follow your heart. We have too little time on earth to live with regrets. That goes for all of you."

As Lonzo shared his plans and Luna talked about her summer classes, I wondered what my life might have looked like if our business hadn't failed. Would I have studied abroad? Would I have followed Mama's footsteps and taken up nursing? Would I still be single?

That old ache in my chest stung. Like every other time I felt resentment creep up, I reminded myself that my circumstances were no one's fault. One day, things would get better, and they *had* gotten better with each passing year.

So what if looking after my siblings at thirteen meant I had lost part of my childhood? At least I helped them enjoy theirs. When Luna and Lonzo were done with school and had stable jobs, then I could take time for myself. Maybe even go back home.

"Tala, what about you?" Mama asked, interrupting my train of thought. "How's work?"

I welcomed the question and its reminder to stay in the present. Looking back at the past was an exercise in frustration. It changed nothing. In the now, I could influence my future, even in the smallest ways.

So I snapped myself out of my funk and told them about my patients.

Things were okay as they were. I was fine.

———

Jason

Armed with sunglasses and an old cap, I strolled through Sterling's University Avenue. The air was thick with humidity, and the weather was warmer than I was used to.

The town didn't get many tourists, and July was the worst time to visit because of its high temperatures. I didn't mind. Here, I could walk down the street without being followed by cameras. The only pedestrians I encountered were older people heading to the grocery store and a handful of students walking to and from campus. A few of them gave me a second glance, but that was it.

Just like I wanted.

Sunlight filtered through the gaps in the palmetto fronds as I crossed to the other side of the road and onto a smaller street. Familiar brick and stone buildings stood around me, none of them higher than the mandated three stories. The college campus lay further down the avenue, but it wasn't my current destination.

My feet found their way to the garden like I had been there yesterday. Turning into a narrow opening between overgrown bushes, I found myself in the place I frequented nearly every day when I was in college.

It was the same...but different. The brick floor was piled with crisp, faded leaves, empty bottles, and crumpled snack bags. The plants I'd once tended had dried out or been overrun with weeds. The rosemary and marigolds I'd cultivated to keep mosquitoes away? Long gone.

Whoever owned the property knew squat about maintenance.

Wincing, I stood in the center and took it all in. Clearing

the trash would be easy. Fixing the plants would take longer. Good thing I had plenty of time.

The garden was silent save for the occasional rustling of leaves and humming of wheels on the nearby street. The silence might have been the biggest change since the last time I was there. It hadn't been this quiet since the day an international student found it.

Tala Reyes.

The girl who blasted tinny music from her battered smart-phone as she danced. She would repeat the same song over and over until she got her dance moves exactly how she wanted them. It annoyed me in the beginning because it was repetitive as hell. She stopped at varying points of a song and replayed it so often the lyrics, when there were any, imprinted in my head even after the music stopped.

It didn't take me long to get used to it. To this day, I played music whenever I read a book, like she had programmed my brain to process faster with background sound.

When she wasn't dancing, we filled the silence with talk. I'd tell her about my games and how my mom got on my case about preparing for the NBA draft. One conversation came back to me so clearly, I took a step back.

"Congrats on the win yesterday," Tala said as I walked in from training.

I grunted. "I was off my game. Good thing the other guys were on fire, or we would've been screwed."

"You scored multiple times."

"I should have scored more. I was sloppy. That free throw I missed? Fucking stupid."

Through my irritation, I noticed she flinched at my words. "I curse, Tal. It doesn't mean I'm going to hurt you."

"I know. I'm sorry."

The swiftness of her apology fed my anger. Not because she was trying to pacify me. She wasn't. That made it worse. "Why are you saying sorry? You have nothing to apologize for."

Her fingers tapped the sides of her thighs the way they always did when she was uncomfortable. "I'm sorry you're upset."

"It's not your fault. You weren't the one sucking ass on the court."

She was silent, her shoulders held tight. Then she said in a low voice, "It sucks to have an off day. But you'll do better next time."

Hell. Now I felt like a legitimate asshole. "I shouldn't take it out on you. I'm sorry."

"It's okay. This is your safe space, right? You can say what you want to here."

The words burst out of me in an angry rush. "It's my mom. She insists I always be at my best because scouts are watching me. Everyone expects me to be as good as Dad. Better. It just—it messes with my head sometimes. You know?"

"Do I know what it's like to have a famous dad? No." She smiled wryly. "But I know a bit about trying to live up to someone else's expectations, especially when it comes to family."

"Would you have moved here if your parents didn't ask you to?"

"No." The answer was immediate. "I never thought of moving away from them. Or living in another country."

I almost asked if she would go back home if she could. But she had already told me what I needed to know, and I didn't like it. I couldn't imagine the garden without her anymore.

"What about you?" she asked. "Would you be playing basketball if your parents didn't expect you to?"

The question threw me. It was the first time anyone had asked. Me playing basketball was a given—there was never a *question of if I would play, only how well I would. Whether or not I could match up.*

It was the same question I asked myself every time I walked onto the court.

Finally, I said, "Yeah, probably. I'm a Meyer. Meyer men play basketball." It hadn't just started with my dad. My grandfather had played too, just not well enough to go pro. He had set the bar. Dad had raised it.

It was up to me to do the same.

She stared at me for a long moment before saying, "You're not just a basketball player, Jason."

The memory of Tala's words seemed to echo in the air, sending a spike of energy through my skin like they had years ago.

Back then, I'd tried to shrug it off, teasing her about how well she knew me. We had only been friends for a couple of months, yet she already seemed to see parts of me that even I couldn't.

Could she still?

I brushed the debris off the step in front of the patio doors and sat. After six long years, I finally looked up an Instagram profile I followed but had stopped checking.

Her following had grown, though she was still short of the five hundred thousand mark. She'd started her account a few weeks after we met. She should have racked up at least a million followers by now.

I tapped her latest post and watched as she danced to an upbeat song that resembled a commercial jingle. Her moves were different from the ones I'd seen her perform before. It was like she'd put on a song she enjoyed and just freestyled to it instead of sticking to a routine.

My lips twitched as she did a silly move imitating a bobbing chicken. She let out a silent laugh right after, executing a perfect twirl that sent her dark hair flying around her.

Damn, she was gorgeous. It seemed she hadn't lost her preference for oversized tees, but instead of the material coming down to her thighs, it was cut to reveal a slice of her stomach over the waistband of her leggings.

And those leggings. They clung to the length of her legs, emphasizing the curves she used to keep hidden.

Fuck. I locked my phone, realizing I was ogling someone who used to be my friend. Aside from Stassy, Tala was the only girl I'd ever considered a friend. She'd never flirted with me, never asked for anything other than my company.

And I'd left her. Ghosted her before it became a trend.

She still lived in town—that much I was sure of. I didn't know if she ever thought about our time together or if she was angry about how I'd treated her, but it was about time I tried to apologize. I just had to get through lunch with Mom first.

5

ikaw – (n) you

Tala

After more than a month of frequent patient turnover and staffing issues, Golden Haven Care Center finally settled back into its normal rhythm. I came in that morning to find nothing urgent reported during the night shift handoff. None of my coworkers were on leave, so I didn't need to cover additional patients. I only had one last stop before I could take my break—on time for a change.

Berna, a seventy-year-old widow with end-stage liver disease, had been with us for almost two years now. Despite her condition, her adult children rarely visited. So whenever one of her friends came to town, I rejoiced for her.

Pausing just outside the room, I knocked twice and opened the door. I smiled at Berna, who was sitting up in her bed. Her regular visitor sat in the chair, but my eyes snagged on the tall man standing behind her.

I froze in the doorway, blinking rapidly. Were my eyes

playing tricks on me? Had I thought about him so many times in the past weeks that I was hallucinating his presence?

"Tala?"

My mind blanked at the deep, familiar voice.

Jason stared at me, looking just as confused as I felt.

My tongue stuck to the bottom of my dry mouth.

Jason was here.

My heartbeat pounded in my ears.

Jason Meyer.

Standing taller than ever in a gray shirt that did nothing to hide his much broader chest and round biceps. His hair was cut shorter on the sides, the blond strands appearing darker. Stubble framed his mouth and continued along his jaw.

The woman in the chair cleared her throat.

My eyes flew her way. Vivian Bateman visited every two months, always with her golden blonde hair immaculately coiffed and wearing a crisp, coordinated pantsuit and red lipstick. Before now, I'd never thought of her as anything other than Berna's honorary niece, but seeing her next to Jason, I instantly knew who she was to him. Her eyes were the exact shade of blue as his.

"Jason. Do you know this...woman?" Mrs. Bateman asked. Only the slight crease on her forehead marred her flawless appearance.

"We were in university together," Jason answered without taking his eyes off me. His stare swept over me from head to toe, lingering on my scrubs and the ID on my breast pocket. "I didn't know you worked here."

"Tala is the best nurse in Golden Haven," Berna declared.

The words drew me out of my stupor. I smiled at her despite my flaming cheeks. "Thank you, Berna."

"It's Miss Berna," Jason's mom corrected.

The sharp, condescending tone was like having a bucket of

cold water poured over me. It took me back to freshman year, to that crawling sensation of judgment as girls with perfect bodies and flawless faces looked me up and down and dismissed me with cutting glances.

I fought the old instinct to lower my head, forcing my spine ramrod-straight instead. Mrs. Bateman had always been aloof, but never this sharp.

Berna spoke up. "You know full well I insisted she call me by my name, Vivian. Tala, I take it you know her son, Jason."

"Yes," I said, relieved that my voice didn't catch.

I am a professional. I've made it through worse. I will not cower.

"Good afternoon, Mrs. Bateman. Jason." I nodded at each of them, keeping our eye contact brief and impersonal. "I'm sorry for interrupting."

Why are you saying sorry? You have nothing to apologize for.

Ignoring the words Jason once told me that rang in my head, I continued, "Berna, I'll just give you your meds so you can enjoy your visit."

I rounded the bed and began preparing her midday medication, pretending I didn't feel Jason staring at me. I held the saucer of pills in one hand and a glass of water in the other. Despite the two pairs of eyes burning through the side of my face, my hands remained steady. I took pride in that.

No matter what they thought of me, I was no longer a helpless little girl.

"Are you feeling alright, Berna? Anything out of the ordinary?" I usually asked more specific questions but patients preferred not to talk about bowel movements and the like around guests.

"No, everything's peachy. Thank you, Tala," Berna said after drinking some water. She patted my arm as though she could tell how unnerved I was.

"Of course. Just buzz me if you need anything. Otherwise, I'll see you later this afternoon." I rearranged the supplies on my tray and looked up at the two visitors. "Have a good day."

As I passed by them, Jason's hand lifted like he was planning to stop me. His mom muttered his name sharply.

I kept my nurse smile on as I approached the door, my breath stuck in my throat. Finally, I stepped into the hallway and closed the door behind me.

My heart raced as I sped toward the staff room. Forget about lunch. My appetite had vanished.

Jason was here in Sterling. After six years.

What were the chances?

Jason

What the hell just happened?

I stared at the door Tala had closed. How had she gone from content creator to caregiver?

"So."

I looked at Berna, who studied me with a mischievous glint in her eyes.

"You know Tala," she stated.

"Yeah," I replied. "Like I said, she's an old friend."

"She's a wonderful girl. Everyone here loves her."

That made me smile. "I'm not surprised."

Our friendship had only spanned months, yet I remembered how she would always ask how I was doing. More than that, she listened—without judgment or ulterior motives.

Tala was caring by nature, and she'd studied nursing in college. But she loved dancing. Despite it being years since we last spoke, I knew it was true. Anyone could see it in her videos. So what was she doing working in a care center?

"My friend tried to set Tala up with her son," Berna said, getting my attention. "He's a doctor. Handsome, but not as much as you."

I feigned casual interest, although the thought of Tala dating someone bugged me. Especially a good-looking doctor. "How'd that go?"

"Tala was gracious about it, but she said she wasn't looking for a relationship then. Maybe she was waiting for you."

Mom sputtered. "She's a *caregiver*."

"She has a nursing degree from Sterling," I replied, annoyed at her disparaging tone. I didn't like the way she seemed to look down at Tala and her profession.

Mom waved a manicured hand. "She's hardly dating material for you."

I opened my mouth to argue, but Berna beat me to it.

"Don't be so judgmental, Vivi," she scolded.

"Pardon me?" Mom gasped. "I am not—"

"You hardly know the girl, and you're already shutting her down."

I almost cheered Berna on. Few people had the courage to call out my mom, and even fewer could do so without consequence.

"If we haven't been through so much, I wouldn't stand for your accusation," Mom told her.

Harrumphing, Berna said, "You tolerate me because I'm dying, not because of anything else."

"You are not dying, Bernadette," Mom said in a raised voice that surprised me. She rarely lost her cool. At least, not in front of other people.

The only other time I'd seen her look less than her best in public was at Dad's funeral. She'd tried to hide it behind a pair of sunglasses and thicker than normal makeup, but the tremble of her lips and hands and the slight quiver in her voice had given her away.

Was she upset now because she was worried about Berna, or was it simply the mention of dying? Death did not exist in her vocabulary.

Your dad passed away. He moved on to a better place. He's gone but we'll keep his memory alive.

Every way you could allude to death without saying it outright—I'd heard them all.

"We're all dying." Berna sounded unruffled. "It's just coming faster for me. And seeing as I don't particularly fear your death stare, Vivian, let me just say that I happen to think Tala would be a fine catch for Jason."

Amused, I answered, "I'll be sure to let her know."

Mom shot me a displeased look.

"Did you two ever date?" Berna pried shamelessly.

"No. We were just friends." Maybe if I hadn't left...

Well. There was no changing the past.

"That reminds me," Mom piped up, her voice bright. "When was the last time you saw Anastassya? Katja told me she's single again. Since you just broke up with that model, it might be a good time to ask her out."

"Like a rebound?" Berna scoffed.

Chuckling, I tuned out Mom's attempt to set me up with Stassy. Again. It was one of the schemes she wouldn't move past, never mind that neither Stassy nor I was interested in the other that way.

My mind drifted back to Tala.

The girl who once hid under baggy clothes and caps, who had been quiet around everyone on campus but me, was all grown up.

I'd known what she looked like, of course. Still, I hadn't

41

been ready for the reality of seeing her in person. Or for that bolt of energy that zinged through me when our eyes met.

Her eyes had always fascinated me. Almond shaped with dark brown irises, they looked calm, even impassive, at first glance. But whenever I'd look closer, they would give away whatever she was feeling.

I'd seen the shock in her eyes when she spotted me inside the room. A second later, she blinked and her gaze became shuttered.

The longer I studied her, I noticed the barely there makeup highlighting her best features—the shape of her eyes, the fullness of her lips.

When we hung out in college, she never wore makeup. Except once, at the party after our team tapped out of regional finals. It was the closest Sterling had come to the championship. From the way we'd partied that night, you'd think we won the damn thing.

It was also the only time I'd seen her in a dress. It had been simple, reaching the tops of her knees and covering most of her chest. But it forced me to acknowledge that the person I enjoyed talking to the most was a pretty girl.

The attraction had hit me like a punch to the gut. I'd been with other girls, but I'd never pictured a future with any of them. At that moment, visions of a life with Tala flashed before my eyes. The scariest part? With her, I imagined just being myself. A science geek who played basketball for fun.

Stupid kid that I was, I made the worst fucking decision because of it.

I needed to talk with her. Needed to fix things between us.

I'd lost her number, but there were other ways to find her. If social media was good for one thing, it was tracking people down. Whether they wanted to be found or not.

6

kapatid – (n) sibling

Tala

A pile of laundry sat in the basket in front of me, but I couldn't focus on it. My mind ran on overdrive, dissecting every second of my unexpected reunion with Jason. Back in college, he'd had charisma in spades. He'd been the golden boy even then, the heartthrob team captain who pulled off being friendly while being way out of league for most girls. Including me.

I had seen him in countless photos and videos since, yet none of those came close to capturing the sheer magnetism he had now. He didn't need flashy clothes, didn't need to speak to dominate the room with his presence. His boyish charm had sharpened with age and maturity, evolving into manly appeal. Maybe I was assuming too much, but he seemed to have lost his softness in more ways than one. He had an invisible heaviness about him, a brooding air that rendered him unapproachable.

Didn't it just suck that I found his darker edge intriguing?

Stop thinking about him.

"Stop thinking about who?"

Realizing I'd spoken out loud, I whirled around to face Luna, who was chopping vegetables on our tiny kitchen counter. "Nothing. Ignore me."

I went back to my ironing, fishing out a pair of scrubs from the laundry basket. It might have been the set I'd worn yesterday.

When I saw Jason at Golden Haven.

I smothered my groan. Couldn't I go ten minutes without thinking about him? Like it wasn't enough that he was all over the news.

Now he was right here. In my town.

Only, was he still here? Maybe he'd come in from Charleston for a day trip.

At first, I'd worried he would try to get in touch with me. But when the hours passed without any messages, my anticipation faded into something else. Something all too familiar when it came to Jason.

Disappointment.

How could I have expected anything else? If he wanted to see me, he would have come back sooner. *Get a clue, Tala.*

"Who are you thinking about?" Luna pestered me.

I concentrated on smoothing out the creases on my pants. "No one."

"Ate!"

Knowing there was no stopping my sister once she fixated on something, I admitted, "I saw someone I knew from college."

"Like a teacher?"

"No. An old friend. He was visiting one of my patients. It's not a big deal."

Liar. My hand clenched the iron as frustration and inadequacy washed over me. His mom had looked at me like I was beneath her. Nothing new, really. Years of snide comments had

44

taught me people's opinions were out of my control. I thought I'd moved past caring about that, but I was wrong.

"You're stressing out about it. That means it *is* a big deal. Who was it?" Waggling her eyebrows, Luna asked, "Was it your secret ex-boyfriend?"

I couldn't help but snort at that. "No."

Despite spending hours alone together, Jason had never shown an inkling that he saw me as a girl. At least, not one he was attracted to. On campus, he hung out with the cheerleaders and basketball players. He only talked to me in that garden, making it crystal-clear all he wanted from me was an after-hours friend.

A metallic clanging drew my eyes to Luna. She was hitting her knife against a metal pot.

"Earth to Ate."

"Stop that," I hissed. "That's dangerous."

"So is not paying attention to the iron," she shot back. Still, she lowered the knife. "Even if this guy isn't an ex, it seems like the two of you have history. Show me a pic!"

"No." The last thing I needed was for Luna to find out about Jason. I would never hear the end of him then.

Pouting, Luna wheedled, "Come *on*. Just one. I don't even know what your type is. Except for the professor."

The professor was my best friend, Gabe Martinez, who taught finance classes at the university. He and Luna took an instant dislike to each other the moment they met. For some reason—and despite my explanations otherwise—Luna insisted he was in love with me.

If she only knew who my type was, and that Gabe was nowhere close to it.

Ignoring the dig about him, I said, "Focus on cooking, Lu."

My phone beeped, signaling I had a new Facebook

message. Turning the iron off, I set it down and picked up my cell.

New message from Jason Meyer.

For a second, my heartbeat stopped. "What the hell?" I muttered.

"What's that?"

Before I could put my phone away, Luna perched her chin on my shoulder. I yelped as her sharp jawbone sank into my flesh. "Luna!"

"Oh. My. God."

I tried to tuck my phone under my thigh, but she reached across me and grabbed it from my hand. It wasn't fair that she had three inches on me, giving her an advantage in both height and arm length.

She hit the power button, lighting up the screen. Her jaw dropped. Eyes wide, she gawked at me. "You have a message from Jason Meyer."

Was there any way I could convince her that he wasn't who she thought he was?

"Why do you have a message from Jason Meyer?" she demanded.

"I don't know," I managed to say. "I haven't read it."

"Ate. Do you know who the second-best player on my favorite basketball team is?"

I sighed. "Of course I do. I hear about him every time you watch their games."

"Why have you never told me that you know Jason Meyer? Did you meet him at one of your influencer gigs?" Her eyes grew even bigger. She shot up. "Is he the guy you saw? Your college fling?"

"He was not a college fling!" I winced as I realized that in denying her second question, I had answered the first.

Looking like she had just been punched, Luna sank onto

the sofa. "Oh my God. Jason Meyer is in Sterling. My sister knows Jason Meyer."

"He's just a guy, Lu," I snapped like I hadn't been freaking out since I saw him. "You don't need to say his name over and over again."

She yanked me to her side and held up the phone. "Read it!"

"Fine." Trying to keep my expression indifferent, I unlocked my phone and clicked the notification.

JASON

> Hey, Tala. It was nice seeing you again. Can we talk? Let me know when you're free for lunch or dinner. Your choice.

Squealing, Luna gave a little jump on the sofa, which groaned under her weight.

"Luna! If you break my bed, you're getting me a new one." The padding already had a permanent butt-shaped indent in the spot where I preferred to sit. The frame might just give out on me too.

"You have to say yes!"

"No. No way." I shook my head.

She studied my face curiously. "Did he break your heart?"

"I told you, we were just friends."

On his side, anyway. When it came to mine, Luna's guess wasn't far from the truth—though I wouldn't admit it.

"Uh huh. You sound *super* convincing," she drawled. "If you were friends, like you said, all the more reason you should say yes. For old times' sake."

"We knew each other for less than a year, Lu. Then he declared for the draft and it was like I was nonexistent to him. One moment, we were friends. Next thing I knew, he was ghosting me and leaving for the NBA."

47

Her gaze softened. "Maybe he wants to explain. Why don't you hear him out? I mean, what's the worst that can happen?"

I mulled over her words, recognizing the logic in them. "I'll think about it."

In the past, I would have jumped at the opportunity to talk to him. To finally learn what had driven him away and get answers to the questions that still hounded me. But now that his invitation stared me in the face, I hesitated. Did I really want to know the truth? Maybe it was better to leave it in the past and continue moving forward. Did I want to give Jason a second chance to mess me up?

No.

I needed to focus on my plan. My career. I had no time or energy to deal with a guy who hadn't even had the decency to say goodbye.

Let him wonder about my silence for a change.

SOMEONE KNOCKED on our front door as I finished setting the table. I frowned, wondering who it was. Was one of Luna's friends dropping by? I hadn't heard her buzz anyone through the intercom.

Luna whipped off her apron. "I'll get it."

"It's fine. I've got it." The door was closer to me, and it only took me four steps to reach it.

"But—"

Reaching for the doorknob, I glanced at my sister. Her protest died. She shrugged and picked up a ladle, staring into the pot as she stirred the *adobo*.

She was acting stranger than usual. Distracted, I opened the door without looking through the peephole like I normally would. I swung it open and my entire body locked up.

"Jason?"

Carrying a pot of colorful flowers in one hand and a bottle of wine in the other, he smiled at me. "Hey, Tala." He stepped toward me.

I stepped back.

His brows drew together.

"What are you doing here?" I asked, still blocking the entryway.

"What do you mean?" The groove on his forehead deepened. "You invited me."

Was he delusional? I didn't invite him. I didn't even reply to his message. My address wasn't publicly listed and I'd stayed in the dorms back then. How did he know where I lived?

"I messaged you this afternoon," Jason said. "Remember?"

"I remember not replying." I'd forced myself not to open the message again, fearing I would give in to the temptation to respond.

"That's strange. I got a message from you asking me to come over for dinner."

A cough sounded behind me.

I exhaled slowly. Luna had borrowed my phone while hers was charging in the bedroom, saying she needed to check the recipe.

Jason's eyes flicked over my shoulder. His brows rose.

"Hi," Luna squeaked as she threaded her arm through mine.

Slowly, I turned my head toward my meddling sister and gave her a narrow-eyed look.

"You must be Luna." Jason's amused gaze moved to me before settling back on her.

I could feel her energy spike. She almost vibrated with excitement.

"You know about me?" she asked, grinning.

"Of course. Your sister used to talk about you often." He looked at me and his face softened. "I'm glad you're together now."

"That makes one of us," I muttered.

Luna jabbed her elbow into my side, and I glared at her in response.

"Come in, Jason." Nudging me to the left, she pulled the front door open and gestured for him to come inside. "Ooh, fresh flowers! They're beautiful. Right, Ate?"

"Right," I answered between gritted teeth.

Her smile stretched even wider as she took the flowerpot and shoved it into my arms. "I think this would look nice on the coffee table."

Jason watched me with hooded eyes. "Should I go?"

"Yes—"

"No way," Luna talked over me. "I cooked plenty of food. And you brought the perfect wine."

"You're underage," I said.

"Nineteen's legal in the Philippines."

"We're in the US." Eighteen was the legal age to drink alcohol back home. Too bad we weren't there.

Turning to Jason, Luna said, "She's only pretending we don't drink cheap wine together because you're here."

"Your secret's safe with me," he told her solemnly.

A groan lodged in my throat. Of course, they would get along. Jason and Luna could both charm any stranger they met.

Looking way too pleased, Luna took the bottle from him and placed it on the dining table.

His eyes met mine. *Do you want me to leave?* they seemed to ask.

I shook my head and led him to the living area. As much as I wanted to demand that he leave, Lola would haunt me if I was rude to a guest, even an unwanted one.

Walking through our tiny apartment, I hid a wince at the thought of how my old, mismatched furniture looked like to him. At least I'd finished my ironing and the space was clean except for the minuscule kitchen, which Luna left in a constant state of disarray.

The flowers in my hand mocked me with their cheerful colors. I didn't even know the first thing about keeping flowers alive. Placing them on the coffee table, I mentally cursed Luna for putting me in this situation.

"Ate," she called out to me and pointedly glanced at my midsection. "Didn't you say you wanted to change after finishing your chores? I'll keep Jason company while you freshen up."

My eyes widened in realization. First, he'd seen me in my scrubs. Now, here I was, in my ratty house clothes in front of the hottest guy I had ever known.

"Jason, do you want water?" Luna diverted his attention, redeeming herself by a smidge. "Then you can tell me all about playing for the best team in the NBA."

Grabbing the opportunity, I excused myself and headed for the bedroom, where I shared the closet with Luna. As the door shut behind me, I ordered myself to get it together. So what if he was a professional athlete and a superstar? This was my place. Invited or not, I could ask him to leave whenever I wanted.

I'd hear him out, let the wine do its job, and send him on his way at the end of the night. I only prayed for the patience to not strangle Luna after he left.

7

adobo – (n) the Philippines' unofficial national dish

Jason

"That was amazing," I said, running a palm over my stomach.

My first taste of Filipino-style *adobo* lived up to its reputation. Garlicky and rich, the chicken and pork stew was at once salty, sour, and sweet. I couldn't remember eating so much rice in one sitting, but it complemented the saucy meal perfectly. No wonder they matched a spoon to their fork instead of a knife.

It was also the first time I had eaten meat in three years. After showing up to their dinner unannounced, I refused to tell them I couldn't eat their food. Even though Luna had technically invited me, she had no way of knowing about my plant-based diet.

Her smile stretched from cheek to cheek. "Glad you liked it. It's our *lola*'s specialty."

"Our grandmother," Tala explained from her seat beside me.

"I remember." She'd taught me the term in the past when she spoke of her favorite relative.

As they had throughout the meal, her eyes shifted to me, only to skitter away when I tried to meet them. I hated that she tried to hide from me when she'd been so open before.

But I couldn't blame her for it.

"Is she still in remission?" I asked, remembering Tala's stories about her grandmother's battle with cancer.

Tala blinked, surprise clear on her face. Then a shadow fell over her features. "She passed away almost four years ago," she said matter-of-factly.

Fuck. I raised my hand to touch her arm, only for her to flinch. My hand dropped back to my thigh. "I'm so sorry to hear that, Tal." The old nickname slipped from my mouth as easily as it used to. "Were you able to see her—"

"No."

She spoke with such finality that I envisioned the stark period at the end of that single syllable. I didn't have to see the stony expression on her face or the sadness on Luna's to know the loss cut deep. Losing a loved one killed part of your soul. Losing someone and not being able to say goodbye? That must have been agonizing.

"So, do you have any special plans while you're in town?" Luna asked in a bright voice. Throughout the evening, she'd kept up the flow of the conversation, engaging me with a series of questions.

Tala, for the most part, only spoke when Luna or I asked her a direct question. I remembered her being timid when we first met, but it hadn't taken her long to come out of her shell. Present-day Tala didn't strike me as timid so much as restrained. Like she picked and chose what she wanted to express, and when.

Much like I did when it came to prying reporters. The realization bothered me.

"I'll drop by the campus one of these days. See my old coach. Other than that, I just want to relax and work on my conditioning. Get some hikes in, maybe go boating." I'd already given my generic reason for visiting Sterling, telling them I needed a break from the limelight.

"If you're going to campus, I suggest doing it on a Friday afternoon to avoid getting too much attention," Luna said. "No one hangs around after class on Fridays."

"That's a great tip. I'll keep that in mind."

"Oh! I just remembered the basketball team's leaving for summer camp soon. I can't remember the dates, but I can ask around for you," she offered.

"It's fine, I'm in no rush. I appreciate the heads-up though." The team being away worked in my favor. It meant I'd be able to go without my appearance causing much fuss. I still had to plan a visit with Coach Tom, but I could push it closer to my departure. I wanted to lay low as long as possible.

Tala reached for the pitcher, her arm brushing against mine. The accidental touch put me on edge. I had never been so viscerally aware of a woman as I had been since she sat beside me at their small square table. Luna hadn't left her a choice, taking the seat opposite mine.

Their apartment was more compact than I expected. The furniture looked worn and uncoordinated, and there appeared to be only one bedroom. Were they sharing it?

I knew influencers and content creators could rake in good money, depending on the size of their following. While Tala's audience hadn't blown up, it was still bigger than most. Based on what I'd seen on her account, she collaborated with brands ranging from independent online shops to household names.

She should have been able to afford a better place, since she had a full-time job too.

Sterling was a safe town, sure, but two ladies living alone needed a secure home. Hell, I'd gotten inside their building by following an elderly man through the front door.

Standing, Tala began to stack the cutlery and dishes. "Thanks for cooking, Lu. I'll wash up," she said.

"Good, 'cause I have to go." Luna pushed away from her seat.

Tala narrowed her eyes on her sister. "Where are you going?"

"Kriz's place." Luna's tone was all innocence. "We're working on a paper together."

I called bullshit.

Tala's raised eyebrow said she wasn't buying it either. "First time I'm hearing about it."

Luna rolled her eyes. "I don't tell you everything. What am I, ten?" Suddenly, she perked up and turned to me. "Speaking of ten...Any chance you can get us an intro?"

"Luna," Tala said sharply.

I chuckled, picking up on the reference. Like me, Miles had chosen his favorite number for his jersey—number ten to my sixteen.

"Miles is my favorite player. After you, of course." Luna's smile was shameless.

"Of course. I'll see what I can do."

"Yes! Thanks, Jason," she gushed.

"No promises, but I'll try my best." Miles was likely in Europe by now, but I could always get him on the phone. Which reminded me—I owed him a call.

Tala shook her head as she placed the dishes in the sink.

Trailing after her, Luna threw an arm around her back. "Don't be mad. I had to at least ask."

Tala's shoulders dropped. "Don't stay out too late, okay?"

"Maybe." Luna gave her a smack on the cheek and whirled away. To me, she said, "It was nice to meet you, Jason."

"Likewise," I replied. "Thanks for the *adobo* and for the invite."

She winked at me and dashed off, only pausing to grab a bag. "Bye, you two," she called out right before the door shut, leaving me alone with Tala.

There was a moment of charged silence. Then Tala spoke up. "Let me show you—"

"I'll help you clean up," I interrupted, knowing where she was heading with that statement.

"It's fine."

"I insist." Moving beside her, I nudged her away from the sink. I tugged my sleeves up to my elbows, picked up the sponge, and scrubbed a set of cutlery.

From the corner of my eye, I saw her hesitate. She sighed and reached for a kitchen towel.

"How have you been?" I asked, going back to the question she had brushed aside over dinner.

"You already asked me that."

"You said you're fine." I scoffed. "That's what I say when I don't want to tell the truth."

Pausing, she glared up at me. "It *is* the truth. I'm healthy, busy with work, and glad to have Luna here. Is that better?"

I passed the washed utensils to her. "She seems to enjoy school."

"She does. She likes her classes and she's found a group of friends." Tala wiped the utensils, her movements jerky. "Kriz, the one she's supposedly meeting, is half Filipino."

"That's great." I contemplated asking the question that had been on my mind since the moment I saw her yesterday. I'd almost asked during dinner but figured it wasn't the right time.

Now that we were alone, I went for it. "Why are you working at Golden Haven?"

Her hand stilled before she resumed drying. "It pays the bills," she said, keeping her head down.

"Are you saving up for another place?"

This time, she looked straight at me. "What's wrong with where I live?"

Shit. Mayday, mayday.

"Nothing." Treading carefully, I picked up a plate. "It's just a bit small for the two of you."

"It's big enough that we have our own spaces."

"You have your own bedrooms?"

"There's one bedroom and that couch," she said, nodding toward the living room.

Glancing behind me, I stared at the worn sofa I'd sat on before dinner. My ass had almost sunk straight onto the frame beneath the lumpy padding. "Where do you sleep?" I asked, dreading the answer I knew was coming.

She went back to the dishes. "Don't look at me like that. I don't owe you any explanations."

Fuck. I was screwing this up so badly. "I didn't mean to offend you. I just—"

"Why are you here, Jason?" she demanded, facing me again. "Just because you saw me at the center didn't mean you had to contact me."

"I was planning to even before I saw you there." I blew out a breath and told myself to just say it. "I wanted to apologize."

Expressionless, she lowered her hands. "For what?"

"You were one of my best friends, and I left without saying goodbye. It was a dick move. I'm sorry." Even before I finished talking, I knew the words weren't enough. I'd imagined that moment multiple times, yet I still couldn't find the right things to say. Like the right combination of syllables and words dangled beyond my grasp.

She didn't even blink. "Okay."

Frustration welled up inside me. "No, it's not okay," I argued, digging my hand in my hair. "You were important to me. I was selfish, and I wish I could change what I did. The least I could have done was talk to you before I moved to California."

"Why didn't you?"

"I was a coward. I didn't know how to tell you I was leaving."

"You could have just said that." Her eyes turned hard. "I knew you would go for the draft. It wasn't a big surprise. I was naive, but I wasn't stupid."

I hesitated, not knowing how to put my reasons into words.

"Look, it's fine." She waved a hand in the air. "It was a lifetime ago, Jason. We've both moved on."

"I've missed you." The truth slipped out before I could think at all.

She shifted her gaze to the dishes. "Okay."

I placed my knuckles under her chin and tipped her head up, waiting until her eyes met mine. "I'm not making it up. Those times in the garden with you are some of my best memories of college. I'm sorry I screwed things up, Tal. I'm sorry I left you hanging."

She swallowed. "Apology accepted."

Then she took a step back, placing an arm's length between us. I fought the urge to bridge that space. Instead, I turned to finish washing the dishes.

"I'll be here for a few weeks." I kept my voice casual. "I was hoping we could hang out like old times."

Efficiently drying the plates I passed to her, she replied,

The Off-Chance of Me and You

"It's not that simple, Jason. We can't just go back to how it used to be. Besides, I'm busy enough as it is."

I heard the rejection loud and clear but refused to give up. "Can I at least get your number?"

"What for?"

"I owe your sister an intro, remember?" When she didn't say anything, I shrugged. "I can always look her up on Facebook too."

She challenged me with her eyes. "It's the same number I had in college."

"My old phone got stolen." Knowing that sounded like a lame excuse, I said, "You can look it up. I left my bag unattended at some bar my first year, and someone nabbed my wallet and my phone. Rookie mistake. The press had a field day writing about it."

Her eyebrow rose, but she snapped, "Fine."

She rattled off her number while I added it to my contact list. A second later, both her phone and her watch buzzed.

I slipped the phone back in my pocket.

She walked to the entryway. "Thanks for the flowers and the wine. I hope you enjoy your break."

Way to let me know she had no plans of seeing me again. It was so unlike the girl I'd known that I couldn't keep from staring at her. Despite the tension in her shoulders, she moved gracefully, like each muscle of her body followed a rhythm only she could hear.

When she reached the door, she glanced back at me expectantly.

"Very subtle," I said.

"I wasn't trying to be," she shot back.

Taking in the stubborn set of her jaw, I decided to let it go. For now. "Fine." I walked to her. "It was great seeing you again, Tal. Thanks for letting me stay for dinner."

Her eyes clouded with what looked like guilt.

I couldn't have that.

Leaning toward her, I cupped her nape and pressed a kiss to her forehead. I caught a whiff of her shampoo—fruity and sweet—and moved away. "Good night," I murmured.

She said nothing as I opened the door and strode to the elevators.

Of the many ways I had imagined the night going, I never foresaw this. Not that Tala hadn't actually invited me, or that Luna was in the picture now. I didn't think Tala would listen to my apology and accept it so nonchalantly. Or that she would turn down the chance to hang out again.

I didn't think I was irresistible, although I'd never had any problems catching a woman's attention.

But...this was Tala. The one girl I'd been able to talk to about practically everything.

As a girl, she had made me feel comfortable. At ease.

As a woman, she unsettled me. Intrigued me.

I stepped into the elevator and stared at her door in the distance. Like I'd told her, I was staying for a few weeks. I had time to try again.

And if she thought I wouldn't, she'd underestimated me.

8

kaibigan – (n) friend

Tala

I chewed on my cheeseburger, my gaze fixed on the tanned neck of the man sitting opposite me. It was much darker than Jason's and hairier too. Jason's facial hair didn't extend below his Adam's apple. Three days ago, I wouldn't have been able to say that for sure, but then I sat through an entire dinner with him beside me—and by *beside*, I mean there had barely been an inch between our elbows.

Our arms had brushed against each other multiple times, and each touch made my skin prickle with awareness. I must've looked like a fool with how often I lost track of the conversation. Thankfully, Luna's social skills compensated for my distractedness.

Though if it weren't for her meddling, I wouldn't have been stuck in that awkward situation in the first place.

I couldn't believe Jason asked if we could hang out like old times. Seriously? I appreciated the apology, as delayed as it had been, but did he really think that changed anything? We were completely different people now.

And that kiss on my forehead.

When we were friends, our physical contact was limited to our arms brushing or palms slapping in a high five. On rare moments, he put an arm around my shoulders, careful to maintain a platonic distance. I never tried to breach it.

But I wanted to then, and hell if I didn't want to now.

"If I were a lesser man, I would be insulted by your disinterest."

Blinking, I lifted my eyes to Gabe's face. He looked back at me with a raised brow, his empty plate telling me just how long I had tuned him out.

I grimaced. "Shit, I'm sorry."

"It's fine. Nothing I don't experience during my lectures," he said wryly.

"Yeah, right. Like you don't have students hanging on your every word."

He shook his head. "If only it were my words they focused on." In his signature style, he wore navy chinos with a white button up and a gleaming silver watch on his wrist. Not a strand of his wavy brown hair lay out of place. Eyes lingered on him as women passed, their curiosity morphing into envy upon spotting me.

I'd long gotten used to that. When we first met in my junior year finance class, Gabe attracted a long list of admirers as a graduate teaching assistant. I had no doubt he continued to distract his students now.

"Some people find your accent sexy," I teased.

The compliment bounced right off him. "And some people might be tricked by your attempt at deflection," he said. "Are you going to tell me what's bothering you, or do you need more time to delay the inevitable?"

He knew me too well.

Releasing a heavy breath, I admitted, "Science guy's in town and he wants to *hang out*." I drew quotation marks in the air around the last two words.

To Gabe's credit, he didn't need a reminder about who I referred to. All he said was, "Explain."

I told him everything, from how I found Jason in Berna's room to dinner with Luna and him texting me the past two days. Gabe listened without interruption, his serious gaze set on me like he was trying to read the emotions I kept contained, even from him.

At the end of my recounting, he flagged down a waitress to order my usual rum and Coke and a beer for himself. I finished the remaining half of my burger in three bites.

"This is good," he told me after the waitress left to fix our drinks. "It's your opportunity to get closure."

My head snapped back. "Closure? I don't need closure. We were just friends."

"He was always the one who got away, and we both know it."

"I've moved on," I insisted.

"Then hanging out with him shouldn't be an issue, should it?"

My lips pressed together in a tight line. "You sound like Luna," I grumbled. It was as if they'd agreed to team up against me separately.

"I hate to admit it," he said slowly, "but your sister makes sense."

"You're only saying that because you agree with her."

He smirked. "Tell me why you turned Jason down when you've said multiple times you wanted to talk to him."

I rolled my eyes. "I was drunk every single time I said that."

"It's easier to say the truth when you're drunk. Am I wrong?"

Of course, he wasn't. I hated when he used his sharp mind against me.

The waitress returned with our drinks, giving me time to think of a response. I wouldn't be able to bluff my way past Gabe. I could put it off for later, but it would only be a matter of time until he pushed me for an answer.

Reaching for my cocktail, I tapped a finger on the condensation clouding the glass. My eyes remained on the dark beverage as I confessed the truth I could barely admit to myself. "It was hard getting over him. I can't afford to risk that again."

Gabe's silence told me he was mulling over my admission. I sipped my drink, grateful the bartender had gone heavy on the rum.

"Both of you were younger then. You know better now."

"Exactly. I know better than to make the same mistake twice." This time, I wouldn't have the excuse of age and naiveté. I would just be stupid.

"So set boundaries."

I met his steady gaze.

"Do what makes you comfortable, whether it's texting or coffee or hanging out on your building's rooftop."

"Why shouldn't I just say no?"

"Because you don't really want to," Gabe said bluntly.

I frowned. "What—"

"If you wanted to say no, you would have said it and moved on. You wouldn't still be thinking about it days later."

His words killed the argument on the tip of my tongue.

He was right. *Again*. Damn it.

His expression remained impassive as he drank, like he was waiting for me to accept the truth he so casually shoved in my face.

Downing my cocktail, I welcomed the burn down my throat. "I hate how well you know me."

He smirked. "You're welcome." Then he turned solemn. "We rarely get the chance to fix things we regret. You know that."

Lola's face flashed in my mind. With it came the long-standing thought that if only I had ditched my finals and emptied out my savings, I could have seen her one last time. Never mind that she would have already been gone.

"Maybe you can be friends again," Gabe continued. "At the very least, you won't need to wonder what could have been."

I groaned. "Fine. I'll think about it." The same words I'd told Luna. This time, I meant them.

"While you're at it, plan for me to meet him. If he's going to hang around you and your sister, I need to make sure you'll be safe."

"*Now* you're concerned."

"When it comes to you, I'm always concerned."

After Jason left, Gabe was the one person I truly opened up to—the only man I trusted outside my family. It didn't matter that he was four years older than me or that people mistook our friendship for something else.

He had kept me sane in the years before Luna moved here. I loved him in the purest sense of the word.

"Have I told you lately that you're the best?" I said.

His eyebrow twitched, a telltale sign I had made him uncomfortable with my rare words of affection.

Neither of us did well with emotions.

"Stop stalling and reply to him already."

"I need another drink," I muttered.

Still, I brought my phone out all the same.

Jason

Panting, I toweled off my face and neck. I'd lucked out with an empty gym, save for a single attendant cleaning the equipment. He'd startled when he saw me but remained respectful and unobtrusive. A welcome change.

As I guzzled water, my thoughts shifted back to the woman who kept me distracted.

Tala still hadn't replied to my texts except for a "you're welcome" after I thanked her and Luna for dinner. If she were another woman, I might have passed it off as a coy attempt to keep me on my toes. Knowing she juggled two jobs, I preferred to think she was simply busy.

I refused to believe she wasn't interested...or, at the very least, curious.

It wasn't my ego talking. I just subscribed to the notion of claiming what I wanted to achieve as reality. Call it the law of attraction, the power of positivity, or plain optimism. Whatever it was, it served me well in my career. I set my goal, put in the work, and made it happen. Even when my body ached and my heart wasn't in it, I hit the court and played to win each time.

That reminded me of how I hadn't touched a basketball since arriving in Sterling. I hadn't gone this long without playing in years—not since a drunk driver hit Dad's car head-on, killing him on impact. He'd been thirty-three years old, fresh from a championship. I was ten.

At first, basketball had been a way to remember him and keep him close. Then it became a matter of continuing his legacy.

I hadn't stopped playing since.

I needed to go back to it. Workouts didn't mean squat if my hands forgot the feel of the ball, if my body lost the motions of the game. I needed to find a court to train.

But did I miss it? No.

Upstairs in my suite, I tossed my keycard on the console table and dumped my gear on the floor. I glanced around the room and frowned. It was well-decorated and clean. Twice the size of Tala's modest apartment. And impersonal. After staying in too many hotels to count, they'd lost any appeal for me, yet I didn't miss my place in Santa Mila either.

The repurposed factory that was my apartment didn't hold much sentimental value. For the most part, it was just a space where I slept, ate, worked, and occasionally fucked. I had more memories in Miles's home than my own.

After grabbing a glass of wine from the minibar, I sat in an armchair and dialed Miles. The line rang twice before he picked up.

"J-man!"

"Took you long enough," I said as I took a sip of wine.

"Miss me?"

"Like I miss my other half."

Miles's voice boomed through the speaker. "I knew you felt the same way! You took your damn time calling. How's life in the 'burbs?"

I chuckled. "Peaceful."

"They forgot you already, huh? Sucks, man."

"You're hilarious."

Apart from a few people giving me second glances or friendly waves, I hadn't received too much attention. It helped that most students were on summer break, and folks in town took celebrity sightings in stride.

It was one of the reasons Dad loved the place so much. As did I.

"So, you coming back anytime soon?"

"I'm actually thinking of renting a place here." I said it impulsively, but the more I thought about the idea, the more I liked it. If I could find a place with a court, even a half one, I'd be sold.

"No shit?" Incredulity filled Miles's voice.

"You were the one who told me to get out of town."

"For a week or two! I didn't think you'd go all hermit mode. You even working out? Fucking hell, if you get soft on me, I'm gonna whip your puny ass into shape."

"I'm in the gym every day."

"Damn right, you should be." Miles talked about a new workout regimen his trainer had him on and made me promise to try it.

"Send me the rundown and I'll check it out," I said. "By the way, I need to introduce you to someone."

There was a loaded pause and then, "Well, I'll be damned. Have you gone and met the one? Is that why you're holing up over there?"

"No, asshole. She's the sister of an old friend."

"An old friend? I'm guessing female. Who are we interested in, the friend or the sister?"

Of course Miles assumed I was talking about a woman. Not that he was wrong. "She's just a friend."

"Wasn't my question, man. Now you've got me hooked. Hold up—" His voice grew louder. "Is this the chick you were talking about that one time?"

Shit. I closed my eyes and rubbed my hand across my face.

"One of those nights you got wasted at a club," Miles continued, confirming my hunch. "Our first year, I think? You were watching some women twerking and said something about how your girl could dance circles around them. I was gonna ask about her the next day, but I got drunk too and forgot about it till now."

I'd hoped he'd lost all memories of that night for good. Too much alcohol loosened my tongue, as I'd learned in my rookie year. It was why I took care to only get wasted with people I trusted, and not in public.

"Tanya!" Miles shouted. "Am I right?"

Too damn close. He had a knack for remembering the most random things. "It's Tala."

"You gonna tell me the score?"

I could count on Miles to keep his mouth shut. We'd covered for each other countless times, both on and off the court. But I wasn't ready to talk yet.

"When I see you," I said instead.

"Make sure you set up a meet when I come over."

I should have seen that coming. He'd never mentioned visiting Sterling before, but the guy was a pit bull when it came to something he was curious about. "You have a date in mind?"

"Let's say second week of September, right before your birthday."

"Sounds good. Let me know when you've booked your flight." That reminded me... "Tell me you're not chartering a plane."

It was bad enough our team insisted on private flights whenever we traveled. Some of my friends refused to fly commercial even with first-class options. The cumulative environmental impact of all our air travel ate at my conscience. My college professors would be ashamed of me.

"Yeah, yeah. Private flights are driving us to the brink of climate disaster. You've told me. A shit ton of times," Miles drawled.

"We're not on the brink. It's already happening." The familiar frustration rose in my chest, strengthening my voice. "You have no idea—"

"Relax, J-man. I'll fly commercial. The sacrifices I make for you," he muttered.

"Planet Earth thanks you," I said drily.

"'Course you think you can speak for our planet. Listen, I've got to run. Underwear shoot."

The excitement in his voice had me snickering. "Enjoy."

"Always. See you next month."

"Counting on it. Later, man."

I hung up and finished my wine. I had over a month to find a rental, convince Tala to give me the time of day, and talk her into meeting Miles.

My phone buzzed. Seeing the notification, I grinned.

TALA

This is not me saying we can hang out.

Maybe not. But her text signaled a step in that direction. All I had to do was keep her walking and meet her halfway.

9

taranta – (adj) rattled

Tala

I strolled into the break room, lunch bag in hand. Bringing food from home was a perk of living with someone who enjoyed cooking. I used to have canteen meals deducted from my salary, and they were decent at best. Now, lunch consisted of packed food most days, and it tasted ten times better than anything from the canteen, even after being microwaved.

Aside from looking forward to Luna's dish of the day, I smiled over the latest messages from Jason. He'd wished me luck at work and followed it up with an infographic about ocean depth. It was completely random yet so typical of the Jason I'd once known. The one who spouted nature trivia out of the blue. That bit of familiarity took me back to simpler times and warmed me to him.

Sneaky guy.

"Hey, Tala." Billie, a fellow nurse who'd become my friend, called to me from one of the dining tables.

"Hi, Billie," I said as I approached.

"Jose asked me to tell you to drop by his office when you can."

I frowned. "Did he say why?"

"Nope. He didn't seem upset or anything, if that helps."

"Alright, I'll go there now." I held up my food. "You mind if I leave this here?"

"Go ahead. Good luck, girl." She gave me a reassuring smile.

After thanking her, I headed down the hall to the supervisor's office. I knocked and entered at his "come in."

"Hey, Jose. You asked for me?"

"Tala. Yes, have a seat." The middle-aged man gestured at one of the chairs in front of his desk.

Sitting, I stacked my hands on my lap.

"I know it's your break," he started. "So, I'll keep this brief. I have some news to share."

"Okay." I squashed the urge to drum my fingertips.

"There's no easy way to say this. We won't be able to sponsor your visa extension."

I blinked. Did I hear him correctly? They *weren't* extending my visa?

Fighting the sudden dryness in my throat, I asked, "Did I do something wrong? I thought you said it wouldn't be a problem."

Just six months ago, I brought up the time remaining on my contract and he'd told me they were definitely keeping me on. He had even mentioned a possible promotion.

I took his word for granted. Other possibilities never crossed my mind.

"No, no. It's not about your performance," Jose rushed to explain. "In fact, we were about to start working on your documents. But while processing Shanti's extension—her visa ends earlier than yours—management put a stop to it. With the state of the economy, they decided to cut costs, including migrant workers. We will, of course, honor existing contracts, but we won't be extending any foreign hires in the immediate future."

"I see." My hands grew clammy. I laced my fingers together to keep from fidgeting.

His eyebrows gathered in. "I'm sorry to break this to you out of the blue. I wanted to give you time to consider other options."

"It's alright," I said, forcing a smile. "I appreciate the update."

"Do you remember how long you have left?"

I had that information memorized, but my brain blanked. "Around three months, I think. I need to double-check."

He nodded and leaned forward. "If you decide to look for another job here, I'll give you a recommendation letter. You can use your remaining time off to interview. I only ask that you give me a heads-up when you decide on what your last day will be, so we can hire and train your replacement."

"Of course."

"Think things over. I'll have HR compute your time off and other benefits you can use. Let's meet in a few weeks to sort things out. Okay?"

"Yes, that's fine. Thanks, Jose."

Standing, I let myself out and closed the door quietly.

Out in the hallway, I opened my calendar app with shaky hands and scrolled down. Too soon, the date marked *Visa expiry* turned up.

October 20.

Just a little over three months from now. Was that enough time to look for another job and get them to sponsor my visa? Would other companies even be open to hiring foreign workers? If Golden Haven, one of the state's most prestigious elderly homes, needed to cut costs, didn't it stand to reason that other companies would as well?

Chill, Tala. Nothing I could do about that problem now. I just had to get through my shift, wrap my head around the news, and come up with a plan B. No need to freak out.

Appetite gone, I went back to the break room to retrieve my lunch. After giving Billie a hasty excuse, I headed for the walking path to clear my head before returning to my patients.

All of a sudden, Jason's unexpected reappearance was the least of my problems.

"AND I-I-IIII—"

I dropped the clipboard I'd been holding as Berna's voice rang through the room.

"Will always love you—"

"Um, are you alright, Berna?" I asked cautiously, picking up her chart.

"Of course. I just had to get your attention somehow," she said.

"Oh." I had been replaying Jose's update in my head, wondering if there was a possibility I'd heard him wrong. But Berna deserved my full attention. "I'm sorry for spacing out. I had some personal issues on my mind."

"Could it have something to do with a certain basketball player who still happens to be in town?" Her eyes gleamed.

At least I could truthfully say no. "Of course not."

I was writing my end-of-shift report when Berna called for me. She did that sometimes when she needed someone to talk to. While it wasn't part of my job description, I tried to accommodate my patients, especially those who didn't get visitors often. Like Berna.

"I called for you because you seemed troubled during your afternoon visit," she explained. "You were so happy in the morning. Giddy, even."

Morning felt like a world ago.

"Can I help you with anything?" Berna said.

For her to ask me that when it was my job to help *her* felt like a warm, invisible hug. Lola used to do the same thing when I took over her chores at home. Chemotherapy had stolen her hair and her energy, yet she still worried about me.

"I'm fine," I told Berna, mustering a smile of gratitude. "Thank you for your concern."

She snorted. "So formal. What am I, a stranger? You've fixed my catheter and cleaned my bedpan. I think you can tell me to mind my own business."

A startled laugh burst out of me. Just when I thought I wouldn't be surprised by anything she said, she managed to catch me off-guard. "It's not like that. I got bad news earlier. It was something I didn't expect and I'm not sure what to do."

"I see." She nodded slowly and shifted, trying to sit up higher.

I leaned over the bed to help her, repositioning her pillow so it supported her back. "Do you want me to raise the top of the bed?"

She waved me away. "No, no. Stop fussing. Where was I? Ah, yes. Well, I'm not going to insist you tell me the news, if you don't feel comfortable. But life doesn't always turn out the way we planned. In fact, it rarely does, or I wouldn't be here."

Despite her matter-of-fact tone, my heart ached for her. "For what it's worth, I'm glad I had the opportunity to get to know you. I wish it would have been under better circumstances but—"

"We take the cards life deals us and make the best out of

them," she said. "I can't guess what's bothering you, and I won't promise you things will be okay. No one can, if you ask me."

I bit back a smile.

"Many things are beyond our control, but how we respond to them, what we choose to do—*that*, you can influence." Her eyes seemed to bore into my soul. "Trust yourself and listen to what your heart says even when your brain argues otherwise. That way, if your world turns upside down, at least you won't regret the choices you made."

My head slowly moved up and down as I mulled over her words. "That's...a lot to process."

"I can write it down for you so you won't forget," she said, reverting to her tongue-in-cheek humor.

I chuckled. "I might hold you to that. Thank you, Berna. I'll definitely think about what you said."

After I had clocked out and caught the bus to my apartment, her words still lingered.

No regrets. I always found it to be a flippant statement—a motto you threw out on the fly that ultimately hit you smack on your forehead with its falseness. It was easy to say when you were high on infinite possibilities to come. But in hindsight, when your chances trickled down to zero, could you really look back on your decisions and say that you wouldn't change a thing?

Jose's news battled with Berna's advice for space in my head, triggering a restlessness in my limbs. The feeling doubled when I found my apartment empty. I'd forgotten Luna told me she'd go out with her friends after class.

Needing to release some steam, I changed into workout clothes and headed for the rooftop.

When all else failed, nothing centered me better than dancing did.

10

taguan – (n) hiding place; hide and seek

Jason

The phone kept ringing in my ear, just like it had the past three times I called.

Grabbing the bag of donuts, I stepped out of my car and hit the lock button on the remote. The entrance of Tala's apartment building stood in front of me, its paint patched over in sections. Unlike the first time I visited, there was no one I could charm into letting me in.

I pressed Tala's unit number on the intercom system and waited for an answer. Again, nothing. Surely one of her neighbors would come around sooner or later. Worst case, I'd wait for her in the car.

That wasn't stalker behavior, was it?

"Jason?"

Turning, I found Luna walking toward me. Perfect timing. "Hey, Luna. Back from school?"

"Yeah." She tilted her head to the right as she adjusted her bag's strap. "Is Ate expecting you?"

"Not exactly. I tried calling but she didn't answer. Also buzzed your unit."

Stopping in front of me, Luna pursed her lips. "She should be done with work. I bet she's on the rooftop."

The rooftop?

My confusion must have been obvious because she explained, "That's where she dances and shoots her videos. Not sure if you noticed, but our place doesn't have much space."

Talk about an understatement. Why hadn't Tala's financial situation improved? In the past, she told me that they'd lost their family business, which prompted them to look for better opportunities abroad. But I assumed her parents had stable jobs now, and so did she. Had anything else happened? There were so many blanks in what I knew about Tala's life, and I wanted to fill them in.

"You think she'd mind if I visited her there?" I asked.

"Honestly? Yes." Luna's face broke into a smile. "But I think you might be good for her. Come on in."

I grinned. "Thanks. I owe you one."

Tapping a fob on the electronic keypad, she unlocked the door. I held it open for her and followed her to the elevator, where she hit the buttons marked *six* and *R*.

Raising the box in my hand, I offered, "Donuts?"

"Ooh. Perfect for my paper writing night."

"Go ahead." I opened the box for her as the elevator lurched up, then I handed her one of those paper napkins that cafes loved to give out in stacks. As though we had an endless reserve of trees.

She skipped the sugar glazed donuts and went for strawberry with sprinkles, carefully lifting it with a napkin. "Don't think I don't know you're trying to get on my good side."

I laughed. "Is it working?"

"Maybe. I'm still waiting for my intro."

Luckily, I had good news for her. "Miles is planning a visit."

Her eyes widened. "Seriously?"

"It's still in the works," I clarified, trying to manage her expectations. Miles usually came through for me, but who knew what might derail his plans. "We need to figure out the details."

Luna's smile lit up her face, her excitement palpable despite my words. "I can't wait. I mean, yeah, I know I shouldn't get my hopes up, but yay!"

We came to a stop and the doors crept open. I pressed the button to keep the elevator open for her. "I'll keep you posted."

"Thanks!" She stepped out into the hallway and hesitated. "And Jason?"

My eyebrows rose.

"You might be a famous basketball player who brings donuts around, but if you hurt my sister, I'll find a way to get back at you."

The threat uttered in her agreeable voice made my lips twitch. I managed to solemnly say, "Copy that. I don't want to hurt Tala, and I'll try my best not to."

"You do that."

"Good luck with your paper."

With one last smile and a wave, she walked away.

I chuckled to myself. Luna was a firecracker. Like her sister, she was beautiful, with long dark hair, tan skin, and striking eyes. But while Tala was reserved and cautious, Luna was bubbly and guileless.

As soon as the elevator opened again, music floated over to my ears. It took me back to the day I met Tala when I was a senior and she was a new international student. This time, there were no palmetto trees, vines, or fountains. There was just the elevator bank, a couple of plastic chairs, and the clear sky.

I rounded the elevator and found her dancing. She wore sweat shorts and a large cutoff shirt. As she threw her arms up, her shirt rose, revealing her flat stomach. She ground her hips to the sensuous beat, dropping her head back.

A bolt of desire zipped through me.

Before I could figure out how to let her know I was there, she twirled.

And shrieked, stumbling.

"Shit, I'm sorry." Dropping the donut box on a chair, I strode toward her.

She dodged me and shouted, "What the hell are you doing here?" Her hand rubbed her chest, like she was trying to calm herself down.

"I didn't mean to surprise you. Are you okay?" Spotting her water bottle, I grabbed it and held it out to her.

She took it from me warily but didn't drink. "How did you know I was here?"

"I ran into Luna outside the building."

"Of course." Her eyes narrowed.

That could only mean trouble later for Luna. I tried to cover for her, saying, "I bribed her with a chance to meet Miles."

"Nice try, but I know my sister." Tala shook her head and opened her water bottle.

"I gave her a donut too."

She sputtered mid-swallow. Holding the bottle away, she coughed.

I leaned over to thump her back.

Wiping her chin, she said, "Are you trying to give me a heart attack?"

"Sorry. I tried calling you several times."

She took a careful sip and capped the bottle. "I disabled my notifications and left my phone in my bag."

The tension in her voice made me pause. "You okay?"

"I'm fine."

Her shifty eyes said otherwise.

"Anyway, you found me. What's up?"

I noticed the strain visible in the corners of her mouth and the line on her forehead. "How can I convince you to give me another shot?"

She sighed. "Why are you in Sterling, Jason? I'm sure you can take a break anywhere in the world. Why here?"

Staring at her, I opened my mouth to say the speech I'd prepared. To my surprise, the scripted words disappeared, replaced by thoughts that I'd tried to rein in. "When we won the ring, I didn't feel anything except tired. I'd been going through the motions but I hadn't really been there in the moment."

The concern on her face prompted me to go on.

"Maybe it's burnout. I don't know, but when Miles suggested a change of scenery, Sterling was the first place I thought of. I always felt like I was fully myself here whenever I visited with my dad, and then when I went here for college. I needed that again."

———

Tala

I studied Jason's face, searching for any sign that he was lying to me. That toothpaste-commercial smile he donned during interviews was nowhere to be found. Instead, his mouth was in a grim line. A deep notch sat between his eyebrows.

Slowly, I nodded. "Thank you for telling me."

He dipped his head.

"What I still don't get is why you keep texting me. Is it guilt? Because I already told you I forgave you. You don't need to worry about that."

"It's not guilt," he said. "Sure, I'm kicking myself for not coming back sooner. For not trying to fix things then. But it's not guilt. It's regret."

My entire being locked in on that last word. Why did it keep haunting me? Was this fate's way of knocking sense into my brain, trying to get me in line with its program?

"We had good times together. I wish we could go back to that," Jason continued.

"We've changed."

"I know. I was a dumbass then," he admitted offhandedly. It reminded me of our first meeting when he called himself an asshole. "I'd like to think I've become less of it."

I snorted. "You weren't so bad."

"Try me now." His voice took on a deeper tone.

My amusement died a quick death. I swallowed.

"You know, Berna said you would be a fine catch for me."

The twinkle in his eye made me wonder if he was joking.

He grinned, seeming to read my mind. "Her words, verbatim."

"I bet your mom didn't agree."

His jaw tightened, a clear giveaway that I'd guessed correctly. "My mom is...protective," he said.

"Well, you can tell her there's nothing to worry about. We're just old friends who ran into each other. Eventually, you'll go back to your world and I'll stay in mine."

"Yeah, no." He shook his head. "I don't like that."

Crossing my arms, I asked, "Which part?"

"All of it. See, the way I see it, I stupidly walked away from one of my best friends. I'm not doing that again."

"What exactly do you want?"

"I want to spend time with you. I can read while you dance, like the old days. I can help you record your videos. We can grab coffee or dinner or, hell, do brunch if that's your thing. Whatever you want."

"So you're inviting yourself to my hideout now?" Trust him to have the nerve to do so. Annoyingly, I found it more charming than not.

He smirked. "I seem to remember you doing the same."

"That's strange, because *I* remember you inviting me to hang out with you in the garden," I shot back, fighting a smile. Damn him for slipping under my defenses. Already, I felt my resolve weakening.

Chuckling, he shrugged. "I wasn't so stupid then, after all."

"I don't do brunch. Coffee or dinner sounds like a date," I grumbled, tapping my foot.

His eyes brightened like he could tell I was softening. "We can table that for later."

"I'm not sure I want that."

He tipped his head to the side as he searched my face. "Tell you what. Why don't we warm up to it? Let me help you shoot. You can order me around. Call me your assistant."

The absurdity of that dragged a laugh out of me. "Since when does a pro basketball player want to be an assistant?"

"Since he wants to make things up to his friend," he replied easily. "Is that a yes?"

He could have asked a hundred other questions; instead, he'd chosen the simplest for me to answer. And the hardest. A yes or no set me squarely between possibilities I'd daydreamed about and an ending that kept me up many nights.

Maybe it was the cumulation of all the advice I'd heard over the past few days, or the thought that my time here might not last the remainder of the year. The realization that things could change when I least expected them to and the desperation for something I could control.

Set boundaries, Gabe had told me. Boundaries I could do.

"Say yes, dance girl." Jason held me with his gaze.

"Fine," I snapped.

"Fine what?"

"I'll let you know next time I'm shooting. If you're busy or you change your mind—"

"I won't." Those lips of his stretched into a slow smile. "Say the word and I'll be there, Tal."

Ignoring the tingle under my skin, I said, "We'll see about that."

A voice in the back of my head told me I was setting myself up for another heartbreak, but I refused to accept it. I had the situation under control. We would do things on my terms. On my schedule.

This time, when our time together ended, I wouldn't be left wondering what could have been.

11

kilig – (n) exhilaration from a romantic encounter

Tala

Blowing out a breath, I looked away from my laptop. I'd been at my job search for the past few hours. Only three jobs stuck out to me as having real potential— one at a bigger facility on the outskirts of town and two located in nearby counties.

I wasn't hopeful about any of them. Bigger facilities often meant cheaper enrollment rates and higher occupancies, which in turn equaled lower staffing budgets. If I went for the other two options, I would end up spending more cash on the commute. That was, if they were even willing to shell out money on my visa.

Not for the first time, I cursed my passport limitations. Without them, I could juggle gigs like waitressing, bartending, or even teaching dance to earn enough money in addition to creating content. Instead, I needed a full-time job that qualified me for an employment visa.

I racked my brain for other options. Being a travel nurse

sounded interesting. I'd always wanted to see more of the world and had barely explored the US in the seven years I'd lived here. Unfortunately, I wouldn't be able to choose where I'd end up. That, and I'd have to leave Luna for long periods of time.

But it would be better than leaving her for good.

Wouldn't it?

Stifling a groan, I decided to go for it. It was easier to have multiple options and narrow them down later instead of having nothing to choose from. I sent applications to the three openings I'd saved, plus a few back-up options. At least one of those should be a good lead.

With that off my checklist, I closed my laptop and got ready for bed. My alarm was set to go off in less than five hours, but I was only working a half shift. Billie had a parent-teacher conference to attend, and she'd asked me to cover for her in the morning.

Then I'd see Jason for the first time after our agreement.

I wanted to be casual about it. After all, he was only helping me with my recording. Did he even know how to set up a tripod and fix camera settings? I'd forgotten to ask.

Then again, he might not even show up. I didn't want to get my hopes up either way. Still, excitement buzzed through me— much to my dismay.

Platonic. I needed to pin that word to my brain in bold, capital letters before it got me in trouble again.

———

AFTER MY SHIFT, I arrived at my apartment building to the sight of Jason standing on the front step next to a plant.

Scratch that. It wasn't a plant. More like a tree in a pot.

"What is *that?*" I asked.

Shoving his hands in his pockets, Jason casually lifted his shoulders. "A belated housewarming gift."

"I didn't know I moved houses since I left this morning."

"Well, it's the first time we're hanging out, aside from that surprise dinner. I thought we should mark the occasion."

Maybe it wasn't the best time to tell him I didn't know how to take care of the flowers he'd given me, let alone an entire tree. Outdoor plants I could do, so long as I had clear instructions on when to water them. But indoor ones? That was another issue entirely. Good thing Luna had a green thumb.

I eyed the tree from top to bottom. "Will it fit inside my apartment?"

"I got it for your hideout, actually. To give it more greenery," he explained.

"That's...thoughtful of you." Up close, the tree was just a few inches shorter than me. "Are you sure you can carry it to the elevator?"

He looked at me like he was insulted. "I bench press more than five times that tree's weight every day."

A laugh escaped me. "Did I hurt your pride?" I teased.

"If I say yes, will you kiss it better?"

I rolled my eyes at his blatant flirting, trying to ignore how his voice sent a tingle down the back of my neck. "Just for that, I'm tempted to make you carry it all the way up the stairs."

"As long as you lead the way."

And give him a front row view of my butt going up nine flights of stairs?

No way.

Unlocking the door, I pushed it open for Jason. He easily lifted the tree, his biceps bunching under his sleeves with the movement. He wasn't overly muscled like some athletes, but he had an undeniable strength that appealed to me.

"Thought we were taking the stairs?" he asked as he followed me inside the elevator.

I lifted an eyebrow at him and pressed the button to hold the doors. "You can if you want to. I'll meet you there."

He met my challenge with a half-smile. "I could, but I prefer the company here." Shifting the tree to one palm, he reached for my hand and eased it away from the hold button. Then he moved it to the one for the rooftop and pressed.

The doors slid shut. He lowered our hands, squeezing once before letting go.

The elevator was small to begin with, and it seemed to shrink with Jason filling up the space beside me. His bicep pressed against my arm, making me hyper aware of his masculinity. True to his word, he didn't seem to be bothered by the tree. Hell, he could probably lift me without issue.

Lift me and hold me against a wall.

He might not even need a wall to give me a good time.

Heat suffused my cheeks.

"How was y—Why are you blushing, Tal?" His voice sounded huskier than usual.

"I'm not. It's just hot in here."

He hummed.

Refusing to check if he was smiling like I thought he was, I stared at the numbers on the elevator screen, willing them to move faster. As if they heard my plea, the doors opened to the rooftop.

"Saved by the elevator," he murmured.

"Very funny." I strode out of the cramped space to my usual spot, dropping my duffel bag on the ground. I'd switched my scrubs for workout clothes at the care center, so I was ready to go.

He looked around before depositing the tree on the far edge of one wall, just beside the full-length mirror I'd propped up there. "How'd you end up dancing here?" he asked.

"I needed a place to rehearse, but I couldn't afford a studio. One day, I went up here out of curiosity." I waved my hands at the space. "My landlord agreed to let me use it as long as I keep it clean and not hold any parties. It's not much, but I like it."

It had taken me a full day to clear out the debris that had built up over the years, and to scrub the concrete floor. A small price to pay for a private space to dance.

"Is it safe for you to be alone here at night?"

I'd asked myself the same question in the past. "Nothing's happened to me yet."

He frowned. "Doesn't mean there's no possibility something won't."

"I don't stay up here late. Besides, Luna and Gabe know about this place."

His body went still. "Gabe?"

"Yeah." Not wanting to get into personal talk, I said, "Were you serious about helping me out?"

He arched his brow, wordlessly telling me he didn't miss the subject change. But he let it go. "Sure am. What can I do?"

"I need to warm up and run through my routines before I start recording." I pointed my toes on the floor and rotated my ankle.

"Alright, I'll do some work on my phone. Let me know when you need me."

With that, he grabbed one of the plastic chairs I kept there. He placed it a few feet from me and sat with his legs spread apart.

Involuntarily, my gaze moved up to where the fabric of his shorts stretched over his groin.

Catching myself, I snapped my head up and fought a wince. What the hell was I doing creeping on him? I hated when men looked at me like I was just a sum of my body parts. There I was, doing the same to him.

He chuckled under his breath, and I summoned the courage to look him straight in the eyes.

"Sorry," I said.

"Don't be. I like you looking at me." One corner of his mouth tipped up. "I like looking at you too."

The admission sent a burst of energy through me, and I couldn't stand still any longer. "I have to warm up," I blurted.

Busying myself with setting up my playlist, I took a deep breath. *Relax.* This was just Jason. I had danced in front of him countless times. No big deal.

I went through my usual exercises, relying on muscle memory. The weight of his gaze electrified my skin, as though my cells recognized his presence and drew too much energy from it.

"This isn't going to work." I cut the music.

How could I have thought I'd be able to rehearse with him watching my every move? I felt so on edge, like I would burst out of my skin in any second.

"What? No." Leaning forward with his forearms braced on his thighs, he said, "I'll work while you dance. It's fine."

"I can't."

"You did it back in college."

"That was a long time ago." My right leg bounced. I was already running behind schedule. No way would I get everything done before dinner, which meant I'd have to push my other tasks to later.

"Hey." Jason leapt to his feet and approached me. His hands rested on my arms, giving them a reassuring rub. "Finish your warm-up. I'll stay over in that corner so I won't disturb you."

He dipped his chin toward the far corner of the rooftop,

which was bordered by a waist-high ledge. From there, he'd be able to see me if he wanted, but I wouldn't see him in the mirror.

An argument rested on the tip of my tongue. Before I could speak, he picked up the chair and walked off.

"Stop slacking off, dance girl," he called out to me.

Stubborn and cocky, just like I remembered him.

He was even more sure of himself now. Secure in his place in the world, confident that whatever he'd say, people would listen. It was both aggravating and enviable.

Fine—it was appealing too.

"I don't hear any music!"

Ugh. "Just giving you time to admire the sound of your own voice," I yelled back.

"Your consideration is much appreciated, but it's time for you to—"

I blasted my music at top volume, drowning out the end of his sentence. Without looking at him, I pictured him grinning. The thought of it made me smile too.

"Let me do that."

I paused in the middle of fixing my tripod and glanced at Jason.

"You should've called me," he said. Ducking his head, he took the tripod from me and unfolded its legs.

"I didn't want to disturb you."

He'd looked engrossed in whatever he was reading on his phone. I studied him longer than I should have as he scrolled up the screen. His lower lip was sucked in, like he was chewing on it. The mannerism reminded me so much of our previous time together that I felt the years blur for a second.

91

"You're not disturbing me. I'm here for *you*, Tal."

My heart tightened. I would have killed to hear him say that years ago. Now here he was, casually dropping those words while he finished setting up my tripod. He reached for the second one and assembled it just as efficiently.

"Do you set up a lot of tripods for your job?" I joked, trying to fill the silence.

"Not really." Placing the second tripod beside the first, he gave me a smile that seemed almost shy. "I looked it up last night."

A warm sensation built in my chest. "Are you serious?"

"Couldn't have you thinking I was dead weight. I promised to help, and I always deliver on my word." He studied me for a long beat. "Give me your cameras so we can get you dancing. I'm not letting you back out of our deal."

It might be for the best if I did. Despite that, I handed him my main camera and tried not to put too much significance on his thoughtfulness in researching the ins and outs of tripods. It was a small thing, but the simple fact that he'd considered it beforehand and taken the time to actually learn how...

It filled me with a feeling embarrassingly close to giddiness.

12

tahanan – (n) home

Jason

I got out of my car and stared up at a narrow two-story brick house. Dark shutters framed white windows, echoing the black door centered on the white entry porch. In traditional Charleston fashion, the porch was set to the right, and it ran the entire length of the house.

The rental looked even better than it had in the photos. Plus, it had a state-of-the-art security system that afforded me the peace and privacy I needed.

I unlocked the front door to find lush planters dangling along the balustrade that bordered two sides of the porch. A pair of wicker chairs stood next to a second door, which opened to a well-lit foyer. I walked down the hall to the central space combining kitchen, dining, and living areas. Everything appeared charming and cozy, but it was the garden that my eyes zoomed in on.

Opening the massive French doors, I stepped out onto a covered patio and took in the trimmed grass, lush bushes and trees, and vines that nearly covered the entire exterior wall. At the end of the property was a half court with a basketball waiting for me at the free throw line.

I lifted the ball, tossing it from one hand to the other. Its weight was heavy and reassuring.

I couldn't pinpoint the first time I held one. From the photos I had seen, I'd gone from a basketball pillow in my crib to a kids' size ball and then to the real thing within a few years. I remembered the wide-eyed wonder I felt watching my dad sink bucket after bucket and the high of making my first shot.

As the ball cleared the net, Dad picked me up in a bear hug and told me, "That's my boy."

The pride in his voice pushed me to do it again and again. Do it better, stronger, more consistently. His cheers fed my enjoyment of the sport, urging me further.

Letting the ball bounce on the ground, I dribbled it. Threw in some footwork—slowly at first, then picking up speed as my body recalled the motions. Moving toward the right of the court, I performed my signature step back jumper.

Swish.

And felt nothing.

When did I lose that joy?

I caught the ball in one hand and tucked it under my arm. Staring up at the hoop, I thought of Tala dancing as if every molecule of her body was attuned to the beat. It had taken time for her to loosen up with me watching, but she eventually lost herself to the music.

Her movements were visual poetry.

Objectively, Tala was beautiful, but when she danced? Fucking hypnotic. She danced like she lived for it.

Looking at the net that swayed in the air, I knew I couldn't say the same about myself and the game. With that truth staring me in the face, I wondered how I could go back to a life-time of basketball.

———

Tala lifted a slice of pizza with her napkin. "What do you do on your phone? While I'm warming up, I mean." Her legs were stretched out across the concrete floor as she rested them after hours of dancing.

"I check my emails. Read contracts and proposals for part-nerships, investments, PR events," I said, picking a vegetarian slice. "The one I was reviewing earlier was from Miles. He's putting together a nonprofit for orphaned kids. Not sure if you know this, but he lost his parents early on."

"I remember Luna and our brother Lonzo talking about that one time."

I nodded. "Miles wasn't adopted until he was twelve. He didn't have the best experience growing up so he wants to help kids in similar circumstances."

"That's amazing."

Amazing was an understatement. Miles put me to shame with his drive to give back. Like I did on the court, I'd give him all the support he needed to succeed in his venture. "The nonprofit's still in the works. We're planning to launch it next year." Luckily, the attention from our championship and Miles's award put us in a good position to see things through.

"I think it's great how you guys are using your platform to help others," she said earnestly. "You have the ability to change lives for the better."

I averted my eyes. The praise felt undeserved. "Thanks. It's Miles's brainchild. I'm just the wingman." I finished off my slice and chased it down with water.

Squinting at me, she commented, "You're still part of it.

Not everyone would put in the effort, especially when it's not your job to."

I shrugged.

"You and Miles are really close, huh?" She switched gears as though she could tell I was uncomfortable. "The whole bromance thing isn't just for show?"

"He's my brother," I said. "I've got his back, and he's got mine."

"You're lucky to have each other."

Our gazes met and an invisible thread pulled taut between us. I'd heard that feeling described in countless songs, and for the first time, it resonated in me.

"I knew it!"

At Luna's voice, we both looked up. She approached with a mischievous gleam in her eyes.

"Lu," Tala greeted her.

"So this is what you guys do up here."

"It's called taking a break."

Ignoring her sister, Luna eyed the pizza boxes and grinned at me. "Hi, Jason."

"Hey, Luna." I tilted my head toward the food. "Knock yourself out."

"Yes! Thank you." Without hesitation, she sat on the floor beside Tala and leaned forward to grab a slice.

I'd ordered two flavors, and both sisters chose the meat option. At their rate, we'd be left with only the vegetarian remaining.

"You splurged on the good pizza," Luna told me between enthusiastic chews. "It's my favorite, but we only have it on special occasions."

Tala frowned. "I got it for your birthday."

"Like I said, special occasions."

Tala's hands jerked in the middle of opening her water

bottle. The sudden furrow in her brow told me their go-to pizza was a matter of budget, not preference. I wanted to promise them all the D'Angelico pizza in the world, but I had a feeling Tala would be insulted by the offer.

Instead, I moved closer to her under the guise of grabbing another slice. "Pizza Hut always hits the spot. Miles and I order that for our cheat meal sometimes."

My knee brushed Tala's thigh. She startled but didn't move away. It was a small touch, yet the connection struck me as keenly as if I'd laid a hand on her bare skin.

"Seriously?" Luna pounced on that tidbit, thankfully missing our silent exchange. "You guys can't eat pizza whenever you want, even though you work out so much?"

"Some players do, but most of us try to be careful with what we eat, especially when it comes to junk food. It's not about our weight but how our bodies process the food," I explained.

With that, Luna launched into more questions about my lifestyle. Like she had during our first dinner together, Tala remained quiet, but this time, she watched me closely. Her gaze gave me the sensation of settling into a favorite sweater—warm and comforting.

As I told her before, I liked having her eyes on me.

Luna jolted upright, pulling my attention to her. She raised a hand with her pointer finger held up. "I have a great idea! You two should do a collab on Insta."

Tala shook her head while Luna continued to talk.

"It's perfect! You hate doing IG lives on your own, and this way you'll have a co-host. You can talk about fitness and healthy living and all that stuff," Luna told Tala.

"No. No way."

"Why not?" I asked. "I think I'm a decent conversationalist, and I do have experience with talking to a camera."

"Yeah, and he has millions of followers. Ooh!" Luna brandished her pizza slice in the air. "You could hype it up with stories leading up to the main event. That'll really boost your viewer count."

Tala set her jaw. "It's not happening, Lu."

"Why not?"

"I'm not using Jason."

I met her eyes. "You're not using me if I'm volunteering. I don't mind."

"*I* mind." Her voice rose, surprising me.

The atmosphere grew thick with tension as Luna and I looked at Tala. Her leg fidgeted against mine before going still.

"I appreciate the offer, Jason," Tala said in an even voice. "But I'm fine. I have a couple of big projects coming up that should help grow my audience."

"Mmm, still. Doing a collab with Jason would be equivalent to working with Nike. It might get you closer to one million followers." Luna reached for another slice of pizza.

"Actually, Nat pitched a Nike campaign to me."

My leg twitched. I stretched it out to my side.

Luna's pizza slice dropped back inside the box. Eyes wide, she asked, "Really? That's awesome! Why am I hearing about it just now?"

"I turned it down."

"What?" The pitch of Luna's voice grew higher. "Why the heck did you do that? Are you going to say you're not using Nike too?"

Tala rolled her eyes. "Of course not. The campaign is in LA."

"News flash, Ate—you can *fly* to LA."

"Yes, but I'd have to take time off from work. Anyway, I already told Nat I can't do it." Turning to me, Tala explained, "Nat's one of my long-time PR partners. She gave me my first big break back in college."

"It's great she found you." Shifting to my left, I broke the contact between us and dusted pizza particles off my shorts.

"Tell me about it."

"I can't believe you passed up that opportunity!" Luna persisted as she leaned toward her sister. "You should call Nat and tell her you changed your mind."

"She'll already have other content creators by now. Don't stress about it, Lu," Tala said dismissively. She switched her gaze back to me. "You okay?"

"Yeah," I answered. Reaching out, I swept back a strand of hair that had escaped her ponytail.

She froze, her breath catching.

I dropped my hand to my thigh even though I wanted to sink my fingers in her hair. To tug her forward, closer to me.

"Alright then." Luna scrambled to her feet. "Sorry to eat and run, but that's my cue to go. You guys done with the pizza? I can bring the boxes downstairs if you are."

"Yes. I'll be there in a bit," Tala murmured.

Stacking the boxes in one arm, Luna thanked me again for dinner and rushed to the elevator. I would have found it funny if it weren't for the emotions stirring inside me.

Out of the blue, Tala blurted, "Are you a vegetarian?"

I blinked at her. "No, but I eat plant-based as much as possible. Why do you ask?"

"I noticed you didn't eat the pizza with meat."

"Right." Was it weird I found it flattering that she'd paid attention? It pleased me more than if she'd complimented me on my appearance. People often focused on the packaging. Few cared to pay attention to the details, or even tried.

"You ate our *adobo* though," she said.

"I was your guest. I wasn't going to say no to food you guys cooked. And I liked it," I assured her. I could almost see the wheels in her head turning.

"It's not public knowledge, is it? Luna would have known if it was."

"No, it's not."

"Can I ask why?"

"I like my privacy. And I don't want to make a big deal out of it."

"Is it for environmental reasons?"

Once again, she caught me off-guard with her perceptiveness.

"I remember you stressing about global warming and how the meat industry contributes to it," she continued. "That was one of the topics that got you fired up."

"That's right. It took me a while to cut meat out of my system, but I finally managed."

It wasn't something I often talked about. Miles and Stassy knew my stance, for sure. When Elena found out about my diet, she took it as a weight loss fad. Mom assumed I did it for health reasons. Here Tala was—a woman I hadn't spoken to in years—yet she could read me better than some people who should be closest to me.

"I'm guessing you have a nutritionist to make sure you have a balanced diet?"

Something shifted inside me as I stared at her. She spoke so casually, like my lifestyle wasn't unusual. Like she understood me.

Maybe she did.

She squared her shoulders. "Why are you staring at me like that?"

"It's just...your reaction wasn't what I expected."

"Oh."

"It's nice," I told her. "Not everyone gets it."

She shrugged. "Maybe it's because I witnessed your science guy era. I don't think I'll ever forget your bee waggle dance."

The memory made me laugh. "Did I actually—"

"Demo the dance for me?" she finished, grinning. "Yes. Yes, you did. I got mad because you wouldn't repeat it."

"You wanted to record it and post it on your Instagram."

"I would've gained hundreds of followers." She pouted.

I wanted to kiss those lips right then and there. Clearing my throat, I said, "I would have lost my reputation."

"Nothing you do would damage your reputation. You always were one of the cool people."

"Says the influencer."

"Content creator. Besides, I have a tiny niche on the internet. You're universal." She dropped her eyes to the concrete floor. "Anyway, we should call it a night. I have an early shift tomorrow."

"Right." Jumping to my feet, I held out a hand to help her up.

Her face held a familiar mulish expression, and I expected her to turn me down. Instead, she slid her hand in mine. I closed my fingers around hers and pulled her up.

I didn't want to let her go, but I loosened my grip anyway.

Dusting off her shorts, she said, "Thanks for the pizza. How much do I owe you?"

"Nothing."

"Jason—"

"It's my treat, Tal."

She let out a gurgling sound. "Fine. I'll get it next time." Her eyes widened comically and she rushed to say, "I mean—"

I grinned. "Same time tomorrow?"

"My shift finishes late."

"I'll wait up."

"If you're not doing anything on Saturday, I'm shooting then. I'm sure you have stuff to do, but just in case..." She shifted on her feet.

She did that—fidgeted—whenever she was nervous or uncomfortable. When we were younger, she would dip her head, using her cap to shield her face. I was glad she didn't do that anymore. Nothing should ever make her feel the need to hide herself.

"My schedule's clear. I'll be here Saturday."

"Fine." She began packing her stuff.

I helped her disassemble the tripods and put away her camera, then we stood and waited for the elevator. She faced straight ahead, avoiding my gaze. Always so eager to get rid of me. It only strengthened my urge to linger longer.

But she needed to rest.

Instead of angling for an invite to her place, I gently tugged on her ponytail. She lifted her head, frowning, and I took the opportunity to kiss her temple.

It wasn't where I would have preferred to place my lips, but it was a start.

She shivered and took a step back. I wanted to pull her in and kiss her properly. Wanted to feel her body against mine.

We'd get there. In the meantime, I'd soak in every second I had with her.

13

alinlangan – (n) uncertainty

Tala

I walked to the break room, my steps light thanks to my parting exchange with Berna. She insisted on singing everything she said and refused to follow instructions unless I sang them out too. Apparently, she'd spent the weekend rediscovering the magic of musicals. Singing made everything sound better, she told me. I didn't have the heart to tell her that was only true if the person singing could carry a tune.

Berna could. Me? Not so much.

She convinced me to do a couple of chassés and pirouettes even though I tried to explain that I hadn't practiced them in years. I did what I could in the small room and earned Berna's delighted giggles for the effort.

The impromptu dance inspired me to brush up on my rusty ballet moves. My routines needed variation, anyway. Since I couldn't compete with other creators when it came to production value, I had to bring something different to the table.

Maybe then I'd be able to break out of the 400k mark I'd been stuck in for years.

As I rounded the corner, I spotted a tall woman with bronze streaks in her curly hair. "Shanti," I called out, hurrying to her.

She glanced at me and smiled. "Tala. Hello."

"Jose told me about your visa." Seeing her smile falter, I added, "Mine's also expiring soon."

Shanti gave me a commiserating look. "The downside of being a migrant worker."

"Tell me about it." I blew out a breath. "If you don't mind me asking, do you know what you're doing next?"

"I signed with a home healthcare company. It was not my first choice, but they were willing to take care of my visa. Beggars cannot be choosers, you know?" Shanti said with a wry twist of her lips. "Next week is my last week here."

"Oh." She had moved fast. "That's great. I'm glad you found a new job."

"Thank you. I am just sad that I have to move to Montana."

"That's pretty far."

"We have to do what we have got to do, yes?"

"Yes," I murmured. "Did you consider going back home?"

Her curls bobbed as she shook her head. "No. That is not an option for me. Things are not easy here, but it is much better compared to where I came from."

"I see."

"What about you? Are you looking for work?"

"Yes. I sent out a couple of applications a few days ago. I haven't gotten any responses yet."

"Did you apply to Merville Park and St. Anthony's?" Shanti asked, naming two of the elderly care homes I applied to.

I nodded.

"They are not accepting foreign nurses right now. I checked."

"Oh." My heart sank. Those were my best options. In fact, St. Anthony's was my first pick since it was nearby and had a good reputation.

"I can refer you to my company, if you like. You will have to relocate, but the money is good. As long as they have not reached their target headcount, they are open to migrant workers."

I hesitated. It was a kind offer, and one I needed. But Montana? That was on the other side of the country. "I'll have to think about it. My sister's still in school, and I don't want to leave her here."

"I understand. How about this? I will give you the number of the recruitment manager. You can call her if you are interested."

I smiled. "That would be great. Thank you."

"You are welcome. I would not think too long about applying if I were you. It is very competitive and options are limited for people like us," Shanti said.

I couldn't disagree with that. After wishing her luck, I headed inside the break room. A few nurses sat together, but I only smiled at them before taking an empty table. I put my food in the microwave and checked my emails while I waited.

An up-and-coming fashion designer wanted to send me clothes for my videos. I marked it as 'follow-up,' wanting to do more research on him. Experience taught me how hard it was to gain a foothold in the midst of bigger and better funded companies. If I could support independent business owners, I would.

The microwave pinged, so I grabbed my food and sat down. Today's lunch was Luna's leftover birthday spaghetti, named after how we usually served it during birthday parties. Kiddie parties, in particular. With sweetened tomato sauce, ground beef, sliced hotdogs, and grated cheese, it was a staple in our family. Luna inherited the recipe from Lola.

My hand tightened around the fork. I missed Lola. My family. Mealtimes were always big affairs in our home, especially on Sundays. After Mass, we'd gather in the kitchen. Luna would help Lola and Mama cook while Lonzo and I took on dishwashing duty. Then we ate together and waited for Papa to call so we could catch up on each other's stories.

If I had known those occasions wouldn't last, I would have savored them instead of looking forward to my afternoon 'me' time.

But it wasn't the moment to be sentimental.

I replied to partnership inquiries, deleted spam messages, and unsubscribed from pushy newsletters. Next, I moved on to Instagram. My latest post had dozens of comments. I used to get overwhelmed by the number of them, spending hours replying to each one. As my follower count grew, I learned to set limitations to keep my sanity, allotting two afternoons a week to clear out my unread messages.

A lot of them were words of praise and encouragement. Some people asked about my clothes, others looked for full versions of my dances. Unfortunately, mixed in were criticisms about my looks or skills, lewd comments about my body, and random spam.

It had taken me a lot of time and positive self-talk to block out the negativity. Even then, I still got affected by haters from time to time.

In the middle of my typing a reply, a new text from Jason popped up.

I smiled. Since we began hanging out—no, since the night he showed up for dinner—I hadn't gone a day without hearing from him. It was like freshman year when we messaged each other constantly. Only now, a heightened level of awareness hummed through me whenever I thought of him.

And I thought of him way too often.

Maybe it was a fantasy, or foolish wish fulfillment. But it was a welcome distraction from reality. From the looming possibility that I'd lose everything I had built here.

Should I take Shanti up on her offer and consider Montana? Relocate again and see if that gave me a better chance at a permanent home?

Did Montana have its own NBA arena?

I slammed the door on that train of thought. Arenas weren't part of my considerations. A list of pros and cons—that's what I needed.

Better yet, I needed an invitation for an interview, stat.

————

Ms. Reyes,

Thank you for your interest in joining St. Anthony's Care Home. Unfortunately, we are unable to process foreign employment visas at this time...

My heart sank. Just as Shanti warned, I received rejection letters from both nearby care centers. The third job listing had been marked closed.

Slumping on my sofa, I tapped the keyboard, listening to the muted beat it created. It actually sounded nice. I should incorporate some tap moves into my next routine.

Focus, Tala.

I sighed and picked up my phone. I ignored the notifications and searched for Shanti's text. After finding it, I created a new email message on my laptop and typed in the address of her recruitment manager.

I paused.

Should I go for it?

My phone lit up with a new message from Lonzo. Thankful for the interruption, I opened our sibling chat group and found photo after photo of the beach. It looked like a perfect day, all clear skies and blue water. Only a handful of people lounged on the sand, along with a lone dog frozen mid-run.

LONZO
Wish you guys were here

I quickly typed a reply.

TALA
You're in LU?

LONZO
Yup. Thanks for the bday gift ;)

A long sigh escaped me. La Union. Would I ever get the chance to visit again?

Another message came in, this time a video. Lonzo had aimed the camera at a group of palm trees on the left edge of the beach, then slowly panned to the right for a panoramic view. The sounds of waves lightly crashing filled my apartment. Then he switched to the front camera and grinned, waving an entire coconut with its top cut off.

"Hello from LU," he said happily.

With a shift of the camera, a girl in a bikini came into view beside him. Was she his girlfriend? He'd never mentioned having one.

She squealed and ducked out of the frame. Laughing, he waved at the camera, and the video stopped.

My heart ached with longing.

Would it be so bad if my visa expired? Then I would have the perfect reason to go back home.

I stared at my laptop.

Research never hurt, right? I opened a new window and searched for flights to Manila. From Sterling, I would have to take three connecting flights. The fastest trip was twenty-two and a half hours. It was also the most expensive at more than two thousand dollars, one way. The cheapest ticket was just under seven hundred dollars, but it involved traveling for over thirty-three hours.

If it meant being home again, I could deal with it.

Indulging the wave of homesickness, I turned on my Filipino playlist. My separation anxiety had tapered down since Luna moved here. I didn't have to rely on video calls and chats to feel connected to my family and our language. Still, the longing remained.

Maybe this visa situation meant it was time to go home.

For a moment, I let myself imagine walking into the airport arrival hall to see Mama and Lonzo waiting for me. Imagined the hugs and tears, even those busy, crawling roads that led to our house. The noise of buses and jeepneys and tricycles honking as pedestrians chatted with each other, clutching their bags. That feeling of walking inside the house I'd grown up in and finally knowing I was home again.

Maybe this was only ever meant to be a temporary stop for me.

Metal jangled outside the apartment. Something thudded on the floor, as was often the case when Luna tried to juggle her stuff while unlocking the door.

Putting my laptop aside, I got up and helped her. We talked about our day as she grabbed a snack. She shared my curiosity about the girl in Lonzo's video and swore to bug him until he told us the whole story.

"Is Jason coming over tomorrow?" Luna asked right before yawning.

Just the sound of his name made my heart skip a beat. I hated it. "No, he'll be here on Saturday."

Or so he'd said. I couldn't believe he didn't have anything better to do.

"It's nice having him around."

"Don't get used to it." It was the mantra I repeated each time I found myself thinking of him.

Luna raised her eyebrows. "Would that be so bad?"

"He's leaving, Lu."

She shrugged and got up. "Anything can happen. Night, Ate."

I said good night as she picked up her bag and went to her room. When the door was securely shut, I opened my laptop again and sent a new batch of applications. But not to Shanti's contact. Not until I had no other option.

I'd give it another week or so. Surely, I'd get some positive replies, right?

Putting the laptop away, I turned off the lamp and tucked myself under the comforter.

Hours after Luna's room fell into silence, I lay staring into the darkness, waiting for sleep to come.

14

gunitain – (v) to remember

Jason

Adjusting my cap, I lowered my head and strode past a group of students. One of the guys shot me a casual glance, then whipped his head back with a wide-eyed stare. On Luna's suggestion, I visited the university on a Friday after spending most of the day cleaning the garden. The campus was emptier than it used to be, but not enough for me to go unnoticed.

Not that I thought a cap and casual clothes would hide my identity. Even with the basketball team out of town to attend training camp, there were bound to be some sports fans around.

I doubled my pace as I followed the familiar path to a squat structure with wide windows. Anticipation thrummed in my veins. Next to the gym, this building had been my home on campus.

The large letters across the top of the facade loomed over me like a disappointed specter: College of Environmental Science & Sustainability. The 'sustainability' part had been a new addition since I'd graduated, and I had no doubt the staff considered it a major win—especially Dr. Robert Johansen, my former professor and advisor. Now dean, he had always advocated for climate change and had shaped my own beliefs.

I stayed after class countless times to ask him to expound on topics he covered during lectures. Net zero, tipping points, carbon taxes. Whatever questions I had, Dr. Johansen always welcomed them, encouraging me to learn more for myself. That was exactly what I did between homework and basketball practice.

Inside the building, the hall was empty except for a dark-haired man walking toward the dean's office. He bent over his phone, oblivious to my presence.

"Excuse me," I called out as I approached.

Pausing in the middle of unlocking the door, he glanced back and narrowed his eyes at me. "Can I help you?"

"Is Dr. Johansen in the office?"

"He's on vacation."

"Are you a professor here?" I asked.

"Yes. Come in." With a quick tilt of his head, he opened the door and let me in.

A wooden desk piled with books dominated the small room. More books filled the shelves that lined three of the walls, while filing cabinets leaned against the fourth. Some titles caught my eye, and I took a mental note of them.

Closing the door, the professor gestured toward the visitors' chairs. I sat in the one on the right and was surprised when he sat opposite me instead of behind the table.

Seeing my expression, he said, "It's Rob's chair."

"I see. I'm Jason Meyer."

He nodded, his expression unchanged. "Gabriel Martinez. Finance professor."

I reached out to shake the hand he held out. "Nice meeting you."

"Congratulations on your championship."

The words took me by surprise. He'd given no hint of recognizing me. "Thanks. You're into basketball?"

A strange look flashed across his face. "I watch on occasion. To be honest, I'm more of a football fan—and I don't mean American football."

"I'm a Madrid fan myself."

"Brazil all the way," he scoffed.

Chuckling, I leaned back. "Too bad about the last couple of World Cups, though."

"We still have the most wins. We'll get the next one."

"I admire your confidence."

He smiled. "What brings you here, Jason?"

"Dr. Johansen used to be my professor, so I thought I'd visit him while I was in the area."

That unidentifiable expression returned. "Too bad about the timing. I'm sure Rob would have been happy to see you. So would the basketball team. You're quite the legend here."

I'd been the best player on my team, and that wasn't just my ego talking. Still, I couldn't help but feel like a fraud. Some of my teammates had been way more into basketball than me. They trained just as much and prioritized the game over everything else, including their studies. But as the luck of the draw had it, I ended up with the Barons while they pursued other careers.

"I had a great coach and an awesome team," I said.

Gabriel drummed his fingers on his thigh. "I'm not sure when the team will be back, but Rob returns to work on Monday. I'll let him know you dropped by."

"Sounds good. I'd be happy to schedule a visit with him."

"If you want to leave your contact info, I'll have him get in

113

touch with you." His mouth lifted on one side. "I promise I won't sell it to your fans."

Deciding to trust him, I gave him the email address I used for business transactions.

He scribbled it on a notepad. "Anything else I can help you with?"

I hadn't intended to ask, but since he had offered... "Actually. Do you have any materials on the college?"

His eyebrows rose, yet it was a testament to his character that he didn't prod. "Of course. Are you looking for any particular information?"

"Anything related to sustainability would be good."

"Alright." Standing, he went to one of the cabinets and brought out a few brochures.

It wouldn't hurt to check them out. I was already there—might as well make the most of my visit. At the very least, I'd learn what Dr. Johansen and his staff had been up to. Maybe find some way to support their department. It would be a good point of discussion for when I met up with him.

Besides, I needed something to do so I wouldn't end up staring at Tala while she warmed up. Just like the old days—me reading while she danced in our own little space. A far cry from how I usually spent my time with women.

Strangely, I didn't mind.

————

A THIRTY-MINUTE DRIVE from the university brought me to Picker Trail, an easy hiking area that cut through Sterling Park. I parked beside a small square building with a vending machine standing between two restroom doors. None of those had been there any of the times I'd visited with Dad. Even though I had only been ten on our last trip, I could clearly remember Dad asking Mom if she wanted to join us on our hike. She'd refused because there were no restrooms nearby.

If she'd known that would be our last vacation with him, would she have gone?

Every time I tried to broach the topic of Dad with her, she'd shut it down. His legacy, we could talk about. Not his death, and never how she felt. I couldn't remember when I stopped asking. Probably around the same time I said yes to trying out for the varsity basketball team, which meant dropping the science team.

I walked under the shade of the oak trees and wondered how many people they'd watched hike the same path. For almost a millennium, they'd stood there, their branches outstretched to the sky.

"*Imagine what stories they could tell,*" Dad said as he stopped and gazed at the trees. "*Nature is the biggest witness to human lives. We think they're just things we can move about, places we can reshape. But they were here before us, and if we don't mess up, they should be here long after we're gone.*"

"*Does that mean we're just temporary?*" I asked, showing off the word I'd only just learned.

"*We're all temporary, son.*" He smiled at me and placed a hand on my shoulder. "*All living on borrowed time. It's up to us what we do with that.*"

My feet came to a stop. Dropping my head back, I stared at the canopy above me and listened to the buzz of insects mixed with lilting chirps. I didn't realize when I'd sat on a stump near a pile of leaves. I soaked in the peace of the moment until my phone interrupted the medley of bird songs.

"Someone's taking a trip down memory lane," Stassy said as soon as I answered.

Hell. That only meant one thing. "They got photos?"

"A couple. People are speculating if it was really you or just a hot new professor," she teased.

That was a new one. "I like the sound of that."

"Don't go changing your day job."

"I'll talk to Sam, smooth things over," I told Stassy, knowing it wouldn't take long for my agent to call.

Sam would find a way to package my visit as an act of good-will. His ability to shine the spotlight on his clients gained him his reputation as one of the top sports agents in the world. I rarely gave him trouble, save for the incessant media fixation on my dating life.

And the time I'd been caught attending a protest for climate change in my rookie year. Sam had stormed into my apartment and reamed me out.

"You can't just decide to go to one of these things on a whim. People know you. The press knows you."

"Exactly. I might as well use that to draw attention to issues that matter."

"I admire the sentiment. I do. But like it or not, your actions reflect on your brand. Your team. They affect people's perception of you and whether you'll be offered a contract extension or get traded at a loss. You cannot make a public stand without discussing it with me first. No matter how good your intentions are. I'm sorry, Jason, but that's your reality now."

I'd been too young to witness how my dad played the game off the court, but I'd quickly learned there was more to professional basketball than just winning the trophy.

"It shouldn't be a big deal. I don't foresee paparazzi going there just to take pics of you on campus," Stassy said.

"Wouldn't put it past them," I muttered.

"Sam will handle it," she said dismissively. "Anyway. How was it?"

She sounded so eager that I faked misunderstanding her question. "Well, Dr. Johansen was out—"

"That's not what I meant, and you know it."

I grinned at her annoyance. "Things are good. Unexpected but good."

"Spill."

I told her about my time with Tala so far. "I can't believe I had no idea she's working as a nurse," I said.

"Who'd have thought, given what she studied in college?"

The heavy sarcasm made my eyes roll.

"When are you going home?"

"Most likely the week before training camp."

"So you have about a month? I'll expect updates, Jason."

I grunted. "Miles is coming over."

"He knows about Tala?" Her voice rang with surprise.

"Just enough to be curious. And I promised her sister an intro."

"You actually agreed to that, huh?" She chuckled. "Sorry to miss the fun. We don't all have an off-season."

"Like you couldn't take off if you wanted to."

"I'll rest when I'm old." That mantra began in her teens, and she repeated it to this day. "Speaking of, I have to go. Work calls."

"Right. Thanks again, Stassy. You're the best."

"Don't you forget it."

Ending the call, I made a mental note to send her a box of her favorite truffles and champagne. She loved to give me a hard time, but I'd always been able to count on her. In my line of work, trustworthy people were few and far between, and despite all the dirt Stassy had on me, none of it had ever gotten out.

Same went for Tala. She'd never tried to cash in on our friendship, even when I gave her a reason to hate me. She didn't

117

try to hit me up for money or get me to buy her things. It was... refreshing. She treated me the same way she always had, though now it was tinged with wariness. Not that I could blame her.

But I could change her mind, and I wasn't leaving until I did.

15

pagtingin – (n) view; favor

Tala

I cursed my laptop and fought the urge to knock it against the dining table. With the old thing freezing every ten minutes, it took me twice as long to edit videos. It didn't help that social media users preferred fancy transitions. Gone were the days when a point-and-shoot video with good choreography and a regular posting schedule were enough to attract an audience. Now, content creation was as much about the production as the actual content, if not more.

As I stared at the spinning pinwheel of death, I forced myself to take slow, deep breaths. No point in losing it or letting out steam on my overworked laptop. Aside from lagging or crashing at the most inopportune times, it was a reliable companion. Still, I needed an upgrade sooner rather than later. Another item to add to the list of things I was saving up for.

It would be fine. I could rearrange my schedule to allot more time for editing. As much as I avoided multitasking because it led to mistakes, I had to compromise if I wanted to sleep.

The second my video finished rendering, I quickly reviewed it. The lighting checked out, but the splicing of clips needed to be refined. Unfortunately, that often triggered my laptop to freeze.

My phone buzzed, distracting me from the frozen screen.

GABE

Guess who visited campus today?

It wasn't tough to figure out who he was talking about. Luna was there regularly, and Gabe had no reason to make a big deal out of it if it was her. That left only one option.

Instead of replying, I called him. "You met Jason?" I demanded when he picked up.

"Hello to you too. I'm doing well, thanks for asking."

I huffed out a breath. "Sorry. Hi, Gabe." I tried to keep the impatience out of my voice, but going by his snort, I hadn't succeeded.

"To answer your question, yes, I did meet your basketball player."

"He's not my—"

"He was visiting his former professor," Gabe continued as if I hadn't spoken. "But Rob's on vacation. I was on the way to his office to check on things when Jason arrived."

"I'm surprised he didn't start a riot on campus."

"If it were the regular semester, he would have."

"Right." Jason had mentioned visiting the university that first night. I wondered if he'd dropped by the garden too.

A rapid tap-tap-tapping on the other end of the line told me Gabe was playing with his pen. "He asked for brochures. Any ideas why he'd need them?"

I squinted at my screen as I mulled it over. "Maybe he's curious. He's always been into that field."

"Yes, you told me. I didn't ask questions, because the guy doesn't know me from Jack. I just found it interesting. Is it your day off today?" he asked in a random change of topic.

"Yeah, but I'm working on edits." Trying to, at least.

The spinning wheel disappeared, and I grabbed the chance to save my file.

"Are you up for dinner later?"

"I'll let you know if I get everything done. My laptop's acting up on me again."

"I told you to replace it. You know I can lend you the cash if that's an issue."

"It's on the list. And thank you, but I'll manage." I could almost see him shaking his head at that.

"Right," he said. "Text me?"

"Will do. Bye, Gabe."

Lowering my phone, I found a new message from Jason.

JASON

Hey, you busy? Can I come over?

Right on cue, my heart raced. It was the stress, I told myself. Not excitement over him texting.

TALA

Editing now. I'll see you tomorrow.

No sooner had I pressed send than my message showed as read. Because I couldn't help myself, I sent a follow up:

Heard you met Gabe at school.

The phone rang. Knowing there was no way around it, I accepted the call.

"How did I not figure out the Gabe you mentioned was the Gabriel I met?"

I let out a reluctant laugh. "I wondered about that."

"So that's the mysterious Gabe. He looks like a fucking model. Or some celebrity."

No arguments there. When Luna started school, she showed me Gabe's fan account on Instagram. We laughed at the stolen photos and comments, then I took screenshots and sent them to him like any best friend would.

"I'll tell him he left an impression on you," I said to Jason.

"Are you two dating or something?"

The darkness in his tone made my stomach tighten. "What's wrong with that?"

His silence was loud over the phone.

Despite my disbelief, I had to ask. "Are you jealous?"

"No," he said immediately. Then, in a reluctant voice, he added, "Maybe."

"You know who you are, right?"

"The idiot who left you?"

My heartbeat thundered in my ears. "Don't say things like that."

"It's true."

"We've moved past that. Besides, things happened for a reason. I—" My laptop screen went black. "Shit."

"What's wrong?"

I tapped on the keyboard, frantically trying to revive it. "My laptop just crashed. I have to go."

"Let me help. I'll go over there now."

"It's okay—"

"You can use my laptop as a back-up."

I hesitated.

"See you in twenty."

Before I could get a word in, he ended the call. I stared at the phone. As much as I tried to, I couldn't deny the thrill his assertiveness gave me.

I definitely needed a back-up plan. But honestly? I flat-out just wanted him here too.

Focus. He was coming to help, not to...do other things. Fixing my attention on my laptop, I went through the troubleshooting techniques that had worked in the past and forced myself not to look at the time. Or to think of the man who was coming over.

———

Jason

The door opened to a frazzled Tala. Her hair was in a bun and she wore a faded muscle shirt and gray sweat shorts. A pair of black rimmed glasses perched on her nose.

"You wear glasses?" I asked, eyes stuck on the metal frames. Had I seen her wear them in the past? I couldn't remember.

"Since I was in high school," she said as she stepped back to let me in. "I only need them when I'm reading or working on my laptop. Near-sighted."

"Oh. I didn't know," I murmured.

"How would you?"

More and more, I realized there was a lot I didn't know about Tala. My memories of her were limited to the moments we'd shared in the garden. I needed more, but now wasn't the time.

"I brought my laptop. And supplies." I held up the iced coffee and sandwiches I bought from a cafe along the way.

Her eyes flickered with surprise. "You didn't have to get me anything."

I handed her the coffee and placed the food on the table. "You sounded stressed. Have you eaten lunch?"

"Oh..." A crease lined her forehead. "I forgot."

"You should eat. I didn't know your usual coffee order, so I had to wing it."

She took a sip and hummed. "Caramel macchiato?"

"Is that okay?"

"I usually get a latte with brown sugar. But I order this when I want to splurge." She peeked inside the box.

"Great. Go eat."

She took out half of a grilled cheese sandwich. "Thank you. For the food and especially the coffee."

"You're welcome." I'd buy her coffee every day to see that delight on her face. "How's your laptop?"

She grimaced and waved at the computer on the table. Around it lay a Bluetooth mouse, an external hard drive, her camera, and several cables. "It's working again but it keeps hanging every couple of minutes. Like now." Walking to the fridge, she asked over her shoulder, "Want something to drink? You didn't get coffee for yourself?"

"I only have one cup a day at breakfast."

"Blasphemy."

I laughed. "Water would be good. Thanks." I bent over her setup and frowned at the frozen screen. "Does this happen often?"

Her laptop still had a built-in CD drive and was an older model of mine. In fact, it looked like the one I'd used in high school.

"Pretty much every time I edit videos these days." She passed a glass of water to me and gestured at a chair.

I waited for her to sit before taking the seat beside her. It was the same one I'd sat on when I ate dinner there. Just like then, I smelled the fruity scent of her shampoo. My fingers itched to undo her hair tie and sink into the dark strands.

Forcing my mind to focus, I asked, "Are you planning to replace your laptop?"

"Eventually. It still does the job. It just takes longer." She said the last few words distractedly as she adjusted her video settings. There was a delay each time she tinkered with something, and the fan whirred louder. Her mouth tightened.

Noting the program she used, I opened my laptop and searched for it. It popped up in the results right away. I clicked on it and waited as it started up. "I've got the same program. You can transfer the file and continue working on it here. My laptop doesn't have a lot of files so it should be fast."

I could almost hear the silent debate going on in her head. Her gaze flitted between the screens.

"I can try that. Let me just save this file," she said.

"Eat first."

She murmured an absentminded agreement as she stared at her screen, waiting for the pinwheel to disappear.

Taking matters into my own hands, I reached for her forgotten sandwich and brought it near her mouth. She startled, eyes swinging to me.

"You staring at it won't change anything," I told her.

She took the sandwich and bit into it. After two more bites, she said, "Do you miss school?"

"What do you mean?" I asked, confused at the abrupt question.

"Your visit to Sterling. Gabe mentioned you wanted to talk to the dean."

The sound of another man's name on her tongue got on my nerves. Particularly that man's. "Right. Yeah, I wanted to say hello. The dean used to be my advisor."

"I remember he was your favorite professor."

"He was the best...even though he had a habit of rambling."

She gave me the side-eye. "I can think of someone else doing the same. Something about how humanity refuses to act before it's too late."

Laughing, I shook my head. "Apparently, I still say that. Miles keeps getting on my case about it."

"I thought you would sign up as an ambassador for WWF or something like that."

"Yeah?" I wouldn't say no if they asked me. I donated to several environmental nonprofits, but it wasn't something I advertised, not wanting people to spin it into a publicity stunt.

"You'd be perfect for it. You have the knowledge, the passion, and the platform." She said it matter-of-factly, as though it was a given.

I stared at her, wondering why she seemed so sure.

"You have more discipline and drive than most people I know. I always knew you'd do great things. Whether or not that involved basketball."

Many people had told me different versions of her first two sentiments. My parents, of course. Sam and my coaches, even some critics. Hell, I told myself the same thing whenever I needed a pick-me-up. But that last bit—*whether or not that involved basketball*. People acted like basketball was my entire identity. Yet Tala saw beyond that.

For that reason, I confessed the biggest issue that had been haunting me. "I've been thinking if that's still what I want to do."

Her brow furrowed. "You mean basketball?"

"My contract is ending next year. It's not confirmed, but they'll likely offer me an extension."

"Of course, they will. You're one of their star players. Plus, you and Miles have incredible chemistry." She stared at me for a few seconds. "Are you considering going into the sciences?"

A sudden silence blared in my ears.

Whenever people asked what I'd do if not for basketball, I always gave a throwaway answer. This was the first time anyone brought up the idea of me pursuing science. The first time anyone thought to mention it. Even my professors had taken for granted that I would go the obvious route.

Tala's hand landed tentatively on my shoulder. Looking at her, I found concern etched on her face.

"Hey." She gave me a gentle squeeze. "You okay?"

"Yeah. Just wondering why I never saw that as an option."

She shrugged and moved her hand back to her lap. "Sometimes it's hard to think beyond people's expectations. Especially when you're used to trying to live up to them."

The words seemed to hold a heavy weight for her. I remembered how she spoke of her family back in college. "What would you be doing if your parents didn't ask you to move here?"

Her gaze lowered to her laptop. "It doesn't matter. Anyway, I have to go back to work."

Disappointment hit me, but she was right. I was there to help her get the job done, not to get her to talk.

"Right." I forced a lighter note into my voice. "Can't be distracting you, dance girl."

One day, she wouldn't be able to hide behind the work excuse. I could be patient until then.

16

tukso – (n) temptation

Tala

"I told you I can handle it!"

Luna's voice snapped me out of reviewing my video. Beside me, Jason stiffened. Both of us glanced at the door.

There came some jostling, and then a deeper voice said, "Focus on unlocking the door, Luna."

My brows flew up. I rushed to the door and opened it to reveal Luna glaring at Gabe as she tugged at one of the two bags he held. It looked like my sister had been out thrifting again.

"Ate," Luna exclaimed. "Can you tell your *friend* to stop being such an ass?"

Gabe raised an eyebrow, unaffected by the death stare Luna aimed at him. "I didn't know offering to help his best friend's sister equated to asshole behavior."

"He didn't even offer! He just grabbed my stuff, dumped it in his trunk, and ordered me to get in the car. I had everything under control, then he went and took my clothes for ransom." She let go of the bag, her hands flying through the air as she vented out her frustration.

He ducked to avoid a flailing arm. "Your clothes are perfectly safe."

"Gabe," I chided him. This was par for the course whenever Luna and Gabe were in the same room.

A cough sounded from the dining table. We turned to Jason, who stood with his hands in his pockets.

"Jason!" Luna skipped to him and threw her arms around his shoulders.

"Ah, hey, Luna." He patted her back.

I bit back a laugh at his awkward expression. He glanced at me with a confused smile, looking like a little boy.

"I didn't know you were coming over today," Luna said as she drew away and went over to the fridge.

"He let me borrow his laptop." I closed the door behind Gabe. "Mine was acting up, as usual."

Gabe deposited Luna's bags next to the door. "It's time, Tala," he told me. Of course he'd use it as another opportunity to bug me about buying a new one. If he didn't know I'd refuse it, he'd gift it to me entirely.

I shook my head. "Thanks for giving Luna a ride."

"Hey," she protested. "Didn't you hear me say he forced me?"

"He was trying to help, Lu."

"Says the girl who hates accepting help from others," she shot back.

Gabe tilted his head. "I hate to agree with her, but she's right."

"Ha!" Luna crowed. "Can you repeat that so I have it on record?"

I looked at the ceiling, wondering what I did to deserve the two of them ganging up on me. I might just prefer them bickering. God help me if they ever decided to join forces.

Gabe's unamused expression told me it wasn't happening anytime soon.

Instead of responding, he walked over to Jason and held out a hand. "Jason. Fancy seeing you here."

Jason shook the proffered hand. "Gabriel. I didn't expect to see you here, either."

Luna looked between the two of them, her eyes wide. "You've met?"

"Yes," I said before either of the men could answer.

Gabe smirked. "Call me Gabe."

"This is so exciting." Luna continued glancing between Jason and Gabe, as though pitting them against each other in her head. "Are you going to beat each other up for Ate?"

"Luna!" I snapped, my cheeks warming.

Chuckling, Jason drawled, "If she wants us to."

"She does not," I insisted. "Oh my God. Don't encourage her, Jase."

He shrugged and winked at Luna.

Gabe narrowed his eyes at Jason before shifting them to Luna. They lingered there.

I frowned. It was the first time I'd caught him eyeing her like that.

"You staying for dinner, Jason?" Luna ignored Gabe. "You should. Right, Ate?"

I met Jason's gaze. "If you're free? I can order food."

"I'd love to stay for dinner. But I'll order," he said.

"No, I insist. It's the least I can do to thank you."

"There's no need—"

"Better to just say yes," Luna told him in a stage whisper. "She's not taking no for an answer."

He studied me, looking like he wanted to argue. His expression softened. "Fine. But I'll get the next one."

I hummed noncommittally. "You guys okay with Thai?" That would give Jason more than enough vegetarian options to choose from.

At their agreement, I asked Luna to take care of placing the order while I finalized my video. "You guys chill on the sofa. I'll join you in a bit."

Gabe and Luna sat with a cushion between them. Meanwhile, Jason settled back in the chair beside me.

"Join them," I told him. "I'm almost done anyway."

"I'm good here," he said.

"By the way, Jason," Gabe called out. "I told Rob you dropped by. He asked me to give you his number so you can set up a meeting. He's looking forward to seeing you. Said you were one of his star students."

"That's nice of him." Jason shifted until his leg rested against mine.

With both of us wearing shorts, I could feel the warmth of his body. The short hairs on his leg were coarse yet soft against my skin, and the sensation gave me goosebumps. I pressed my thighs together, trying to be subtle about it, but his gaze flew to me.

"Tal?"

I yanked myself out of my thoughts, my cheeks flaming when I spotted the secret smile playing on Jason's lips.

"Yeah?" I asked, relieved that I sounded completely unbothered.

"Luna was asking if you're getting chicken pandan or pad thai," he said with mischief in his eyes.

"Pad thai for me," I called out to Luna.

"Got it!"

Trying to ignore Jason's nearness, I saved the file and began exporting the video. Not worrying about the laptop hanging was such a welcome change. Maybe I could find a decent second-hand model that worked better than my clunker.

"By the way," Jason said. "You never told me how you and Gabe met. Was it at school?"

"Oh, don't you know? They hooked up when Tala was in his class." Luna spoke as if I hadn't corrected her version of the story multiple times.

Jason's stare bore into me.

"We never hooked up," I clarified. "Gabe was a graduate teaching assistant in my finance class. I needed to do some extra credit to make up for a bad grade, and my professor had me talk to him."

"It's like the setup for a cheesy porn," Luna said without looking away from her phone.

I ignored her. "Gabe gave me a couple of assignments that helped me better understand the lesson. After that semester, I came across him at the coffee shop where I worked."

"You came on to me," Gabe corrected, smirking.

Having heard that before, I rolled my eyes. "Please. You were the one who asked me out."

Jason stilled.

"I thought you needed a friend," Gabe said. "It seemed fitting that we outsiders look after each other."

"I'm still rooting for you, Jason," Luna chirped as she got to her feet and skipped over to me. "You done?"

Blinking, I saw that the file had finished exporting. "Yeah." I verified that it was saved in the right folder and air-dropped it to my own laptop.

"Check out what I got." Luna linked her arm through mine and dragged me to the shopping bags. She pulled out one piece of clothing after another, telling me about the style and fit and how much she got it for.

As she talked, I glanced back at the men and found them talking about sports. Jason's brooding expression cleared, but his shoulders looked tense. Was he bothered by what he'd heard? Instinct told me yes, and that same voice said he'd ask me about it soon.

———

I CLOSED the door behind Gabe and exhaled. Luna had excused herself after washing the dishes, leaving me and Jason alone in the living room. After the nonstop conversations and laughter, I felt more relaxed than I had in a while.

I already knew that Luna and Jason got along, and I was pleased that Jason and Gabe found plenty of things to talk about. Aside from sports and business, they discussed green technology startups that Gabe was looking to invest in.

Seeing the three of them come together was like seeing different parts of my life converging. I wouldn't have imagined it in a million years, but it worked. It gave me a warm, fluttery feeling inside.

"Thanks again for the laptop," I told Jason as I leaned my hip against the kitchen counter. "I erased my files so they wouldn't take up space."

He mirrored my stance, leaving just a few inches between us. "You didn't have to. In fact, keep the laptop. I don't use it much anyway."

"Oh no, it's fine. Thank you, though."

His brows drew together, like he was getting ready to insist. Then he said, "So...you and Gabe."

There it was. Shaking my head, I crossed my arms over my chest. "Still stuck on that?"

"Nothing ever happened between the two of you?"

"We kissed." The admission slipped out of my lips before I could think. Seeing his shoulders go rigid, I clarified, "Once. It was enough to tell us we were better off as friends. I didn't have a lot of those at school."

Understatement of the century.

"Gabe's mostly a loner too. He spent most of his time back then studying and working. We just understood each other, I guess."

The room was silent as he brooded over my words. I stared at my toes as I slowly rotated my ankle.

He stepped closer to me and nudged my chin up with his knuckle. When I looked at him, he murmured, "I'm glad he was there for you when I wasn't. I hate that I wasn't."

"Don't. You were always going to leave Sterling, even without the NBA."

"I just wish..." His voice trailed off as he seemed to take in every inch of my face.

I licked my lips unconsciously, my gaze dropping to his mouth. Was it just my imagination, or did he move even closer?

"Tal." He swept his fingers across my jaw.

My eyes fluttered closed at the whisper-soft touch. Goosebumps broke across my skin and without thinking about it, I leaned into his hand.

He cupped my cheek and I opened my eyes to see him lowering his face toward mine. Slowly, like he was giving me a chance to stop him.

I didn't want to stop him. Instead, I stood on my tiptoes, my breath in my throat, and—

"Ate!"

The door to Luna's bedroom swung open as Jason and I sprang apart. Smothering a gasp, I fought to regulate my breathing.

Luna stopped in the middle of the doorway, her eyes going

so wide that I would have laughed if I weren't mortified. "Oh my God, I'm so sorry. I thought Jason left." Her gaze bounced from me to Jason and back. "I was going to show you this jacket I bought, but never mind."

I glanced down at the leather jacket in her hand. "It's fine, Luna," I said to her disappearing back.

"No, no. Forget that happened. Carry on!" She punctuated her words with the slam of the door.

I moved away from Jason. "We shouldn't have done that." My hands fidgeted with the hem of my shorts.

"We didn't even do anything," he said calmly. "But I understand if you need time."

"That's not—"

"I know you're not sure if you can trust me, and I deserve that. I'll wait."

Speechless, I stared at him.

"Thanks for dinner, Tala." Quickly, he ducked and pressed a kiss to my forehead. Just like he had that first night. "Good night."

I murmured good night as he let himself out. It was only by force of habit that I locked the door.

What had just happened?

I had always been attracted to Jason, and a part of me knew he returned the interest. Still, I couldn't reconcile myself with the idea that he'd almost kissed me.

Now, he was saying he'd wait for me to be comfortable with him. That he wanted me to trust him.

Was I dreaming?

As I walked to the dining table, I noticed his laptop still sitting there. He'd left it, and I had no doubt he'd done so intentionally. Of course he had. Where college Jason had been all about limitations and friendly distance, I was learning that the grown-up version of him enjoyed getting under my skin. He was confident but secretly unsure, charming yet guarded, and too generous for his own good. The same science geek I'd known then, but more mature. Complicated.

And I was dangerously close to liking him more than I should.

17

landas – (n) path

Jason

Aglass of whiskey in hand, I sat on the couch in Dr. Johansen's house. He'd suggested meeting there instead of his office since students were back for the fall semester.

My former adviser had welcomed me with a warm handshake, saying, "It took you long enough." Like he'd always known I'd be back. "Call me Rob. You're no longer my student."

We opened with small talk about my season and his vacation in New Orleans. From there, we moved on to developments in the environmental industry. In particular, Rob told me about the equations being created to predict how quickly certain ecosystems were degrading, which would help scientists determine the most urgent issues to address. Those would be game changers, since the systems at risk were growing faster than people could triage them.

I found it both alarming and fascinating—the first because

the need for such equations pointed to the sheer volume of climate emergencies at hand, and the second because it gave me hope for the future.

Before I realized it, our thirty-minute appointment neared the hour mark. My whiskey was long gone and Rob had that ruddiness to his face that I knew came from talking passionately for so long.

"I lost track of the time," I said when he took a breath. "Do you have another meeting?"

Wrinkling his brow, Rob checked his watch. "Not for another hour. Plenty of time. Gabriel told me you asked for our brochures."

I nodded. "Yes. I'm considering exploring the field."

"Said very decisively."

Hearing the wryness in the older man's voice, I replied, "It's not an easy decision to make."

"I'm sure it isn't. Especially not for someone like you." He studied me closely. "In the event you decide to explore it further, I can tell you that with your degree, you would simply need to submit the proper documentation and pass the admissions test. If, hypothetically, you want to join our graduate program, it will take two years of full-time study. We also have a certificate program that can be finished within six months to a year. Of course, there will be variations based on the specific track you intend to pursue."

"I see." It wasn't anything I hadn't figured out while studying the brochures. I'd pored over them while Tala edited her video the other night and did additional research when I went back to my place.

Rob adjusted his glasses and tucked his chin between his thumb and forefinger. "May I be candid?"

"Go ahead."

"Of all the students I've taught, there were only a handful

whom I thought had the passion to go deeper into the field. You were one of them."

That stunned me into silence.

"But I also knew you were the least likely to do so."

I blew out a breath and looked down at my shoes. It was the same pair I'd worn for the quarter finals. Now they felt too tight around my feet.

"I was wrong."

My gaze flew up to meet his.

"You don't have to rush, Jason. Some specialists don't pursue this path until later in their lives. You don't even need further studies to support the cause. With your following, you can spread awareness and promote initiatives that might just drive impactful policy changes."

I knew he was trying to reassure me, but his words seemed to double the pressure in my chest.

"If you plan to go the academic route, it will be difficult— near impossible, I'd say—to balance with your career."

My shoulders dropped, but I hitched them back up. "Right. Well, as you said, there are many ways for me to be involved. I'm just looking into the possibilities."

Sam would've been proud of my diplomatic answer, even though he'd bust a nut if he learned the context. I trusted Rob to keep the matter between us. Gabe was a safe bet because of his friendship with Tala, but the more people who knew what I was considering, the higher the risk someone would slip.

"I'm glad to hear that. If you have questions, you have my number. Whatever you decide, you're always welcome in our college," Rob said.

"Thank you, Rob. I appreciate you taking the time to talk."

"Of course. Are you planning to visit the campus again?"

"Yes, I need to see Coach Tom." I ran my palms down my thighs. "Any chance you have his number?"

"No, but I'll ask my secretary to get a hold of it and send it to you."

"That would be great. Anyway, I'll let you get ready for your next meeting." After thanking the professor again, I said my goodbyes and promised to keep in touch.

As I drove back to my rental, I mulled over our talk. On the one hand, I felt energized because, finally, here was a topic that mattered to me. Yet on the other, I was disappointed that Rob affirmed what I'd already figured out.

It boiled down to a choice between the career that had been planned for me and the one I actually wanted. A decision between safety and risk, and a question of now or later.

I needed to talk to someone, and only one person came to mind.

Dialing Tala, I waited for her to pick up. She'd told me she had the day off and she was spending it running errands and working on her admin tasks. We weren't supposed to see each other until Saturday, but I couldn't wait.

"Hello?" Her voice filled the car, instantly flooding me with warmth.

"Hey, Tal. You busy?"

"Just putting away my groceries. What's wrong?"

How could she tell something was off? Did my voice give me away? "I just finished my meeting with Rob—Dr. Johansen."

"Oh yes, how did it go?"

"I was hoping to tell you in person. Can I come over?"

There was a rustling in the background and a slight thump. It sounded like she was closing her cupboard. "I have an online meeting in thirty minutes, then I need to catch up on my emails and messages."

Right. Just because I was on vacation didn't mean everyone

else was. It being her day off didn't mean she didn't have work to do.

I forced my voice to remain casual. "Alright. I'll just—"

"We can talk over dinner if you want. I mean, if you're free."

She always did that—gave me an out. Like she thought she ranked low on my list of priorities, when she was one of my top two reasons for coming to Sterling.

"Dinner sounds great." My mood lifted, and I didn't want to dwell on the reason why. "Don't worry about the food. I'll take care of it."

"I can—"

"I'll take care of it, Tal."

I could picture the scowl on her face, and the thought of it almost had me chuckling.

"Fine," she said begrudgingly. "Seven p.m. okay?"

"Perfect. It's a date."

"It's not a date—"

"See you later, dance girl."

She gave an aggrieved sigh before saying goodbye. This time, I laughed out loud.

Her reluctance to breach the friend zone amused and frustrated me at equal turns. I'd made no secret of my attraction to her. Despite her misgivings, she obviously felt the same way about me.

If it hadn't been for Luna, Tala would have kissed me, and I would've lifted her onto the counter so she'd be in the perfect position for my mouth.

Good thing Luna interrupted when she did. Tala could barely look at me after, and I didn't want her to regret anything that happened between us. When the right moment came, I'd take my time with her. No potential interruptions, no time limitations.

As I turned onto the road for my rental, my phone rang. The name on the car display sent my thoughts to a screeching halt.

Mom.

I bit back a groan. She hadn't stayed in town for two days before flying out with my stepdad Phil for a series of business trips. It was my first time hearing from her since she'd left.

Accepting the call, I said, "Hey, Mom. How's your trip?"

"Jason. It's going wonderfully. Phillip bought me a new purse. It's stunning."

Of course he did. I couldn't guess how many bags she had acquired since they'd met. Luxury bags were Mom's weakness, despite me telling her she didn't need another one made of real animal skin.

"Congratulations," I told her, knowing it was the only response she would welcome.

She hummed. "What have you been up to?"

"Not much. Working out and reviewing contracts. I visited campus the other day."

"Do you mean to say that you're still in Sterling?"

"I told you I was staying here." I parked in my usual spot and transferred the call to my phone from the infotainment system.

"What are you really up to, Jason?" she asked, disapproval clear in her voice.

I slid out of the car, locked it, and entered the gate. "I'm just taking a break, Mom. There's nothing for you to worry about."

"You're being evasive."

"There's nothing to tell." Not yet, anyway. I wasn't opening that can of worms until I was ready to deal with the shit it unleashed.

"Are you seeing that girl?" Mom demanded.

I scowled at her tone. "I know a lot of girls," I said to annoy her.

"You know who I mean. The one who works for Bernadette."

"Her name is Tala, and she works for Golden Haven."

"Bernadette pays Golden Haven, and they pay that girl. It's the same thing."

"Mom. What's your problem with Tala? Is it that she works for a living, or that she's Asian?" Either way, she sounded judgmental.

"Of course not. I have no problem with her race. I do have a problem with my son dating her."

"I didn't say I was dating her."

"You didn't deny it, either."

I sucked in a breath and fought to keep my voice level. "I told you, Tala and I are friends. There's nothing to get worked up over."

Guilt pricked at me. True, Tala and I were friends, but my feelings for her went way past platonic. Not that it was any of my mom's business. She'd already gotten her way when it came to my career. I wasn't about to let her dictate my dating life too.

"Fine," she grumbled.

I let myself inside the house. "I've got to go."

Now that she'd gotten me riled up, I needed to get another workout in before my dinner with Tala.

"I assume you're celebrating your birthday there," she said. "If so, let's have brunch or dinner."

"Send me your travel plans and I'll make arrangements."

"Alright."

"See you then. Bye, Mom."

"Goodbye, Jason."

My breath escaped in a whoosh as I ended the call. Mom's reaction to Tala bothered me. She commented on the women I dated in the past but stayed uninvolved for the most part. All of a sudden, here she was being overly concerned about Tala. Despite her denial, I couldn't help but correlate her behavior with Tala's job and ethnicity—two things that marked Tala as different from my previous partners. Subconsciously, I'd gone for women with high-profile careers. Women the public considered sophisticated and successful in their own fields. The expected partner for a pro athlete.

I'd accused my mom of being prejudiced, but what did my choices say about me?

The conversation left a bitter taste in my mouth, a far cry from the talk I had this morning. I rubbed my hand over my face, feeling the bristles of my beard scrape my skin.

Damn it. I wasn't going to let my mom of all people ruin my first date with Tala. As far as I was concerned, the women in my past were just that—part of my past.

Except for Tala. I'd made mistakes with her, and now that I had another chance, I couldn't screw it up. Not again.

18

panliligaw — (n) courtship

Tala

I stared at the food Jason spread out on the table. A mixed greens salad, roast chicken with herbed rice, cauliflower steaks, pesto pasta, assorted breads, and a bottle of wine. On top of those, he'd placed a dessert box in the fridge.

I raised a brow at him. "Are we having a party? Should I call Luna and Gabe to join us?"

He rolled his eyes as his mouth quirked up. "I wasn't sure you'd eaten today, so I got a couple of options. Besides, everything keeps well in the fridge."

A couple of options? More like a buffet. "Uh huh. Or you wanted to make sure I eat my veggies." I laughed and sat in my usual chair. He didn't need to know I'd only had a sandwich.

"I got you chicken in case you needed meat. But hell yes to you eating more vegetables." He hesitated, glancing at the seat beside me to the one opposite. "I can't decide if I want to sit beside you or facing you."

"I can eat on the sofa if that makes it easier." It would definitely be less distracting for me. I couldn't look at him without remembering how we'd almost kissed.

"Ha ha," he deadpanned, finally moving around the table to sit across from me.

I rubbed my hands together and gazed at the food. "Where should we start?"

"Wherever you want," he said, waving a hand at the spread.

"I'm trying everything." I scooped salad onto my plate and paired it with a fluffy dinner roll.

Soon, both our plates were loaded with food. Holding out the wine in front of me, he waited for my nod and filled my glass halfway.

"So, how'd your meeting go?" I asked him in between bites of bread.

"Pretty well." He told me about his conversation with the dean and how Rob encouraged him to get involved in the field.

Genuine excitement filled his voice, lighting up his face. It made him seem younger. Less hardened. It was like getting a glimpse of the boy I used to know.

"Did it give you a better idea of what you want to do?"

His smile faltered. "Not really. He basically confirmed that if I wanted to study again, I'd either have to give up my career or wait until I'm ready to retire from basketball. I won't be able to juggle both."

"Have you told Miles you're thinking about retiring?"

A dozen emotions flitted across his face before he shut them down and put on his public mask.

I hated that.

Even before he spoke, I read the denial in his expression.

"No," he said.

"You changed your mind?"

"I never made it up in the first place." He twirled pasta

around his fork and dropped it on his plate. The metal clanged against the ceramic. "It would break my mom's heart. My career's her only link to my dad. The only way to keep him alive."

"Even if you quit, you'd still be here."

He frowned. "What do you mean?"

"I mean, you are literally made from your dad," I said. "Whether or not you play basketball, he's still there in you."

Shaking his head, he picked up his fork. "Mom doesn't see it that way."

"Do you know that for sure?"

"She's been talking about me following in Dad's footsteps since I can remember. She won't entertain the idea of me retiring while I can still play, let alone when I'm at my peak."

"Have you ever told her you're more interested in science?"

"I tried to in college. She was convincing me to declare as soon as I was eligible, but I told her I wanted to finish my degree. That was my nonnegotiable. Then senior year came, and I brought up the idea of not joining the draft. She stared at me like I'd lost my mind and continued the conversation as if I'd said nothing. Trust me, she would not be on board that train."

He shoved his fork inside his mouth and chewed mechanically, looking defeated.

If I were the touchy-feely type, I would've hugged him. Instead, I stood and walked over to the canvas bag hanging near the entryway.

"What are you doing?" he asked.

I pulled out a book and returned to the table. Holding it out to him, I said, "I got this for you."

He took it and stared at the cover. Then he raised his eyes to me. "It's the book Gabe recommended."

"I found it while I was browsing in the bookstore. I remembered you said you hadn't read it." Avoiding his gaze, I cut a portion of the cauliflower steak and transferred it to my plate.

"I remember seeing a copy in Rob's office. You didn't have to buy it," he murmured.

"It's not a big deal," I said, annoyed that my cheeks were burning. "Just say thank you and let's move on."

He burst into laughter. Rising from his seat, he bent over the table, cupped my cheek, and kissed my forehead softly. "Thank you, Tal. I appreciate it."

"You're welcome." I tapped my fork with a finger. "You should try the cauliflower. It's delicious."

His mouth twitched as he sat back. "You haven't even tasted it."

Glaring at him, I speared a bite and ate it. "You should try the cauliflower. It's delicious."

He laughed so hard, I dropped my fork and ended up laughing too.

———

Jason

I couldn't wipe the smile off my face. I glanced down at the book and up again at Tala. Her features were twisted in a scowl, but my attraction to her didn't wane.

She bought me a book. It probably cost less than twenty dollars—less than the price of the salad I ordered—but it meant a lot, knowing how careful she was with money. More than that, she'd thought of me and what I liked. I had forgotten the title of the book, yet she'd taken note of it and looked for it.

I'd received plenty of gifts over the years. Designer clothes, luxury watches, even a special-edition car. This book was one I'd remember all my life.

"If you don't stop looking at me like that, I'm taking it back and exchanging it for a romance novel," she threatened.

"Hands off," I said, pushing the book out of her reach. "I didn't know you were into romance novels."

"I'm not. But I could always give them a try."

"Or you could just experience it in real life and give me a try."

She stared at me. Then she howled with laughter.

"Hey. I thought that was smooth." I flicked a leftover piece of lettuce at her.

"More like cheesy." Picking up the lettuce from where it landed on her shirt, she ate it. "Also, I thought you were against food wastage."

"You need more vegetables in your diet. And I meant what I said."

Her cheeks flushed. Standing, she gathered the plates and stacked them in one hand. "Thanks for dinner. I've been wanting to try Claudette's for a while. Now I know what the hype is about."

I wished we could've dined in the restaurant, but it was better this way. Fewer distractions, less noise. Just the two of us, and she couldn't see the prices and refuse to order.

"Don't forget dessert." I stood to go to the fridge for the tiramisu and almost bumped into Tala. At the last second, I caught her by the arms and steadied her. "Whoa. Sorry about that."

"It's okay." She sidestepped me and put the dishes in the sink, running them under the faucet.

"Let me help you."

"I've got it," she said.

"You've always got it, don't you?"

No answer came.

Leaning a hip against the counter next to her, I placed one hand on the small of her back. "Tal. Look at me."

She stiffened, shooting me a look from the corner of her eye.

Stubborn woman.

"Would it kill you to accept some help from time to time?"

"I let you help me shoot," she argued as she rinsed the plates and stacked them in the sink. Water splashed onto the bottom of her shirt, but she didn't seem to notice.

"All I do is fix the position of your cameras and press play."

"I'd let you star in my videos if you do your waggle dance," she said. Some of the tension in her shoulders eased.

"Let's not break the internet like that."

Watching her carefully, I stroked my hand up her back and stopped at her nape. She held herself so still that I wondered if she was breathing.

I brushed the fine strands of hair under her ponytail and felt her shiver.

"What are you doing?" she whispered, turning to face me.

I dropped my forehead on hers. "Ask me to kiss you, Tal." Holding my breath, I waited for her to speak.

When she didn't say anything, I dropped my hand and lifted my head. I took a step back. But then she reached out, grasped the back of my neck, and tugged me down to kiss her.

Fucking finally.

This was no tentative kiss. Her lips pressed firmly against mine, seeking me out. I wound my arms around her and deepened the kiss. My tongue slipped inside her mouth, caressing hers. She tasted like a dream—delicious food, fine wine, and uniquely *Tala*.

Her hand moved down my chest, stopping where my heart thudded in rhythm with hers.

I jolted, struck by the force of my emotions. My mouth

broke away from hers, and she gasped, sucking in air. Panting, I gazed into her eyes. Searching. I saw the desire and desperation I felt reflected there.

"Tal—" My voice came out rough and deep.

Tightening her fingers on my shirt, she pulled me toward her until our bodies pressed together. Our lips met again. One tug on her updo and her hair fell down her back. My fingers tangled through it, drawing her nearer, while my other hand traced the curve of her waist.

Without breaking the kiss, I lifted her onto the counter. She let out a little yelp and wrapped her legs around me. I dipped down, placing open-mouth kisses down her throat.

A guttural moan escaped her. Throwing her head back, she ground against me. Her hands clutched at my back. I kissed along her collarbone, loving how her scent was stronger near the crook of her neck. The heady sweetness of it sent my blood rushing through my veins. I thrust against her, and we both groaned at the friction.

"Jase," she whispered as she locked her ankles tighter around my ass. Her eyelids dropped, those long lashes fluttering.

The sight of her pleasure amped up my own. And yet, something nagged at the back of my mind. I hesitated.

This was too fast. Too soon.

She blinked and stared at me, her brows drawn together. "What's wrong?"

"Nothing," I said quickly. "I just—Luna might come home anytime."

"Oh. Right."

I could feel her walls coming up as she dropped her hands and legs, releasing me. My arms tightened around her. "Tal. Don't think I don't want this."

She stiffened within my hold and shifted her gaze.

"Tala." I waited until she met my eyes. "I want you. But I don't want to rush this." If she were any other woman, I wouldn't hold back. I'd lose myself in her body for the night.

And there was the catch.

With Tala, I didn't want just one night. I didn't want just her body.

"Who says I'm giving you another chance?" she challenged me with a lifted brow.

Fucking hot.

"Is that how you want to play it?" I nuzzled her neck, savoring how she shivered in response. "You should know I bet on myself, dance girl."

She scowled at me, but amusement twinkled in her eyes. "You are so full of yourself."

"If I don't believe in myself, who will?" Before she could say anything else, I leaned in for a kiss—a brief one this time. Then I helped her down from the counter. "Now it's time for tiramisu."

Her sharp inhale drew me back to face her.

"What is it?" I asked.

She swallowed, all traces of teasing gone. "Nothing. It's just...that was Lola's favorite dessert. She fell in love with it the first time Mama brought some home. It wasn't even the fancy tiramisu, just a cheap version from a fast-food restaurant. But Lola asked for it during special occasions."

Grief colored her voice. It stirred the same emotion I'd buried deep in my chest, awakening that phantom ache. Standing in front of her, I took her hands in mine and squeezed them. "I'm glad I chose it then. We'll eat and toast to your *lola*."

Her lips quivered as they lifted in a hint of a smile. "Thanks, Jason."

"No, thank you for telling me that. I'd love to hear more about her if you're ready to share."

As we devoured half of the cake, Tala talked about their video calls and how her grandmother had worn a hair turban in a different design every time. Her *lola* had kept it as her go-to look even after her hair grew back.

"I told her about you," Tala admitted as she lowered her glass of wine.

My stomach tightened. "Did she hate me because I left you?" I hoped she didn't. Even though I hadn't met her, I didn't like the idea that she'd had a bad impression of me.

"No. She reminded me that you were just a kid too and you had to make the best decision for yourself at that time." Tala smiled. "Of course, she was right."

Was she though? I played it like I was tough when in reality, I'd chosen the path of least resistance. I played basketball to satisfy everyone's expectations. Dropped Tala to keep from looking back at who I'd been in that garden with her. If I hadn't, would I have done more important things with my life? Made a bigger impact?

"So how do I buy in?" Tala said out of the blue.

Had I missed what she was talking about? "Sorry, what?"

"We're taking bets on you, right? I want in."

My earlier words came back to me: *You should know I bet on myself...If I don't believe in myself, who else will?*

Her hand reached across the table for mine, pausing an inch short of contact.

I bridged the distance, catching her fingers. They were delicate yet strong—just like the woman herself. I didn't know why she had such faith in me, but I damn sure wanted to prove myself worthy of it.

19

nais – (n) desire

Tala

"Ate! They're calling!"

I looked up from my laptop, thankful for the reprieve from going through my emails. I'd received another rejection letter, this time from my second batch of applications. Four others still had not been answered, but it wasn't looking good.

In my desperation, I bit the bullet and reached out to Shanti's contact. I even applied to night shift openings in nearby hospitals. I didn't know what I wanted more—for them to reply, or for them to ignore me.

So, I welcomed the temporary escape that our family catch-up provided.

"Coming," I yelled as I put my computer aside and headed for the bedroom.

Luna was lying on her stomach with her laptop plopped on the bedspread. Glancing at me, she said, "Here she is!"

"Hi, Mama." I smiled as I settled in a cross-legged position beside my sister.

Mama smiled back at me through the screen. "Tala. How are you?" Her dark hair fell in a thick curtain to her shoulders. The last time I saw her in person, she had a few white strands. Were there more of them now?

"I'm okay. How—"

Luna interrupted excitedly, saying, "Ate's dating a basketball player, Ma."

I elbowed her. "We aren't dating. We're just friends."

"He brought her so much food from the fanciest restaurant here," Luna continued as if I hadn't spoken. "Including wine and tiramisu."

"Does this guy have a name?" Mama asked, her head cocked.

"Jason Meyer," Luna said. "The second-best player on our favorite team."

I smothered the urge to pinch her.

Mama frowned. "You mean he's a professional player?"

"He's not a *player*," Luna rushed to correct her, throwing a sidelong glance at me. "Well, he is a player in the sense that he plays basketball, but he's not a player like a playboy."

"That's good to know." Mama studied me closely. Then something on her side of the screen caught her attention. "Alonzo. Do you know a Jason Meyer?"

"Do I know Jason Meyer?" Lonzo's voice was distant yet audible. "He's only the second-best player in my favorite NBA team."

Luna nudged my shoulder. "See," she whispered.

"Luna said your *ate* is dating him," Mama said, her eyes still focused above the laptop.

"What?!" Lonzo shouted.

I should have seen his reaction coming. After all, he played

155

basketball as a hobby and watched it as a fan. It was something he and Luna had bonded over since they were kids.

A second later, his face popped up next to Mama's. "Are you serious?" he demanded as he glanced from me to Luna.

"Hello, brother," I said.

"Hello to my sister who is dating one of my favorite players without telling me." He glared at me, the expression at odds with his usual mellowness.

"Like I said, we're just fr—"

Luna cleared her throat loudly and raised an eyebrow at me. I read the look as: *Tell them the truth or I'll tell them what I almost caught you doing last Friday.*

Good thing she hadn't walked in the other day. There would be no denying anything then. "We're hanging out," I admitted.

"So you *are* dating," Mama said slowly. "Or is there a new term for that now?"

"Depends on what they do while hanging out," Lonzo muttered loud enough for everyone to hear.

"Alonzo!" I chided him while Luna burst into giggles.

My siblings would be the death of me.

Mama still looked confused. "How did you become friends in the first place? Is it easy to meet athletes there?"

"Don't say you met him at a party." Lonzo snickered. "Or on a dating app."

Scowling at him, I said, "We met in college."

He gaped. "You've known him that long and you didn't tell me?"

"*See,*" Luna said louder this time.

"We lost touch when he graduated."

"He came over a few weeks ago and they reconnected. Now he's helping her with her videos. They're so cute." Luna fiddled with her phone as she explained. Then she held it up in front of the camera.

Mama's eyes widened. "He's handsome."

"Holy shit. My sister's dating Jason Meyer." Lonzo's tone was almost reverent.

Mama glared at him. "Language!"

"Sorry, Ma," he replied distractedly. "Can you send that to me? I need to show my friends."

"Don't," I ordered Luna. "Give me your phone."

"No way. I'll show you myself so you can't delete it." Luna turned the phone around and moved it closer to me.

She had stolen a shot of me and Jason checking my video the previous week. We were sitting at the dining table, heads huddled together as we studied the screen.

Well, I was studying the screen. Jason was looking at me, and the side of his mouth that faced the camera was tipped up in a smile.

Based on the photo, one might guess he liked me.

No kidding, Tala. You were there when he kissed you, right?

Blushing, I shifted on the bed and tried to clear my head.

"You're so red, Ate," Lonzo said with a cheeky grin. "Wonder what you're thinking about."

I answered quickly, "Nothing."

Luna dropped her phone and sang out, "Ate's in love."

"I am not."

No way was I going down that road with him. He was leaving. Even if he decided to leave the NBA, his world was so far from mine. Whatever we had, it was just for the moment.

"Just promise me you're being safe," my mom said, effectively derailing my train of thought.

I groaned. "Mama."

Was she actually telling me to use protection? My conservative mom who believed in waiting for marriage to have sex?

"That's not so bad. Mama gave me a long lecture when I

started dating Dani," Lonzo said, referring to the girl he'd been with in LU. "It was like a repeat of reproductive health class, but more brutal because it was my *mom*."

"Hey," Luna complained. "Why did you guys get the safe sex talk? Meanwhile, I got the no-sex-before-marriage rule."

"I would have gotten the same talk if Mama wasn't too busy before I moved here." I patted her slumped back.

For as long as I could remember, my mom had never been as protective of me as she was with my siblings. Maybe it was because I acted more like a co-parent than a daughter. Taking care of my siblings, my grandmother, and our home didn't leave me much time to hang out with friends or attempt to date. Then I moved away for college.

"I prefer that none of you have sex before marriage, but I know I can't control what you do. So I am trusting you—all of you—to make smart choices and to be responsible for your actions." Mama looked at each of us, but her eyes seemed to linger longest on me.

I felt antsy, like she could see right through me. I wanted to reassure her that I hadn't had sex with Jason. But if he hadn't stopped...

I'd never know for sure.

Regardless, it wouldn't be my first time. That honor had gone to a random guy I hooked up with one drunken night in college.

The memory of it still hit me with remorse. It was one part Catholic guilt—the product of being raised in a religious household—and one part personal pride. When I moved here, I promised not to just go along with what my classmates were doing. Then one night, I'd tried to drink my loneliness away only to wake up naked in someone else's bed.

I couldn't even remember his name.

An elbow to my arm brought me back to the present. I jerked upright and glanced at Luna.

"Mama has news," she told me, nodding at the screen.

My eyes switched to my mom, who was grinning. "What is it?"

"Your papa's coming home!" Pure joy shone from Mama's face, making her look years younger.

"For good," Lonzo added.

My jaw dropped. "Are you serious?" I looked between them as they nodded.

Luna scrambled to a sitting position and grabbed my arm. "That's great!"

Dazed, I nodded. "Finally."

Papa planned to resign over a year ago, after receiving his ten-year loyalty award. But then Mama lost her job. With Luna moving to the US and Lonzo preparing for law school, Papa decided to extend his contract again. Luckily, Mama had found a new job with better working hours since then.

"He talked to his boss about resigning and looking for work here, and they offered him a desk job. The pay won't be as good, but we'll manage. He'll be here by late October."

"That soon?" I asked.

"It's been in the works for a few months now. We didn't want to tell you until we knew for sure."

"That's great, Mama. I'm so happy for you and Papa." The back of my eyes stung, but I blinked the tears away.

Papa was finally going home for good after more than eleven years abroad. No more long-distance calls, yearly visits, and missed occasions. At least not for them.

We spent the rest of the call talking about how Mama was preparing for Papa's arrival and how Lonzo's schoolwork was going. Mama asked about Luna's classes and my work. I gave vague answers, saying what my family needed to hear—that everything was fine.

They didn't know I was in danger of losing my visa, or that I needed to find a new job and fast. Nor did they know that I wished I was returning for good too.

After we said our goodbyes, Luna closed her laptop and flopped back on the bed. "I can't believe Papa's going home," she said as she stared at the ceiling.

"Me too." Watching her, I murmured, "What if I did too?"

Her head popped up. "What? What are you talking about?"

I picked at a loose thread on the bedspread. "You know. What if I went home?"

"Like, for a visit?"

"No. To stay."

Luna shook her head fiercely as she sat up. "You can't."

I raised my shoulders. "Why not?"

"Why not?" she cried. "Why not? What would I do without you?"

"You'd be fine, Lu. You have your scholarship. You have this place. I can pay the rent for the rest of the year so you won't have to worry about it. And you mentioned wanting to get a job, right?"

Her brows furrowed. "Yes, but I don't have one yet."

"I can wait until you do." Internally, I winced. I didn't have the luxury of time, but Luna didn't know that.

"No. I can't stay here without you." Luna set her jaw. "Besides, you came here so you could get a green card and maybe bring everyone else here. Are you really going to go home when you're so close to doing that? And what about me? We were supposed to do this together."

My stomach churned with guilt. "You're right. I guess I just got caught up in the news."

She relaxed and gave me a sideways hug. "I know you miss home. But we have to keep our eyes on the goal."

"Yes. You're right."

"Maybe you can plan a visit for later this year?"

I patted her arm. "Maybe."

It was easier to say that than to tell her the truth. Because I'd come to realize that beneath the frustration I felt from my job rejections was...relief. It started as a kernel and grew with each new 'no.'

Even as I sent out resume after resume, a big part of me hoped for another answer I could add to my list of reasons for why it was time to go home.

———

Jason

Tala's sharp curse yanked me out of the article I was reading. She steadied herself in front of the mirror, breathing deeply with her eyes closed. I could almost hear her railing at herself in her head.

She'd been at it for over two hours now, moving from one song to the next before settling on a heavy techno beat. Then she tried out different moves and mixed sequences, only to shake her head and start all over. Some thirty minutes ago, she announced she was ready to shoot but told me to stop recording after she messed up the fourth take.

She just didn't seem to have her mind in it.

"You okay, Tal?" I asked as I rose from the chair and walked to her. I slipped a palm behind her neck and rubbed the knots I found there.

Head falling back, she moaned.

"What's up? You seem distracted." My free hand brushed

161

back her loose wisps of hair while the other continued massaging.

She relaxed into my touch, her eyes still closed. "Just tired."

"From the care center?" My thumbs pressed two points below the base of her neck and kneaded the bundle of tension.

"Yeah. One of the nurses left. We're in the middle of training her replacement."

"Is the newbie any good?" I asked.

"He just graduated so he doesn't have much experience. He's eager to learn though. Follows instructions."

The longer I massaged, the shorter her sentences became. Her muscles grew more pliable beneath my fingertips.

"Hopefully he picks things up easily," I said. "How are things on the social media side?"

"Same. Engagement dropping. Need new ideas."

"I'll do some research for you. See what's trending."

She murmured a thank you.

My gut told me I was missing something. I'd seen her stressed over work before, but it didn't distract her from dancing. If anything, she got even more sucked into the movements when everything else was going sideways. "Is anything else bothering you? How's your family?"

Just like that, the stiffness in her body returned in full force. "They're fine," she said, stepping away from me.

My hands fell uselessly to my sides. "You know you can talk to me, right? You already know my shit. I'm not going to go spilling yours."

The seconds ticked by. Indecision shadowed her eyes and an entire conversation seemed to take place in her head.

"What—"

I forgot the rest of my question as she pulled me down to her mouth.

The kiss was desperate, tasting of anxiety and frustration. I met her lips' demands with my own. Took the torrent of emotion she unleashed and held her steady in my arms. Maybe she didn't trust me with the words yet. But she trusted me enough to share this side of her—raw and untethered, without her usual mask of composure.

Too soon, she lifted her lips from mine and dropped a few inches lower. Only then did I realize she had been standing on her tiptoes.

"You're too tall for this," she said with a hoarse laugh.

"Not if you're sitting on top of me." My cock liked that idea, straining beneath my shorts.

Her cheeks flushed redder. "That's an interesting hypothesis. But I need to go back to work. I'm so behind."

Disappointment hit me, but I nodded. As much as my erection protested, my brain knew it wasn't the time or place to take things further.

She took my hand and squeezed it, like she understood my feelings. Then she let go and reached for her phone. Probably to prepare her music again.

An idea occurred to me.

"How do you feel about a change of scenery?" I asked.

She glanced up. "What do you mean?"

"I was thinking you could practice at my place. A new location might inspire you."

"You mean your hotel room? I don't think that would be a good idea," she said slowly.

"I rented a house. It has a garden and everything," I explained. "It'll be a bit like the old days."

Her eyes widened. "You rented an entire house for yourself."

"I wanted privacy."

"Right." She gave a slight shake of her head.

"I can come pick you up tomorrow morning. Spend the day

there, get some videos done. I'll cook for a change."

Her lips pursed to one side.

"Come on, Tal," I said, using my best pleading eyes.

She snorted. "Fine. Give me the address and I'll meet you there."

"I'll pick you up. It's on the other side of town."

"Of course it is," she said.

In the end, it took her three more takes to get the dance right. As I shot a fourth clip—her insurance, she called it—I thought about what I needed to prepare for her visit.

I didn't lie that it was for her work. But I couldn't deny hoping for more.

20

labis – (adj) excessive

Jason

As we drove through Crescent Hills to my rental, Tala grew stiffer with every house we passed. "Nice neighborhood," she said.

"It's a bit over the top," I admitted. "But it's secure."

"It better be. Have you had any problems with reporters in town?"

"No. There are random people sneaking pics, but nothing too bad. Mostly students, I think."

"What's your worst experience with your fans? Or paparazzi?"

"With fans, women sneaking into my hotel room. Guys— and girls—offering me three-ways with their girlfriends."

She gawked. "Are you serious?"

I nodded. I'd never taken anyone up on one of those offers, though I knew some players who did. "It's the rival fans who can be intense. Spitting, bottle throwing."

She inhaled sharply, but I only shrugged.

"Par for the course. With reporters, I don't really get into too much trouble aside from the random intrusive questions and offhand insults. Well, except when I date..." I trailed off, realizing I was drifting into dangerous territory.

"Supermodels and actresses?" she said, filling in the blanks. "You don't have to tiptoe around it, Jason. I know you've dated tons of beautiful women."

"Not tons," I argued.

"Mm hmm."

I pulled into the spot in front of my gate. It served as the perfect interruption to a conversation I wasn't ready to have.

She gaped. "This is your house?"

"My rental, yeah."

"Jase...it's incredible." Leaning forward, she stared up at it through the windshield.

"I knew it was the one right away," I said as I undid my seatbelt. "You can get out, you know. I didn't bring you here just to see it from the car."

"Right."

"Hold on." I hurried out of the car so I could open her door.

True to her nature, she didn't wait for me. Stepping out of the car, she gave me an amused look. "I can open my own door, Jase. I don't have your muscles, but I have a working hand. An arm."

"Funny." I snagged her bag before she could protest. I didn't need to rush—she'd gotten distracted by the house again.

"I can't believe you get to live here."

It didn't come close to Miles's house in terms of extravagance, but there was no denying it had a unique charm of its own. "I definitely hit the jackpot with finding it. Come on, I'll give you the full tour." Unlocking the gate, I swung it open for her and trailed behind.

"I love the brick. And the contrast of the shutters against the windows."

"Me too." I opened the front door and watched her face light up.

Her eyes ping-ponged across the space while her mouth hung slightly open. Her awestruck reaction continued as I walked her through the rooms on the first floor. When we reached the great room, she drew in an audible breath, her gaze instantly going to the garden beyond the tall windows.

I grinned at how her pace quickened. She was practically skipping to the arched glass doors.

"May I?" she asked, her fingers already latched around the handle.

In response, I placed my hand over hers and pushed the door open.

"Wow," she breathed out. "How will you leave this place?"

"I'm not sure." My gaze traced over her face, and her tell-tale blush made another appearance.

She averted her eyes. "Can I shoot here?"

"That was the idea," I said. "But first, snacks." I took her hand and tugged her back inside and into the kitchen. "Have a seat."

"How can I help?"

"I've got it covered." Opening the fridge, I took out the pitcher of cold brew lemonade I prepared earlier. I filled two glasses with ice and lemonade, and uncovered the platter of pastries on the center of the island. "Take anything you want," I told Tala as I handed her a plate.

She leaned closer to study the baked goods. "You went all out."

"I was excited to have you here," I said simply.

Despite the house's luxury, it didn't feel complete. Not until she stepped in.

This was what I'd been missing when we won the finals. Someone to share it with. Even though I'd enjoyed the house on its own, the feeling paled next to my pleasure at seeing Tala enjoy it too.

As I watched her scrutinize the pastries like they were precious jewelry, realization dawned.

I was in love with her.

The feeling staggered me. Not because it came out of nowhere, but because it felt...natural. Like some space inside me had just been waiting for her to nestle right there. It was unlike anything I'd ever felt with anyone else.

Oblivious to how my world had just shifted, she let out a little "ooh" and fished out a *pain au chocolat*. Her gaze darted to me.

This woman. "Go for it," I said as much to her as to myself. *Don't you dare mess this up.*

She took a bite and smiled, and I wondered if it was too much to ask her to stay with me forever.

Suddenly, she paused. "What is it? You're looking at me weird. Why aren't you eating?"

I picked up a random pastry and bit into it without tasting what I was eating. White powder fell over my fingers, cascading down the front of my shirt.

Laughter bubbled out of her. She reached out to wipe my chin with a napkin. "Good thing you wore white today," she murmured as she swept her hand across my shirt to dust the sugar off.

"I can always change my shirt. Or take it off." I raised my eyebrows at her.

"Then I won't get any work done," she said between a mouthful of her pastry. "And your garden's the perfect backdrop."

Her eyes shifted over my shoulder to the view. Was it stupid to be jealous of my own garden?

"It's not going to disappear," I told her.

"But the lighting is perfect."

"I don't think anyone has ever chosen a garden over me," I muttered before finishing my own pastry.

She laughed again. It was becoming one of my favorite sounds in the world, even when it was at my expense.

"That's what you get for inviting me to shoot here."

And with that, she smacked a kiss on my cheek, drained the last of her coffee, and traipsed to the patio.

"Time to get to work, assistant," she called out over her shoulder.

My eyes dropped to the curve of her ass. I washed down my groan with cold brew. As much as it killed me not to finally continue what we started in her kitchen, I'd promised to help her film.

So I picked up her equipment bag and followed her outside.

——

Tala

I looked up from Jason's laptop where I'd been going through my video files. In front of me, the window offered an uninterrupted view of his garden. I'd been out there all day and still couldn't believe it was his house.

If his rental was this amazing, I couldn't imagine what his actual home must look like.

I knew he had money. Between his parents' careers and his own, he had to be more than well-off. Then there were his endorsements and investments. I had never tried to find out how much he made and honestly didn't want to know.

I didn't need to know exactly how wide the gaps between us were.

He never flaunted or bragged about his wealth, so I even found myself forgetting about it sometimes. If I asked him for help, I knew he wouldn't think twice. That was why I wouldn't ask. I didn't want to be one of those people going to him for handouts—didn't want to be indebted to him, or for him to think I was after his bank account.

Like I did whenever it came to something I didn't like, I avoided thinking about it. Limiting our time together to my place helped. It was a safe space. My domain.

Then I agreed to visit him.

I'd never been in this kind of house before. It was gorgeous, with all the charm a professional designer could bring and all the comforts money could buy.

After mentally freaking out for the first couple of minutes, I'd calmed down. In fact, it scared me how quickly I'd fallen at ease.

Because of Jason.

We spent the afternoon shooting a full video and multiple thirty-second clips, then I settled in at his desk while he made dinner. He'd said he wanted me to try his favorite home-cooked vegetarian dishes.

While I tried to focus on my edits, he puttered around in the kitchen. Music played low through the speakers, and soon, the mouth-watering aromas of lemon, basil, and other spices filled the space.

I swiveled the chair and observed him sprinkling ingredients into a pan. The salt and pepper shakers looked small in his hands, like toys that came in one of those kiddie cooking sets.

Chuckling, I stood and stretched. Jason lifted his head, his eyes snapping to my midsection and slowly tracking their way up. I felt his gaze as though his hands were on me, caressing my skin. My breasts tingled with awareness.

All day, I'd felt his eyes on me. Even though we'd been at it for weeks, him watching through the camera as I danced, the sensations felt more acute now. Maybe it was because this wasn't my space and there was no one who could interrupt us.

The air around us felt charged.

Swallowing my nerves, I walked to him. His eyes held mine each step of the way. Some distant part of me noticed him turning the stove off and moving the pan. He wiped his hands on a kitchen towel.

I stopped in front of him, an arm's length away. His mouth twitched like he was amused by the distance I'd left between us.

He leaned against the counter. "Done with your videos?" he asked, his voice low. Deeper than usual.

"For now."

Reaching out, he hooked his fingers into my waistband and pulled me closer. My aching breasts pressed against his muscled abdomen, and his length strained against my stomach.

"I think you've worked long enough," he murmured as he pressed a kiss into my hair.

To hell with playing it safe. I'd always lived within the lines, bending to people's expectations. Now, it was time to go after what I wanted.

Bracing my hands on his shoulders, I jumped and wound my legs around his waist. He caught me, squeezing my butt. The contact made me groan. He ducked his head toward mine and kissed me as though he needed me to breathe. All the while, our lower bodies ground against each other.

His lips left mine to trail down my throat. He shifted my weight to one arm as his free hand cupped my breast. Keeping his gaze locked on me, he kissed the top of my chest. He drew the strap of my tank top down my shoulder and grazed his lips across the skin he uncovered.

"No bra, dance girl?" he murmured.

"It's built into my—" My words ended in a moan as his mouth came into play.

My hands moved restlessly, one digging into his hair while the other traced his abs. His muscles contracted beneath my touch.

"Jase," I said as I dipped my fingers into his waistband.

Turning, he sat me on the island and proceeded to pull my tank off. For what felt like forever, he stared at me. "You're beautiful."

I squirmed under his attention. "Are you talking to me or my chest?"

His eyes pierced through me. "I'm talking to all of you, Tala. Beautiful."

The wonder in his voice was unnerving. I shook my head at the emotion that filled my chest to bursting.

"You are," he said. "But since you don't believe me, let me convince you."

With that, he stepped in between my legs and kissed me again. Slower, taking his time. His mouth moved against mine as his hands brushed up my sides, coming just short of the bottom of my chest.

I broke the kiss. "Stop teasing me."

Smirking, he dipped his head and hovered above my left nipple. His tongue licked around it. "This what you want?"

"Yes!"

There was a flash of a smile. Then he alternated between my breasts, his hand plumping them up for his mouth. I never thought my nipples were sensitive, but they seemed to have a direct line to my core.

"So good. I want to taste you everywhere."

I tugged at the hem of his shirt, pulling it up.

"Fuck. Wait." His voice was the roughest I'd ever heard it. Reaching behind his neck, he yanked his shirt off in one move.

I'd seen him half naked in photos, but now he was right in front of me. His muscled torso gleamed under the lights, and I couldn't help but map it out with my palms. Leashed energy— that's what he felt like.

As I traced the grooves of his abs, he swept a hand up my thigh. The higher he went, the faster my breaths came. Finally, his thumb brushed against my soaked underwear and rubbed the perfect spot.

I groaned as pleasure zipped through me. My hips shot up, seeking more of that friction.

He grinned. "You want this, Tal?"

My head bobbed, my hands moving aimlessly across his warm skin.

His hands left my body for a second, only to haul me up and remove my shorts and underwear. One moment, he was standing. Next thing I knew, he was propping my heels on the marble counter, opening me to his gaze. He kneeled on the floor.

I froze, my eyes wide. "Y-you eat here."

His breath caressed the most sensitive part of me as he said, "I'm about to."

The first swipe of his tongue had me crying out. It didn't take long until I was grinding against him, fingers tangled in his hair.

"Yes. Right there," I urged him on, all self-consciousness forgotten.

The tension within me built as he licked, sucked, and thrust. My brain couldn't process what we were doing, but my heart thrilled to be with Jason this way. My body shuddered with pleasure and I moaned as I came, my thighs pressing against his head.

When the waves subsided, he eased my legs apart. My eyes fluttered open and landed on his flushed face.

"Did I smother you?" I asked as I tried to catch my breath.

"Just like I wanted." He kissed my clit and drew away, hands stroking my thighs. Taking his time, he gazed at me from head to toe, lingering on the parts where I was aching. "You look like every fantasy I've ever had," he murmured before he stood.

I dropped my feet, letting my legs dangle. "Your turn." I reached out to unbutton his pants and push them off his hips.

His erection sprang up, long and hard. My mouth fell open. "You don't have to—"

"I want to." I gripped him in my hand.

"Fuck."

I tightened my fist and added a squeezing twist when I reached his tip.

Our lips crashed together. Desire overwhelmed me as he played with my breasts and moved his tongue against mine. Pushing at his shoulders, I jumped off the counter. He caught me by the waist, but when he set me on my feet, I went down on my knees.

His groan came loud as I wrapped my lips around him. He throbbed in my mouth, his fingers tunneling into my hair. With one hand on his trembling thigh and the other around the base of his erection, I sucked him as deep as I could.

His words urged me on. Soon, he was thrusting into my mouth.

Just when I thought he was about to come, he pulled away. I wrapped my hand around his length and stroked until his entire body went rigid.

"Tal," he moaned.

Had my name ever sounded hotter?

Gently, he pulled me to my feet and embraced me. "I brought you here so you could dance and I could feed you."

My mouth twitched. "I mean, you kind of did."

Silence.

"If that's your version of an appetizer..." I lost the battle with my amusement.

To my delight, his laughter joined mine.

21

kisapmata – (n) blink of an eye

Jason

I couldn't stop touching Tala. Her hand, her hair, her thigh —I touched any part of her I could reach. After we cleaned up and got dressed, I heated the food on the stove, my eyes darting to her as she set the table. She glowed, her smiles coming easier than usual. Her lips were swollen, reminding me of how they'd looked around my cock.

Said appendage twitched beneath my shorts. Even though I'd come less than an hour ago, it wouldn't take much to get me ready to go again. That state of semi-arousal was fast becoming a constant when I was around Tala. Now that I'd gotten a taste of her, it took every ounce of my self-control not to push for more.

It would have been easy to sink inside her. Her body was ready for it. But the momentary satisfaction wasn't worth it if she'd only push me away right after. I wanted her all in, no regrets or second guessing.

So I contented myself with being with her like this, soaking in the warmth of her beside me.

She took a bite of my plant-based General Tso's chicken. "I can't believe this is tofu. It's so good. So meaty."

Her enjoyment of my cooking filled me with relief and pride. "Glad you like it. I figured you'd want a rice dish after all your dancing."

"You figured correctly." She scooped another spoonful of tofu. "I'm trying to imagine my family's reaction if they tasted this. We're not big on tofu at home."

"I can give you the recipe," I offered. "Are you planning to visit them anytime soon?"

A cough sputtered out of her. She grabbed her glass and drank in big gulps.

"You okay?" I patted her on the back.

She lowered her glass. "Food went down the wrong pipe. I'm fine. Actually, I want to go home but I'm not sure when." She hesitated, then said, "I just found out my dad's going back for good."

"Seriously? That's great news. How long has he been abroad again?"

"Going on twelve years. We're happy he's finally coming home. Especially my mom." She smiled, but it didn't hold the lighthearted joy she'd had earlier.

I pulled her hand into my lap and ran my thumb over her knuckles. "Then it's the perfect time for you to visit. A family reunion."

"Yeah. Maybe." Her voice was soft, and she looked at our joined hands. "Do you ever wonder what your life might have looked like if your dad were still here?" Her head snapped up. "Shit, I'm sorry. I shouldn't have asked. That was insensitive of me."

"No, I don't mind." I squeezed her hand. "I used to, all the time. I try not to think that way now, because it's like I'm holding a grudge against him when none of what happened was his fault. But sometimes...Yeah. I wonder if I still would've gone pro. Or maybe I'd be more like Gabe, only in the science field."

"Do you think your dad would've been okay with that?"

I'd thought about it so often in the past that the answer came easily. "I know he would have. Dad always encouraged me to go after what I wanted. He might bug me about working on my game, but he'd support me either way."

"I can imagine you as a teaching assistant for Dr. Johansen while you work toward your master's." She giggled. "Students would cast votes for the hottest TA between you and Gabe."

I grunted. "I better have your vote."

"Well, I'd need Gabe's math skills more than yours," she said with a teasing smirk.

"But my *mouth* skills—"

Her loud groan cut me off. "You are so lame."

"It's part of my charm." Leaning back, I slung my arm around her chair and traced the line of her shoulder.

"So full of yourself," she grumbled even as her skin pebbled underneath my touch. "Ooh. You could be like a real-life Captain Planet, advocating for sustainability."

I laughed. "I haven't heard that name in a long time."

"It's a great concept for a cartoon. I didn't realize it back then, but talk about addressing real issues."

Her words sparked a forgotten memory. "Dad was the one who got me watching that. He convinced Mom it was educational."

"I mean, it was." Tipping her head back so it rested on my forearm, Tala stared into the distance. "If we were living our alternate lives, I'd still be in Manila. I'd probably teach dance on the side while working a desk job."

"If you wanted to teach, you could do that here and earn more than you could over there."

"Yes, but in another life, money wouldn't be an issue. I wouldn't have a reason to move here."

"I'm here."

Her eyebrows lifted. "But I wouldn't know you then."

At that very moment, I realized just how lucky I was that our lives unfolded as they had. How thankful I was that the turns I took led me to her.

I just had to find a way to convince her that our reality was better than the alternative.

—————

Tala

Hand in hand, Jason and I walked down the hallway to my apartment. I tried to persuade him to drop me off at the building's entrance, but he insisted on walking me to my door. Since it was past midnight, I agreed. Really, though, I'd take any excuse to spend more time with him.

He told me about the hikes he'd been going on in and around Sterling. Sometimes, he ran through them as part of his conditioning. Other times, he took it slow, leaving his phone in the car so he could disconnect like he used to with his dad.

In return, I told him about the beaches and mountains we had back home. How I wished I'd seen more of them.

"We'll see them together one day," he'd said.

I'd hummed in response. Maybe we would, but I was ninety-nine percent sure it wouldn't be with each other.

Like he'd read my thoughts, he said, "I'll let you get used to the idea of it."

Ideas, I was used to. I was also used to scrapping those that were unrealistic.

When we reached my door, I gave in to the impulse to reach for him.

He took a sharp breath as our lips met. Cradling my face in his palms, he deepened the kiss. I moved closer to him, and he backed me up against the wall.

Then he stopped. "You need to sleep," he said, caressing my cheek.

I leaned into his touch. "So do you. Don't you have to get up early to work out?"

"Don't care. I'd give up sleeping to be with you."

"You'll have a hard time going back to your routine."

"It'll be hard to go back regardless."

In the dim light of the hallway, we stared at each other. The tenderness in his eyes made my heart tighten.

"Thanks for today," I murmured. "I had a great time."

"Me too. And trust me when I say any time."

I smiled and forced myself to step back. "Good night, science guy. Drive safe."

"Night, dance girl. Sleep well."

He walked away as I unlocked the door. I glanced at him right as the elevator door opened. He looked back at me, smiled, and stepped inside the elevator.

I was still smiling as I entered the apartment, only to startle when I found Luna on the sofa. She looked up from my laptop, her gaze flat.

"Hey," I said. "Why are you still up?"

"I have a paper due later. My laptop overheated so I borrowed yours. I texted you," she answered stiffly.

Nodding, I deposited my bag on the floor. Luna borrowing my laptop wasn't unusual. We borrowed each other's things often. So why was she acting so strangely?

"Is something wrong? Do you need help with your paper?"

"I opened your browser."

I cocked my head. "Okay..."

"Your email was open."

My inbox just contained collaboration opportunities, contracts, fan mail, newsletters. None of that was cause for alarm.

Then a lightbulb went on in my head.

Yes, my content creation email was all business. But my personal account? That held messages about the job hunt I hadn't told Luna about.

My exhilaration faded in the face of her accusing glare.

"You're looking for work? Were you fired?"

"Not exactly..." I sat on the other end of the sofa.

"Well, tell me what it is exactly," Luna snapped. "Because I've been spending the last hour trying to figure it out."

"Golden Haven can't afford to sponsor my visa extension," I admitted.

Her brows squished together. "I thought your boss already told you they would?"

"He did, but he spoke to me again last month. They had to cut their budget, including foreign workers who need visa sponsors. Instead of paying more to keep foreigners, they'll hire locals."

"Don't you have a contract that says they need to honor their word?"

"I have a contract, but it doesn't guarantee an extension."

"So you *are* getting fired," Luna said in a flat voice that sounded nothing like her usual bubbly self.

"I prefer the term 'let go,'" I said, trying to lighten the atmosphere.

Her face remained grim. "When?"

"My visa expires on October 20." I told Luna what Jose had told me and that I'd been applying for other jobs.

"Most of your messages are rejections."

I couldn't blame her for going through my inbox so thoroughly. "Everyone's affected by inflation. I have an interview scheduled." Shanti's contact had finally replied with an invite yesterday morning, just before Jason picked me up.

"The one based in Montana."

"Yes, well, beggars can't be choosers."

"Why didn't you tell me?" Luna asked.

I lifted my hands. "I didn't want you to worry."

"But I could have helped." The words escaped her in a burst of exasperation.

"I've checked out the possible options nearby. They all said no."

She bit down on her bottom lip. "Is that why you mentioned going back to Manila?"

The question knocked me into silence. Luna's eyes drilled into mine, and I wanted nothing more than to look away. But I couldn't hide from her any longer.

Shaking her head, she murmured, "That's it. You *are* thinking about going back."

"You know I miss home," I said quietly.

In contrast, her voice grew louder. "What, so you're just going to give up? Like that?"

"I'm trying, Luna. I'm doing the interview via video call this week. And I'm waiting for other responses. It's not that easy to find work."

"I know it's not easy," she shouted. "That's why I would have wanted to help."

"You can still help—"

"You're saying that now because I caught you. Were you going to wait until the last minute to tell me?"

"I wanted to wait until I had a plan. I was working on it."

"You're not my mom."

I reared back, stunned. "I know that."

"Then stop acting like it. You don't need to protect me from everything." Luna closed my laptop and placed it on the table. "Does Jason know?"

"What?"

"Does. Jason. Know."

My chest tightened. "No."

"Of course. Why would you tell the guy you're dating? And don't give me the *we're-just-friends* shit." She pointed a finger at me. "It's almost one in the morning. You spent the entire day at his place and your lips look twice their usual size."

Said lips pressed together tightly.

"I'm glad you're not denying that, at least."

"It's a recent development," I murmured, bouncing my leg.

"If you care about him, don't let him find out the way I did. He deserves better than that." Standing, Luna muttered, "I thought I did too."

"Lu—"

Anything I might have said was cut off by the slam of her door.

"Shit." I sank lower into the sofa. Any traces of the butterflies I'd felt with Jason had disappeared, leaving behind a heavy pit in my stomach. And a sinking feeling of dread.

I couldn't fault Luna for getting mad. In her place, I would be too. I had plenty of chances to tell her and chose not to under the guise of protecting her. Was I protecting her by thinking about leaving?

All of a sudden, the aches in my body screamed at me. A stinging in my chest joined them. I'd never seen Luna look at me like that before. It wasn't just hurt and anger on her face. There was disappointment too.

As I stared at a point behind the wall that separated me from my sister, I asked myself what to do next.

22

indak – (v) to dance with the music

Jason

Closing the car door, I smiled. I couldn't wait to see Tala. It had been three days since I brought her to my place, and the hours had dragged on longer than usual. We texted like we normally did, and I called her every night just to hear her voice. Clingy wasn't my style. But I couldn't get her off my mind.

I circled the car and opened the passenger side door. I was taking out a potted yucca palm when I spotted Luna. She had just stepped out of their apartment building, her usual canvas tote slung on her shoulder.

"Hey, Luna," I called out.

Her head turned to face me, and the frown on her face disappeared. "Jason. Hi." Amusement flashed on her face when she noticed what I had in my arms. "Adding another plant to the collection?"

"Tala liked the one at my place," I said as I approached her. Shifting the pot to my left arm, I gave her a side hug.

"Right." Her smile faltered. "She's up on the roof, as usual."

I studied her, noting the corners of her mouth were stiff. Her eyes couldn't seem to meet mine. "Everything okay?"

"Of course," she answered with what sounded like false cheer. It fell flat. "It's nothing."

"Is it Gabe?"

Her eyes snapped up to meet mine. They were wide with alarm. "What do you mean? Why would it be Gabe?"

I lifted an eyebrow at her.

"Oh my God." Luna buried her face in her palms. "Is it that obvious?"

"I don't think Tala knows." At least, she never mentioned it.

"Do you think Gabe does?"

I answered carefully. "Not that I'm aware of." My guess? *Yes.*

She groaned. "Great. Like my week didn't suck enough as it is."

"Did anything happen between you two?"

"Of course not. I'm just his best friend's annoying little sister." She harrumphed and adjusted the strap of her bag.

I wasn't sure about that, not with the way Gabe looked at her when she wasn't looking. "If it's not him, then what's the matter?"

"Just girl problems." She averted her eyes. "Did Ate talk to you?"

"About what?"

She opened her mouth then hesitated before saying, "Nothing."

I frowned. "Is she okay?"

"I guess so. Busy, but what's new?" She gave me a side-eye. "Be careful with her, Jason."

"Of course I will."

"Don't forget to wrap it up."

My eyebrows shot up. "That's...unexpected."

"She would say the same thing to anyone I dated. No, actually, she would probably threaten them if they dared to touch me."

I chuckled. "She's not that bad."

"Ha," she snorted. "Anyway, I've got to run."

"Thrifting?"

"No. I have a job interview."

I smiled at her. "That's great. Where at?"

"University store. At least it's some place I know, and it's extra money. If I get the gig." She shrugged, but I saw through her front.

She was nervous.

"Hey." I gently squeezed her shoulder, trying to encourage her. "You'll kill it. I know you will."

"Thanks, Jason."

"Need a ride?"

"Nah. Kriz is picking me up on the corner." Her phone started ringing. "That's her. Got to go."

"Good luck," I called out as she jogged down the sidewalk, waving back at me.

A second later, a car honked. I heard Luna yell, "Hold on!"

I waited for the sound of a car door closing before I walked to the building's entrance. I keyed in the code Tala gave me, then headed for the elevator, punching the button for the rooftop.

As soon as the doors opened, Tala's music streamed in. Unlike her usual tracks that ranged from hip-hop and EDM to pop, this one was slow, focused more on vocals with distinct sounds of piano, electric guitar, and drums.

It wasn't a song I recognized, and the reason for that was simple. It was in Filipino.

My breath caught when she came within view. Her hair

was loose for a change, and it whipped around her as she turned and spun on her bare toes.

She wasn't dancing the way she typically did. Instead, she moved with outstretched legs and sweeping arms, executing multiple turns with breathtaking ease.

I stepped forward. Then I halted as her face became visible. Her emotions always showed when she was fully involved in her dancing. This time was no different. I read the conflict and indecision on her face, and it tugged at my chest.

Suddenly, her eyes landed on mine. Just like that, her walls slammed into place, her face rearranging to smile at me.

"Jase." She cut the music. "Another plant?"

I glanced at the yucca in my arm. I'd forgotten about it. "I thought you could put it in your room. Or here, to add to your backdrop."

"It would look nice next to the sofa," she said.

We stood in front of each other. I bent, pulling her close by the waist. She stretched up to kiss me. And yelped.

I drew back to study her. "What's wrong?"

Rubbing her neck, she laughed and nodded at the plant. "One of the leaves poked me."

"Shit, sorry." I squatted and placed the palm on the floor. As I straightened, I caught her waist again and lifted her so we were the same height. Her ankles locked behind my back.

"You keep doing that, you'll break your back."

I scoffed. "What did I tell you? I lift heavier weights than you, dance girl."

"I forgot. You're a big, strong athlete." Her lips twitched as if fighting the urge to laugh.

"Looks like I need to remind you."

I kissed her again, pouring out my feelings the only way I knew wouldn't scare her.

Her lips were soft, tentative at first. Stroking up her neck, I held the back of her head and tipped it as I traced the seam of her mouth with my tongue. She opened for me, sliding her tongue along mine.

We kissed like we had been doing it our whole lives. Like we had all the time in the world.

"Why didn't I kiss you back in college?" I murmured when we broke for air.

Her laugh ghosted across my face. "Because you were a hotshot athlete and I looked like a lost kid." She looked down at her oversized shirt, her mouth twisting wryly. "Guess nothing's changed."

"Wrong. I'd like to think I've finally gotten my head out of my ass."

"Ha." She rested her face in the crook of my neck.

Her lashes fluttered against my skin, her breath spreading goosebumps across my body. I was already primed from feeling her against me. My jeans grew uncomfortably tight, but I wasn't going to press her.

"What was that song you were dancing to?" I asked.

"It's called '*Indak*,'" she murmured against my skin. "It's by one of my favorite Filipino bands."

I rubbed her back. "What does it mean?"

"I'm not sure about the exact translation, but it's basically to dance with the music."

"I see. It sounded...not exactly sad, but not like your usual songs."

She nodded. "It's conflicted. It's about being torn between two people."

"Is that your way of telling me you have another man in your life?" I asked drily.

"Actually, now that you bring it up..." She wiggled her eyebrows.

I laughed even as I shook my head. "Smartass."

"Like I have the time to juggle two guys. Or the energy."

"Glad to hear that." A thought struck me. "Does Luna know you and Gabe kissed?"

Her eyebrows furrowed. "No. Why would I tell her that?"

"I thought you two talked about everything."

A cloud passed over her face. "No, we don't."

"Are you two okay? She seemed off when I saw her."

"You went by the apartment?" she asked.

"No. I ran into her out front as she was leaving. That reminds me, it's great she got that interview."

She stiffened in my arms. Drawing back, she stared at me. "What interview?"

I frowned. "Her job interview for the university store?"

Had Tala forgotten? That didn't seem like her.

Her shoulders dropped. "Oh."

That one word, coupled with her reaction, told me she hadn't forgotten—Luna hadn't told her.

"Maybe she wanted to surprise you when she got hired," I suggested as I stroked her back. It was the only reason I could think of.

Shaking her head, she laughed humorlessly. "No. She just didn't want to tell me."

"She seemed nervous. Maybe she didn't want to disappoint you in case she didn't get it."

To my surprise, her eyes welled with tears.

"Hey." I hugged her, wanting to ease whatever was troubling her.

She swiped her eyes with the heel of her hand. "Oh, God."

I gently tugged her arm down and wiped her cheeks. The circles under her eyes were darker than usual. What was going on? First Luna's shifty behavior, now Tala was crying.

She wiggled in my arms, trying to free herself. "You can put me down."

Instead, I carried her over to a chair and sat with her in my lap. It was the first time I had held her that way. I liked her weight on top of me and how she automatically snuggled into my chest.

But I didn't like the slump in her posture.

This was the girl who created her own space to dance when the college team refused to let her audition because she didn't fit their vibe. The woman who juggled two jobs and still carved out time for her family.

I hated seeing her look so defeated.

Placing my knuckles under her chin, I tipped it up so she faced me. "You and Luna fought?"

She sighed, her gaze dropping. "She...I was keeping something from her, and she found out before I could tell her."

"Was it connected to us?"

From what Luna said, I assumed she knew Tala and I were past the friend zone. But Luna hadn't seemed upset by that. Random threats aside, I hadn't gotten anything but support from her since she invited me for dinner under false pretenses.

"Something like that." Tala refused to look at me.

That told me she was keeping a secret from me. I wanted to press but knew from the tension in her body that I'd get nowhere except booted off of her rooftop.

So I put aside my suspicions and focused on her. I stroked her back in a slow, repetitive motion that I hoped would comfort her. "Whatever it is, I know you'll work things out. You love her, and she obviously loves you too."

She looked past me. "Yeah," she murmured. Then, finally, she met my stare. "I'm sorry. I killed the mood."

"You don't have to say sorry. I'm here to help with anything you need, whether it's shooting videos or talking. Anything, Tal."

After a few beats, she said in a soft voice, "You're too good for me."

"The hell?" I glowered at her. "Fuck that."

"You deserve better."

"There's no one better for me than you." I could feel her trying to put emotional distance between us, and I held her tighter in response.

She whispered, "I don't think we should go on with this."

"I disagree."

"We'll ruin our friendship."

"We won't."

I couldn't tell her it was too late—I'd never be able to think of her as just my friend anymore. I was all in, but she already had a foot out the door. In fact, she seemed far too ready to dance out of it.

"Look," I said in a calmer voice. "We can take it one day at a time. Okay? Let's enjoy what we have."

For a moment, she was quiet. Then she wound her arms around my neck and nuzzled my ear. "Can we go to your place?"

I had her things packed up and ready to go before she could change her mind.

23

mahal – (n) love; (adj) costly

Tala

My bags fell on the floor as Jason pinned me against the door, lifting me up in one effortless swoop. "I guess that's one way to close the door," I managed to gasp out. Between his mouth ravaging mine and his hands roaming under my shirt, I couldn't catch a breath.

That's what I got for running my hand up and down his thigh on the drive here.

"Best way ever." He pulled my shirt off, using his hips to support my weight. As soon as my shirt cleared my head, he lavished kisses on my breasts.

The parts that were uncovered by my sports bra, anyway.

"I hate these things," he grumbled.

I laughed. "They're good for support." Nudging his hands away, I took the bra off myself.

Jason made an appreciative sound deep in his throat. With a naughty glint in his eyes, he cupped one breast and lowered his head.

I moaned at the wet heat of his mouth. My head banged against the door, and he lifted his hand to cushion it.

"More," I breathed out as his lips moved to the other nipple.

"What do you want, Tal?"

"Everything."

He brought his mouth to my lips, kissing me long and slow. When we were both gasping for air, he leaned his forehead against mine. "My room?"

I nodded.

"I'll get your stuff later." Still carrying me, he strode to the stairs.

I took the opportunity to kiss his neck and lick the spot right below his ear.

He stumbled but caught himself on the handrail. "Fuck. Do you want to kill us both?" He passed two doors in the upstairs hallway.

"You never gave me a full tour," I teased.

"Later," he said as he swung the last door open. He walked me to the center of the room before letting me slide down to my feet.

His eyes looked intently into mine. While we'd been full of frantic energy in the kitchen, here things fell hushed. I heard nothing but the pounding of my heart in my ears and Jason's ragged breaths as he lifted a hand to my hair.

Standing half-naked in front of him, I felt no shame or shyness. I wanted to bare myself completely to him, and him to do the same for me.

"Dance girl," he murmured, palming my cheek. "I've wanted you for so long."

I slipped my hand in between our bodies, sweeping it up his chest. "You have me now."

His free hand caught mine and held it over the spot where his heart beat quickly.

Staring into his eyes, I rose to my tiptoes to bring my face close to his. Never had I wished so much to be taller than in that exact moment.

He figured out what I wanted, bending until we were eye to eye.

One hand clasped in his, I lifted the other and traced from his temple to his chin. I cupped his face, mirroring his hand on my own, and whispered, "I want you."

His eyes closed tightly. When they opened, they shone with an emotion that echoed in my chest.

"Tala. Are you sure? I don't want to take advantage of you."

Even now, he put my needs first. The sincerity in his face gave me the confidence to do what I did next.

Dropping to my feet, I slipped my thumbs in my waistband. I held his gaze as I dragged my leggings and underwear down in one go, letting them fall in a heap. All of me was revealed to him, and still he stared into my eyes as though searching for a sign of hesitation.

"In case it wasn't obvious," I said, "Yes. I'm sure."

Jason

At Tala's words, I let my eyes lower. Various tan lines marked her golden skin, highlighting the curves of her breasts. Her stomach was defined by years of dancing, her waist flaring into generous hips that called to my hands. Below that, athletic thighs enveloped her bare pussy.

Tala was strong and sexy all at once, and she stole the breath right out of me.

"You're perfect for me, Tala," I told her in a voice that wasn't quite steady. Hell, my legs didn't feel steady either. They felt weak, the way they did after a brutal game.

She bit her lip, her first show of nerves since we entered my room. "Why am I the only one naked?"

Holding out my arms, I said, "Have at it."

Her eyes flashed with desire. She stepped forward and tugged my shirt up. I bent so she could get it off, both of us laughing when the neckline caught under my left ear.

My laughter died as she traced my dips and ridges, setting my body on fire. I fisted my hands.

"Am I giving you a hard time?" she asked slyly.

Hard was the right word, alright. I was the hardest I had ever been in my life. But I'd let her take her time.

"Do your worst," I said, my voice way raspier than I'd ever heard it.

Tala kissed my chest, right over my heart. She continued pressing her lips across my pecs, drifting to my left nipple, then the right. As her lips moved downward, her hands lowered to the button on my jeans. The backs of her fingers brushed against my erection, making me hiss. Then she was undoing my pants and pulling them down along with my boxer briefs.

I held back a curse as my cock sprang free. Her hands grasped it in a tight fist and stroked down. My hips surged forward. "Later," I managed to say as I tugged her up. Too much of that, and I'd lose control. She had to come first.

She rose and I met her halfway, crashing my lips on hers. Her fingers dug into my hair, and the feel of her nails on my scalp and her taut nipples on my chest sent my senses into overdrive.

I filled my hands with the firm curves of her ass and lifted her. This time, when our lower bodies met, no fabric lay between them. My cock slid against her bare, wet pussy. I groaned, every molecule of my being aching for her.

"Jase," she moaned as her hips moved with mine. One hand left my hair and clutched at my back. Her nails bit into my skin. "I need you."

Her words wrapped around me like a sensuous embrace. I buried my face in the crook of her neck and reached for her hair tie. One tug and her hair fell loose as I carried her to the bed. I laid her down on the bedspread and took a moment to savor the sight of her.

Finally, she was here. And she wanted me.

She shifted on the mattress, appearing restless. I climbed onto the foot of the bed and settled between her legs, planting my forearms on either side of her hips. My lips roamed across her skin, eliciting those moans I could listen to forever.

As I kissed a line down her center, her spine arched to meet me. The flick of my tongue in her navel drew out a breathless laugh that turned into a whimper the lower I went. I felt drunk on her scent, her body.

My palms smoothed up her legs to the juncture of her thighs. Then I brushed the back of my knuckles across her pussy.

"Is this all for me, Tal?" I asked, letting my breath caress her skin as I watched her reaction.

Her eyes were low-lidded with pleasure, mouth swollen from our kisses. "Mmm."

Moving lower, I traced the V between her legs with my tongue. Her breathing grew shallow.

I braced my arms under her legs and placed her thighs on my shoulders. A flick of my tongue on her clit, and her back bowed.

She grasped at my hair, thrusting against my mouth. I licked along her opening, then I made love to her with my mouth, her body meeting my every move. I slipped a finger inside her and groaned at how wet she was.

Circling my tongue around her clit, I added another finger. I ground my erection into the mattress, needing the friction. Her inner muscles squeezed around my fingers, and I couldn't wait to feel her do the same around my cock.

"Jase. *Please.*"

"I want to feel you come for my mouth," I said, breaking for air before I resumed my mission. Her cries rose, thighs trembling as I thrust my fingers inside her. She writhed uncontrollably, and I clamped one hand on her waist to hold her still. Her breath grew shorter as she got close. I moved faster, sucking her clit until she came with a gasp, her muscles clenching around me.

I licked her through the aftershocks. Then she grasped my shoulders, trying to pull me up. After one last kiss on her pussy, I hauled myself up. My cock was so hard, it hurt. She caught it in her palm and stroked.

Through my haze of pleasure, I spotted the worry that flashed across her face. "We don't have to—"

"I want you," she repeated. "Condom?"

Reaching for the nightstand, I yanked the drawer open and grabbed the unopened box. Tala began grinding on me, and I nearly dropped the box. I fumbled with the lid and snatched a gold packet, tearing it open. Then I rolled it over my erection.

She wrapped her legs around me, urging me down until my cock nestled between her folds.

I thrust against her. Once. Twice, rubbing my length across her clit. Moaning, she reached between us and positioned me at her opening.

Our eyes met, and in hers, I read longing and a hint of nervousness.

"I'm sure, Jason," she told me.

I kissed her gently and took her hand. "I'll take care of you," I promised as I twined my fingers with hers over her head.

She nodded.

Watching her face for any trace of pain or doubt, I slowly slid the tip of my cock into her. She stiffened, and a filthy sound escaped her mouth. I stopped. "You okay?"

Tala's eyes fluttered shut as she bit her lip and nodded.

"Talk to me, Tal. I want to make this good for you." My body strained with the effort of holding back, but I did. For her.

Her eyes snapped open, hazy with need. "You feel amazing. Don't stop."

She kissed me then, and as our tongues met, I pushed all the way in. Her wetness eased my motions as I thrust carefully, going deeper each time.

"More," she demanded, digging her heels into my ass as her hips bucked against mine.

She felt like heaven, her lush heat surrounding me. "Fuck," I groaned. "You feel so good." Sitting up, I lifted her hips off the mattress and thrust harder. I alternated them with heavy grinds on her clit, loving the breathy sounds she made. Then I hooked my arm under her knee. "Is this okay?"

The corners of her lips curved upward. She raised her leg onto my shoulder, and the change in position opened her further, allowing me to sink deeper inside.

Fuck, yes.

I sped up, driven by her moans. The headboard slammed against the wall. Her inner muscles squeezed me tighter, and the bottom of my spine tingled, signaling I was almost there.

"Jase," she cried out.

"Come with me, Tal," I told her.

She whipped her head from one side to the other, launching her hips up in sync with mine.

Lowering myself until our chests met, I kissed her with my

eyes open. Her glazed eyes met mine for a beat before she threw her head back in a silent scream.

The feel of her clenching around me was too much. I thrust twice and came deep inside her. Unintelligible words burst out of me as pleasure so bright flooded my body. I held there, reveling in the rapid thumping of her chest beneath mine.

I love you.

"Can't breathe."

"Sorry." Releasing her leg, I shifted onto my side. I pressed a kiss to her lips and whispered, "Be right back."

Then I removed the condom and headed to the ensuite bath. After disposing of it, I grabbed a washcloth and returned to the room. Tala was sprawled out on the bed. Her eyes were closed, lips curved into the slightest hint of a smile.

I sat beside her and carefully wiped her clean.

She sat up. "I need to use the bathroom."

"Okay." I lifted her off the bed.

"I can walk, you know," she told me as I carried her to the bathroom doorway. "You didn't break me. I think."

I laughed and placed her on her feet. Her legs wobbled, so I wrapped an arm around her waist. Catching the wince on her face, I asked, "You okay? Did I hurt you?"

"It's been a while. And you're not exactly small."

Shit, I should have been gentler with her. "I shouldn't have been so rough."

"I liked it. I just need to get used to it." Her eyes widened. "Not that I'm expecting we'll do that again. We don't have to. We shouldn't."

This woman. Always so quick to assure me that she didn't expect anything from me—so sure that she was just temporary. The irony of it was that I wanted the exact opposite.

Holding her hands, I rubbed my thumbs across her knuckles. "Tal. This isn't just a one-night stand."

Her forehead creased. "But—"

"Did you really think I'd do that to you?"

Her teeth worried her bottom lip. I wished I could read her mind. She held her thoughts so close to her chest, only giving up control when I had my hands on her body.

"Fine," she said.

I raised my eyebrows. "Fine?"

"Only for the summer. While you're here," she stressed. "When you go home next month, it'll be a clean break."

"That's not what I had in mind."

"That's all I'm ready for. If you're not okay with that, that's alright. We'll go back to how we were before."

Did she seriously believe I could forget what we had just done? That I could spend time with her and not want to kiss her, touch her? Now that I'd had her, I wasn't letting her go.

I could wait until she was ready. In the meantime, I'd play it the way she wanted to.

"Fine," I said.

She blinked. "Okay."

There at the doorway to my bathroom, we stared at each other.

Heat flushed her cheeks. "I need to pee now."

"Okay," I said without moving.

"Out, you perv." She dropped my hands and playfully pushed me, closing the door behind her.

I laughed quietly as I headed back to bed.

We belonged together. I knew it down in my bones. Now, I just had to convince her too.

24

akap – (n) embrace

Tala

I trudged up the fifth flight of stairs to my floor. Shanti's replacement had been missing in action, only to send in his resignation over lunch. That left us understaffed right when two new patients arrived.

I spent the morning getting them settled in between attending to my usual patients. I couldn't even stay to chat with Berna because I'd scheduled my interview with Shanti's contact over my lunch break. I'd expected it to take thirty minutes max, but the interviewer felt the need to ask me every single question on the recruitment manual. We said goodbye minutes before my break ended, leaving me with just enough time to guzzle down some water, freshen up, and dash to my next patient. I barely sat until I clocked out at quarter to nine— almost two hours after my shift should have ended.

The upside of leaving work late was snagging a seat on the bus. My eyes shut the moment we started moving, and the sole reason I woke up for my stop was that the passenger beside me nudged me awake.

I trekked to my building half asleep, only to find the elevator closed for maintenance. By the time I unlocked my door, my feet were crying for a massage. My shoulders were stiff, and my head was woozy from hunger and exhaustion. As soon as the door shut, I rested against it, my eyelids drooping.

I had to do this all over again tomorrow.

"You look like crap."

My eyes flashed open in surprise. I hadn't noticed Luna on the sofa because she left the ceiling lamp off, only using the corner light.

"Hey," I said carefully. It was the first time she had talked to me in a week. When I got back from Jason's place, she was nowhere to be found. She had been eating out, only staying at home to sleep and do her laundry. Her replies to my texts were straight to the point, devoid of her trademark emojis.

I didn't think I'd miss my sister's frequent calls and texts, but I did.

Hanging my bag on the coat rack, I walked over to the sofa. "I'm sorry, Lu. I know that won't change what happened, but I am. Tell me what I can do to fix this," I pleaded.

Luna closed her laptop and put it aside. She nodded to the coffee table, where a folded garment lay. "I got that for you."

I sat on the edge of the sofa and picked it up. Holding it open, I recognized the number in front and the name on the back. I gaped at her. "It's Jason's jersey?"

"From his rookie year. It's men's sized and there was a huge hole that I had to repair, but it's a rare find. The store owner didn't even know it was there. Guess she's not a basketball fan."

I found the patch near the hem and traced it with my finger. My vision swam.

"Are you crying?" Luna sounded incredulous.

"No." I wiped the bottom of my eyes. I didn't cry often and this was twice in seven days. What was happening to me?

Her arm came around my shoulder.

"Thank you for the shirt. I'm so sorry I've been a sucky sister."

She sighed. "Why didn't you tell me? I get that you didn't want me to worry but did you really think I wouldn't want to know?"

"It's not that. I just..." I smoothed the jersey as my leg bounced beneath it.

I hated having to confront my feelings. Even worse was baring them for someone else and risk being judged. It made me feel naked and vulnerable when I'd tried for so long to be strong.

But this was my sister.

"I've gotten used to being alone," I admitted, raising my eyes to her. "I had to look out for myself and decide on my own for years. It's a hard habit to break. Besides, you have your own problems to deal with. You didn't need more from me."

"That's just it—you don't know that's what I was feeling. You assumed it."

"I..."

"I would have wanted to know what you were going through. Even if there wasn't much I could do, I could at least listen. Maybe I'm making assumptions too, but I'd bet Mama and Papa and Lonzo feel the same. Just because you live far away doesn't mean you matter any less to them. And just because you don't tell us about your problems doesn't mean we don't worry about you."

Swallowing the lump in my throat, I opened my mouth but nothing came out. I didn't know what to say.

"I know you're a strong, independent woman. I've always

admired you for that. But sometimes, I wish you could just be my sister, and that you would let me be a sister to you too."

"You are—"

"Almost twenty," she interrupted. "Not ten. If you need to look for a new job, I can help. I'll pitch in for the bills. I mean, can't I be strong and independent like you?"

I stared at her and wondered how I hadn't seen her, *truly* seen her, in a while. Why hadn't I seen how Luna had stepped out of her comfort zone when she moved here? How she tried to be a friend to me even when I treated her like my duty? Yes, she was the fun, outgoing one. But she was more than that too.

Taking her hand, I squeezed it. "You're right, Lu. How did you get to be so wise?"

"I grew up. You weren't paying attention."

"I'm sorry." I moved closer and rested my head on hers.

"I forgive you, and I'm sorry for giving you the cold shoulder. So much for being mature, right?"

"It's okay. I understand."

"Don't take it so easy on me, Ate. Someone told me I was being a brat."

I scowled. "Who told you that?"

"Who else?" She used the exasperated tone she reserved for only one person.

"Gabe?"

She rolled her eyes but replied, "He's right. Though I'll deny I ever said that."

"You're not—"

Luna cut a glance at me.

"Fine. You can be a brat sometimes," I admitted, my mouth twitching.

Her glare burned into me. "I can't believe you said that!"

"You just said..." I shook my head. "Fine."

"See? You let me off the hook too often. Don't, or I'll

become a bigger brat." Scrunching up her face, she added, "I mean, you can take it easy on me sometimes."

I laughed with relief. Luna was back to her usual self, and it felt good. "I'll remember that. Thanks again for the jersey. I love it," I said as I folded the shirt.

"I was thinking you can surprise Jason. It's long enough to be a dress on you. No one will be able to tell you're not wearing underwear."

My jaw dropped. "I wear underwear!"

"With Jason?"

"Of course." Heat spread across my cheeks and other parts of my body as I remembered what I hadn't been wearing in his house two days ago.

Luna's loud laughter told me what she thought about my answer. "Right. Because I'm not always a brat, I won't accuse you of being a liar."

My mood dropped. Her words reminded me that I'd slept with Jason despite knowing I was hiding something big from him. I searched for what to say—a truth that I could offer my sister. "I had my interview earlier."

She sobered. "How did it go?"

"Fine, I think. They're scheduling another interview with one of the senior staff, but the recruiter I met said it looks very promising."

"This is the one in Montana?"

"Yeah. They have another location..."

Her face brightened. "Where?"

"...in Vermont," I finished.

"Oh." She slumped against the couch. "Well, at least that's on this side of the country."

"Yes, but I don't think I'll be able to pick the location. It will depend on wherever there's a need for a stay-in caretaker."

"Right."

"I got an interview scheduled with one of the hospitals in Charleston, though," I said, trying to sound optimistic. "So that could be an option. I'll send more applications tonight."

"Do you want to stay?" Luna asked suddenly, her voice quieter than usual.

"What do you mean? Of course. I need to be here with you."

"But do you *want* to stay?" she repeated. "If I weren't a factor, what would you want to do?"

I could lie about it, but she deserved my honesty. "I'd want to go home. I miss Papa and Mama. And Lonzo. I want to visit Lola's grave." The one I'd helped pay for but never seen outside of photos.

She picked at a loose thread on her shirt. "You'd work as a nurse in Manila?"

"If I had to. But I want to open a studio someday. I'd start with giving dance lessons at one of the schools and figure out how to earn more money." I tried to chuckle but it turned into a cough.

Sighing, Luna looked me straight in the eyes. "Maybe you should do that."

Was I so tired I was imagining things, or had she told me to go back home?

As if she'd read my mind, she said, "Maybe you should go home. Be with our family. Focus on dance. You should do it all."

"I can't, Lu. You told me yourself—I can't leave you behind."

"I got a job," Luna blurted out. "At the university store. I don't know if Jason told you, but I went for an interview and got the position. I started yesterday. I'm actually pretty good at convincing people to buy more than they planned to."

"That's great. I'm so proud of you." I smiled, even though I felt a pang of guilt.

"Don't give me that look. You didn't force me into it. I wanted a job. Luckily, I got one that has decent pay. Who knows, I might even enjoy it."

"I'm glad to hear that. And it's on campus, so at least you won't have an extra commute."

"Exactly," Luna said. "That's why it was my first pick too. But my point is...you were right. I can make it on my own. No." She shook her head and corrected herself, "I *need* to make it on my own. I need to prove that I can do it."

"You don't need to prove anything to me."

"Yeah, but I need to prove it to myself."

I understood exactly what she meant. It was the one thing that convinced me she wasn't just doing it out of obligation. "Okay. Okay, Lu."

"Though I'll probably still need you to pay the rent for a few months." Luna grimaced.

Laughing, I hugged her. "Of course."

"You should tell Jason."

The words deflated me. I ran my thumb across the hem of the jersey. "I don't want to distract him. Anyway, we didn't commit to anything long-term."

"Uh huh. More like you don't want to admit that you have feelings for him and you don't want to consider being in a relationship."

Luna had it wrong. I knew what I felt for Jason. I wouldn't have had sex with him otherwise. And I *had* imagined what it would be like to be in a relationship with him—often. But it would never work out.

"It's only for the summer, Lu."

"Did he say that, or was that something you assumed?" she shot back at me.

My sister knew me better than I thought.

"I need to eat," I said in the most obvious deflection. "I haven't eaten since breakfast." I barely had the energy to keep my eyes open, let alone argue about Jason.

She sighed. "There's *longganisa* fried rice in the fridge. But for the record, I'm pretty sure Jason's serious about you." Leaning over, she gave me a smack on the cheek. Then she stood and picked up her laptop. "I need to finish my homework. Think about it, okay?"

Like I could stop. "I will. Thanks, Lu. Good night."

"Night!" she called back.

The door closed behind her, leaving me with my thoughts. My watch vibrated with an incoming call.

"Hey," I answered on speakerphone.

"Are you home? You didn't reply to my text." Jason sounded worried, so unlike his usual calm self.

"I fell asleep on the bus. Then when I got home—after climbing up the stairs, by the way—Luna was here. We made up."

"I'm glad you guys are good again." He paused. "Wait, the elevator wasn't working?"

"The memo said it will be out until tomorrow. Hopefully, it'll be back to normal by the time I finish work."

"I can always give you a lift up the stairs."

I laughed, and some of the exhaustion drained out of me. This was my favorite part of the day—chatting with Jason.

"You sound tired, dance girl."

"Long day. At least Luna's talking to me again."

"I knew you'd work things out."

"Mmm." I walked to the refrigerator and removed the container of rice with *longganisa*, a popular type of sausage back home.

We continued talking while I heated the food. He asked

208

about work, and I asked about his day. After I finished eating and washing up, I sat on the sofa and stretched my legs out on the coffee table.

"By the way," he said. "When are you shooting the video for '*Indak*'?"

The question took me by surprise. "I'm not."

"Why not? I loved that dance."

"It's Filipino. It's not my usual style." I thought that was obvious.

Silence, and then, "*You're* Filipino. And it's good that it's not your usual style. It stands out. Going by my research, that's going to help you gain visibility, especially with your Filipino audience."

"I don't want to alienate my followers who don't understand our language."

"I've seen people dance to songs in different languages. It shouldn't be a problem. In fact, I think it's nice to show another side of you. The way you danced then? It felt genuine."

Of course it did. It was me, unfiltered. No thoughts or planning, just raw feelings. I got enough hate when I danced to music people knew. How much more would I get if I used a song they didn't? "I'll think about it." I said the words only to appease him.

"Good. One more thing—guess who's coming to visit this week?"

I closed my eyes and let the sound of his voice soothe my headache. "Who?"

"Miles."

My eyelids popped open.

"He's coming over for the weekend."

"Oh! I'm glad you'll have company." I drummed my fingers on my lap. "You guys are turning Sterling into the next 'it' place."

He grunted. "I'll tell him to keep a low profile."

It would be near impossible to hide who Miles was. Aside from him having one of the most recognizable faces in sports, he was massive. If Jason drew attention on his own, I doubted Miles would go unnoticed.

"Is he staying at your place?" I asked.

"Yeah. I want you to meet him."

My leg bounced on the coffee table. "Jase...I'm not sure that's a good idea."

He took a minute to respond. "He's one of my best friends, Tal. It would mean a lot to me. Besides, I promised your sister an intro. I can't do that without introducing you too, right?"

"Right." How could I keep Luna from meeting her favorite player when she had the rare chance to do so?

I couldn't.

"I'll make sure he's on his best behavior," Jason told me.

"Alright. I'm working on Sunday, but Saturday's free."

"Great. I'll set it up and let you know the plan before then."

I could already imagine Luna's reaction. My mouth broke into a grin as phantom squeals rang in my ears. It would be a nice surprise for her, though I wouldn't tell her until the schedule was set.

That reminded me of something I needed to ask Jason. "Have you told Miles you're thinking about studying again?"

"Not yet," he said, his voice tight. "I don't know if I should mention it. I don't want to stress him out over something that might not happen."

"Have you heard anything from the dean?"

"He sent me Coach Tom's number and a couple of interesting articles. It's just..." He huffed a breath. "Can I really walk away from what I have? It's a once in a lifetime opportunity that only a few people get. Everyone will think I'm insane if I quit."

"Lonzo told me athletes have a less than one percent chance to go pro."

Jason snorted. "It's close to nil, Tala. How can I give it up?"

I tried to imagine myself in his position. "I guess it depends on what matters more to you. Yes, you have a career that most people can only dream about, but does it count if your heart's not in it? Everyone has their own opinions. But at the end of the day, you're the one who has to deal with the reality of your decision."

"So you think I should go for the option I'll regret less?" he asked.

"Don't take my word for it. I'm not an expert."

"I don't need an expert to tell me what to do. It's your opinion I care about."

I took my time answering him. "There are things I wish I could have done differently, but I don't regret them because they were for my family. That said, if you have the freedom to decide for yourself—if no one will suffer from your decision—then I think you should go for what you really want. What fulfills you. And figure out the rest along the way."

"Just like that?"

The words tasted bittersweet. "Easier said than done, right?"

We settled into silence, and I imagined he was deep in thought. "Jase?" I murmured.

"Yeah?"

"Thank you. For calling. For listening."

"Of course," he said softly. "You know I'd be there if you asked. Just say the word, Tal."

"I know."

Later, when I was freshly showered and tucked in bed, I wondered how to tell him the truth. And how I'd handle him walking out of my life for the second time.

25

barkada – (n) a group of friends

Jason

My gaze slid to the passenger seat in time to catch Tala checking her reflection in the side-view mirror. I bit back a chuckle, but I must have given myself away. She turned and narrowed her eyes at me.

"Stop it," she warned in a low tone.

"I didn't say anything." My face split into a smile.

Tala was nervous. Aside from when she was naked, she never seemed to be self-conscious about her looks. Not that she should be.

When she opened her apartment door earlier, she stunned me into silence. She'd traded her typical athleisure clothes for a printed wrap dress with a slit showing glimpses of her right leg. Instead of sneakers and a ponytail, she wore strappy sandals and left her hair loose. The last time I'd seen her hair like that, it formed a curtain around my face as she rode me in one of the lounge chairs.

No matter what she was wearing—or not wearing, for that

matter—she stole my breath. It amused me that she might worry otherwise.

Taking her hand, I placed it on my thigh. "You look amazing, Tal."

"It's not that," she grumbled.

"Then what is it? You're not getting starstruck on me, are you?"

Her glare burned into the side of my face. "Of course not."

"Okay..." If that wasn't the problem, I had no idea what was. Since Luna wasn't in the car with us, I'd get no clues from her.

Tala had invited Gabe to the party, and he'd offered to give Luna a ride from school. I wondered if him coming was less about meeting Miles and more about watching over Luna.

Picking at her skirt, Tala said, "Miles is your best friend. I'm worried he might not like me."

I never saw that coming. Her caring about what Miles thought gave me hope. Maybe she did see me as more than just a summer fling.

"You don't have to worry. He already likes you. I just hope you won't like him too much." I pulled up behind a shiny silver convertible parked in front of my gate. Noticing Tala's interest in the car, I explained, "That's Miles being subtle."

"I think we have different definitions of the word," she murmured, tapping her foot on the floor mat.

"He loves his flashy cars, but he's as down to earth as they come." Unbuckling my seatbelt, I turned to her. I drew her hand to my lips and placed a kiss on her knuckles. "Thanks again for agreeing to this."

"It wasn't just for you. Luna would kill me if I said no," she said as she tried to wriggle her fingers free.

"Still." Hand firm on hers, I leaned closer and gave in to the urge to kiss her.

Much too soon, she drew away. "You're going to be late to your own party."

"Miles can wait."

She unlatched her seatbelt, making me sigh. I hurried out of my seat to open the door for her.

"Thanks." She stepped out of the car—beating me to it *again*—and grabbed her bag. "Could you get the cake?"

"Sure." I got the dessert box from the backseat. I'd told her not to bring anything, but she insisted.

After locking the car, I slipped my fingers through hers and led her down the pathway.

She tried to tug her hand away, but I held onto it tighter. "What are you doing?" she demanded.

"Holding your hand."

She stopped in the middle of the path. "Miles might get the wrong idea."

I shrugged. "As far as I'm concerned, it's the right one." And I didn't care who knew.

"Finally!" a familiar voice said.

We were so focused on each other that we hadn't heard the front door open. We turned to find Miles smiling at us from the entryway.

"You couldn't wait for us inside?" I groused, letting go of Tala's hand only to slip mine on the small of her back.

My best friend grinned wider. "You cut the engine a decade ago. I wanted to check that you guys didn't suffocate inside your car."

"Asshole." I shook my head and laughed.

Miles jogged down the steps and met us halfway. Without hesitating, he embraced Tala and lifted her like she weighed nothing. She inhaled sharply as he held her in the air.

"Stop manhandling my woman, Miles." My words held no heat to them.

He glanced at me. "So that's how it is, huh?" Setting Tala back on her feet, he said to her, "Since J-man here has no manners, let me introduce myself. Miles Gomez at your service."

She smiled and shook his hand. "I'm Tala. Nice to meet you, Miles."

"I've been waiting for you for hours." Miles slung a massive arm across her shoulders and ushered her up the stairs.

Midway to the landing, Tala glanced back at me and gave me a small smile. It hit me squarely in the chest.

As I followed them into the house, I wondered how I had gone without her for so long.

———

Luna and Gabe arrived not ten minutes after we did, and it was the perfect excuse to tug Tala away from Miles. Luna had indeed been starstruck by Miles, but Gabe's brooding presence seemed to keep her from bouncing off the walls. Tala, for her part, responded to Miles's easy-going nature with friendly reserve.

To keep our get-together under wraps, I opted against hiring a catering team and ordered food instead. Tala helped me set up the spread on the patio table while Gabe stood by Luna as she chatted with Miles.

The weather was perfect for an outdoor picnic, sunny but not so warm that the overhead fans couldn't do the trick. We settled outside and chatted over glasses of iced sweet tea. Tala and I sat on the short end of the sectional sofa with Luna and Gabe on the other side. On my left, Miles lounged in one of the armchairs.

"I can't get over how cool this place is," Miles said, looking around. "It's so different from your apartment. You should see

215

it, Tala. It's a renovated shoe factory with concrete floors and exposed beams and windows and plants everywhere."

"That sounds interesting. Of course he'd have plants there too." Tala smirked at me.

"You hired some green architect, right?" Miles looked to me for confirmation. "Added those solar panels and everything. This place is more, like, historic looking. But with high-tech security."

"I'll hire the same guy to make this place more sustainable."

Tala frowned while Miles did a double-take.

"You're gonna renovate a place you're renting for a few weeks?" Miles asked.

"Of course not. I'm going to renovate a place I bought."

Tala froze while everyone else made varying sounds of surprise.

"Bro. You bought this?" Miles gaped at me.

"Seriously?" came from Luna, who had been busy exchanging angry whispers with Gabe.

"I put in an offer yesterday, and the owner verbally accepted this morning. Our lawyers should be in discussions as we speak."

Tala coughed.

"You okay, Tal?" I put my hand on her thigh.

"I'm fine." She shifted her leg, her eyes darting to her sister.

"Are you, like, planning to move here?" Luna asked.

I shrugged, trying to play it casual. "It's a vacation house. I might rent it out most of the year. I'll play it by ear."

"Good on you, man. Always said you should diversify your portfolio," Miles said.

As he engaged Gabe in financial talk, I studied Tala's profile. She seemed to be having an entire silent conversation with Luna, and the strain on their faces told me it wasn't about anything good.

I wanted to pull her aside and ask her about it, but I'd wait until I had her all to myself. Over the past week, she'd become more open during our phone calls. Hearing her share her thoughts so freely gave me a high not unlike that of dropping the perfect dime.

Throughout lunch, Luna sparkled from chatting with Miles, who was more than happy to indulge her. Gabe unclenched as we talked about soccer—football, to him—though he might as well have pissed on Luna with his body language. On Luna's insistence, we set up a video call with Lonzo, who looked like his head would explode.

While we ate, I touched Tala in one way or another. Brushing her hair back. Placing my hand on her leg, my thigh against hers.

I couldn't help it. Everything in me was drawn to her. Despite her earlier protest, she didn't flinch away from my touch. Whether she noticed it or not, she gravitated toward me too. She'd lean her shoulder against my arm, and her eyes sought me out when we weren't beside each other.

We could make this work. One final season playing with the NBA, then I could settle here and work toward my MBA—maybe. Tala wouldn't have to continue working as a nurse. If she wanted to, she could focus on her dancing and content creation full-time. That would give her a lot more flexibility, and she wouldn't be so stressed all the time.

Hell, she wouldn't even need to keep renting her place. She and Luna could move into my house, or Luna could keep the apartment if she wanted her own space. I'd check if it was possible to buy the unit outright for her, so she wouldn't have to worry about payments.

The more I thought about the idea, the more I liked it.

Now I just had to sell it to Tala. At the very least, I could count on Luna to back me up.

It was past sunset when we wrapped up the party. Miles excused himself for a quick drive to Charleston, where one of his foster sisters lived. He promised to be back in a couple of hours.

"That went surprisingly well," Tala said as she put the left-over food in a glass container.

Luna snorted. "Luckily Miles wasn't offended by *someone's* bad mood."

Three guesses who she was referring to.

"I like him," she declared.

"Of course you do." Tala shifted on her feet, drawing my attention to her sandals.

They didn't seem too comfortable, so I swept her up and carried her to one of the stools at the island.

"Jason!" She swatted my shoulder and tried to jump off.

My hands on her waist kept her in place. "You look tired," I said as I sat her down.

"And on that note, we should get going," Gabe said. "I'll bring your sister home, Tala."

"What? But—" Luna started to protest.

Tala spoke up. "I'll go with you two."

"Hell no," I told her, amused she even thought I was letting her leave. "You're staying with me."

"Jason," she hissed before looking at Luna and Gabe.

Luna only rolled her eyes. "Like we don't know that Jason isn't just helping you with your videos."

Gabe snorted.

Laughing, I caged Tala with my arms.

She pushed at me. "Not in front of my sister! Also, Miles will be back in a bit."

"I'll move him to the room farthest from ours," I said.

"No way. I'm going home with Lu and Gabe, and you're staying to bond with your best friend."

218

"You can bond with him too."

"Ooh, that should be interesting," Luna interjected, her eyes gleaming with mischief.

Tala cut a glance at her. "Who are you, and what have you done to my sister?"

"What about this? Stay for a bit, then I'll bring you home later," I offered, knowing when I was fighting a losing battle.

She sighed. "Fine. But you're helping me edit."

"Deal." I'd taken an introduction to video editing class online, and while my skills were nowhere near hers, I could do the basic stitches and adjustments when she needed to work on something else.

"Glad that's settled." Gabe walked over to us and clapped a hand on my shoulder. "Thanks for lunch, Jason. Enjoy the rest of your night."

Tala slid off her stool and hugged him. "Thanks for coming, Gabe. Take care of Lu."

"Of course."

"I don't need a guardian," Luna grumbled.

Tala embraced her too. "See you later."

"I won't wait up." Luna gave me a conspiratorial smile as I kissed her cheek.

"Good to know." I winked at her.

Tala and I accompanied them to Gabe's car and waved them off. Before driving away, Gabe and I exchanged pointed looks.

"What was that about?" Tala asked as they pulled away from the curb.

"Just guy stuff." With that wordless exchange, Gabe basically told me to take care of Tala, and I warned him to do the same for Luna.

"Oh no. You've bonded."

I chuckled. "Maybe."

Placing my hands on her shoulders, I ushered her back inside. I meant to ask her about the weird moment between her and Luna that afternoon, but she climbed me as soon as we entered the living room.

With her lips on mine and her hand sliding down my chest, it didn't take long for all thought to leave my brain.

26

balita – (n) news; rumors

Tala

As I entered the staff room the next day, my shift mates looked up and stared at me in unison.

"You're dating Jason Meyer?" Billie asked, eyes unblinking.

Only then did I notice they had their phones in their hands. Dread mounted in my chest. All sound receded as my heartbeat thumped right in my ears. My hand tightened around my bag. "What?"

"It's all over social media." Billie flashed her phone at me.

The photo of me and Jason had been taken from a distance but our features were recognizable. We were stepping out of his house, his arm around my waist and my head resting on his bicep.

"There's a video too," one of the other nurses added.

Swiping at her phone, Billie showed me the clip of the two of us walking to Jason's car. He kissed me on the forehead before helping me into the passenger seat. There was nothing scandalous about it. In fact, I'd found it achingly sweet in that moment.

But it had been meant for us alone. Now, it was plastered on other people's phones. The post had already generated more than a hundred comments after being published thirty minutes ago, and the day had barely even begun.

"You didn't know?" Billie asked me in a softer voice.

"About the posts? No."

I avoided checking social media first thing in the morning, knowing how it affected my mood and productivity. I usually spent the bus ride to work going through my calendar and personal messages, but I'd had no clue of what happened. Probably because most of my friends were still sleeping and hadn't seen it yet.

I tried to shake off the buzzing in my head.

"Tala? Are you okay?"

Was I? I'd known the risks of being involved with Jason—known there was a chance people would find out about us. I already had a fair share of critics and trolls on a regular day. I didn't want to read what people would say about me now.

For a moment, I felt transported back to freshman year with strangers staring at me. Speculating about me and snickering about my accent.

I blinked and grounded myself in the present, focusing on the striped walls and linoleum floor of the staff room and the locker that had been mine for nearly three years.

I was at work. Even though I was being let go, I still had to be professional.

No time to lose it.

"I'm fine," I said to Billie, flattening my palms against my thighs to keep them from shaking. "Thanks for letting me know. I should get ready."

As if she could read my mood, she gave me a nod and stepped aside. "See you at the huddle."

Most of the other nurses trailed out of the room with Billie, giving me curious glances as they went. Left with one of the newer hires, I breathed in deeply. As I exhaled, I tried to release my anxiety and forget about the gossip that was undoubtedly making the rounds.

Everything would be alright.

It wasn't the end of the world. I was stronger than my insecurities.

Later, I'd deal with the chaos on the internet. For now, I needed to be professional. So I put my phone on mute and prepared for my shift.

———

"I DIDN'T KNOW you were involved with a celebrity," Jose said as he leaned forward and steepled his hands on his desk. He had called me into the office right after our change-of-shift huddle for what he called 'a quick chat.'

There was no way to ignore the bomb Billie had dropped. Eyes tracked me as I walked down the hallway, and whispers followed. Where I had once been just another nurse, now I was an object of curiosity.

"He's an athlete," I said despite the fact that Jason *was* a celebrity. If he wasn't, no one would care about who he was seeing.

"Yes, well, he's all over the internet and so are you."

"We knew each other in college. Is that going to be a problem?" I didn't give away the nature of our relationship. How could I when I didn't have a name for it myself?

Summer fling? Friends with benefits?

Better to keep it vague.

Jose clucked his tongue. It was one of his tells whenever he was contemplating something.

My immediate termination, maybe.

"As long as he doesn't interfere with your job, it's none of my business," Jose said. "I've known you long enough to have faith in your work ethic. I trust you to look out for our patients."

My hands that had been gripping my thighs relaxed. "Of course."

"To be completely transparent, I'm foreseeing that the attention on you will provide free publicity for the center. I'm not sure what management will think about it, but given your work status..." He hesitated, seeming to realize he had raised a sensitive topic.

"It's fine. As long as something good comes from this, right?"

"That brings me to my other concern. Were you able to find a job? Or will you no longer be working now that you're with Mr. Meyer?"

"No!" The word erupted from me, surprising us both with its force. I lowered my voice. "I mean, no to both. I'm still... considering my options."

To Jose's credit, he didn't pry. Instead, he said, "If you need my help with referrals..."

"I'll be sure to let you know. Thank you for the offer."

"Have you decided on your last day?"

"I'm looking at October 12." I hadn't decided about going home, but if I did, I wanted to spend my last few days here with Luna without work getting in the way.

"I'll take note of that. Thanks for the heads-up."

"Alright. Well, I should go—I'm running late for rounds." I stood.

"You take care, Tala. Unfortunately, there's a lot of people talking, and we can't control what they say."

"I know. I'll be fine." With a nod, I left and went about my work. Wishing that the more I said the words, the more likely they'd come true.

———

Jason

"I'm sorry, man," Miles said for the tenth time that morning.

I had just gotten off a call with Sam, who had been blowing up my phone even before I woke up. It was a toss-up who left me the most calls and texts: Sam or my mom. Stassy was a far third. All of them revolved around the same topic —Tala.

Apparently, some enterprising fan spotted Miles in Charleston and decided to stalk him back to my house. Then, because said person had nothing better to do, he parked on the opposite street and waited until I stepped out the door with Tala to bring her home. The photos of Miles getting into his car had gotten buried under those of me kissing Tala.

The only bright spot was that the wannabe paparazzi didn't follow us to Tala's apartment. Whether it was past his bedtime or he just had a skewed sense of decency, it was the one thing that kept me from suing the hell out of him.

Still, it hadn't stopped people from identifying Tala. By the time I checked social media, her name and accounts had been blasted. There was no chance she didn't already know about it.

"I told you, it's not your fault," I reassured Miles.

We were well aware of the lengths some fans went to when it came to their so-called heroes. Not for the first time, I wondered if they knew the attention could do more harm than good.

Of course, I was grateful I even had fans. But I never went

into basketball for the fame or the money, and at the end of the day, I wasn't sure either one was worth it.

Rubbing my temples, I headed for the fridge. I usually had coffee around this time, but it wasn't even nine a.m., and I already had a headache.

"I shouldn't have visited Charley," Miles grumbled as he swung himself onto a bar chair. "Still no word?"

I chugged down an entire glass of water and refilled it. "No. She's probably busy with her rounds."

As soon as I found out what happened, I'd wanted to drive down to Golden Haven and talk to Tala. See how she was doing. I might have been the reason for the public interest, but she was the one bearing the brunt of it. People criticized me for slumming it. But Tala? She was getting torn apart, even on her own accounts. I wanted to reply to every one of those trolls—hell, I wanted to get them reported.

Fuck it.

Grabbing my phone, I checked my messages again. Still none from her. Luna texted to say she hadn't heard from her sister either but that it was normal for her not to text when she was working. I'd try to call during her lunch break and hope it was one of those days she could actually take her break on time.

I wanted to get her away from it all.

Miles looped his arm around my neck. "C'mon. Prove to me you haven't lost your touch." He walked to the patio, dragging me along.

Twenty minutes later, I was panting while Miles bounced from one foot to the other, barely winded.

"The fuck was that, J-man? Did you even try?" he demanded in a half-horrified, half-joking tone.

I grunted as I pulled my shirt off and used it to wipe my face. That was the fastest Miles had ever owned me in a one-on-one game. Any other day, and I could have held out longer. Not today. And I wasn't the least bit bothered.

Glancing at him, I cataloged the way he absentmindedly dribbled the ball. It almost seemed like a natural extension of him. His passion for the sport rang clear in his movements, and it made him a joy to watch on the court.

Just like Tala and her dancing.

"You're freaking me out with your silent treatment shit." Miles bounced the ball off the floor and caught it, tucking it under his arm. "Don't tell me you're pissed I crushed you."

"'Course not. You beat me fair and square."

"I know I was the one who suggested you get away, but man, I didn't think this place would mess you up worse."

"It hasn't." My stomach rumbled, reminding me I hadn't eaten yet. "Hey, you hungry? I'll make breakfast."

"Won't say no to that." Miles followed me to the kitchen. "Is Tala messing with your game?"

"No." Was I distracted by her radio silence? Yeah, but I couldn't pin my shitty play on her. A large part of basketball was mental, and my head wasn't just out of the zone, it actually resisted the thought of it. As if it was on strike or something.

"You talk to your old coach yet?"

"Nope." I kept putting off calling him, but now that my being in town was all over the news, I didn't need to slink around. Maybe seeing my old coach would help kick me back into gear.

That gave me an idea.

"Are you up to meeting a couple of college basketball players?" I asked Miles as I boiled water for oatmeal.

"Hell, yeah. But don't forget I fly out tomorrow night."

"I'm sure they'll make it work." A surprise visit from the current MVP? I'd bet the entire team would show up no matter what it took. "I'll call Coach after we eat."

"Sounds good. You calling your mom too?"

I looked up from the bananas I was slicing.

"I saw you've been ignoring her calls. What's that about?"

"She doesn't like Tala." I told him about the first time Mom met Tala and everything she'd said about her since.

He frowned. "That sucks. Never thought your mom was that type. She seems to like me fine."

"Apparently, it only matters when it comes to who I'm dating." Since most of the women I dated in the past were celebrities, there had been no reason for her to complain.

The realization came to me earlier as I read Mom's outraged texts, and it soured my image of her. I stirred oatmeal into the boiling water and lowered the heat. How many of her prejudices had I unconsciously lapped up?

"Joke's on her 'cause you have me for life," Miles said.

A reluctant laugh escaped my throat. "Is that your idea of a proposal?"

He shrugged. "It's more than I'll be getting from your lazy ass. This what Tala has to put up with?"

"Can it," I said half-heartedly. I turned off the stove and scooped the oats into two bowls.

"I'm kidding. Jeez. Let's get some food in you so you stop being such a grump. Then we can figure out a game plan."

"You're on."

27

sundo – (n) someone who fetches another person

Tala

I hiked my bag on my shoulder as I pushed through the staff exit. It was an hour past the official end of my shift. I had stayed under the guise of overseeing our newest trainee, but I really only wanted to avoid questions from my coworkers.

My strategy worked. The staff room had been empty when I went in and no one interrupted me on my way out. Just one day of this, and I was already sick of the attention.

Letting my shoulders drop, I trudged down the pathway. The weather was getting cooler. Soon, the temperatures would drop even further. I wondered if it would snow come winter. I'd only experienced it once—a flurry that left the ground wet and slippery. At that time, I thought I'd have plenty of chances to play in the snow. If I knew then what I did now, I would have danced in that flurry despite the risk of breaking my neck.

It never crossed my mind that I wouldn't have more years here. I had so much more to see and experience.

Maybe someday I'd save up enough money to visit Luna and Gabe. We could take that road trip we'd dreamt about, driving from east to west and stopping at charming B&Bs like we always saw in movies.

My feet faltered. When did I start to think of going home as a sure thing?

A car door slammed in the distance, drawing my head up. My eyes narrowed as a tall man wearing a cap exited a familiar car.

Jason.

My heart leapt at the sight of him, only to drop in panic.

"What are you doing here?" I hissed as he met me a few feet from the car. Catching his elbow, I tugged him away from the building, far from any prying eyes.

He went along with me to the passenger door. Pulling it open, he held my stare. "I'm not leaving without you," he told me, none of his usual playfulness on his face.

Instead, he looked mad.

Well, that was fine, because I was mad too.

Letting go of his arm, I glared at him.

"The longer you refuse to come in, the higher the chance someone will see us."

I wanted to shout out my frustration. But that would only make things worse. Besides, I was a calm, mature, professional woman.

I repeated that mantra in my head as I ducked inside the car. And again when he tried to take my bag and I fought the urge to pull it away from him. And yet again when he sat behind the wheel only to study me.

"Why are you here?" I demanded as I yanked the seatbelt across my midsection.

"To pick you up." He locked the doors.

It felt like the walls of the car were closing in on me. "God, Jason. We're already on the news. Is this how you do subtle?"

"Considering my first instinct was to wait for you inside—yes. This is me being subtle." He grimaced. "Like you said, people already know anyway."

Dropping my head on the head rest, I blew out a breath. "You and Miles need to check your definitions. Let's just go."

Something landed on my lap—a paper bag bearing a familiar fast-food logo. My eyes flew to Jason's profile while he stared straight ahead.

"You got me a burger?" I asked in disbelief. Now that it sat on my thighs, I smelled the undeniable aroma of fried meat and grease.

He put the car into gear and pulled away from the curb. "Figured you might have skipped lunch."

Opening the bag, I pulled out the burger. "It's my favorite."

"Consider it a one-time pass." His eyes touched on my face briefly before returning to the road. "Got you orange juice too."

My throat grew thick. How had I ever convinced myself I'd gotten over Jason Meyer? Loving him was like dancing an old favorite routine just to realize I'd been missing the heart of it. I'd loved Jason in the past, but that feeling paled next to the depth of my emotions for him now.

I swallowed, the sound seeming to echo in the car. "Thank you for the food."

He sighed. "I'm sorry for earlier. I worried about you all day, then I got pissed that you never replied to my messages."

"I'm scared to check my phone," I admitted. "I kept it in my bag and put my watch on 'do not disturb.'"

I had to face the issue sooner or later, but I would put it off for as long as I could.

It was cowardly and only postponed the unavoidable. But as ashamed as I felt about hiding, I did it all the same.

He reached out and wove his fingers with mine, and somehow, it felt like everything would be okay. Like nothing else mattered as long as he was with me.

"I understand this is overwhelming, and I hate that I got you into this shit. But please lean on me, Tala." His hold slightly tightened. "You're not alone. We'll get through this together, but you have to let me be here for you."

I bit my lower lip.

He glanced at me. "Don't shut me out, Tal."

This time, it was my turn to squeeze his fingers. I brought them to my lips and kissed them—a silent apology for everything I hid from him.

Would he forgive me when I told him? Would he understand my decision?

Placing our intertwined hands on my thigh, I rubbed my thumb across his skin. What could I tell him without lying outright?

"I'll try." That was all I could say. I needed to sort through my thoughts, figure out if I was making the right decision and that it wasn't just my emotions getting the best of me.

"Alright. Eat before your food gets cold. I tried to keep it warm with the car heater, but it's been here for over an hour."

"You waited that long?"

"Since quarter to seven. I wanted to be here before you left."

The thought that he'd waited in his car for me sent a pang through my chest. "You didn't have to. The bus is just—"

"Of course I didn't have to. But I wanted to," he said. "Eat."

————

Jason

I regretted telling her to eat when she let go of my hand to unwrap the burger. Instead of moving my hand away, I kept it on her thigh and wished I was touching her skin.

It was a struggle to keep my attention on the road, especially when she took a bite and gave a little moan. The same sound she made when I pushed inside her.

Get your mind out of the gutter, I told myself.

"It's so good. I'm sorry—I know this is against your code. But this is too good." She bit into it again and sighed.

Fuck.

I'd told her the burger was a one-time thing. Truth was, I'd get it for her anytime she wanted one. That was how far gone I was.

Couldn't she see it?

Lowering the burger to her lap, she turned to face me. "I'm sorry I shut you out. Luna tells me it's my defense mechanism."

"I've noticed. I'm not going anywhere, Tal."

Technically, I was. I had to. But I'd do everything in my power to convince her to go with me. If she said the word, I'd hold a damn press conference and introduce her to the world as my girlfriend.

"I spoke with my agent, Sam. He's trying to keep the news —" I rolled my eyes at the absurdity of calling the gossip *news* "—out of the mainstream press. It's harder to control what's circulating on social media. Our options are to post about each other on our own channels or just ignore what they're saying."

She stiffened.

I didn't tell her that Sam suggested a third option—for me to fly back to Santa Mila and go on public dates with another woman. Someone who was used to the spotlight and would deflect attention away from Tala.

According to him, it was the best solution. It was also out of the question.

"What do you think?" I asked Tala, hoping she was on the same page even though my gut told me otherwise.

She tapped her index finger on the burger's wrapping. "I think we should just ignore it."

Once again, my gut checked out. I'd never resented it more than I did at that moment. "Are you sure?" I prodded. "You're going to ignore the comments on your posts? The hashtags?"

She flinched, and I almost regretted what I said. But it was the reality we had to face. Unfortunately, her more than me.

"It'll be fine," she said. "I've gotten hate before. At least it's no longer in person."

My fingers tensed around the wheel. I'd known she didn't have an easy time at school. In a city that had always been predominantly white, Tala stood out—and some people could be cruel to those they considered outsiders. We didn't see each other around campus often because our schedules were so different, but whenever I spotted her, she'd been alone and wearing massive headphones that covered her ears. When I asked if she was okay, she'd play it off with her default line: "I'm fine."

Except for that time when the dance team kept her from auditioning.

I'd noticed her slumped shoulders and unusual stillness as soon as I entered the garden, and I'd felt so damned ashamed of myself because I'd been hooking up with the dance captain. I'd offered to talk to Fallon for her, but Tala shot me down, saying it would only make things worse.

"Did things get bad after I left?" I braced myself for her reply.

She shrugged half-heartedly. "Not really. I think they got used to me being around."

There was more to it, but one glance at her clenched jaw warned me not to dig. Anger flared in my stomach, and it was directed at myself as much as the assholes who'd bullied her.

"I wish I could've been here back then," I said, hating that she'd gone through it at all. Hating even more that I hadn't been around to help her.

"Don't worry about it, Jason. I like to think of it as a character-building experience." She glanced out the window as we rounded the block to her building's parking lot. "You brought me to my place?"

One corner of my mouth tilted up at the confusion in her voice. She'd expected me to bring her to my house. I wished I could, but Miles was staying one more night. And I had a feeling she needed her space.

"Can I come up for a bit?" I asked, hoping for more time with her. I wanted to ask about her day and tell her about mine, wanted to hold her without the damn car console between us.

I wanted her, period. No conditions, no restrictions, no time limits and intrusions. Just her.

Her lips curved the slightest bit, her eyes going soft. "I'd like that."

———

Tala

Jason kept a respectable distance from me as we went up to my apartment. As soon as we closed the door, he swept me off my feet and carried me to the sofa.

"Does this mean you missed me?" I teased as he sat with me on his lap and buried his face in my neck.

Peppering kisses on my skin, he moved a hand under my shirt and swept it up and down my side. "You could say that."

I sank my fingers in the short strands of hair at his nape, holding him closer. "I'm right here." Maybe not for much longer, but for now, I needed to get as close to him as possible.

Plastering myself against him, I ground on his growing erection.

"Your sister," he whispered.

I groaned. Luna wasn't home yet, or she would have checked on us already. But she might walk through the door any moment now.

Jason shifted his hand to my back, soothing me. I rested my cheek on his shoulder. He was hard beneath me, yet he did nothing more than stroke my back. My heartbeat slowed down, syncing to the rhythm of his.

"Social media aside, how was the rest of your day?" he asked.

I talked about my patients, including Berna, who was ecstatic about the photos. Told him about the trainee I was supervising and how he was steadily improving. Everything I could say, I did...except what he actually needed to know.

When I asked about his day, he told me about the meet-up he'd arranged with Miles and the university basketball team. He admitted he was excited and nervous about it. I reassured him the players would appreciate the chance to see him, no matter what he did or said.

After Jason left and Luna settled on the sofa beside me, I finally voiced the realization I'd had earlier. "I think it's time to go home."

"Are you sure this is the best time to decide that?" Luna asked.

"I can't afford to put it off anymore. And I knew what I wanted even before this mess happened."

She studied my face. "As long as you're not just running away."

"I'm not. I'm sure." It was the truth, even if part of me was already agonizing over saying goodbye to Jason.

Taking my hand, Luna squeezed it. "You know what you have to do."

I nodded.

Deciding was one thing. Telling Jason was a whole other battle.

Then again, we'd always had an end date, hadn't we?

Seven years ago, it had been one school year. Now, it was one summer.

I'd known it wouldn't last. The most I could do was wrap things up as tidily as possible and make sure there were no hard feelings.

If only my brain could get my heart on the same page.

28

pangarap – (n) dream

Jason

I had to give it to the Sterling U basketball team—they knew how to give a guy a warm welcome. They'd closed off the court, decorated it with streamers and a *Welcome Back* banner, and even set up a buffet table with fast food and soda.

Like I predicted, the entire roster showed up, and they brought a ton of stuff for Miles and me to sign. Coach Tom stood at the forefront of the celebration, greeting me with a hearty bear hug and the words, "Fucking finally, Meyer."

"Good to see you too, Coach," I replied, clapping a hand on his back.

"Had to find out from the envi-sci dean that you're here. Can't believe you waited so long to see me."

"You guys were out when I dropped by," I said. "Coach Tom, meet my friend Miles—"

"Miles Gomez. Of course I know the guy. Welcome, Mr.

238

Gomez." Coach Tom held out his hand to Miles, who shook it immediately.

"Call me Miles."

Nodding, Coach Tom rubbed his hands together. "Hope you two are ready. I've got a bunch of guys chomping at the bit to meet you."

Sure enough, the players gathered around us, jostling each other to introduce themselves and snap selfies on their phones. We made it a point to talk to every one of them and sign whatever they wanted. It was chaotic but I knew it was a dream come true for many of them.

The first time my dad brought me to the court to meet his teammates, they seemed larger than life. I imagined that was how this moment felt to these guys. Seeing the joy and excitement on their faces humbled me.

When Coach Tom suggested a pick-up game and tasked me to lead the blue team against Miles, I was hit with a sense of inadequacy. I felt like a fraud as I rallied my teammates to a two-point loss. More so when they asked me for tips, and I spewed out the same tired lines.

Work hard, train consistently.

Be better each time.

Shoot your shot.

Did I mean the words? Sure. I used to think I'd lived by them too, but now I knew the NBA and all it entailed was never my dream. And there were shots I regretted not taking.

Looking at the younger players with stars in their eyes, I wondered if it was time to really put my money where my mouth was.

We were coming up to the end of our allotted two hours when one of the guys, their starting small forward, spoke up. "Since you're dating that dancer chick, does that mean you'll be in town more often?"

Their team captain gave him a slap on the back of the head. "No personal questions, dumbass." He glared at his teammate.

The other guy shrugged and looked at me expectantly.

"The season's coming up, so we'll have to see," I said, reverting to my interview persona.

"Ball over babes, huh?"

Instinct urged me to ream him out for disrespecting Tala, but I held back my anger. He was a kid trying to act like a man in front of one of his idols.

"It's up to you to define your priorities," I replied. "But pro tip? Don't refer to women as 'chicks' if you want them to take you seriously."

A chorus of "oohs" sounded as the guy winced.

Trying to soften the burn, I clasped his shoulder. "Tell you what, next time I'm in the area, I'll come say hello. For now, it's time for us to hit the road."

"You forgot something," Miles told me.

The players lit up, standing straighter than before.

Right. "It didn't arrive in time, but we've got some merch heading your way. Coach, we'll coordinate with you to make sure you get it," I announced. We'd ordered Baron caps, T-shirts, and basketballs for each of the team members, as well as the supporting staff.

Cheers went off. We ended up staying for a couple more minutes to say goodbye. Coach Tom gave us an out by blowing his whistle and herding us through the gym doors.

"Thanks for dropping by, you two. You made those guys' year," he said as he walked us to my car.

"Glad we could pull this off," I told him. "Thanks for having us, Coach. They seem like a good bunch."

He swept a hand down his face, reminding me of the count-less times I'd seen him do that when he was frustrated, disappointed, or tired. "Eh. They have some growing to do, but you know how it is. You live and you learn."

"Growing never stops, right?"

"Not till we're six feet in the ground," Coach agreed.

Miles spoke up. "I'd prefer to be cremated and have my ashes shot into space myself."

Coming to a halt, Coach stared at him with a dumbfounded look on his face. Having dealt with rowdy teens for so long, he wasn't one to easily be caught off guard but Miles had that effect on people.

Laughing, I quipped, "Now you've met Miles."

They exchanged half-hugs, thumping each other's shoulders. Then Coach turned to me and gave me a sober nod. "You grew up good, Meyer. I'm proud of you. And I'm not just saying that because you won the championship."

I swallowed the lump in my throat. No one could ever take Dad's place, and I'd never sought a replacement. But I'd hit the jackpot with my mentors, and I couldn't be more grateful for them.

"Thanks, Coach," I said, tugging on the brim of my cap. "I appreciate it."

"There's always a place for you here. Don't be a stranger."

———

BEFORE HEADING TO THE HOUSE, Miles and I dropped by the garden. I'd told him Tala and I used to hang out there and he wanted to see it for himself. For the first time ever, I drove there from campus. Walking with Miles was an invitation to be mobbed, especially now that people knew we were both in town.

Over the past two months, I'd slowly restored the garden to its former luster. A fresh layer of leaves covered the stone floor, while the vibrant colors from hollyhock, hydrangea, and marigold blooms complemented the lush greenery. I couldn't wait to bring Tala there soon.

I pictured her dancing in the exact spot she used to while I watched behind the camera. Wouldn't that be the perfect full circle for both of us?

"Trust you to find yourself a garden while everyone else was hanging out in frat houses," Miles said as he wandered around the place. "How'd you keep your friends from tagging along?"

I raised a shoulder. "Told them I had tutoring sessions and ducked out while they were in the showers."

"Tala must've really liked you to put up with your dirty ass self." He snickered.

"I always took a shower, asshole. Just a quick one."

"Hey, no judgments here, man. Not gonna blame you for wanting to get with her."

"You know it wasn't like that." I'd been too stupid to recognize what was right in front of me then.

"Yo," Miles called out. "You seen this?"

I joined him in front of the patio doors. A piece of paper was taped to the glass—a crude 'For Sale' sign.

My eyebrows swung up. Who knew someone actually owned the place? They sure hadn't put in the effort to keep it in shape.

A name and contact number were scribbled in black ink.

"Up for another investment?" Miles asked.

I had just signed the contract for the house that morning. Though money wasn't an issue, I preferred to approach investments one at a time and only after plenty of consideration. Question was, could I stomach the idea of someone else taking over the garden?

Technically, it wasn't mine to begin with. But it might as well be.

Maybe I should make it official.

I snapped a photo of the sign.

"Well, damn. You're whipped." Slinging his arm around me, Miles ruffled my hair. "Never thought I'd see the day."

We drove back to the house for a quick lunch before he had to take off for the airport. Melancholy crept over me. I wasn't getting on that flight with him, but it was only a matter of days until it was my turn. Until it was time to step back into reality.

The past few months felt like living in an alternate world, one where I could be whoever I wanted and be with whomever I wanted without worrying about the consequences. But reality was catching up. Already, it left a crack in the relationship I was trying to build with Tala. I hated that my career had the power to negatively affect hers.

People always had a lot to say about my dating life, but I never expected this much buzz. It wasn't just the rumors either. It was the hate that pervaded them. Trolls targeted Tala because she didn't fit the mold of who I usually dated. They said all kinds of shit about her looks, her body, her skill—fuck, even her character. I knew because I read them, even though I had a personal rule to never read comments.

Despite the vitriol she received, she refused to turn off the comments on her accounts.

My knuckles turned white as I gripped the steering wheel, wanting to punch something.

"J-man," Miles said. "What's going on in that head of yours?"

"I fucking hate social media." It wasn't just the actual reporters you had to watch out for. Anyone fabricate toxic headlines and set off a shitstorm.

"Ahh. What are you gonna do about Tala?"

"Try to convince her to come with me."

He did a double-take. "Are we talking about her moving to Santa Mila, or her following you on the road?"

"I'll take whatever I can get." My chances were slim but not impossible. I just had to work harder, and fast.

I had less than ten days until I had to be back for training camp.

"I'm rooting for you. Whatever you need, just say the word."

Miles's voice rang with sincerity, and once again, I marveled at how lucky I was that he had my back.

"Thanks, man." I wanted to tell him about the career change I was contemplating. We'd talked about retirement, but it was always as an inevitable outcome in the distant future. Of all the guys on our team, Miles was the only one I trusted with my thoughts. He deserved to be the first to know.

Only, how could I spring it on him just before his flight? Talk about a dick move.

No, I'd wait until I was back in Santa Mila. I needed time to decide if it was in the cards; otherwise, I'd freak him out for no reason.

One step at a time.

First, I had to convince Tala to join me in California. Deadline: ASAP.

Next, figure out my career direction. Deadline: before my contract came up for renegotiation. The earlier the better.

29

takipsilim – (n) nightfall

Tala

For the second night in a row, Jason picked me up from the center. This time, he told me beforehand, reasoning it was near his hike anyway. It didn't take much convincing for me to agree. I knew he'd show up regardless, and now that people already gossiped about us, there was no need to hide.

Truthfully, I didn't want to argue. Not when we only had a few days left together. Jason hadn't brought up his flight home, but it was coming. He and Miles talked about training camp the other night. It was scheduled at the end of September, which gave us two weeks—less, if he had to be back earlier.

Until then, I wanted to spend as much time with him as I could.

"How was your meet and greet?" I asked as we drove to his place by unspoken agreement.

"Good. The whole team showed up."

I chuckled. "Of course." Like any basketball fan would miss

that opportunity, especially when it came to meeting someone they considered a hometown hero.

"We had a pick-up game. Coach Tom split them into two groups, and Miles and I led each of the teams."

"And...?"

"My team lost," he said matter-of-factly.

"Sorry to hear that."

"I didn't mind losing. I was more disappointed for my guys, but I think they enjoyed just getting to play with us."

"I imagine that's a dream come true for most of them."

His head jerked in a brief nod. He cleared his throat. "Yeah."

Sensing the tension pouring off him, I asked, "So how do you feel about that?"

"Honestly? I felt like a fraud. Some of them said they wanted to declare for the draft. There I was, encouraging them to go for their dream and to keep working hard. Telling them to never give up. Meanwhile, I'm thinking about how much I'm dreading getting back to the court."

My heart ached at his obvious struggle. Reaching out, I placed my hand on his. "Just because basketball isn't your dream doesn't mean you're a fraud for encouraging them to pursue it. You can want something for someone else while wanting something completely different for yourself."

"I know that. It's just...I could tell how much they live for basketball. Same way I see it in my teammates. The more I see it, the more I realize I never felt that way, even though I've tried to." He wound his fingers with mine. "I keep trying to hack it, Tal, but I can't. It's just not in me."

"Did you ever love basketball?"

"I loved learning from Dad and sharing his passion for it. It's a part of him I can hold on to, you know? Even though he's not here, I remember him when I play. And I love my team, being part of something. Working with them toward a common goal. I love seeing the fans happy and making my mom proud."

Did he realize that all the things he mentioned weren't about the sport itself but the experience around it? Celebrating his dad. Belonging to a team. Pleasing other people.

"If you retired, do you think you'd lose that connection with your dad?"

"No," he answered instantly. "Not playing professionally doesn't mean I wouldn't play at all. I'd still play because I enjoy the game. It would just be less pressure. More fun. Like it used to be before..."

"Before what?"

"Before I decided I had to keep Dad's dream alive."

"Do you think that's what he wanted for you?"

His fingers jerked around mine. In silence, he navigated the car to his house, though he seemed to be directed more by habit than actual thought. Miles's convertible was nowhere to be found as Jason parked in his usual spot.

Thinking he wasn't going to answer my question, I startled when he spoke up.

"He always told me I could be anyone I wanted. And he made me promise not to take that privilege for granted."

I squeezed his hand. "He sounds like a great dad."

"He was." His throat bobbed. "He was the best."

"I wish I could have met him."

Facing me, he gave me a half smile. A sad one. "I wish you could have too."

———

IGNORING Jason's insistence that I rest on the sofa, I joined him in the kitchen and washed the lettuce while he cooked a mushroom dish. He'd put on some music, a playlist that made me think of mornings in a cafe in a European countryside.

Not that I'd ever experienced that.

"I didn't know you were into French music," I said as I turned the handle of the salad spinner.

"I found this playlist when I was preparing for a road trip in the South of France. I drove from Lyon down to Provence and the French Riviera. Even caught the tail end of lavender season." He threw me a smirk. "Perks of not getting through to the semis that year."

"That must have been amazing. Did you go alone?"

"Met up with Miles in Nice."

He said it as casually as if he'd met someone at the coffee shop around the corner. Like there were no visas or budgets to worry about—because for him, there weren't.

"I'll take you there one day. We'll fly into Paris, take a train to Lyon, and drive the same route. You'll love it."

I snorted. "I wish."

He put down the spatula and turned to me with an earnest expression. "I mean it. We'll do it after the season. Who knows, we might get there in time for the lavender. I'll take care of all the arrangements."

Avoiding his stare, I spun the lettuce again. "It's not that easy for me." More like near impossible.

"Hey." He took the spinner from me and set it on the table. His palms enveloped my face and tipped it up to him. "We'll make it work. I promise."

I forced a smile and nodded. "You might burn the food."

His eyes searched mine like he wasn't convinced by my response. He lowered his head and kissed me slowly, as though relishing the feel of my lips. Too soon, his mouth moved away from mine. "You might not believe me now, but I'll prove it to you, dance girl."

Then he turned back to the stove and stirred the food in the pan.

I wanted nothing more than to believe him, to look forward to a European summer with just the two of us. I'd go with him if I could.

But we only had two more weeks, and I had to savor our last days together.

On a whim, I said, "We've never danced, you and me."

His head swiveled toward me. He raised an eyebrow. "You asking, Tal?"

I stepped beside him. Turning off the stove, I draped my arms around his neck. "Can I have this dance?"

A smile crept across his face. "I thought you'd never ask."

Wrapping his arms around my waist, he pulled me close until there was no space left between us. A new song began. It was quieter than the previous one, with a melancholic feel that perfectly matched my emotional state.

In the middle of the kitchen, we swayed together, my cheek against his chest, head tucked beneath his chin. His pulse was the perfect counterbeat to the tripping piano keys and occasional rasps of a violin.

"I don't like this song," he muttered, clasping me tighter.

I pressed my trembling lips together, thankful he couldn't see my face. "I think it's beautiful," I said.

"It's sad."

"Some of the most beautiful things are."

"It's the wrong song," he insisted, trying to move away like he wanted to change the music, but I kept him in place.

"Just dance with me, Jason."

He let out an indignant huff but indulged me. Our bodies moved from side to side, turning in a slow circle. Too soon, the song ended in abrupt silence.

"Thank God it was quick."

My mouth quirked. "That's what she said."

Rearing back, he stared at me and burst out into laughter. It broke the heaviness blanketing us, and it was exactly what I needed.

"Your sister's rubbing off on you," he remarked. "You owe me another dance. I'll pick a nicer song next time."

"And you owe me a redo of your waggle dance. Let's just call it even."

My laughter trailed off as he looked into my eyes like he wanted to see into my soul. A deep furrow settled between his brows. I shifted, trying to distract him before he saw too much, but he held fast to me.

His hands stroked my arms slowly. "One day," he murmured, "you'll trust me enough to let me in."

The words pierced through my chest. I closed my eyes against the emotion I glimpsed in his face, and shut my mind to the feelings that surged within me—

Guilt and shame over the truth I hid from him.

Bitterness that I'd gotten a taste of how things could be.

Regret that I had to impose an expiration date on the only relationship I'd ever longed for.

"Tal..." Jason slid his palms up my shoulders and sank his fingers in my hair, urging me to look at him.

Helpless against the need in his voice, I opened my eyes.

"Take a chance on me." His every word came as a whispered breath on my lips.

I rose to my tiptoes, stretching to meet him. Pressed my entire being against his in a kiss that said everything I couldn't. *I love you. I'm sorry. I know I'm not meant for you, but I want you anyway.*

As I clung to him, I wished I never had to let go.

Jason

That night, I made love to Tala in my bed with the curtains drawn open to the stars.

I undressed her carefully, kissing and caressing each sweep of skin I revealed. Taking my time on the swell of her breasts, I held out until she was breathless before taking her peaks in my mouth. Then I teased her clit with light circles, waiting until she cried out my name to sink my fingers inside her. As she climaxed, I kissed her, letting her steal my breath.

When I thrust inside her, I held for a beat, enjoying how her body let me in and embraced me in her warmth. It was my version of heaven, the highest high I'd ever felt, and I'd give everything I had to stay there forever. We moved together, stoking the flames inside me into a heady mix of pleasure and torture until my body tightened with the strain of holding back. As I felt the familiar ripple of her muscles clenching around me, I let go and joined her in release.

Our breaths came in pants in the aftermath, joining the whisper of the evening breeze. I held her in my arms, tucking her head in the crook of my shoulder with one leg wrapped around her waist. Her skin was flushed with satisfaction, lips slightly swollen from my kisses. I wanted to keep that picture engraved in my memory.

Tell her now.

"Tal..."

Her head jerked up, the drowsiness in her eyes replaced with wariness.

I opened my mouth to tell her I loved her, but I lost my nerve at the last second. Instead, I said, "I'm flying back to Santa Mila early on the twentieth."

Something flickered in her gaze before she blinked. "Oh. Your training camp starts the week after, right?"

"Yeah. But I have a couple of meetings before then." I'd tried to push them back as much as I could. As things were, most of the five days before camp were loaded with commitments that demanded my attention.

"Right. Of course." She nodded and gave me a small smile that didn't reach her eyes. "Time flies, huh?"

"Come with me."

She went still.

"I'll handle the flight and everything. You can stay at my place and explore the city while I'm at camp. I'll get you a driver so you can go to San Fran—"

"I can't. I have work."

"You get time off, don't you?"

"Yes, but it's not that simple."

"Is it about the money? Because I have money, Tala. You don't have to work if you don't want to. Hell, you can quit the care center to focus on your dancing."

She pulled away from me. "Are you saying you want to be some kind of... a sugar daddy?"

"What? Of course not." I sputtered. "I just don't want you stuck in a job you don't like. And I want you with me."

She cocked an eyebrow. "And what happens when you get tired of me?"

"That's not going to happen."

"How do you know that?"

Because I love you, damn it. Because I've been with plenty of other women before and none of them worked out because they weren't you. Because you see in me what others don't and you make me believe it's okay to be myself.

As much as I tried, I couldn't get my mouth to form the right words. I'd spoken to dozens of reporters on camera and given speeches in front of crowds, but when it came to emotions? My damn tongue tied itself into knots. "I just know, Tala."

Shaking her head, she chuckled darkly. "It doesn't matter. I can't just leave my job and go with you because you asked. That's not the kind of person I am."

Every semblance of afterglow disappeared at her words. I wanted to keep her in bed until she agreed to come with me. But common decency held me off.

"I don't want to fight," I said. "Just...think about it. You don't have to quit your job if you don't want to. But come with me to Santa Mila, even just for a couple of days. We can take things from there."

Her lips pursed and her leg bounced, shaking the bed. As soon as she noticed what she was doing, she held herself still.

"Come on, dance girl. Can you think about it, at least? It'll be like a vacation for you."

She seemed deep in thought, almost conflicted. Finally, she sighed. "I'll think about it. Okay?"

"Alright." I snuggled her back against my chest. "So, did anything unusual happen at work today?"

As she told me about another trainee who was scheduled to join them tomorrow, I decided to enlist Luna to help convince Tala to go.

I wasn't saying goodbye to her on the twentieth. Not if I had anything to do about it.

30

banta – (n) threat

Tala

If there was ever a time I needed the frenetic energy of the understaffed care center, it was now.

Jason had insisted on giving me a ride after I spent the night at his house. We stopped at my place for a quick change of clothes, and I thankfully didn't wake Luna.

I hit the ground running as soon as I clocked in. One of the night shift nurses asked me to help with a patient who had dementia, and it didn't take long for my troubles to sink into the back of my mind. Work was so chaotic that the staff didn't stare at me or hound me about Jason. I even forgot to feel self-conscious.

After we pacified the man who mistook his nurse for a threatening stranger, I caught up with the nurse log and reviewed the calendar for the day. We only had two visitors scheduled. One of them was Jason's mom.

I hadn't seen her since that unplanned encounter with Jason. With rumors about our relationship plastered all over social media, I dreaded seeing her today. She hadn't hidden her disapproval during our initial meeting, and I doubted she'd changed her mind about me since then.

Had Jason known his mom was back in town? He hadn't mentioned it to me—not that I could fault him. Between Miles's visit, the media debacle, and his meet-up with the basketball team, he had his hands full. Then he had to prepare for his trip home, which apparently included convincing me to go along.

Part of me was elated he'd asked, but my guilt and dread outweighed it. I should have told him the truth. It was the perfect opening, yet I didn't have the courage to do so. Just when I was trying to work myself up to confessing, he talked about me resigning.

I'd forgotten everything aside from my mortification. I had read comments accusing me of being a gold digger, speculating that I was with Jason for the money, the citizenship, the fame. Despite knowing Jason meant well, I couldn't help but resent that he thought I'd be alright with relying on him financially.

It cemented my belief that we couldn't be together in the long run. Not when he didn't see me as his equal.

He was used to a different lifestyle, a completely different world. I was content to remain in mine. It might be harder and less luxurious, but it was what I knew. It was where I was safe.

Tomorrow. I promised Luna a girls' night, but tomorrow I was having dinner with Jason. I'd tell him then. Better to lay the cards on the table so we both could move on.

Then again, it was his birthday tomorrow.

I told myself I'd decide tonight. For the moment, I focused on getting through my task list and preparing to see Mrs. Bateman.

I KNOCKED on Berna's door at a little past nine. Her voice rang out as I came in smiling despite the glare that blasted me from the visitor's seat.

"Good morning, Berna. Mrs. Bateman," I greeted. "How are we doing today?"

I walked to the side of the bed and prepared the blood pressure monitor.

"Tala!" Berna grinned at me while Mrs. Bateman pierced me with cold eyes. "I was just telling Vivi that you and Jason make a gorgeous couple." She positioned her arm so I could take a reading.

Mrs. Bateman cleared her throat and gave her friend a sharp look.

"Don't try those evil eyes on me, Vivi. After almost thirty years, I'm immune to them," Berna said, appearing unbothered.

I worried the exchange would affect her blood pressure, but the reading turned out normal. "One nineteen over seventy-five," I said, jotting it down.

"See?" Berna said smugly. "Immune."

Mrs. Bateman sighed. "Why do I put myself through this?"

"Because you need someone to call you out on your nonsense. And because you would hate yourself if you didn't see me before I kicked the bucket."

"Stop saying that!" Mrs. Bateman snapped at her.

"It's true." Berna popped the pills I gave her and washed them down with water.

I took the glass and handed her a napkin, which she used to dry her lips.

"As I was saying—" Mrs. Bateman spoke to Berna, but her stare dug into my skin.

I refused to look up from Berna's chart.

"Phil and I are flying out to Santa Mila for Jason's first game. After that, we're having dinner with him and Anastassya.

I haven't seen her in ages, but the two of them have always been close. She's just as beautiful as Katja. The perfect match for Jason."

"You're the only one who thinks so," Berna said in a sharp tone. "And you are not being the least bit discreet or respectful."

"They'll realize it sooner or later. And I don't have to be discreet. It's just between the two of us."

Mrs. Bateman's casual dismissal of my presence shouldn't have hurt. More than one patient or relative treated me like I wasn't worth acknowledging, so it was nothing new. But after all the insults I kept getting on social media, her blatant disdain was like pouring alcohol over an open wound.

"Vivian!" Berna admonished her.

"Fine. If I must acknowledge this girl, let me say that I hope you're enjoying yourself. Just don't get comfortable," Mrs. Bateman told me head-on.

"I beg your pardon?"

"You have Jason's attention at the moment, but not for long. He won't throw his life away for you. What is it you want? Money? Fame? A green card?"

I stepped back like I'd been shot.

"That is enough, Vivian!"

I'd never heard Berna sound so angry before.

"You've crossed the line," she said to Mrs. Bateman in a low voice. "I've never been so ashamed of you."

"Why, I never—"

Worried that Berna's blood pressure might shoot up, I tried to diffuse the situation. "It's alright, Berna. I understand Mrs. Bateman is concerned about her son." I turned to Mrs. Bateman and said, "You're right that I came to the US for a chance to live here permanently. But I always planned to do it through studying and working hard. I never considered marrying someone so I could stay here. Not before Jason and not since him."

Her mouth tightened.

"I work two jobs to help support my family, but I've never asked for a handout, especially not from Jason. And believe me, I never wanted people to talk about me. I only joined social media so I could share what I love to do."

Mrs. Bateman's eyes remained stony, her face unmoved. But she was listening. If this was the only time she would, I'd say everything I needed to.

"I know you only have my word to go by, but you don't have to worry. Jason's leaving in a few days, and I won't see him after that. I'm not going to stand in Anastassya's way." Whoever she was.

"If you do anything to compromise my son's future—" Mrs. Bateman started.

"That's the last thing I want to do. He deserves the best. That's something we can agree on." My throat closed and I was horrified to feel my eyes stinging. I held back my tears with sheer, stubborn will.

Berna spoke up. "Vivian, can you give us some privacy while Tala checks my vitals?"

Without saying a word, Mrs. Bateman picked up her purse and walked out of the room, her heels clicking on the linoleum floor.

"Don't listen to her," Berna said as soon as the door closed.

"I'm fine," I answered. "She just wants what's best for Jason."

"Vivian wants what's best for herself, and she won't listen to anyone who tells her otherwise," Berna corrected. "Anastassya—who actually prefers to go by Stassy, not that Vivi cares—is her friend's daughter."

"You don't have to tell me—"

Berna ignored me. "She grew up two houses away from Jason, so they were bound to be close. But aside from a brief flirtation when they were teens, they never showed romantic feelings for each other. Of course, I haven't seen them together for years, but I'm quite sure they aren't going to date just because their mothers want them to. In fact, I'm certain that would be a huge reason for them not to."

"You don't need to explain anything to me, Berna. It's really none of my business."

"Vivian wanted you to hear about Stassy. That gives me all the right to make sure you know the full story. The part I'm aware of, at least. It's up to you to get Jason to fill in the blanks."

"I'm not going to ask him." He'd never mentioned Stassy. But even if he had, he didn't owe me an explanation. We weren't in a real relationship anyway.

"I wish you would, but that's your prerogative. Jason is a good man, and he couldn't do better than you. You should believe that."

Gratitude overwhelmed me. I smiled, saying, "Thank you, Berna. I really appreciate it."

"I mean it too." Berna laughed, but there was a slight sheen to her eyes. "Now you should get going before Vivian comes back and starts World War Z."

Chuckling, I gave her hand an affectionate squeeze. I didn't know what I'd done to deserve her kindness, but I was beyond thankful for her. She reminded me that there were still good people out there, and that I wasn't insignificant.

As I finished taking her vitals and left for the nurse station, I tried to hold on to that thought. But Mrs. Bateman's cutting remarks remained like a persistent mosquito buzzing near my ear.

At least I said my piece and didn't cower. I was honest.

Whether or not she believed me—whether or not my words made a difference—I tried. That was all I could do.

———

Jason

I sat facing Mom in Claudette's, the Michelin-star restaurant where I ordered food for my first date with Tala. While I would have preferred that my first time there was with Tala, my mom told me to meet her there for dinner. Since Tala had plans with Luna, I didn't mind the schedule change. It meant I could spend my entire birthday with Tala.

Mom cut a piece of her baked salmon and brought it to her mouth. She had spent the entrée and half the main course talking about her recent trips to Boston and New York.

I acted the part of the dutiful son, nodding along and asking the questions she led me to ask. But the prolonged chit chat grated on my nerves. It wasn't that I didn't want to catch up with her. It was that she was clearly holding back the most important topic in some pointless attempt to build suspense.

I wasn't in the mood for mind games.

At the first lull in our conversation, I asked, "What was so urgent that you wanted to meet tonight?"

She gave me a look of thinly veiled annoyance. "Must we talk about unpleasant matters now? I was enjoying my meal."

"Did you want to talk about it in the car instead?" When she only arched an eyebrow at me, I shook my head and scoffed. "There's no point in delaying it. Just tell me, Mom."

"Fine." She took her time patting her mouth with a napkin. Her red lipstick didn't even budge. Then she placed the napkin back on her lap and finally said, "I visited Bernadette this morning."

The significance of her words flew over my head. She visited Berna regularly. Why did she make it sound like a big deal?

My eyes widened.

Golden Haven.

Tala.

In my preoccupation with figuring out how to convince her to go to Santa Mila with me, I completely forgot to warn her about my mom's visit. Given how cagey Mom was acting, I guessed she'd seen Tala and shit had gone down.

"What happened?" The last time I spoke with Tala was about an hour ago, on my way to pick up Mom at her hotel. Tala had just clocked out and was walking to the bus stop. She didn't mention seeing my mom.

"I brought Bernadette her favorite chocolates and that tea that helps calm her nerves. Then we talked."

"Tala," I snarled. "What did you say to Tala?"

Her mouth pinched at the corners. "You mean that nurse?"

"I mean, the woman I'm dating." *The woman I'm in love with* was more accurate.

She glared at me. "Shush. We're in public, Jason."

"I didn't say anything that people don't already know."

"I can't believe you let yourself be photographed with her. You should have known better," she hissed before grabbing her wine glass.

"I didn't *let* it happen. We didn't know anyone was watching us." Not that I cared about people knowing. I just hated how it had been exposed like it was some seedy affair.

"Honestly, Jason. You could have any woman you want. How could you go from Elena Carson to...her?"

"Her name is Tala, Mom. Tala Reyes. If you insist on forgetting it every time we talk, I'll have to keep repeating it until it sticks."

"For heaven's sake. That girl—"

"Call her that girl one more time," I snapped, too far gone to hold my tongue any longer.

Some of the waitstaff and other diners glanced our way, curiosity painted on their faces.

Mom colored but she forced a tight smile to her lips. "Mind yourself, Jason."

"Say her name."

Her mouth flattened.

"I don't care about making a scene. Say it," I demanded louder, refusing to back down.

"Alright. Tala," she said just above a whisper. Her eyes, a mirror of mine, burned into me. "I don't know what's gotten into you. I raised my son with better manners than this."

"And I thought my mother had the basic decency to be kind to anyone—regardless of their race or socioeconomic status. Guess we're both disappointed." I took a long drink.

When my glass ran empty, I reached for the bottle at the center of the table and poured another round. I started to do the same for her, but she cut me off with a slash of her hand.

"You're so quick to judge me. But tell me—did you know that your Tala lost her job?"

My eyebrows drew together. "What are you talking about? You just saw her at the center."

"Yes, and I heard the other nurses talking about how her work visa won't be renewed. Apparently, she'll be out of work next month," she shared with a hard gleam in her eyes. "They were saying how smart she was to get involved with you. How you were the answer to all her problems."

That didn't add up. Tala never hinted she was having problems with work. In fact, she had too much of it. No way that was true. "That's just a rumor, Mom. You know how people say what they want to say."

"Hmm. Maybe so." She finished her wine, letting her words linger in the air. After blotting her mouth again, she said, "Why don't you ask Tala about it?"

"I will."

"Good. I'd be careful, if I were you. You don't want to get stuck with an unplanned pregnancy and a hanger-on. Then what will happen to your reputation? Your career?"

I wanted to tell her there was more to life than that. She didn't know Tala. She didn't know I'd given her the perfect opportunity to use both my money and my fame, and she'd turned me down without hesitating.

But Mom had planted a seed of doubt with her talk about Tala's visa.

Could it be true?

The woman I knew wouldn't even consider taking money from me. I couldn't imagine her trying to trap me with a baby for a green card. Still, she seemed to be keeping secrets behind walls I couldn't scale.

And I couldn't wait until tomorrow to get to the truth.

31

taning – (n) time limit

Tala

L una and I sat on the sofa watching our favorite Filipino movie about ex-lovers who kept going back to each other. We'd seen the film so many times that we'd memorized the pivotal confrontation word for word. Luna even had the characters' facial expressions down pat.

A few minutes before the dramatic scene, the doorbell rang.

Luna groaned as I paused the video. "I was ready to emote!" she complained.

So was I.

"Let me check who it is." I walked to the door, half hoping it was Jason.

Swinging the door open, I came face to face with him all dressed up in a collared shirt and chinos. I smiled at him, that familiar warmth spreading across my chest.

Then I noticed the tension in his shoulders. His hands were buried in his pockets. And the biggest giveaway that something was wrong? The blankness in his eyes.

Warning bells went off in my head. "Jason. What are you doing here?"

"Hey, Jason!" Luna called from the sofa.

He looked over at her and nodded. "Luna," he said, then looked back at me. "I had dinner with my mom."

Oh no.

"She told me you saw each other at the care center."

I took a step back and fiddled with the hem of my shirt. "Yes, we did. I was going to tell you later."

"Were you also going to tell me that your visa's expiring?"

I froze, my eyes going wide.

Shit. Shit, shit, shit.

"Ah, I'm going to my room," Luna announced.

I heard her scrambling to her feet, then the bedroom door slammed.

Jason swore, the single word like a crash of thunder. "It's not a rumor, is it?"

"Come in," I said. It felt like my heart was on the verge of thumping right out of my chest. How had he found out?

Shaking his head, he stormed inside. I locked the door behind him and turned as he whirled around to face me.

"Tell me everything," he demanded.

And I did. I told him about Jose's reassurance early this year that they would renew my visa, and the news that they couldn't. About the job applications and rejections. About Luna finding out by accident and how that caused our fight. And then I told him about the out-of-state job offer I received.

He moved closer, clasping my arms. "Why didn't you tell me?"

"You didn't need to know." I caught his flinch and hurried to explain. "I didn't think you'd hang around this long. I figured it wouldn't matter to you what happened to my visa."

"To hell with that," he blurted out. "I get why you would

think that then. But we've been spending all this time together. These past weeks, I'm inside you as often as I can be. When I'm not, I'm dreaming of the next time I can be with you."

I winced at his explicit words. "You're only talking about sex."

"Fuck that!"

A tremor ran through my body. I stepped away from him and wrapped my arms around my stomach.

"Jesus. I'm not going to hurt you, Tala."

"I know."

He would never hurt me physically. But his anger stabbed deep into me, even though I deserved it. I shouldn't have let things go so far. I should have told him when we began sleeping together.

I shouldn't have had sex with him to begin with.

"I'm sorry I didn't tell you. I—"

"I'll have my lawyer look into your visa situation." His gaze moved past me, like he was mentally adjusting his plans. "You can live with me, and I'll help you find a job in Santa Mila."

"Jason..."

"I'm not sure if there are many care centers in the city, but maybe we can find one in San Francisco. Or in one of the hospitals—"

"Jason!"

His eyes swung back to meet mine.

"I'm planning to move back to Manila."

He gaped at me. Then he said, "There are other jobs out there, Tala."

"I know. But I want to go home. You know I've been home-sick for a while. This whole visa issue is a sign that it's time."

"It's a sign that it's time for you to switch jobs—not that you need to leave."

His voice grew louder with every word. There was no chance Luna couldn't hear our argument from her room.

"You call it leaving. I call it going home." I spoke as calmly as I could. "I told you this was just for the summer."

This time, he stepped back. "What exactly are you saying? Was I just an item you wanted to tick off your bucket list? One last fuck before you go back home?"

Guilt hit me so hard, I felt nauseous. I couldn't find the words to defend myself. Not when part of what he said was true.

Pain flashed in his eyes. "Jesus, Tala."

"I'm sorry," I said quietly, holding myself tighter.

"Does this really not matter to you?"

Do I not matter to you?

I heard his unspoken question. "Of course you matter to me. These months with you have been the best of my life."

"Then stay."

Swallowing, I said, "I can't."

"Yes, you can. I'll find a way. I could have helped earlier if I'd known—"

"I don't need your help."

His face hardened. "You never needed it, right? You can do everything on your own."

The mocking words cut me right where I was most vulnerable. "I have to. I can't count on anyone but myself."

"Because you don't *want* to," he shot back. "Even when other people want to help. When *I* want to help."

"Jason—"

In one step, his body was against mine, my face caught between his hands.

"I love you, Tala."

My heart stopped.

At that moment, it seemed my entire world narrowed down

to him speaking the words I'd longed to hear for so long. They were everything I needed and everything I didn't, all at once.

"I'm in love with you," he said, enunciating each word.

My head moved from side to side. "N-no, you're not."

He chuckled humorlessly and dropped his hands. "So now you're telling me how I feel?"

"I'm leaving, Jason."

"You don't have to."

"I want to."

He reared back as though I had slapped him. "Even after what I told you?"

"I thought I loved you too. Back then."

Swiping a hand across his face, he made a rough sound deep in his throat.

"You left," I shouted. "You left and I didn't hear from you again for *six* years."

"I told you, it was the biggest mistake of my life."

"Don't say that. If you hadn't left, you wouldn't be where you are now."

"I don't care. I don't want to lose you again, Tal."

My mouth mimicked the curve of a smile without any of its feeling. "You never really had me. Just like I never really had you."

———

Jason

I stared at Tala, wondering how she could think that. She had more of me than anyone else ever had. The real part of me. Even through the years and the distance, that part of me had only ever been hers.

But I didn't want to tell her. Not now. She'd just brush it off.

"So that's it? You're not even considering going to Santa Mila with me?" Maybe I was a glutton for rejection, but I couldn't stop myself from asking. Couldn't keep from hoping that if I asked enough times, I'd get the answer I wanted.

"I think it would be better if I didn't," she said without looking at me directly. "A clean break, you know?" She blinked rapidly, but no tears fell.

"Right. A clean break." I scoffed. "You know, for someone so strong, you can be such a coward."

She looked back at me, her jaw slack. "What did you just say?"

"You heard me. You're so scared of the possibility of getting hurt that you would rather play it safe. You'd rather close yourself off." I remembered something she'd told me earlier and laughed. The sound was harsh even to my own ears. "So much for you telling me to come in. You never let me in once, did you?"

A tear trailed down her cheek. "That's not fair."

"Don't talk to me about fair. Was it fair that I was all in with you when you had zero plans to take a risk on me? Was it fair that I stripped my soul to you, told you things no one else knows, and you couldn't even bring yourself to tell me your fucking visa was expiring?"

"You're right. I should have told you. There's no excuse for that. I'm so sorry you had to find out from someone else."

I willed her to say more. To tell me she wanted to fix things, that she wanted to talk it out. Anything, damn it.

Instead, there was only silence. I didn't know that was the sound a heart made when it shattered into a million pieces.

My shoulders fell. "You're not even going to fight me on

this, are you?" I whispered as adrenaline drained out of my body.

"What do you mean?"

"You're not going to try to argue with me or find a way to move forward. You're just calling it quits."

"I—"

My phone rang, and she clammed right up. As I dug it out of my pocket, I saw Stassy's face on the display. I quickly rejected the call but heard Tala's gasp.

"Is that Nat?" she asked, her brow drawn in confusion.

Fuck. I hoped she hadn't seen the name on the screen.

"Stassy..." Her eyes widened. "Anastassya? That's the woman your mom was talking about?"

What the hell did Mom tell her about Stassy? And why, of all times, did Stassy choose that exact moment to call?

"Jason." My name came out sharply from Tala's mouth. "Is Anastassya my PR contact Nat? The woman your mom believes is your soulmate?"

I shoved my phone back in my pocket. "Yes, Nat is Stassy," I admitted. "But she's not my damn soulmate. She's one of my closest friends. I've known her since we were kids. That's it."

"Why didn't you tell me you knew her? I mentioned her a couple times. You never said a word." She held herself still.

I saw the wheels in her head turning.

"Did you tell Nat to hire me?"

"Of course not," I said firmly.

Her body relaxed but a shadow of doubt remained in her gaze.

"I showed her your account back then. She was the one who wanted to work with you."

"Did you—"

"Call in any favors? No. I just told her I had a friend who had talent and sent her the link. You know Stassy. Do you really think she would put her job and her reputation on the line for a favor?"

She hesitated. "No..."

"She wouldn't do that for me, and I wouldn't ask her to. I didn't tell you about her because of this right here." I gestured at her. "I didn't want you to doubt that your success is all yours. You put in the work. You deserve the recognition for it. I just wanted you to have a chance to be seen because you didn't have connections here. Don't think for one second you didn't get to where you are fair and square."

She dropped her gaze and scuffed her toes on the floor.

"Tala. Did you hear me?"

Her head bobbed.

Despite my anger, I couldn't help but want to comfort her.

I pulled her into my arms and hugged her tightly. Her head rested against the part of me that beat for her, and she wrapped her arms around my waist.

"I'm sorry I didn't tell you," I murmured against her hair.

"I'm sorry I didn't tell you either," she whispered back.

"You're not going to change your mind." I knew it for certain, yet I still hoped. "Are you?"

She took a shuddering breath that reverberated through me. "Can we just make the most of the time we have left? Like we planned?"

"It was never just a fling for me. I can't pretend otherwise."

And I couldn't go on being with her when I couldn't have her. Not the way I wanted.

Tightening my embrace, I breathed in her scent. Memorized the feel of her in my arms, her body against mine. It might be the last time I'd be with her like this.

I thought we'd have all the time in the world to be together. How could I have known things would end this way? Joke was on me.

"Jason, I..."

Say it.

If there was ever a moment I needed reality to bend to my will, this was it. I needed her to tell me she felt the same way.

Take a chance on me, dance girl.

Again, silence.

Feeling a stabbing pain in my chest, I kissed the top of her head. Held her a second longer.

Then I let her go.

"Jason," she said as I walked to the door.

"I can't do this, Tala," I answered without facing her.

And I left.

32

dalamhati — (n) anguish

Tala

Sunlight seared my eyes the moment I opened them. I groaned, moving gingerly. My head pounded like it had been hit by a truck, and the room teetered from side to side.

Bile rose up my throat. Fighting the lethargy dragging down my limbs, I launched myself off the couch and ran to the bathroom in time to expel my stomach's contents. It was a revolting mash of solid and liquid. The stench sent me heaving into the toilet again.

I distantly remembered taking shots with Luna. When we ran out of tequila, I'd chugged wine straight from the bottle...a bottle that Jason brought over the previous week.

Despite my attempts to drown out the memories of our last conversation, they rang clearly in my throbbing head.

Luna heard most of what happened. To her credit, she didn't brag that she told me so. Instead, she unearthed her hidden stash of tequila and drank with me as I sat through the rest of our movie in silence.

I didn't cry when Jason walked out of the apartment. Not even during the film's climax when the characters reunited. Or when I crashed on the sofa.

It was only after I washed out my mouth and checked my phone that tears fill my eyes. That it was almost ten in the morning—the latest I had woken up in years—barely registered. Notifications crowded my screen but none of them were from Jason.

These past few weeks, I always woke up to his messages. Losing them left a hole inside me, and I had no one to blame but myself.

Leaving my phone on the coffee table, I went back to the bathroom and into the shower. As water cascaded over me, I finally let go. My shoulders shook as I sobbed with the tiled walls as my witnesses. I cried for the words I said, but more for the ones left unsaid. For his declaration that came too late—those three words that changed everything and nothing at the same time.

Regret tasted like salt on my lips, sharp and stinging. When my tears ran out, I stepped out of the shower, dried myself, and brushed my teeth. In the kitchen, I found a fresh loaf of bread and aspirin waiting on the table.

As I heated the bread in the toaster, I retrieved my phone. I had two messages from Luna.

LUNA

> I didn't want to wake you up coz you need to rest. Drink medicine and lots of water! I'll be home right after my shift.

> Love you, Ate xx

They were exactly what I needed. No questions, no false

274

promises that things would be okay. Just straight-up information and a reminder that I wasn't alone.

I replied with a short *Thanks, Lu. Love you too*, and proceeded to eat breakfast. Two pieces of toast, one painkiller, and a gallon of water later, I typed out another text.

TALA

Hey, Jason. Can I come over later?

Any other time, he'd reply right away. But after I cleaned the dishes, reviewed my schedule, and worked through my emails, there was no response. I went on to edit the last video we filmed together. Despite my laptop hanging every few minutes, I finished without hearing from him. My phone calls went to his voicemail.

I hadn't even known he used voicemail.

Frustrated, I grabbed my keys and made the commute to his house, only to find his car gone. I stood outside the gate and called him again. This time, his phone rang twice before it disconnected.

He'd rejected my call.

I texted him again.

TALA

I know you're mad, but I really think we should talk. I'll wait outside your gate.

Trying to work off my nerves, I walked up and down the sidewalk. The aspirin eased my hangover, but agitation replaced my headache.

Fifteen minutes later, still no response.

I didn't have Miles's number, so I decided to try another route. Standing beneath the shade of a palmetto tree, I waited for Nat to answer my call.

"Tala?"

My muscles loosened in relief at hearing the familiar voice. "Hi, Nat," I said. "I'm sorry to call out of the blue, but I didn't know who else to contact."

"It's alright. Is something wrong?"

I bit my lip. "Have you heard from Jason? He hasn't been picking up. I just want to check that he's okay."

"No, I haven't. I actually tried to call him last night, but he didn't answer." Nat abruptly went quiet. "Wait. How did you know I know Jason?"

"I was with him when you called," I admitted.

She said something in Russian. "No wonder he hasn't called me back. Did he explain our relationship?"

"He told me you're childhood friends and that he's the one who sent you my Instagram account."

"Did he also tell you he didn't ask me to contact you?"

"Yes."

"Good. Because I wouldn't jeopardize my name or my clients for anyone," Nat said in her usual no-nonsense tone.

"That's what he said."

"As long as we're clear on that."

I remembered how he'd made it a point to reassure me that I didn't get to where I was because he'd intervened on my behalf. He'd even apologized for hiding it from me, when *I'd* kept a much bigger secret.

No wonder he was avoiding me. After what I did to him, he didn't owe me a response, let alone the time of day.

Still, he said he loved me. If that was true, he wouldn't just leave like that. Would he?

"You said he isn't answering your calls. Did you get into a fight?"

"We were arguing before you called." Figuring I had nothing more to lose, I told her about my visa situation and how Jason found out.

When I finished talking, Nat said, "I'm sure you're kicking yourself for hiding it from him. But it's not the end of the world. You could always get married."

It was the last thing I expected her to say, and it left me speechless.

She sighed. "Or you could get a different job, but that's the boring option."

"Actually, I'm going back home."

There went that Russian word again. "I'm sure that didn't sit well with him."

"No." An understatement.

"That explains why Vivian texted me out of the blue. She said Jason needed to talk to me and I should call him ASAP. She must have guessed he'd go over to see you."

Of course she had. It should have upset me, but I didn't have the energy to spare. Mrs. Bateman meddling didn't negate the fact that I shouldn't have kept the news from Jason in the first place. It was my mistake, and I needed to make things right. To do that, I needed to talk to him.

"It doesn't matter," I said. "I just want to check on Jason. I'm at his place now and his car's gone."

"I'll call him. If he doesn't answer, I'll try Miles."

"Thank you, Nat. I appreciate your help."

"Don't mention it. I'll get back to you as soon as I talk to him. And we'll have to schedule a meeting to talk about your plans moving forward," she added, ever the businesswoman.

"I'll set it up."

"Do that."

"By the way, did you know Jason's mom thinks you two are soulmates?"

A choking sound burst from the speakers. "Vivian has been living with that delusion since forever. Don't buy into it. God knows we don't."

Loud whispers came from my right, where a trio of college-aged girls stared at me from across the street. Jason's address had been leaked, and I wasn't being discreet by hanging around outside his gate without a hat or sunglasses.

One of the girls aimed her phone at me. I took off in the direction of the bus stop and hoped they'd leave me alone. "I need to go, Nat," I said, keeping my face averted from the road.

"I'll be in touch."

"Thanks again."

Luckily, the girls didn't follow me, and the bus rolled in with barely a wait. I spent the ride replying to comments on my latest post, automatically skipping over those mentioning Jason or using any derogatory language. If anything good had come out of the media storm, it was that I was becoming immune to insults and slurs.

That, or I was deep in denial.

Jason's radio silence blasted me back to the past. To that Monday afternoon I went to the garden and waited for him to get there. All day, the entire campus buzzed over the news of him officially declaring for the draft and how he'd likely be the first player from Sterling to get signed. I'd been so excited to talk to him about it. I waited in the garden until it was too dark to stay any longer. He didn't come, and he didn't reply to any of my messages.

Two days later, I saw him in the cafeteria with Fallon, the captain of the dance team. We'd been at opposite ends of the room, but I could have sworn he saw me. And he'd turned away.

Before Jason, I'd thought the term heartbreak was just an exaggeration. He'd taught me otherwise. It was a lesson he drilled into me every day for the rest of the month that I kept going back to the garden, hoping he'd show up.

Who knew heartbreak would hurt worse the second time around?

Two stops away from my apartment, my phone vibrated.

New message from Jason Meyer.

On cue, my pulse went haywire. I fumbled with my phone, dropping it in my lap. Tightening my grip, I opened the message.

JASON

> Stassy said you called. I'm on my way home.
> Clean break, right? Take care.

I read it twice. Once more. Each time, the text remained the same, and each time, my anger mounted.

The message was short, but perfectly calculated. The subtext unmistakable.

Stassy said you called meant he wouldn't have texted otherwise.

I'm on my way home said Sterling was just a temporary stop for him.

Clean break, right? was a big, sarcastic 'fuck you,' throwing my words back at me.

And *take care?* That meant 'have a good life,' but not really.

Put it all together, and it equaled him not planning on talking to me again. Not only that, but him not saying my name once was a deliberate move to underscore that I could be any other woman he'd hooked up with.

Forgettable and easily replaceable.

Locking my phone, I turned it face-down on my thigh. My broken heart hardened, its aching wounds crystallizing into jagged edges.

Forget sadness and regret. I was furious. Whether I was angrier at him or myself, I couldn't tell.

All I knew was I needed to dance or I'd lose it. As soon as I got off the bus, I hightailed it to my building and took the elevator straight to the rooftop.

33

kumalas — (v) to break away

Jason

The massive oak door swung open even before my feet hit the porch steps.

"J-man!" Miles boomed as he loped toward me in a pair of basketball shorts and nothing else. The full force of his weight knocked the breath out of me. Embracing me, he thumped my back and then pulled away. Gave me a once-over. "Birthday boy. You look like shit. The hell happened to you?"

Hell might just be accurate.

"Drove from Sterling."

Miles stared at me. "You drove. From Sterling."

"That's what I said."

"That's almost three thousand miles, man. You got a thing against commercial planes now?"

"I needed to drive." I didn't even swing by my house before leaving. Not when it held so many memories with her.

Besides, there was nothing in Sterling that I didn't have in Santa Mila. Nothing except for the one woman I couldn't have.

Then again, she wouldn't be there much longer.

I drove out of town right after our blowup, continuing until morning broke and my eyes grew too bleary for me to safely stay behind the wheel. In a small town in Alabama, I checked into a decent-looking inn run by an old woman who barely blinked at me. There I crashed until the afternoon, had a quick shower and a late lunch, and went on my way. That summed up how I spent my twenty-eighth birthday.

The next day went the same, only I drove longer and stopped in New Mexico. Because I couldn't stomach wearing the same clothes again, I raided the gift shop attached to the boutique hotel I'd checked into, and bought a pair of generic shorts, a value pack of boxer briefs, and a souvenir shirt.

"Let me guess," Miles drawled. "You left all your shit at your place, which is why you look like a walking ad for Villa La Pacita."

I grunted in response.

He looped an arm around my neck and led me inside the house. "Gym or court?" he asked, proving how well he knew me.

"Bathroom, then court." I'd been on my ass the majority of the past three days. I needed to move. Needed to blow off steam.

I had to drive my body to the point of exhaustion so I'd stop thinking of her.

Without missing a beat, Miles turned in the direction of the pool and the basketball court beyond it. "I'm done with drills, but I could always do more. Let's go."

Sweat poured down my body as I charged past Miles to do a layup. The ball went through the hoop with a soft, satisfying swoosh. After forty minutes on the court, I smiled.

"There he is," Miles said as he swiped a hand across his face. "Who knew you only needed a free shot to make you smile?"

Catching the ball in one hand, I pointed it in my friend's direction. "That wasn't a free shot."

"You're welcome." His white teeth flashed in a grin.

I threw the ball at him. "Asshole."

"Just for that, I'm done taking it easy on you."

He proceeded to beat me by five points. No surprises there. When we went one-on-one, the most I could manage was to make him work for his win. Didn't matter that it was twice as brutal for me than it was for him.

Walking to the chairs on the sideline, I grabbed a towel and mopped my face and neck. I'd lost my shirt fifteen minutes into our drills, and my shorts were drenched in sweat. I didn't need to look in a mirror to know what shade my face was. My heart rate was up and my muscles hurt like I'd taken a beating.

It felt damned good.

"Better than last weekend," Miles remarked as he dried the side of his face with one hand and lifted his water bottle with the other. "A little more and we'll have you ready for camp."

"I've been thinking of retiring."

He froze with his bottle tilted to his mouth, water spilling down his chin and chest. He spat out the sip he'd just taken.

I side-stepped to avoid the spray. "Man."

"You're fucking with me now, right?" Miles demanded as he carelessly wiped himself.

"Nope." Sitting down, I stretched my legs in front of me and drank some water.

He stared, slack-jawed. "Something happened with Tala."

"No."

Lie.

I sighed and leaned forward, elbows braced on my thighs. "Well, yes. But even without her in the picture, it's been in the back of my head for some time. You know it was never my dream to go pro."

That was another secret I unloaded on Miles the night we got flat-out drunk. We had never talked about it again.

Until now.

"Fuck. I convinced myself I was just dead wasted that night." Sitting, Miles angled his body to face me. "We won the championship, man. You're at your peak."

"I know."

"So, what? You're just going to let that go?"

I clasped the back of my neck with both hands and leaned back. "I don't know. Maybe." I forced myself to say the words out loud. "She's leaving."

"The fuck?"

I recounted our last conversation, feeling the same emotions roiling inside me. They were no duller despite the time that had passed. To the contrary, they were compounded by memories of moments we shared. I kept wondering whether things would have worked out differently if she had been honest with me from the start.

"Wait. You never told me about the Stassy connection," Miles said.

"I didn't want to make a big deal out of it. It was Tala's talent that got her in. I just introduced them, in a way."

"So now she needs to find a way to extend her visa without having to move to a different state?" Miles clarified. "Simple, marry her. You're in love with her anyway."

Why did people automatically resort to marriage as the solution? Even Stassy brought up the idea when she called to ream me out for my disappearing act. If Tala and I couldn't get our shit together while dating, how would we manage something more permanent?

"It's not simple," I ground out. "She wouldn't say yes to coming here with me. What are the chances she'd agree to getting married? Even if I asked, she'd see it as a handout. I can't get her to accept money from me, so why would she accept a ring?"

"From what I could tell, that woman's gone over you. Maybe she just hasn't realized it yet. Or maybe she's in denial."

Hope stirred in my chest. Then I remembered her silence. How I asked her multiple times to try and work things out, and she shut me down. I laid my heart out on the floor for her, and she fucking stomped on it.

And she had the nerve to say we needed to talk. I'd given her time to talk to me. She had over two months, damn it.

My resolve hardened. "It doesn't matter. She asked for a clean break. Who am I to deny her what she wants?"

"You're Jason fucking Meyer, man."

Damn right. And Jason fucking Meyer didn't beg for anyone's affection. So Tala didn't want me. There were plenty of other women out there, and they would battle it out to be with me. I wouldn't even have to lift a finger.

That was exactly what I found when we arrived in Ellipsis hours later. The exclusive club was one of the hottest places in the city, mostly because of the athletes and celebrities who hung out there. Miles and I both owned shares, giving us unlimited access to the VIP area, which overlooked the dance floor and the women who filled it. Some glanced toward the raised section, maybe out of curiosity, or trying to catch someone's attention.

None of them made me look twice.

Sitting on the couch beside Miles, I sipped my wine. His

bodyguard stood watch from the corner. I preferred to go without one unless the situation demanded it, but Miles's superstar status meant he needed a lookout in bigger cities, especially in our home base.

In an attempt to distract myself from my phone, I watched the crowd below. Tala quit trying to reach me after my text two days ago. I had my assistant hire a moving service to pack up my stuff at the house and deliver my laptop to her place. A new one waited for me at my apartment. This morning, I learned that Tala refused to accept the laptop, telling the movers to send it to me with my boxes.

Stubborn woman.

She didn't say a word to me about it either. No doubt she'd read the hidden message in my text.

I told myself it was for the best.

Still, I broke my self-imposed promise to steer clear of her and clicked on her Instagram account.

She hadn't posted since yesterday. It was the last video we shot in my garden the day before Miles visited—her version of a dance trend I'd found. She took three takes to be satisfied with the footage, and then I satisfied her on the outdoor sectional.

I fucking missed her.

I missed the way she zoned into the music and how she blinked rapidly when she ended a routine, as if she was coming out of a trance. When she looked at me through the camera lens, one corner of her mouth would lift in a smile like she couldn't believe I was there.

I missed the taste of her lips, the feel of her body against mine. Her breathless sighs and moans when I touched her. The scent of her skin when she was flushed with sweat or snuggled next to me.

I missed hearing her talk about her day, the antics Berna got up to, and the updates she received from her family. Missed telling her about something interesting I read about and how her face twisted in confusion, her lips pulling tight when I got too technical.

If she were with me right now, she'd be curled up in my arms, fast asleep. She would make those little murmuring sounds that told me she was dreaming, her brows furrowed until I smoothed them with my fingers.

Miles's voice broke through my recollections. "She didn't post today."

"Yeah."

As far as I knew, it was the first time she'd skipped a day. I wondered how she was doing.

After I sent that message to Tala, Luna texted me a scathing tirade about how I shouldn't have left like that. I asked how her sister was and the only response I got was *Ask her yourself.*

I tucked my phone in my pocket and swore to keep it hidden. I needed to move on. That wouldn't happen if I fixated on a piece of metal and glass.

"Jason, right?"

Looking up, I caught a mile of leg and a red dress. The brunette smiled at me. She looked vaguely familiar. Could be I'd seen her on a show or billboard somewhere.

"Yeah," I answered.

Miles gave me a discreet but sharp elbow to the side.

Unbothered by my curt response, she said, "I'm Kaylee."

"Nice to meet you. Unfortunately, I'm leaving." With that, I pushed up off the couch and turned to Miles.

"You want some company?" she asked.

I took a longer look at her. Objectively, she was a knockout. Too bad I only had one woman on my mind.

"No, but thanks for the offer. Maybe you'll have better luck with one of the other guys." I met Miles's amused gaze.

"Hitting the sack already?" he said.

"I've been driving for three days. I'm beat." With that, I took a few bills from my wallet and tucked them under my quarter-full glass.

Miles rose and did the same. "Nightcap at my place?"

Pausing, I muttered just loud enough for him to hear, "You don't need to babysit me, you know."

The last thing I wanted was someone feeling sorry for me. I was just having an off day. A few more days in Santa Mila, and I'd be back to normal.

"Yeah, well, this is me trying to get you plastered enough that you'll tell me your deepest, darkest secrets. Since I'm your bro, I won't even post videos on the internet. They're all for me. And maybe a certain dancer too."

"Fuck off."

The crowd surged around us as we headed out of the club with help from Miles's bodyguard and a few bouncers. As soon as the doors opened, lights flashed, and voices drowned out the music. Reporters shouted over each other, asking about things they weren't entitled to know.

"Jason! Can you confirm your relationship with Filipino dancer Tala Reyes?"

"Where's Tala? Have you called it quits?"

"Is it true that your girlfriend moonlights as an elderly care nurse?"

I was back in reality, alright. It hadn't taken me twenty-four hours to remember exactly why I'd tried to escape. This was far from the life I wanted, this place where my personal issues were someone else's entertainment and a person's worth was directly commensurate with their status.

After experiencing a different world, I wondered how much longer I could stomach living in this one. Especially when I didn't have Tala by my side.

34

bumangon – (v) to rise

Tala

I stared at the tall iron fence enclosing a small garden. The palmetto trees on the left were familiar, and so were the vine-covered wall, the old patio doors, and the three-tiered stone fountain in the center.

But the sign that said, *Private property. No trespassing*—that, along with the fence, was new.

"This is where you met Jason?"

Glancing to the right, I found Luna walking toward me with a scowl on her face. The reason for her irritation became clear when I saw who trailed behind her.

"Gabe," I said. "What are you doing here?"

In a single step, he overtook Luna. "I followed your sister." His dark gaze studied me as he stopped in front of me. He enfolded me in his arms.

After Jason left, Luna had apparently been so worried about me that she'd texted Gabe. He came over the same day I learned Jason was gone, and we'd spent hours talking on the roof.

Gabe forgave me for not telling him because he, of all people, understood what was going on in my head. Only he had seen me at the worst points of my homesickness.

"How are you?" he murmured. "And don't say you're fine."

"Okay. I'm better."

It wasn't a lie. The first two days after Jason left, I walked around in a bitter haze. Luckily, I'd been off-duty, which should have meant I focused on my content creation. But even dance, my go-to outlet, failed me. Social media grew more toxic with people tagging me in photos of Jason with other women. Like it wasn't enough to hurl invectives and baseless accusations at me.

In the end, I decided to take a social media break—my first since I started my accounts. Then it was back to the care center, where I threw all my energy into working.

Gabe straightened and raised an eyebrow at me. "You haven't posted in a week."

"Technically, the day isn't over yet. So it's only been six days," Luna said, shouldering him. She wove an arm around my elbow. "She can still post today. Right, Ate?"

I gave a halfhearted murmur of agreement.

With our arms linked, Luna and I stared at the sign.

"When was the last time you were here?" she asked.

"Graduation." Three years ago.

The garden was the first place I felt at home when I moved to the US. Although I stopped shooting my videos there a few months after Jason left, I still came by whenever I needed an escape or felt particularly emotional. It witnessed not just our short-lived friendship, but also my solo celebrations when I got good grades and my angsty moping sessions when I felt over-whelmed and out of place.

After I received my diploma, I returned with a wine cooler,

sat on the folding chair, and toasted to surviving college on my own.

How fitting was it that I ended up there the second time Jason left?

"So this is where you'd hide out," Gabe murmured from my other side. "I assume it wasn't off-limits then."

"If it was, it didn't have a sign." Spotting a man moving about on the other side of the fence, I called out, "Excuse me! Hello?"

His head swung in our direction. He dropped something on the ground and ambled toward us. Judging by his soil-streaked overalls, muddy boots, and gloves, he was a gardener.

My heart pinched.

Once upon a time, it had been Jason taking care of that garden. I'd tried my best to clean it up and clear some of the weeds whenever I visited, but I never had much of a green thumb.

"Hi," I told the stranger. "I was wondering if it's possible to come in for a visit?"

"This here's private property."

"I see that. But I used to come here when I was in college, and I'm about to fly back home. Is there any chance I can visit one last time?"

He squinted at me and glanced at Gabe and Luna, as if weighing the damage we were capable of. His gaze returned to me. "You look familiar."

Internally, I winced, but I kept the same friendly expression. "Maybe you've seen me around town. I've lived here for a while."

He snapped his fingers. "You're that woman. With Jason."

Just my luck the property's gardener happened to be a Jason Meyer fan. I shrugged, seeing no reason to deny it. At the very least, I had Gabe and Luna with me, and the man looked harmless enough.

"You two broken up?"

Feeling Luna bristle beside me, I tightened my arm around hers.

"That's none of your business," Gabe said in his professor's voice.

The gardener held up his hands. "I didn't mean no disrespect. Just wonderin' if you could get me an autograph."

"He's in California." And going by the photos circulating online, he'd jumped right back into his real life. I'd seen multiple photos of him out with Miles, signing autographs and waving to his fans. In a couple of the shots, he was with different women, each of them gorgeous.

I had no right to complain. It was nothing I didn't expect, and I knew not everything on social media was as it seemed. Also, I'd been the one to ask for a clean break—as he had so bluntly reminded me.

Yet seeing that killed me, especially when he cut off all communication. I hadn't even been able to greet him on his birthday.

The stranger was saying something about the upcoming training camp. "...Heard he's tryna get his mind back in the game. But I guess you know that?"

I nodded in response, having missed the first part of his statement.

"I'm so sorry to interrupt," Luna said in her perkiest voice. "But we have to get going in a bit. Any chance you can let my sister in even for just five minutes? It would really mean a lot to her."

Luna was laying it on thick, giving him the sweet smile with batted eyelashes that she often used to get her way. As always, it worked. The gardener drew the metal bar locking the fence and swung the gate open.

"Five minutes," he told us as he let us in.

I slipped inside before he could change his mind, saying, "Thank you!"

The sound of Luna chattering with the man faded as I walked deeper into the garden. Some parts of the ground were freshly dug, a sign that the man had started working on it recently. The wooden chairs were gone, but I remembered exactly where Jason used to put them. There had only been one in the beginning and then he'd brought another for me.

A crack splintered the layer of ice I'd put up around my heart as memories bombarded me.

He would sit there by the corner, where he'd hung a battery-operated lantern over a rusty nail, and read his textbooks while I danced in front of the patio doors. Their wavy glass panels had served as my makeshift mirror. Sometimes, in the middle of my dance, I'd catch him watching and stumble over my own feet. He would smirk at me and share bits of trivia, and I'd momentarily forget he was a hotshot basketball player and the most handsome guy on campus.

Hey, dance girl. Did you know there's such a thing as an immortal jellyfish? Too bad most of them get eaten by other fish.

Did you know the earth is four-point-five billion years old? Scientists estimate that we have one-point-five billion years left before it's too hot for humans to live here.

And my favorite—*Did you know honeybees do a waggle dance to lead other bees to where there's food? Maybe you can add that move to your routine.*

There, right by the hydrangea shrub, was where he did a spontaneous demonstration of said dance. To this day, I regretted not capturing it on camera.

I had a lot of regrets when it came to him.

My ice shield shattered into minuscule shards that pierced my chest until old scars bled with the new ones. I took a staggering breath to ease the constriction in my lungs but still felt like I couldn't get enough oxygen.

Keep it together, Tala, I ordered myself. This might be my last time here, so I had to make the most of it.

While Luna continued to distract the gardener, I brought out my phone and took a quick recording. The fountain stood in the forefront with the hydrangeas peeking out on the left and the vine wall and patio door in the background. I caught a few leaves of the shortest palmetto tree swaying in the upper right corner of the video.

All it was missing were the pair of chairs and the overturned wicker basket he'd used as a table.

And Jason.

If all of that were there—if *he* was there—it would be perfect.

My hand trembled as my vision grew blurry. Blinking back the tears that threatened to spill, I lowered my phone. I took one last look around the garden that had been my safe space. And finally said goodbye.

THAT EVENING, I nibbled on my salad while waiting for Luna to finish reading my drafted post. It was a testament to Jason's influence that I had chosen to eat vegetables. After weeks of eating healthy dinners with him most nights, it had become a habit.

Gabe, on the other hand, inhaled the instant noodles he'd bought. Between him and Luna, they'd almost finished the entire value pack.

Turning in my chair, I prodded Luna. "So?"

"It's perfect." She nodded and passed the phone back. "And that video? Inspired."

Gabe reached across the table and plucked the phone from her.

"Hey!" She glared at him. "I thought you didn't care about social media?"

"I don't," he said while studying the screen. After a few seconds, he tapped on it. "You have a typo here. I'll fix it. Otherwise, it looks good."

I took the phone from him and reviewed the draft one last time. "Thanks, guys. I'm posting it now."

"You're not scheduling it?" Luna asked as she dug into her noodles.

"No. I might overthink it." I took a deep breath and, ignoring how my hand wasn't quite steady, clicked *Share*.

Two seconds later, my post went live.

I exhaled and put my phone down. "That's that."

Luna toasted me with a wine cooler. "I'm proud of you, Ate."

Drinking from my own bottle—the same drink I'd had after graduation—I wondered if Jason would see the post. Maybe he had blocked me already.

Or maybe he had just moved on, like the photos made it seem.

"I need to book my flight," I mused as my foot bounced under the table.

I felt more than saw Luna go still. From the corner of my eye, I caught the look she exchanged with Gabe.

"The airfare's going to get more expensive the longer I put it off," I said.

"Are you sure you want to go home?" The question came from Gabe, who contemplated me with an inscrutable expression. "I know that's what you told Jason, but you can still change your mind."

These past restless nights, I'd gone through the different possibilities in my mind. Even without Jason in the picture, I could get help. Gabe and Nat already offered their respective networks and, between the two of them, I was sure I'd find a decent job.

I'd asked myself over and over again if I just latched on to the idea of leaving so I could escape the backlash from my relationship with Jason. The more I thought about it, the more I knew that regardless of the situation, I needed to go home. I'd wanted to for years now.

Maybe it wouldn't be permanent. Maybe I'd return after a year. All I knew for sure was at this point in my life, I belonged with my family.

So even though a part of me wailed at the thought of moving back to the other side of the world, I looked Gabe in the eye and nodded. "Yes. I'm sure."

His expression didn't change—like he'd expected my answer and had wanted to ask just the same. "Alright, then. Let's go book your flight."

35

anino — (n) shadow; trace

Jason

My days in Santa Mila were filled with an endless lineup of workouts, practices, meetings, and social events. I went from spending two hours a day on a half-court to triple that time in the arena. When I wasn't training physically, I was conditioning my brain to switch to competition mode.

I'd played through my mental resistance before. I could do it again.

The difference was I now knew how my life could be, which made it harder to put on my old act.

As I sat in our training center's holding area and waited for Miles to finish his interviews, my mind drifted away from the chaos of media day and landed back on Tala.

Where before she only crossed my mind when I let myself remember the past, thoughts of her haunted me now. More and more, I intentionally left my phone buried in my bag to keep from checking if she'd reached out. Never mind that I'd been the one to cut her off.

Hiding my phone also stopped me from monitoring her Instagram account despite her announcement that she was taking a break. I'd been in bed when I saw the post, and it had me sitting up.

Instead of a twenty- to thirty-second video of her dancing with a short caption below it, this post featured a clip of a garden—our garden—along with a lengthy writeup.

I started this account so I could have my own little corner in a place that was completely foreign to me. It's always been about dancing and creating a community around that shared passion. And until recently, it's always been my safe space.

After almost eight years, I'm taking a short break to think about the kind of content I want to create. Lots of changes coming, but I'm excited for this chance to go beyond my usual and discover what else I can do.

Maraming salamat / thank you for your support. I can't wait to dance with you again.

Hanggang sa susunod / until next time,
Tala

I read it so many times that I memorized every word—even the Filipino ones. Guilt plagued me that she needed to take a break from what she loved. At the same time, I admired her for speaking up and taking back control of her account.

Of all the unexpected things in her post, I was most surprised that she'd included her own language. It might have been an insignificant detail to most, but I knew she struggled between trying to please her audience and showing her authentic self.

Maybe it was a sign of what was to come. Whatever the

case, and despite the knowledge that she was leaving, I was proud of her. She'd been brave enough to be true to herself. I wondered if I could do the same.

That post had been four days ago, and there had been nothing from her since. No messages from Luna either, angry or otherwise. Even Luna's account, where she posted stories taken around campus or at their apartment, was quiet.

Was Tala already preparing to fly back?

I tried asking Stassy, but she snapped that I should ask Tala directly. In fact, Stassy used our old agreement not to talk about Tala as an excuse to avoid my questions.

So much for my friend being on my side.

Media day was the part of our off-season duties that I dreaded the most. The morning had revolved around photos and playing it up for the cameras. Now I waited for my turn to be grilled by the press. Most days, I barely felt the jitters when I sat with a mic in a room of people hanging on my words. But this time, tension filled my body.

As a rule, invited press usually limited their questions to revolve around basketball or the team. However, there was a chance they'd ask about Tala this time. Sam prepared me for it, giving me vague lines to spout if the questions came.

Still, everyone knew reporters loved to catch their subjects off-guard for the sake of a viral sound bite.

One of the team assistants caught my eye and mouthed, "You're up."

The door opened and Miles strode in. "Good luck, man," he told me, slapping my shoulder.

"Thanks." Standing, I smoothed a hand down the front of my jersey and cleared my mind. I pasted a casual expression on my face as I entered the press conference room.

About twelve people made up the audience. They sat in

black chairs, some with a pen and notebook in hand, others with a camera. All of them had their phones at the ready.

I nodded to them as I walked to the long table placed front and center and sat in the single chair.

The first question was the same every year: How was my off-season? I spoke of getting plenty of rest and incorporating more weights and swimming into my usual routine.

"It looks like you were up to more than just training and recovery," one reporter said. "Word is, you've been getting cozy with a certain dance influencer."

"There's a lot of news floating around. I can assure you that I put a lot of time and energy into preparing for this season," I answered.

"It's your seventh year with the Barons. What are you looking forward to going into training camp?"

"Playing with my team never gets old. We've built a great rhythm and established a solid sense of trust in one another. Now we have three new players, and it's going to be interesting to see how dynamics change. How we'll push each other to do better. Our coaches have worked hard on this program, and I'm excited to dive into it."

I answered a few more questions about my expectations for the season ahead and the teams I was most concerned about. Then the mic was passed to one of the veterans on the sports reporting circuit who was known for creating breaking headlines.

"Hey, Jason. We know you're up for an eighth season by player option. Do you see yourself taking that? We have a source claiming that you might be retiring soon. Can you verify that for us?"

Immediately, the energy in the room spiked. People sat up taller and whispered to each other while their eyes dissected me.

I stilled. I'd been so focused on what I would say if Tala was brought up that questions on my potential retirement never even crossed my mind.

Who the fuck had leaked it?

Channeling my best poker face, I answered as evenly as I could manage. "Like I mentioned, I love my team, and that includes the people I work with both on and off the court. Do I see myself taking that eighth year? Sure. As for the latter question, I can confirm that I have made no decision to retire. I'm at the peak of my game, and I'm not stopping yet."

"So it's not true that you visited Sterling University with the intent of entering a graduate program?"

The buzz grew louder. For the first time, I was thankful that the staff kept the air conditioning on full blast. The last thing I needed was for those sharks to see me sweat.

"Some of you may know I majored in environmental science. I've always been fascinated with that field, and I'm especially concerned about the state of our environment. That's why I visited the university—to reconnect with my old professor who happens to be a major figure in the climate change movement."

Leaning back, I chuckled before continuing. "Now, unless you guys want to hear me give a lecture on the reality of climate change, I think we should move back to basketball. I will say that this issue is very real and very important, and I do hope to get involved in it someday. But for now, the game's my number-one focus."

The reporter looked like he wanted to press the topic further, and other hands popped up in the air. But our team assistant stepped on stage, saying, "That's all the time we have with Jason. Next up, we have Corey Payton."

I gave my two-finger salute in farewell and stood, ignoring the questions and interview requests that followed me out of the room. I thought I did a passable job despite the unexpected offensive. Good thing my mom trained me to give diplomatic answers even before I signed my first contract.

Back in the holding room, Miles eyed me with concern. Before we could talk, our coach appeared by the doorway and barked out, "Meyer. My office. Now."

Miles winced and mouthed another 'good luck' to me as Coach Jenkins stormed off. The sports center bustled with staff, reporters, and photographers alike, but they automatically parted for Coach and me. They shut their mouths because Coach wasn't a man you wanted to cross, but they'd talk the moment we disappeared.

Inside his office, Coach settled into his chair and waited for me to close the door. As soon as I sat down, he said, "Sam's on the way. I'll ask you now—is it true?"

Faced with his steely gray eyes that seemed to drill into me, I had no choice but to admit it. "I haven't made any decisions. But I am considering it."

"Is this because of the dancer? Because I have to tell you, of all the players on our team, you were the last one I expected to be influenced by a woman."

"No," I said firmly. "If I decide to retire, it won't be because of anyone other than myself. I promise you that."

Coach scrubbed the back of his neck. "Hell. I thought we'd get through this media day without any scandals. Now we're trending for the wrong reasons."

"I can post a statement."

"Wait for Sam. He's the expert."

"Of course."

"Do I need to remind you that I'm counting on you? We all are."

"No need, Coach. I take my job seriously."

"Good." He leaned back and pinched the bridge of his nose

with his thumb and index fingers. "You know the press is having a field day with this, right?"

Pressing my lips together, I dipped my head.

"Your woman's going to get heat. I hope she's ready for it."

Fuck. He was right. How had I not thought of that? Of course the press was going to look at the rumors and draw their own conclusions. My fans had blasted her accounts when our photos made the circuit. What more would they do if they thought she was the reason I was supposedly retiring?

I dug into my pocket, only to remember I'd left my phone in my locker.

Damn it.

I was about to excuse myself to get it, but a knock sounded on the door. It opened and Sam strode right in, and I resigned myself to a long, painful conversation before I could get to Tala.

As expected, we spent almost an hour formulating our game plan. I admitted Tala knew about my career thoughts, and when Sam broached the possibility that she'd talked, I instantly shut it down. She might have been less than honest about her own plans, but I didn't doubt she would keep my secrets.

I didn't consider Gabe a threat either, since he wouldn't let Tala get caught in the crossfire. Likely, the leak had come from Rob's office, though I refused to believe it was the dean himself.

In the end, we agreed a casual approach would work better than an official interview or press release. I would set up a live video with Miles to address the controversy and play it off as an absurd rumor rather than something serious.

I had another motivation for the video, but I kept it zipped.

As soon as I left the office, I retrieved my phone, locked myself in a private restroom, and dialed Tala.

The phone rang four times before she picked up. "Hello."

Her voice made my stomach tighten. "Tala. Are you okay?"

"Yes, I was practicing," she said, sounding like she was trying to catch her breath.

I heaved a sigh of relief. "Good." She was alone and as safe as could be.

"What's up, Jason? I thought you didn't want to talk."

"I had media interviews earlier. They asked about you...and about my rumored retirement."

She inhaled sharply. "Shit. Are you okay? How—wait. Do you think it was me?"

"Of course not."

"How are you sure?"

"Because you're good at keeping secrets."

She went silent, and I grimaced at my word choice.

"I didn't mean it how it sounded," I said.

"Didn't you?"

"No. I—fuck." Exhaling, I dragged a hand down my face. "I just wanted to check on you, okay? They might come after you. Who knows what people will think."

"I'm fine. I'm taking a break from social media, and I turned my comments off."

"I know." The admission slipped before I had time to think about it.

"You do?"

I figured I had nothing to lose by being honest. "Just because we fought doesn't mean I don't care."

There was that weighted silence again. Then she said, "Thanks for checking in. How are you doing? Are you in trouble with your team?"

"I had to tell Sam and my coach, but it's okay. They needed to know anyway. We already agreed on our strategy, so don't worry about me."

"Like you said—just because we fought doesn't mean I don't care."

Hearing her say that settled the churning in my stomach. Hell, just hearing her voice made my problems seem inconsequential. "Are you going to work tomorrow?"

"Not until Sunday."

I nodded even though she couldn't see me. "When's your last day?"

"October 12," she whispered.

That was the official end of preseason. Did she know that?

Someone knocked on the door, unknowingly saving me from coming up with a response.

"You have to go," she said, apparently hearing it too.

"Yeah. Will you let me know if anyone messes with you?"

"I'll be fine. They'll get tired of me soon. Focus on yourself and training camp."

Did she really think my career mattered to me more than her safety?

As soon as the thought popped up in my head, I cursed myself. Why wouldn't she think that after I'd stormed out of town and practically told her to lose my number?

After a stilted, awkward goodbye, I exited the restroom and found Miles leaning next to the door, arms crossed over his chest.

"Done with your meltdown?"

I rolled my eyes and walked to the locker room, ignoring the nosy stares from people around us.

"Heard we have a video to prep for," Miles said as he kept pace beside me. "You ready to put on a show?"

No, but I'd do it all the same. If it had just been about me, I'd let the gossip die on its own. But since Tala was involved, I'd suck up my pride and play the game. Only now, I'd play it my way.

36

taya – (n) bet; also, the "it" in a game

Tala

I was trending again. Like last time, it was in relation to Jason—but unlike then, the accusations were completely false. Since people couldn't comment on my account or tag me in their posts, they took to creating new accounts and using hashtags. There was #GoHomeTala, #CancelTala, and my personal favorite, #FreeJasonMeyer. Like I had trapped him somehow.

After scanning some posts, I decided to delete the app from my phone, at least for now. I didn't need the distraction or emotional assault, not when I had to plan my next steps.

I sat at the dining table brainstorming ways to add a Filipino touch to my content. It could be the music or the moves themselves, maybe from the traditional dances I learned in high school.

A few weeks ago, Jason had brought up the idea of creating a tutorial series, something he'd found that people enjoyed. As I considered it, a rough plan took shape in my head. I'd break

306

each routine into easy steps and post tutorials on YouTube. The more complex dances could be offered on a subscription basis to supplement my ad revenue and sponsorships.

It wouldn't be enough to compensate for my nursing salary, so I still had to find a regular job, ideally as a dance instructor. If all else failed, I'd work as a nurse until I got my bearings.

Hopefully, things wouldn't come to that.

"Ate!" Luna burst out of her room in a flurry of energy and crashed into the chair next to me. "You have to watch this."

She plopped her phone between us, open to Jason's Instagram account. He was chatting with Miles on an empty basketball court. Unlike the team jersey he wore in this morning's media interview, he was dressed in a plain white shirt and gray shorts.

"...You really know how to steal the limelight, don't you?" Miles was saying to Jason as he straddled a backwards-facing chair. "You trying to show me up, man?"

Jason raised his shoulders, looking unbothered. "I'm just living my life. I don't know what to tell you."

"Well, guys." Miles switched his attention to the camera and talked to his audience, which the number on the screen showed had already surpassed ten thousand. "The reason I convinced Jason to do this live was so we could set the record straight. This way, you can get the truth directly from his mouth."

One corner of Jason's lips curved up in that smirk I loved. "You're really milking this, aren't you?" he said to Miles before facing the camera. "There's nothing to get excited about."

"Shh, I'm trying to give people what they want. Let's start with the off-season. You spent it in Sterling."

"Yeah. It's where I went to college. But before that, my dad loved to bring me there during his off-seasons. It's where he taught me to fish, to pitch a tent...and to do a crossover, among

307

other things." Jason chuckled, his eyes moving beyond the camera as he reminisced. "I must have practiced for hours before I got it right."

"Your old man sounds like the dream trainer," Miles commented.

"He was the best." There was a softness in Jason's face that was usually absent when he appeared on camera. He gave a brief nod. "So yeah, Sterling's special to me. After last season, I wanted to revisit it, you know?"

Miles pounded a fist on Jason's arm. "Always the sentimental one. I got you."

"Exactly. I wanted to go back to my roots. See old mentors, friends. Take a breather." He was speaking to Miles, but I could tell he meant the words for the public. "There were no ulterior motives to that trip. So when I heard what people were saying —" he shook his head "—I've got to tell you, I didn't see that coming."

"You mean about you retiring?" Miles jumped right in. "I was pissed when I heard. You quitting without telling me? What's that bullshit?" His eyes flew to the camera. "Excuse my French."

"Exactly. You know me. I'm a science geek, but I'm not going to leave the team hanging like that."

Nodding vigorously, Miles said to their viewers, "He *is* a geek. If you guys knew how many times he's gone off about greenhouse gasses and melting ice caps—"

"You're going off-topic, man."

I had to laugh at their totally natural exchange.

"I'm making a point. And that is you're into science, but you're also into basketball."

Jason tilted his head. "That's one way to put it."

"You're not retiring. Say it with me."

"I'm not retiring," Jason echoed agreeably. "That said, I do want to support the climate change movement. You already know I feel strongly about that, but I don't discuss it publicly. I think it's time to change that."

"Does that mean you'll be showing up on Insta more often?"

He gave a cryptic smile. "Maybe. But basketball will still be my priority."

"Damn right." Miles slapped the back of Jason's shoulder. "By the way, I noticed you've got a little hashtag going on. You got anything to say about that, or you going to dribble around it like you always do?"

My heart raced. He wasn't going to talk about me, was he?

Jason chuckled. "You know I rarely talk about my personal life."

"Forget about the thousands of people watching right now. It's just you and me, man."

"All I'm going to say is that there's a special woman I care very much for. I hate that she's being targeted for various reasons, including my fabricated retirement." His jaw tightened while his eyes grew flinty. "She doesn't deserve that. She's a talented, hardworking woman, and a genuinely good person. I'm asking everyone to please lay off her."

My entire world went still.

"Well." Miles cleared his throat. "You said a lot more than I expected."

"My dad taught me a lot of things. That includes taking a stand for the things and the people that are important to me."

They continued talking, but I couldn't hear a word. Not a minute later, the video ended with Jason frozen in his usual half-smile.

"Sooo...did Jason just declare his feelings for you on the internet?" Luna's eyes were wide as she gripped my arm.

I barely felt it.

My emotions were all over the place. I didn't know if I was happy and grateful that he defended me openly, or whether it had upset me. Pent-up energy bubbled just beneath my skin. I had the overwhelming urge to get up and dance or run or do...something.

Eyeing me, Luna put her phone down. "It's too late to go up to the roof. You won't have enough light."

My right leg bounced rapidly. Jumping to my feet, I paced the length of the room and sorted through my thoughts.

When Jason called, he'd hinted he still had feelings for me. Now, he announced it for the world to hear. He hadn't spoken of love, but him saying he cared for me was more than I ever expected after I hurt him so badly.

It convinced me to find a way to work things out with him. Of all the loose ends I needed to tie up, our relationship was the only one I would regret not fixing.

Coming to a halt in front of Luna, I blurted out, "I think I should go to Santa Mila."

"Yes!" Luna threw up her hands. "Hallelujah!"

"I can book a flight going to Santa Mila, then change my current booking so I'll leave for Manila from there instead of here." I dropped back into my chair and opened a new tab on my browser. It was going to end up costing more, but I'd rather go broke than live with regret. "I just need to check the dates when he'll be in town."

"Their first game is on the sixteenth, and it'll be at their arena. So you can fly there on the day of, or earlier," Luna said helpfully.

"That means I'll have to leave you earlier than I planned to." Unless I brought her along. Could I afford to?

"It's okay." She waved a hand. "We still have the next couple of weeks. It's more important that you see Jason.

Besides, I'm a working adult now, you know. I can't just go AWOL."

"Are you sure?"

"Yes. In fact, you should book your flight now so you won't have time to change your mind." Luna danced in her chair. "This is so exciting!"

It was. Scary too, but fear was something I could deal with if it meant I'd have another chance with Jason. This time, I wasn't going to let him walk away without telling him how I really felt.

I owed him that much. And I owed it to myself too.

37

kanlungan – (n) shelter

Jason

"Nice going out there, bro." Miles snapped his soggy towel toward my left shoulder.

I ducked so it missed. "Not bad for day one," I said as I sank into my assigned chair in the locker room.

Our teammates milled around us in various states of undress. Everyone was in good spirits, having kicked off training camp with a day of drills and scrimmages. So far, we were meshing well with our latest additions, and there hadn't been any big surprises aside from mine.

The past week of training with Miles put me in my best shape, especially since I'd channeled my frustrations into working out. We had three more days of practice before we'd go head-to-head with our first preseason opponent on Saturday.

"Dinner at my place?" Miles asked.

I considered it, but I'd been camping over at his house nearly every day since I got back. It was high time I used my own apartment. "Rain check. I'll crash at home for a change."

"Nothing from her?"

"Yeah." Tala was taking a break from social media, but surely she'd seen the video. At the very least, Luna would have seen it and told her about it.

Had Tala finally gotten sick of the hassle I kept getting her mixed up in? Maybe I underestimated her feelings for me. Or maybe she held a grudge against me for leaving like I did.

After I posted the video last night, Rob called to apologize about the leak. Apparently, his secretary saw my response to his email, which included the updated syllabi for the master's programs. She put two and two together and sent her conclusion to the press in time for media day.

Rob asked if he could do anything to help, but I told him it might just add fuel to the fire. Nothing stopped word of mouth from spreading other than the arrival of newer, bigger stories. At least now I knew the rumor's source. I'd deal with whatever happened next when it came.

I showered off a day's worth of sweat and spent half an hour in the ice bath with Miles and our other teammates. When my legs no longer felt like they'd seize up at any moment, I got dressed, said goodbye to the guys, and headed to my car.

Glancing in the passenger side mirror, I got hit by a flashback of Tala sitting beside me on the way to Golden Haven. Our hands had been linked together on the center console, her head turned to the window as she watched the darkness lifting from the sky.

I should have switched to my usual ride, but I couldn't let go of the one I'd rented in Sterling. Even though it felt like stepping inside a mental torture chamber, I couldn't bring myself to return it.

In fact, I asked my assistant to contact the rental company so I could buy it off them.

Was it a form of self-inflicted punishment?

Maybe. But I couldn't let it go.

I was outside my apartment when my phone rang. Unfortunately, it wasn't the caller I'd been hoping for.

It was my mom. I'd been avoiding her calls, but it was only a matter of time before she stormed into town. No way did I need that extra headache, so I unlocked the door and put the call through speakerphone.

"Hey, Mom," I said, toeing my shoes off. I dropped my bag on the bench in my foyer and hung my keys.

"Finally!" Her voice echoed in the open concept living area. "I've been calling you for days, Jason. You've been avoiding me."

Barefoot, I walked to my favorite armchair, sank into it, and kicked my feet up onto the matching ottoman. "Sorry. It's hectic with training camp and everything."

"You could get through camp in your sleep. It's her."

"She has a name." I bit the words out.

"Yes, Tala," she snapped. "Like talons, which is fitting, given the hold she has on you. Seriously, Jason. What were you thinking? Not only do you get yourself tangled up with her, you did that video willingly? And that retirement scandal—"

"There's no scandal, Mom. That was the point of that video." *In case you missed it,* I held back from saying.

"The point of the video was to stake your claim on Tala, and both you and I are well aware of that. You forget I was the one who taught you about public relations and perception. Your tactics might work on other people, but not me."

If I thought my tone was cold, hers was arctic. Another thing I'd picked up from her.

"Of course. I shouldn't have expected otherwise." Fatigue hit me. After more than a week of stress and sleepless nights, coupled with the physical strain I subjected my body to, I felt depleted.

"Is there any truth to that rumor?"

I should have reassured her there was none. Any other time, I would have. But I was tired of lying. I lied to the world every day. I shouldn't have to do the same with my only remaining family member.

"I'm not retiring this year, but I'm thinking about it," I said.

"Are you mad?" she whispered, horror clear in her voice. "Why would you do that? Why would you throw away every-thing you have? You have everything you've ever wanted, and you're just going to throw it down the drain?"

She couldn't have said anything more to cement the fact that she didn't know me. At all.

This wasn't what I wanted, and it never had been. Sure, I'd wanted to follow in Dad's footsteps, but not because he was a famous athlete. It was because he'd been happy and content with his life. Short as it was, he'd lived a full one, and he'd shaped it to fit his ideals. Not anyone else's.

That was exactly what I wanted too.

"Is it because of Tala?" Mom demanded, her voice rising.

Closing my eyes, I leaned back. "No, Mom. It's something I've been thinking about for a while, even before I went back to Sterling."

All Tala did was help me see that I was more than a basket-ball player. Realizing I couldn't keep up this act forever...that was on me.

"Whatever it is you're thinking, it will pass. Don't decide in the heat of the moment. I'm flying there in a few weeks; we'll talk about it then."

"Like I said, I'm not retiring this year. That's one thing I'm sure of, so there's no need to worry," I told her. "And Mom?"

"Yes?"

"Stassy and I are never happening."

She inhaled sharply.

"You're my mother and I love you, but I'm in love with Tala."

For the first time in my memory, I managed to stun her into silence.

Then she breathed out, "You can't mean that. You're not in love with her. You're confusing it with lust. It'll pass."

I slowly inhaled through my nose and exhaled through my mouth. She still had the gall to assume she knew how I felt. "You saying that doesn't make it true."

"She isn't the right woman for you," she bristled.

"You don't know her at all. Everything you think you know is just from your own assumptions."

"I was right about her visa, wasn't I?"

Setting my jaw, I spoke through my teeth. "It doesn't change the way I feel about her." Before she could say anything else, I continued. "Mom. I know you're trying to look after me, but I can take care of myself. I can make my own decisions, and if they're the wrong ones and they bite me in the ass, then I'll deal with it. I just need you to respect my choices and let me live my own life."

"We'll talk when I'm in town. Until then, don't make any rash decisions."

Then she cut the call.

My anger fizzled into something worse. Hurt.

After Dad died, I'd consoled myself with the thought that I still had a mom who loved me. Now I wondered if I had fooled myself. Would she treat me the same if I chose a different path from the one she wanted?

I needed a drink. Someone to talk to.

Tala. I needed Tala.

Pushing myself up, I strode to the fridge and took out a

pitcher of water. It wasn't the beverage I wanted, but I had training tomorrow. Even though my heart wasn't in it, I had to do my best. That entailed keeping my body in top shape. God knew my mental state was already fucked up—I didn't need to add a potential hangover to the mix.

As I poured a second glass of water, my phone pinged. My eyes moved to the screen and my chest damn near squeezed.

New message from Tala.

I opened it to find a link to a video entitled, *How to Do the Bee Waggle Dance.*

TALA

Was looking for dance ideas and came across this. It reminded me of you.

Thanks for looking out for me, Jason. Are you okay? I hope you didn't get in trouble with your team.

I nearly shook from wanting to embrace her. Since I couldn't, I settled for the next best thing. Would it help me move on from her? Nope—and I didn't care. That wasn't an option when it came to Tala, anyway.

Hitting the call button, I waited for her to pick up. She did after a single ring.

"Hi." One word, and she soothed every aching crevice.

"Hey, Tala," I said as I headed back to my chair.

"What's wrong?"

"What makes you think something's wrong?"

"Your voice sounds tight. Tired," she murmured. "Did you watch the video?"

"Not yet. To be honest, I just wanted to talk to you."

"I'm glad." She hesitated, and then, "I miss you."

"I miss you too, dance girl. You have no idea."

"I'm sorry I couldn't go with you."

"It's okay. I get it."

"You do?"

"You're committed to your job, just like I am to mine," I said. "I was wrong to insist that you drop everything and leave because it suited me."

It had taken me some time to yank my head out of my ass, but I realized Tala's independence, her hard-headed focus on her goals, were traits that made her who she was. They were some of the reasons why I'd fallen in love with her. I couldn't hold that against her when it meant she wouldn't simply fall in line with what I wanted.

She was silent, likely thinking over my words. "That's part of it, and I appreciate you understanding that. But...I wanted to go with you. I could have, but I was scared."

"You weren't ready. I can't fault you for that—not when I didn't give you much time to get used to the idea."

"You're not the only one. I didn't give you time to get used to me leaving, either."

"Yeah, well." I gave a rough laugh and dug my hand through my hair. "I left as soon as you told me. So that's on me too."

She sighed, and I almost imagined I could feel her breath coasting across my face. "I don't want to throw blame, Jason. We both made mistakes. I just want to fix things."

"I want that too."

She asked about the team's reaction to my interview, and I told her how Rob cleared up the mystery behind the leak. Although it hurt to talk about it, I spoke about my argument with Mom. Tala said she didn't want to be a source of conflict between us, but I insisted it wasn't just about her.

"She doesn't know who I really am because I always let myself be what she wanted," I said. "After Dad died, I tried too hard to please her, and I lost myself in the process. It's something I need to work on, but I can't fix it overnight."

Tala hummed in agreement. "I hope you two get to talk when the tension isn't so high. If there's anything I can do to help, just let me know."

There was an utter sense of rightness in this, in simply talking with her at the end of the day. A quiet comfort in knowing she was there to listen, and I'd be accepted as I was, flaws and all.

Right then, I discovered that love wasn't just in the big moments, in the overwhelming feelings of attraction and likeness. It was also in the everyday things—in leaning on the other person when the load got too heavy and willingly taking on that weight when they needed help.

As our conversation turned to Tala's job and the new hire she was training, I wondered if I would be able to see her before she flew home. Even if I could, was it possible to maintain a long-distance relationship?

It was tough enough to maintain a relationship when we lived in the same city, given that I spent half my time traveling and most of the remaining hours in practice or recovery. Throw in the distance, time difference, and media, and it was an equation for disaster.

But the flip side meant saying goodbye to Tala. If there was one thing I learned from the past weeks, it was that I could live without her, but my life was better with her in the picture.

I just had to figure out how to make that happen.

38

despedida - (n) a farewell party

Tala

In the weeks that followed, I split my time between working at the care center, shooting content for my social media relaunch, and wrapping up my life in Sterling. I wrangled an agreement from Jose to cut back on overtime and emergency shifts. It was time to rearrange my priorities. Besides, the team had to get used to me not being there to take up the slack.

On my days off, I met with my PR contacts to discuss my move. Luckily, none of my commitments were affected by my break, though I had to turn down two campaign offers. While the sudden media attention brought me a wave of new followers and engagement, it also impacted my public perception. So I prepared an entire deck outlining the changes I planned for my platform and the types of content they could expect from me going forward.

The first partner I set up a video call with was Nat, since she already knew about my upcoming move.

"I still can't believe you're leaving," she told me. "I'm happy you get to go home and be with your family, but I've always been rooting for you and Jason."

"We only started dating recently."

Nat shook her head. "Jason never talks to me about girls, so when he sent me your profile back then, I knew you were important to him. He made me promise not to tell you how we knew each other and not to talk to him about you. I thought it was because he cared about you but couldn't allow himself to. You remember how I kept asking you to tell me when you're ready to date?"

Reeling from the revelations she shared, I nodded.

"He was the guy I wanted to set you up with. I guess it was a good thing you never agreed. It wasn't the right time."

"And you think now is?"

"Uh huh. I'm betting on you two. You'd better work things out."

"I'll do my best," I said with a confidence I was starting to feel. "Actually, can you keep a secret?"

"I never told you about Jason, did I?"

Right.

I told her I was planning to visit Jason before my flight home. She was completely onboard with the surprise. When I admitted I didn't have tickets to the game yet, she told me she had it covered and ignored my protests.

"Consider it my sendoff gift to you," she said. "But it's also for Jason."

Since I was practicing the art of accepting help when it was offered, I took her up on it. "Thank you, Nat. I wish we could see each other before I leave."

"You never know. I might just end up going to Santa Mila," she teased before we moved on to work-related topics.

The rest of my meetings went smoothly, save from the

inevitable questions—discreet and otherwise—about Jason. When I wasn't working, I spent most of my time with Luna after her shifts at the bookstore. We did chores together and bought souvenirs for me to bring home, and I accompanied her on one last thrifting adventure.

Sometimes, Gabe picked us up from our errands and joined us for dinner. He and Luna seemed to have a truce going on, but I sensed a different kind of tension between them. One night after Gabe left, Luna and I were washing dishes side by side when I brought up the topic. "So, about Gabe."

The plate Luna had been washing clattered in the sink. "Wh-what—" she stammered, her eyes wide with alarm.

"Lu." I nudged her arm with my shoulder. "You know I don't have feelings for him. We're practically brother and sister."

Luna's entire body slumped on her exhale. "He's not like a brother to me."

"I know."

"Are you mad?"

"Of course not. Gabe is a great guy, but I was never into him."

"Never?" Luna raised her eyebrows in challenge.

Well, since she asked... "There was a super brief time when I considered it. But we quickly found out that we're really just friends."

Biting her lower lip, she said, "Did you ever..."

"No!" I shook my head vehemently. "We kissed once, and we agreed it would never happen again."

Luna picked up the plate and resumed scrubbing it. "Do you think he knows?"

That she had a thing for him? Probably.

No, definitely. Gabe didn't like to be involved in other people's business, but he rarely missed a thing.

"He's never brought it up." I picked my words carefully, not wanting to seem overbearing like I had in the past. *You're her sister*, I reminded myself, *not her mom*. "Lu, I won't tell you what to do or what not to do when it comes to Gabe. Just...be careful. He's one of the best guys I know, but he has some baggage he needs to work through."

She handed me the plate so I could dry it and said, "You don't need to worry. He doesn't see me like that. Anyway, it's just a stupid crush."

Sure, it was. I wanted to intervene but knew I had no right to. Still, that didn't mean I wasn't going to remind Gabe to look out for her.

"Anyway, how's it going with Jason? Are you sure he doesn't know about your visit?" Luna asked in an obvious attempt to change the topic.

If that was what she wanted, I was happy to oblige. "Things are good. I don't think he suspects anything. If he does, he's good at hiding it. He keeps talking about wanting to come over though."

What began as a sudden phone call became a continuation of our old routine. On the fourth night, he apologized that he couldn't set a fixed time for us to talk since his schedule kept changing. But I didn't mind waiting.

"How can he come over? Isn't he busy with practice and games?"

"He is," I answered. "I told him to focus on training, especially with everyone watching him so closely."

Since rumors of his retirement had circulated, people questioned if he'd start slacking off. Instead, he played consistently and ignored the gossip. He told me what strangers said was out of his control. All he could do was focus on the things he could, like how he prepared for his games and worked with his team.

I missed being with him, but the good thing about being

apart was that we were forced to talk without sex distracting us. We discussed everything except for the elephant in the room— our relationship. Aside from that initial night, we didn't speak of our feelings for each other. I was waiting to tell him when I saw him in a week and a half.

Nat pulled through with courtside tickets after telling Jason she planned to bring a date. She also invited him for a post-game dinner. Little did he know he'd be having dinner with me, not Nat.

I just had to hold out until then and pray he'd say yes to my proposal.

———

ON MY LAST day of work, I woke up to a bouquet of stargazers and dandelions on the kitchen table. A note beside it read:

> *For the woman named after the goddess of the morning and night star,*
> *I thought these flowers were perfect for you—vibrant, resilient, and passionate. No matter what you do next, I know you'll shine like the star you've always been.*
> *Yours, Jason.*

The doorbell rang before I could process the words. Wondering if I was still dreaming, I answered it and found a delivery boy holding two cups of coffee and a takeaway box from my favorite cafe.

Footsteps padded behind me and Luna's head popped over my shoulder. "Aww, he got me coffee too. He's such a keeper. I hope someone gives me flowers someday."

In my daze, I stared at the items in the stranger's hands

until Luna nudged me aside, taking them herself. She told him to hold on while she got a tip, but he waved it away, saying it was taken care of.

When we closed the door and were alone, I asked, "Am I dreaming?"

"Nope," Luna said cheerfully as she pushed a cup into my hand. "I've been chatting with Jason since a quarter to five because he wanted to make sure the flowers were here."

If it was past five our time, it would be two a.m. over there.

"You should call the poor guy so he can finally go to sleep."

Stumbling over to the sofa, I did just that. He picked up on the first ring, sounding wide awake.

"Tal?"

"Why are you still up?" I blurted out.

He chuckled. "I wanted to check that you got everything okay. Good morning."

"Good morning," I echoed. My heart felt close to bursting. This man was the sweetest, most thoughtful guy I had ever known, and I wished I could teleport to his place and hug him. "I...I don't know what to say."

"Do you like the flowers? You know I don't usually buy cut ones, but I made an exception for you."

"I love them. I love that you thought of all this even though you're so busy." *I love you,* I almost admitted, but I didn't want the first time to be over the phone. Instead, I said, "Thank you, Jason."

"You're welcome. I wish I could be there, but this is the next best thing. Ready for today?"

"Yes. It feels bittersweet...but it feels right too."

"That's good. I'm glad you're not stressed about it."

"You should go to sleep. Workout is at seven?"

"Yep." He yawned. "Good to hear your voice, Tal."

"You too. Sleep well, Jase. Thanks again."

"My pleasure. Talk to you later."

Distracted with admiring the flowers he sent, I left my apartment later than usual. Luna packed a few pastries for me, and I ate one on the bus with my coffee. I didn't really need the caffeine to boost my mood, although it was a happy bonus. Just talking with Jason was enough.

At the care center, everything was business as usual until lunch time, when Billie, Jose, and a handful of my friends surprised me with a cake in the break room.

"What is this?" I asked.

"Our send-off." Billie lowered the chocolate cake onto the table in front of me. *Bon voyage* was written in frosting across the center, on top of which sat three stars.

"You guys." I glanced from the cake to each of their faces. I'd prepared for this day, but the reality of it only sunk in now. "You didn't have to."

Standing, I hugged and thanked them one at a time. When I reached Jose, he shook my hand.

"Thank you for your hard work, Tala. You're one of the best we've had here," he told me. "I'm sorry we couldn't keep you."

"There's nothing to apologize for, Jose. I appreciate every-thing you've done for me."

"I hope everything works out for you in Manila. And with your celebrity." He gave me a rare smile.

I laughed. "He's an athlete."

But he was so much more than that. He was an avid geek, an unexpected gardener, a steadfast friend, a generous lover. Everyone else might love the golden boy with his reserved charm, but only I got the conflicted man with his random trivia and passionate speeches.

Even though he'd never admit to being a superstar, he couldn't be ordinary if he tried.

"So, this is it," Berna said when I visited her room one last time.

"I know. I still can't believe it."

Nostalgia rolled over me as I stood next to her bed. For years, Berna had acted like a godmother to me, dispensing jokes and advice as I administered her treatments. Through the busyness of the care center, Berna had always been a shining spot, and I would miss seeing her regularly.

I felt a heaviness in my throat, but Berna tsked at me.

"None of that, Tala. I know I'll see you again," she told me sharply despite the sheen in her eyes. "You're not getting rid of me that easily."

"I'll definitely come visit next time I'm here. And I'll keep in touch. I'm counting on you to share your adventures on social media," I said with a laugh.

"Of course. The same goes for you. I love your dances but I want to see more of your life too. Never mind those haters."

"I'm working on that."

"Remember, long distance relationships aren't impossible. Not if you both put in the effort and commitment." Berna's eyes grew cloudy and, for one brief moment, I got a glimpse into the loneliness that lurked behind her devil-may-care facade. "In this life, you don't get many do-overs. You have to make every chance count, even if it doesn't work out the way you want it to."

I stared at her hand, frail and wrinkled with age. Reaching out, I held it and squeezed lightly. "I will. I promise."

It was unfair that Berna would likely be stuck here for the rest of her life with only the rare visitor. A part of me felt guilty over leaving her, especially since I didn't know when I'd be back.

"I told you, none of that. I've lived my life outside these walls. It hasn't ended just because I'm in here."

"I'll miss you, Berna."

"I'll miss you too." Squeezing my hand back, she gave me a watery smile. "Now go get your man."

I laughed. "I will."

———

LATER THAT EVENING, I clinked wine glasses with Luna and Gabe at Claudette's. Despite the restaurant's fancy ambience, I was wearing the leggings and T-shirt I'd changed into at the center. I thought we were eating in as usual, but Gabe picked me up with Luna in the backseat and said we were celebrating my last day at work.

"Are you all packed?" Gabe asked after the waiter served the main course.

"Mostly. I just have my daily stuff, some clothes, and my video equipment left." The rest of my belongings were tucked away in my suitcases, minus the things I was leaving behind for Luna.

Gabe nodded and turned to Luna. "Can you pack quickly?"

She frowned. "What do you mean? I'm not going anywhere."

"You're going with Tala to Santa Mila."

"Um, no, I'm not. Did you get beamed to an alternate reality where I can afford to buy a ticket?"

"I bought you one," he said.

We gaped at him.

"Well, two if you count the flight back."

"Are you serious?" I asked when it looked like Luna was lost for words.

"I thought you'd want company, and since I can't leave, Luna might as well go with you."

"B—but I have classes. And work," Luna stammered, blinking rapidly.

"It's just two and a half days. I got you on the same flight as Tala on Monday, then you fly back Wednesday at noon so you can make it to your shift," Gabe said.

Luna just stared at him, dazed.

"I know I should probably tell you that you shouldn't have —and you shouldn't have," I told him. "But I'm so glad that you did. Lu and I have always wanted to visit the West Coast together, and now we're getting to do that. Thank you, Gabe." Even though everything about the restaurant seemed formal and proper, I leaned up from my chair and gave him a hug.

"Sound the alarm. Tala Reyes is finally accepting a gift without protest," he quipped, squeezing me back.

"I was so nervous about the trip, but I feel better now that Luna's going," I said as I sat down.

"I talked with your boss," Gabe told Luna. "She'll swap your Monday shift with another employee. And I'll get you notes for any classes you'll miss."

"I can take care of my own notes," she snapped. "Also, you didn't have to talk to Marge. It's my job, so it's my responsibility. You're not my keeper."

Shocked at her angry outburst, I said, "Lu—"

"It's alright." Gabe was unruffled. "I saw Marge on campus and thought I would save you the trouble. That said, I'm glad you can take care of your notes."

Luna harrumphed and grabbed her glass, downing her soda in one gulp. "Fine. Thank you, professor."

"Can you believe it?" I told her. "We're going to California! Wait, I have to tell Nat you're coming. Hopefully she can help us get another ticket."

Finally, her scowl transformed into a grin. "Lonzo is going to freak. We're going to watch the Barons play live." She wiggled in her seat. "I can't wait to see Jason's reaction when he finds out you're there."

Neither could I.

39

dahilan – (n) purpose; reason

Jason

I set up a tripod in the middle of Miles's garden. The sky was clear and a steady breeze cooled the air despite the heavy rays of sunlight. Since Miles's house was tucked away from the city center, there was no traffic or noise, making it the perfect place to shoot.

"You sure about this, man?" Miles asked, attaching the clip-on microphone to his shirt. "I thought you hated social media."

"It's not the media I hate. It's how people use it," I said as I mounted my phone to the tripod. When the right time came, I'd buy an actual camera with the right specs for videos. For now, my phone would work just fine. "Tala once told me I have the platform to make a difference. Might as well take advantage of it."

"Hell, yes. Thanks for inviting me along."

After weeks of planning, we were finally ready to shoot the first episode of 'Beyond the Hoop.' The seed for the live video series came from Tala and Rob, and their confidence in my ability to bring awareness to important causes. The positive response to my video with Miles proved the idea had legs, and him agreeing to partner with me clinched the deal.

I took the extra step of meeting with Sam, Coach Jenkins, and our team manager to cover all my bases. Luckily, they gave me the go signal so long as we avoided certain topics and stated that our views were not reflective of our team's.

Sitting in the chair next to Miles, I took a drink and settled myself. A glance showed me he was completely relaxed. I envied him.

Nerves stirred in my stomach. It felt like I was about to expose myself to the world. No wonder Tala felt leery about posting that Filipino song.

"We got this, man," Miles told me without a trace of doubt. "Ready when you are."

Clipping on my mic, I nodded. We did a quick sound check, then I counted us down. At one, I hit the Bluetooth remote control to get the video rolling.

"Hey, guys," I said, smiling at the camera. "Happy Sunday. I'm Jason Meyer."

"And I'm your man Miles Gomez."

"Welcome to the official premiere of 'Beyond the Hoop,' a weekly video series where Miles and I share the things that matter to us outside of basketball."

"Jason enjoyed the spotlight so much he wanted a repeat," Miles joked. "But kidding aside, we wanted to chat with you guys about topics that hit us hard. This week, we're gonna be talking about Jason's love affair that's got everyone buzzing."

Pausing, we exchanged grins before I said, "My love affair with the environment, that is."

For the next twenty minutes, we talked about how my dad got me into the outdoors with backyard camping and stargazing. I spoke about studying environmental science and discovering just how the state of the earth was deteriorating. We'd decided not to use a script but had an outline to guide the flow of our conversation. Despite the seriousness of the topic, Miles's additional commentary kept the tone light.

When we hit twenty minutes, Miles made a circling motion with his finger below the camera's range—our sign that it was time to wrap up.

"If you'd like to hear more on sustainability, I'll share some resources and tips on my account," I said. "We'll also talk more about this and other topics in the coming weeks."

"We hope you enjoyed this first episode of 'Beyond the Hoop.' Next week, it's my turn to drive. Lemme tell you, you won't want to miss it." Miles winked at the camera.

"Thanks for joining us, everyone. Till next week."

As Miles said goodbye, I did my two-finger salute and pressed the remote. The video cut out, and a long exhale left my mouth.

"Whoa." Eyes wide, Miles shoved his phone in front of me. "Fifteen thousand viewers. Not bad, considering we didn't even post a teaser."

I scanned the numbers on the screen and smiled. "I'd say that was a success for our second amateur livestream."

Standing, I walked to the tripod and removed my phone. Among the notifications, I zeroed in on the one person I wanted to hear from.

TALA

Looking good, Mr. Influencer.

My smile grew so wide, I felt like a lovestruck goof. I called her and switched on the camera, needing to see her.

When she accepted, I saw she was on the rooftop, sitting in one of the chairs we used to share. Of the places I'd been to around the world—and there had been a lot—that was my favorite spot. It had nothing to do with the place and everything to do with the woman.

She grinned at me with pride shining in her eyes. "Hey, you. Congrats on the livestream. That was such a brilliant idea."

"Thanks. I—"

"Tala!" Miles jostled his way to me and leaned his head into the camera frame. "You saw our debut?"

Her eyes left mine. I almost shoved Miles away so I could have her all to myself.

"Hi, Miles. Of course I did, though I missed your intro. If Jason had told me about it, I would have set an alert. You guys are naturals," she said to him.

"The cam loves me so much that my magic rubs off on this guy." Miles chuckled, elbowing me.

She laughed. "I happen to think that guy looks pretty good himself."

Didn't that make me feel ten feet tall?

"You're too nice for your own good, Tala. Anyway, I'm gonna go before your man knocks me out. See you around, hey?" Miles winked at her.

To my surprise, she blushed. I narrowed my eyes at Miles, who gave me an innocent look. I knew he would never try to poach my woman. Still, that didn't stop me from wanting to clock him.

"Bye, Miles," Tala said.

"Chill, I'm going," Miles told me before walking toward his house.

Turning to Tala, I said, "Sorry I didn't tell you about what I was planning. I wanted it to be a surprise."

"It's alright. I'm just so proud you did it. Your passion really came through while you were talking, and you and Miles always have great chemistry."

"Thanks. I'll take some tips if you have them. We're just winging it here."

"Of course, any time."

"Were you dancing?"

"Yes, I'm shooting my last batch of videos here. I was checking one of my takes when I got the notification that you were live."

"Good timing. I wish I could be there to help you shoot."

She gave me a soft smile. "You know I'm used to doing it alone, right?"

"Yeah, but I also know you enjoyed it more when I was on the other side of the camera."

I expected her to play off my bluster as usual, so she caught me by surprise when she said almost shyly, "Maybe I did."

It was the closest we came to talking about our feelings for each other since that phone call nearly three weeks ago. Like we'd both agreed to hold off on the serious talk.

But we were running out of time. She was flying out in four days, then I'd lose my chance of seeing her in person until the season ended. My schedule barely allowed for days off, let alone trips across the world.

I knew players whose relationships imploded with rumors of cheating and jealousy. Mom claimed her marriage with Dad worked out because she traveled with him as much as she could, sacrificing her career in the process. Just these past weeks, tabloids and social media pages posted stolen shots of me with various women and speculated on how many of them I was screwing. Didn't matter that I'd barely even spoken to them, let alone met them past a single sighting.

Suddenly, a wave of desperation crashed over me. All the words that had been brewing inside flooded out.

"Look, I know you need to go home, and I completely understand that," I said as my heartbeat raced. "I did some research and I learned you can stay here for six months on a tourist visa and petition to extend it for a year. So I'm thinking when you get to Manila, you can apply for a new visa, catch up with your family and everything, then fly back here."

The glow of happiness on her face dimmed with every word.

Still, I kept talking, my mouth too far gone to be stopped despite the sirens blaring in my head. "Like I said before, you can stay at my place here or at the house in Sterling whenever you want to visit Luna. You living here makes sense for your career since most of the clients you work with are based in the US. Then we can work on getting you permanent residency. I've already asked my lawyer to look at our options, and she has some connections who can help us out. I'll set up an online meeting to discuss them."

That sounded reasonable, right?

She shook her head. "So, your solution is for me to live with you and rely on your connections and money?" she asked in a tight voice.

"It's called maximizing resources, Tal. Exhausting all options to achieve our goal."

"Our goal being?"

Was she seriously asking that? "Fixing your visa so we can stay together." When she flattened her lips and said nothing, I continued. "Look, it's a win-win solution. You get to go home and spend time with your family. Then we can make it so your visa won't be a roadblock for us."

Silence.

My frustration boiled over, and I heaved an aggravated breath. "So? What do you think?"

***

Tala

What did I think?

I didn't even know where to start.

My fingers felt stiff from clenching my phone. "Jason." I tried to keep my voice level. "I don't think we're on the same page here."

"What do you mean? We both want to work things out. Or did I get that wrong?"

"No, of course not. Of course I want to work things out."

"Okay, so I'm suggesting a way we can do that."

"You don't get it. Manila is my home. I'm not going back for a visit. I'm going *home*."

The frantic, almost feverish glint in his eyes disappeared, his stare going hard. "I do get it. I'm not telling you not to go, but you don't have to stay there permanently."

"You don't understand. I *want* to stay there, at least for the immediate future."

He cursed. "Stop telling me I don't understand."

"Then stop telling me not to stay in my home," I shot back, determined to stand my ground.

"How many months are you talking?"

"I don't know, Jason. A year? Two?" Too restless to remain still, I started pacing. "I have interviews with a couple of schools and dance studios scheduled."

His frown deepened. "What about us?"

"I mean, we have phones and the internet. We've kind of been doing the long-distance thing these past weeks, and it's worked out okay."

"Sterling is three hours ahead of Santa Mila. Manila is sixteen." His voice grew louder. "Sixteen hours, Tala. And that's if I'm here. What about when I'm traveling?"

"We can come up with a schedule. I'll do my best to adjust,

but we don't have to talk everyday if we're busy. I'll save up to visit you, then you can come over after the season."

"That's a year from now."

"It's not like you'll be sitting here doing nothing," I argued. "You have eighty-one games left, right? Also, you'll be traveling half the time."

His video bobbed as he scrubbed his free hand down his face. "Do you know how hard it is for NBA couples to stay together? The odds aren't good, Tala—and that's when they live in the same country."

"You make it sound like being in a relationship with you is impossible."

"Not impossible but damn near it. That's why we need to eliminate any other complications in the equation."

A complication. He boiled down my need to be with my family to a complication when to me it was a necessity.

Releasing a shaky breath, I said, "I'm sure it'll be hard. We'll have to work on it. Compromise."

"Right." He gave a single, insistent nod. "So come back here."

"Jason." I closed my eyes for a moment, struggling with my rioting emotions. Maybe it would be easier to cave in. But what happened when the honeymoon phase wore off and I began to resent him for making me put off my needs again?

I might not be an expert, but I didn't believe you could build a relationship on rocky ground.

"Why can't my plan work? Spell it out for me, Tala."

"Because you're deciding about our relationship, *my life*, without me. Even if I want to give in, I'm scared that means I'll put myself last again. If that happens, we might be together, but I might end up hating you. You're asking me to give up something I've wanted for years. Something I need. I need to be with my family again, to be home. I missed being with Lola for the last years of her life. I'm not missing out on more."

"Like I said, I get that."

Going still, I looked him dead in the eye. "Do you? Because if you did, if you truly understood how I feel, you wouldn't be telling me to change my mind. I don't know if I'll stay for good, but I want to see what life there could be like."

He grimaced and broke eye contact. "If I could go with you, I would. I'd fly back and forth so we wouldn't have to be apart for too long. But I can't. I'm under contract, Tala."

"I know. That's why I'm not asking you to do that. All I'm asking is that you respect my needs and try to make this work."

"Women throw themselves at me. People say all kinds of shit. You know this already. They'll talk about me and you, and I won't be there to smooth things over."

"So we learn to communicate more. To trust each other," I insisted. "I know it won't be easy. It scares me too. But I think you're worth it. I think this, you and me, is worth it. At the same time, I know I can't give up something that's so important to me. Please don't ask me to."

He turned quiet, pressing his lips into a firm line. "You're telling me I don't get a say in this."

"You do. Of course you do."

"But you're going to do what you want no matter what I say. Aren't you?" He shook his head. "I can't deal with this right now."

"Are you seriously going to freeze me out? Again?"

"I have a game in two days, Tala. Everyone's going to be watching me, waiting for me to fuck up. I need to get my shit together."

"Fine," I snapped. "When you have the time to deal with my complication, you know where to find me."

And I cut the call.

I didn't know how long I stood there gripping my phone. The sound of a door snicking shut cut through my heavy breaths. Glancing toward it, I found Luna watching me cautiously.

"Well, that did not sound like a happy call," she said.

"He wants me to get a tourist visa and come back to live with him. He said he'll have his lawyer figure out a way to get me a green card."

Biting her lip, Luna nodded. Then she came over and pulled me in a hug. "So what do you want to do?" she asked, her chin perched on my shoulder. "Should I tell the professor to get a refund on my flights?"

Maybe I should have said yes. My pride demanded that I not be the one to beg for Jason's attention when he had a track record of walking away from me. But my heart told me not to give up so easily. I might be setting myself up for the biggest rejection of my life, but at least I'd know I'd given it my best. If he decided to walk out of my life for good, he'd hear everything I had to say first.

Lifting my head, I met Luna's concerned gaze. "We'll push through with the plan. Even if Jason turns me down, at least we'll have the trip together."

She smiled at me. "Have I told you how proud I am to be your sister?"

"Not that I can remember." I tightened my grip around her waist.

"Well, I am. Now let's get you ready to knock some sense into your man."

40

ilahad – (v) to reveal; to offer

Jason

I walked into our temporary dining hall and sat at an empty table. My nerves were tighter than usual. Maybe it was the significance of being part of the season kickoff. As the reigning champions, we had all eyes on us. Already, the bets had started, with people speculating whether the Barons were ready to defend their trophy.

I also had a nagging thought in the back of my head that this might be my last season. Possibly. Despite the persistent rumors—especially in the wake of our video series—I hadn't made up my mind yet. My team deserved my entire focus every time I hit the court. I couldn't give them that if I already had one foot out the door.

But my brain was miles away from the game. In roughly forty-eight hours, Tala would be on a plane heading to an entirely different country, an ocean away from me. And we hadn't spoken since our argument.

I was close to saying to hell with it and just taking the

earliest flight to Sterling. Never mind that we'd be getting our championship rings tonight.

Grabbing my phone, I pulled up a flight booking app. I could catch a morning flight tomorrow, then return early the next day to travel with the team for our Friday match. I'd have to miss a day of practice, but it was still early enough in the season that it shouldn't be a huge deal. Coach would understand. Hopefully.

Fuck it. I couldn't let Tala leave without seeing her again and talking things out. If it was a lost cause, at least I would know for sure. Better than being stuck like that spinning wheel of death on her laptop.

Without letting myself think twice, I booked my flight and shot a text for my assistant to arrange a rental car. The tension in my shoulders eased. Maybe the trip wouldn't solve anything but neither would sitting on my ass and sulking.

I headed to the buffet and loaded a plate with my usual—salad with a ton of vegetables and pasta with broccoli. Nodding at my teammates, I returned to my table and systematically cleared my plate. Miles was MIA for some reason, but I welcomed the solitude. Later, all sorts of noise would blast my ears, so I soaked in the relative silence. My eyes stared through the TV as I tried to psych myself up for the night ahead.

A soft ping penetrated my mental train of thought. I checked my phone and found a notification that Tala had a new post. Her first in almost a month.

The video was shot on her rooftop, with a dusky sky in the background and the plants I'd given her in the corner of the frame. A lantern similar to the one we used to have in our garden added light to the space. In the center, Tala was barefoot, wearing beige leggings and a matching tank as she danced to a song I had never heard before, in a language I was still trying to learn.

The song was slow, like a ballad with a staggered beat and layered instruments. I couldn't understand a word that the male singer was saying, but God, did I feel it.

She moved gracefully, all outstretched limbs and sweeping gestures. Her eyes were low-lidded and filled with so much emotion, she glowed with it. Her body flowed with the music as if she had been created solely for that purpose.

I'd watched her dance countless times, but this was different. This was a side of her I'd never seen, and it entranced me completely. I fell in love with her all over again.

When the last few notes of the song faded away, she looked at the camera for the first time. Smiled. And flashed a familiar salute.

I almost staggered with an overwhelming sense of awe.

Under the video was a short two-liner:

Mahiwaga, pipiliin ka sa araw-araw. / My love, I will choose you every day.

My breath stopped on an inhale. I read it over and over again, double- and triple-checking that my eyes weren't tricking me.

"You saw it." Miles's voice came as if from a distance. "Good."

I turned toward him.

He glanced at my phone and smiled like he knew a secret. "Check her stories."

I snapped out of my haze and did just that. Her first story had a screenshot of her video with the words *Link to the lyrics and translation here* below it. I was about to click on it when I noticed her second story—a boomerang video of her and Luna jumping in front of a metal arch trellis with curling grape vines.

My eyes widened. I knew that structure well. It marked the

entrance to Santa Mila's most famous park, where tourists flocked for that iconic photo op.

"She's here?" I went back to the story, wondering if I was hallucinating.

Miles laughed and slapped my shoulder. "Call her, man."

He didn't have to tell me twice. I dialed her and requested a video call, needing to confirm she was really here.

Tala's face filled my screen. The video was blurry and the audio was noisy, but I recognized the grounds behind her. Then she smiled at me.

God, I loved her.

"Shouldn't you be in practice?" she asked without preamble.

I stared stupidly back at her. "It's our lunch break. Also, someone almost gave me a stroke."

"I thought you were made of stronger stuff than that."

My heart jammed in my throat. Shaking my head, I said, "Fuck, Tala. You're here."

"I am. I'm sorry I hung up on you."

"I'm sorry I was an ass."

It was her turn to shake her head. "Let's talk later. We came to watch you play, and we're counting on a good game."

"I'll make it good any time you want," I murmured.

Despite the poor video quality, I could see her blushing.

"My ears were so not ready for that," Luna yelled.

Miles laughed. "Hot damn, man. Didn't know you had it in you."

"Hi, Luna. Welcome to Santa Mila." I waited for her to shout back a greeting before asking Tala, "Do you have tickets?" I'd given two to Stassy and set aside the remaining pair for my mom and Phil in case they decided to watch.

Mom hadn't spoken to me since we launched our video

series. But it was ring night, one of the pinnacle moments in the NBA. Would she really miss that milestone?

"We do. Thanks again, Miles. We really appreciate it," Tala said.

My head whipped toward him.

"Stassy asked if I had spares," Miles told me. "You know I got you."

I hooked an arm around his neck. "Thank you."

He thumped my chest in response and peered into the screen. "Glad you finally showed up, Tala. Got to give my bro's right hand some rest."

I elbowed him and searched Tala's face, worried Miles's wisecracking ass had gone too far. He knew about our argument and still acted as if everything was okay.

But Tala only laughed. "No resting for you guys until after you win the game."

"J-man's not breathing at all until you're properly reunited." Miles avoided my punch and stood. "You've got to work off your aggression, bro. See you later, Tala."

"Good luck," she replied.

In the background, Luna shouted, "Kick their asses, Miles!"

Miles barked out a laugh. "Count on it." He beelined to the buffet, leaving me to talk with Tala.

"I still can't believe you're here," I said to her. "I thought you were pissed at me."

"I am. But I couldn't leave without forcing you to hear me out." Tala's brow lifted in a silent challenge.

Fuck, but I loved this woman. She fought for me as fiercely as she fought with me, and I didn't know what I did to deserve her. She brought me to my knees, and I'd happily stay on the ground if it meant she'd be with me.

"I can't wait to hear it, dance girl." Clearing my throat, I added, "I loved your post."

345

Her lips curved. "Thanks. Someone suggested I show a different side of me," she said, throwing my words back at me. "I thought it was time."

"You are amazing." Her courage gave me the kick in the ass to admit the truth. "I miss you, Tal. All I can think about is seeing you. I booked a flight to Sterling tomorrow morning."

She blinked. "I hope you can get a refund."

Of course she'd think of that. If it were up to me, I wouldn't care either way as long as I could be with her. But I knew she hated the thought of throwing away money like that. "I'll see what I can do. How long are you staying?"

"I fly out to Manila Thursday afternoon."

That gave us two days, and not enough hours together between the game tonight and practice tomorrow.

Screw it. I'd skip practice and deal with the consequences after.

"Look, we need to go grab food before Luna gets hangry," Tala said. "Meanwhile, you have a big night to prepare for."

As far as I was concerned, I already won. I didn't need the ring to feel like a champ. Not when I had her. That said, she deserved to watch a great game, so I'd give it my hundred percent.

"I'll see you after?" I asked.

"You'd better. I came all this way."

We stared at each other, and she smiled.

"See you later, Tal."

"Later, Jase," she whispered. "Go get them."

The call cut off.

I paused to center myself, a grin splitting my face. My woman was here. Now all I had to do was get my act together and win the first game of the season.

41

salubong – (n) welcome

Tala

With a minute and thirty-nine seconds on the clock, the Green Valley Archers were up by two points. The Barons led the game in the past three quarters, only for the Archers to take the lead when one of the Barons fouled out at the start of the fourth. The energy in the arena had grown to a fever pitch, with the crowd cheering on the Barons to score. Miles's and Jason's names were called out so frequently and so loudly that I wondered how they could focus.

Sitting a few feet from the court, I saw how they were completely zoned in. When their eyes weren't tracking the ball, they were bouncing from their teammates to their opponents. Their chemistry was undeniable. They seemed to know where the other person was at all times and anticipated their next move. It allowed them to pass the ball with ease, to position themselves exactly where the other needed them to be.

At that moment, Jason was guarding the Archers' power

347

forward. The guy took a step back and released the ball, only for Jason to jump up and block the shot with an open palm. With an audible whack, the ball flew halfway across the court to where Miles was waiting. Leaping up, he snatched the ball and turned to face their basket.

Luna grabbed my hand and gripped it so tightly, my fingers tingled. "Make the shot, make the shot," she chanted.

Miles planted his feet, crouched low, and shot the ball high. It arced in the air and swooshed through the net.

"Yes!" we screamed along with the majority of the crowd.

And we were tied.

Jason and Miles slapped hands, exchanging words that made them laugh. The opposite team called a timeout, and they walked to the sidelines. Jason grabbed a towel and sat on a chair. His eyes landed unerringly on me. My lips stretched in a giddy smile.

"They've got this," Nat said on my other side.

The seats beside her remained empty—the two Jason reserved for his mom and his stepdad. Vivian had skipped opening night, even though there had been a ceremony to award Jason and his team their championship rings.

The president of Santa Mila's basketball operations called out Miles and then Jason to give a short speech, and it filled me with pride to see him in the spotlight, laughing it up with his best friend. Basketball might not be his big dream, but he'd worked hard for that ring. I hurt for him that neither of his parents were there to witness it, especially since Vivian had the chance to do so.

Would she regret missing it? I would have. Witnessing Jason's milestone was worth maxing out my credit card and facing public scrutiny.

While we waited for the game to resume, I felt people watching us, as they had been since we wound our way to our third-row seats. Even the courtside cameras found us and flashed our faces on the big screens.

Maybe I should have chosen a different date to post my video, but I didn't want to let other people influence my schedule. I posted it when I had to send a message to Jason. His reaction was the only one that mattered.

The buzzer sounded, and I watched Jason jump to his feet and stride onto the court.

Forty-eight seconds remaining.

The Barons had possession of the ball, but the Archers stole it three seconds in. They drove the ball to their court, with Miles guarding the holder. He attempted the shot. It hit the rim and bounced off. Multiple hands reached out to grab it. One of the Barons claimed the ball and passed it to Miles.

Jason ran to their basket, an opponent close on his heels. Miles threw the ball straight at Jason. The opposite player leapt to intercept it but Jason tapped the ball away. Then he followed its trajectory to the right, swooping it from the air on its way down.

Nine seconds.

He bent and aimed the ball at the hoop. Shot...and scored.

I jumped onto my feet and cheered along with the crowd.

Two points up. We'd won.

Luna and I shrieked as we hugged. I couldn't remember another time when I had felt such a thrill. The crowd's energy fed into mine, and my entire body buzzed with it.

Standing on tiptoe, I searched for Jason on the court. He was sandwiched between Miles and another player—the one who'd fouled out earlier. People jockeyed to catch their attention, yet his gaze passed over them. Before Jason turned to the reporters, he gave me a quick wink.

The butterflies in my belly went into a frenzy.

Nat leaned close and whispered, "That guy has it bad."

I smiled. "The feeling is mutual."

We waited for the crowd to thin out before making our way out of the stands. Nat led me and Luna to a heavily guarded hallway where security checked our badges before letting us pass.

"Miss Reyes," one of the men said. "Jason told us to expect you. I'm Lex and I'll show you to the lounge where you can wait for him."

"Thank you, Lex." I looped my arm around Luna's and followed him.

He brought us to a large, fancy room with sofas and armchairs on one side and a buffet and dining tables on the other. There were more people than I expected—players' family members and stunning women, some of whom I'd seen on television or in print ads.

"Feel free to sit anywhere and grab some food," Lex told us. "Jason might take a few hours."

We thanked him and snagged an empty table near the back of the room. Luna took off for the buffet, but I was too keyed up to eat. Forget about butterflies—it felt like there was an entire menagerie of animals tumbling around in my stomach.

"It's not always this packed, but since it's ring night and the first game of the season, everyone's here," Nat said as she placed a cup of tea on the table and sat beside me. "There's coffee if you want." Eyeing me, she chuckled. "There's alcohol too."

"I'm fine. I'll get some water in a bit."

"Get comfortable. I don't think he'll be out for another two hours or so."

An hour and a half later, I was spreading butter on the last bite of my dinner roll when my skin prickled with awareness. Glancing toward the door, I found Jason zeroed in on me as his legs swallowed the distance between us. People called out to him, but he didn't take his attention off me.

When he stopped next to me, I rose to face him.

We stared at each other. It had been weeks of wanting to see him, and then two days of dreading his reaction when he saw me. Now that we were separated by mere inches, I stood frozen in place, incapable of speech.

His hair was damp from his shower, and he wore a striped shirt and dark gray pants with white sneakers. I took in every inch of him, feeling a sense of incredulous disbelief that he was there, close enough to touch.

"Okay, this tension is killing me," Luna blurted out.

Nat burst into laughter. "Same here, Luna." Standing, she hugged Jason and said, "Congrats, champ. You did good."

"Thanks, Stassy. For everything. I owe you big time." He patted her back and released her. He went to Luna next, hugging her also. "Hey, Lu. Glad you made it out."

"Me too. Thanks for the show out there. Lonzo is dying that we got to watch you in person."

"I'll get you guys tickets whenever you want. Just let me know."

Then he was back in front of me, his mouth curled in a smile that was mine alone. "Dance girl," he murmured. "Nice jersey."

"Luna got it for me," I answered. "Congrats on the win."

He shrugged. "It was a team effort. But also, I promised."

Neither of us made a move toward the other.

"We should get going before you two really give people something to talk about," Nat announced.

Jason's eyes flicked to my plate, where my bread lay forgotten. "You done, Tal?"

"Yes," I said.

Grabbing the piece of bread, he popped it in his mouth. "Come on."

My heart raced as he took my hand and led us through the hallway. He didn't let go once despite the people who talked to him and the phones that snapped photos of us together. Even though he was clearly eager to leave, he stopped to introduce us to teammates we came across, wrapping a protective arm around Luna as he did so.

When we finally emerged into the private parking garage filled with luxury cars, Luna was high with excitement.

"This is the best day ever," she gushed, her eyes bright.

"You can meet the rest of the team at practice tomorrow," Jason told her. "Miles and a couple of the guys got held up with the press."

"They let you skip interviews?" Nat asked.

He raised one shoulder. "I did two and begged off. I'll make it up to them next time."

"My flight's at noon," Luna said, frowning.

"No problem. We can swing by the gym on the way to the airport. I can't promise all the guys will be there, but most of them will."

"You have training tomorrow," I murmured and winced at the disappointment in my voice. I'd been so stuck on seeing him that I forgot I wouldn't have him all to myself.

He stopped walking, his hand tightening around mine. "Tal—"

"Oh, I just realized I need to go to the restroom." Nat caught Luna's elbow. "Luna, you wanted to go too, right?"

Luna's eyes widened. She nodded. "Right. Too much soda."

"We'll go and meet you back here in a bit. Ten, maybe fifteen minutes." Nat was already walking back to the tunnel with Luna in tow.

"That was weird," I said to Jason, laughing.

Then I wasn't laughing anymore because he pulled me into his arms and laid his mouth on mine.

It was like coming home.

My nerves disappeared as his warmth and strength surrounded me. He smelled of soap and tasted of mint and longing. My heart ached with love for this man.

Our kiss softened as we remembered where we were. He dropped his head beside mine and breathed deeply. "Damn it, Tal. I missed you so much."

Part of me, the prideful part, wanted to hold out on him. But the logical side of me argued that it contradicted the entire reason for me being there.

My rational brain won out. "I missed you too," I admitted.

"Come home with me tonight."

As much as I wanted to, I couldn't ditch my sister on our last night together. "Luna..."

"Where are you staying?"

"We got a hotel room near the city center."

"I'll book a suite at the Concorde so we can drop by the gym tomorrow morning. It's just one block over. We can get your things before dinner. I'm guessing you're the date that Stassy told me about?"

"Yes. You don't need to get us a suite though."

"Tal. I understand you want to spend as much time with Luna as possible," Jason said patiently. "But we need to talk, and we can't do that in a shared room. So we can either stay at my place where I have a guest room for your sister, or at a hotel suite with adjoining rooms. Your choice."

When he put it that way, the answer was obvious. "Fine," I said. "But we don't need to get the best suite."

His answer came in the way of a smirk and a raised eyebrow while he pulled out his phone and typed.

He was definitely getting the best suite.

42

mahiwaga – (adj) inexplicable

Tala

After dinner at the Concorde Hotel's restaurant, we had dessert and wine sent up to the lavish suite Jason booked. It was almost midnight when we wrapped up our celebration, and Nat returned to her room on another floor. Jason excused himself to check his emails, which I took as his way of giving me and Luna time alone together.

"I know this sounds weird, but I'm happy to see you so happy," Luna said as she polished off her wine. "Seeing you and Jason try to work things out gives me hope for myself."

The singsong tone in her voice told me she was buzzed. "Thanks, Lu. I don't know where this will go, but I want to find out. Fingers crossed that when it's your turn, things won't be as messy."

Luna harrumphed. "I highly doubt that. Most guys suck. And you know who sucks the most? Your best friend."

I laughed. "Okay, enough wine for you."

"I'm good. Great, even." A sober look fell across Luna's face and her body deflated. "I'll miss you, Ate."

"Same here." I wrapped an arm around her shoulder and nudged her hip aside so we could share her seat. "You can always text or call me, you know. Anytime, even though I might not be able to reply right away."

"I know. Is it weird that I'm also kind of excited to be alone in the apartment?"

"Not at all. If there's one thing I learned from moving here, it's that living alone can be nice. Freeing. You learn to be alright on your own and find out what you're capable of."

She hummed in agreement. Then her mouth opened in a wide yawn. "Okay, that's it for me. I need to sleep the wine off, and you need to join your basketball player. Just keep it down, will you?"

My mouth fell open. I pinched her arm and was about to deny her innuendo, but I shrugged instead. "No promises. It's been a while."

Letting out a sound that was between a laugh and a shriek, Luna tried to push me off, but I held on in a hug. "Who are you, and what have you done to my sister?" she used my past words against me.

The door to the master bedroom opened, and Jason peeked out, revealing his bare shoulders. "Everything okay?"

"Yes," we replied in unison.

He blinked at us and said, "Okay then."

Once the door was closed, Luna and I looked at each other.

"I hate you," she told me. "I'm sleeping with earplugs."

"Oh, come on. You don't need to do that." I grinned slowly. "The walls look thick enough."

She shoved me away, laughing. "Good night, Ate. See you tomorrow."

"Sweet dreams," I sang out as she walked to her room and shut the door.

Still chuckling, I headed to the master. With every step, my amusement faded and was replaced by a mounting sense of nerves and anticipation.

The moment I opened the door, Jason caught my arms and backed me up against it, pinning my hands above my head. He kissed down my throat, and I moaned as my body thrummed with excitement.

"I know we need to talk," he said hoarsely, "but I've been holding myself back all night."

He pressed against me, and I fought the temptation to wrap my legs around his waist. "Jason," I groaned with a half-hearted protest.

Dropping his forehead against mine, he exhaled. "You're right. We need to clear the air so next time I'm inside you, you'll know I'm all in. Not just for tonight or for as long as you're here. I'm in this for the long run, Tal."

The flush of arousal softened as my heart seemed to swell from his words. I stroked the stubble lining his jaw. "I'm in this too. I want to work this out."

He skimmed his palms down my arms and twined his fingers through mine, then led me to the foot of the bed. I sat in a cross-legged position, and he mirrored it so we were facing each other, my knees touching his shin. If not for the softness of the mattress, we could have been sitting on the floor of my apartment rooftop, or maybe even the grass in our garden.

"Tala." Jason captured my eyes with his earnest gaze. "I'm sorry for playing down your need to be with your family. For making it sound like our relationship's contingent on you being here. I shouldn't have disregarded how you feel and insisted you give up what you need when I can't do the same. It was selfish and entitled of me."

"Jason—"

"Please let me finish before I wuss out."

My lips twitched at the wry smile on his face, but the thread of nerves in his voice tugged at my chest. Jason always put up a confident, unbothered persona in front of others. It felt like the biggest privilege to witness him being vulnerable.

I claimed his hand and squeezed it, giving him a nod to go on.

"I knew there was something special about you since the day we met at our garden. You were so easy to be with, the one person I could talk to about my family and what I was really into. You still are," he said. "But back then, I told myself I needed to focus on what came after graduation. The truth was, I was a coward. I didn't want to pursue you because a part of me knew that if I did, that was it. I wouldn't be able to walk away from you, and I wouldn't be able to do what I had been working for all my life.

"So I told myself we were just friends. When the deadline to declare came up, I didn't talk to you about it or second-guess myself because it would have made it harder. I knew going pro meant being on the road more often than not, having tons of obligations, and being watched by so many people. I didn't want to put you through that only to fail in the end."

"Wait a minute." I held up my hand. "Sorry to interrupt, but I have to get this out."

"Go ahead."

"I get that you made a choice based on what was better for you then. But don't use your perception of my ability to handle a relationship as a reason to walk away. You can't decide what I can or cannot handle, and you can't speak for me if we haven't even had the chance to discuss the issue."

He swallowed but nodded. "I agree. It wasn't my call to make. I took the easy way out, and because of that, I lost years with you. I thought I'd learned my lesson, but I made the same mistake again."

"I've already forgiven you for what happened when we were younger. We had to grow on our own, and I don't regret how my life turned out," I reassured him. "I also understand why you left last month. I kept something important from you. Then you told me you loved me, and I disregarded it. I'm so sorry for that. I felt put on the spot. I needed to process not just with what you were feeling, but what I was too. When you left that night, I thought you needed space. But it turned out you left Sterling completely and ghosted me for the second time. It was like reliving freshman year, only it was worse because we weren't just friends anymore."

His face twisted in a grimace. "I was too caught up in my own frustration. I guess I was so used to the idea that if I put enough effort and time into something, I would get what I wanted."

"Things don't always work that way."

"I'm learning that now." Jason took a deep breath. "Tala. I didn't know it then, but I fell in love with you years ago because you saw me and you accepted me for who I was. These past months, I fell in love with you again because I saw all of you. You're beautiful on the outside, but you shine brighter because you're true to who you are. You love so deeply, and you inspire me to do the same."

My eyes welled, and as I blinked, tears slipped down my cheeks. The words felt like balm on the wounds that had festered inside me for so long.

Reaching out, he cupped my face in his hands and gently thumbed my tears away. "I'm sorry for leaving you again. For asking you to choose between me and your needs. I love you, Tala, and I won't pass up this chance to be with you, even if it means having to be without you for a while. No matter how hard it is, no matter what the odds are, I want to take this shot."

My heart hammered in my chest. "You know what that means, right? We need to trust each other and be honest with each other. Even when I'm uncomfortable and you're frustrated, or vice versa."

He huffed a breath and pressed a brief kiss to my lips. "I know, Tal. I know there'll be days when one of us is extra tired or sad, and we'll get upset and fight. Then you'll cry and I'll—"

"Why am I the one who cries in this scenario?"

His chin trembled like he was holding back laughter. "Right. Forgive me for that sexist comment. I'll cry and you'll punch your fist into the wall."

I rolled my eyes even as a chuckle burst out of me. "That sounds about right."

"My point is," he said in a determined tone, "I'll willingly go through it all for the sake of being yours. Who cares what people say about long-distance relationships? We'll show them how it's done."

A weird blend of laughter and sobbing poured out of my mouth. "Of course, you'd act like it was your idea. Also, that was over-the-top cheesy even for you."

"What can I say? I'm shameless. But you love me anyway." He feigned confidence, but I saw through it to the insecurity he kept hidden.

I wrapped my hands around his nape and leaned close. "You're right. I do love you, Jason Meyer."

It was the first time I'd ever said the words to someone outside my family, and it felt exhilarating and terrifying all at once. My admission unlocked a lifetime of possibilities, but it also gave him the power to hurt me more than anyone else could.

But wasn't that what love was? Opening yourself to the risk of pain because life without it had no reward. No meaning.

Suddenly, Jason tugged me forward, and I squeaked as we tumbled on the mattress with me on top of him. "I love you too, Tala Reyes. I feel like I've waited forever to hear you say that."

He kissed me deeply, until I felt drunk on the love and adoration he poured into my lips. Then he stroked his hands up my legs to my thighs. "Now I believe we have some celebrating to get to."

We proceeded to do that all night long.

43

araw araw - (adv) every day

Jason

Hours before the sixth game in the finals, I sat in front of my locker, staring at my jersey.

Months of training, playing, and travel boiled down to this point. We were down two to three, and the next few hours would determine the need for a game seven or if the trophy would go to the Archers. Whichever way the game went, I'd made my peace with it.

I kept my word to pour my all into the season. With every match we played, whether we won or lost, one thing grew clearer in my mind.

This was the last season I would play.

"This is it, J-man," Miles said from the chair beside mine. "You nervous?"

"More like excited."

He smirked. "She here?"

Just as I did every time I thought of Tala, I smiled. "Yeah."

I'd just been with her two days ago, but I couldn't wait to see her again. She had flown into Santa Mila for our fifth game, and I'd left the next day to travel with the team to Green Valley. After months apart, I wanted to be with her twenty-four seven.

The first few weeks had been the toughest. Not only did we have to figure out a new rhythm for our relationship, but we also got hit with rumors left and right—as expected. Despite the misunderstandings and frustrated outbursts, we pulled through to the tail end of the season. Only one, maybe two games to go, and we could make a new set of plans. One that hopefully meant being together in person more often than not.

"Good to see you happy, bro," Miles told me. "Whatever happens tonight, it's been an honor being your teammate."

I slapped the back of my hand against his chest.

He didn't even flinch.

"Don't start with me, man."

With an agreeable expression on his face, Miles tipped his chin. "I get it. You're not ready to do emotions right now. Let's win this thing, and then we'll talk."

I knocked fists with him. This time, I wasn't playing for the title. I was playing for the sheer honor of being part of this team. If this was to be my final game, I would enjoy every last second of it. No matter the outcome, I knew my dad would be watching on with pride—and so would Tala.

Tala

The Barons didn't win the championship.

Jason and his team fought hard through four quarters and two overtimes, but they lost by three points. No one could deny it had been a remarkable battle, with either team refusing to let up. Despite the crowd's disappointment, I was proud of the guys, many of whom I'd gotten to know since Jason and I officially started dating. They put on their smiles as they embraced one another and congratulated the Archers.

Out of all his teammates, Jason looked the happiest. He had a lightness about him that gratified me.

"I've never seen him like this," Mrs. Bateman said from beside me. Her red lips pursed. "So...content. Even though they lost."

I glanced at her, noting the way she stared at Jason. As usual, not a strand of hair was out of place, but there was a softness in her brow that hinted at emotion.

She and Jason hadn't fully mended their relationship, but they were working on it. The counselor that Phil suggested had already helped. Although Jason's schedule kept them from meeting often, the online sessions they attended put them on the right track.

"He played well. They all did," I replied.

"It would have been better if he won another championship. That might have made it harder for him to retire."

Nothing would have changed Jason's mind, but his mom was still learning to accept that he wanted a different path for himself than what she'd envisioned.

A loud whoop came from the court, drawing my attention back. Beyond the ongoing celebrations and commiserations, Jason and Miles had their arms around each other. Miles had his back to me and he seemed to be saying something to Jason, who wore a solemn look.

Then Jason's eyes landed on me. The creases in his forehead smoothed as a slow smile crept across his face. Just like he had that first game, he winked at me. My lips curved upward in response. His gaze lingered a second longer before shifting to his mom. He gave her a nod.

"I have to give it to you. You lasted longer than I thought you would," Mrs. Bateman told me.

From her other side, Phil chided, "Sweetheart..."

"Oh, don't give me that tone. It was a compliment." A second later, she sighed. "I meant it was an observation."

Not something I wanted to hear from the mom of the man I was in love with, but at least we'd sat through the entire game without incident. I considered that a major win.

"It's fine," I said. "Sometimes, I'm surprised by it too."

"I'm glad. You make him happy." Mrs. Bateman's words stunned me into silence. They were only loud enough for me to hear, and she didn't look away from the court. Still, it gave me hope that one day she might warm up to me.

"Thank you. He makes me happy too."

And it was true. I looked forward to our phone calls every day and kept a countdown for the rare times we got to see each other in person.

Our long-distance relationship had been even more challenging than I expected. It demanded sacrifice, patience, understanding, and a whole lot of trust. I had to battle my insecurities and nearly broke down multiple times. My parents became my pillars, talking me through the worst of my anxieties when the time difference meant I couldn't reach Jason. They understood what I was going through, having been separated for a decade themselves.

Now that Jason and I were in the same place and time

zone, I knew that every choice and outcome was worth it. Because now, we could finally create a future where we could be together.

———

ONE WEEK LATER, Jason announced his retirement from the NBA in order to pursue a new role.

That of being an environmental crusader.

"I wonder if I should call you Captain Planet now," I told him.

In addition to signing up for his master's degree in sustainability, Jason was launching a solo podcast and vlog that focused on environmental education. He and Miles continued recording 'Beyond the Hoop,' but it had turned into a monthly series since they both had their hands full.

Jason and I sat together in our old garden—the one I had just learned now belonged to him. That gardener we met during my last visit? It turned out Jason's assistant had hired him to bring new life to the space.

"Don't start," Jason said, pausing from kissing his favorite spot in the crook of my neck. "Blue does not suit my skin tone."

That was a blatant lie, but I went with it. "You're right. Green fits you better. I told you, you should have used 'Green-Minded' for your podcast title." I snickered. He'd been all for the suggestion until I confessed that it was a term we Filipinos used to describe someone who added a sexual spin to the most innocent things.

Raising his brow, he asked drily, "And risk having *Pinoys* think I have a dirty mind? I'll pass."

He ruined the sentiment by slipping a hand under my waistband.

"I don't think you're proving your point here," I said with a breathless laugh.

"I'm proving us both right. I *am* the captain of your planet... and you're the only woman my mind goes dirty for."

I groaned. "That's the cheesiest thing you've ever said to me. And you've said a *lot*."

"You love me anyway."

He was right; I did.

A month later, Jason launched 'Real Green Minded.' He received plenty of comments from Filipinos poking fun at his title, but he said they didn't bother him at all.

Epilogue

tadhana – (n) fate

Jason

Slouching into the shadows, I tried to make myself as unobtrusive as possible—to no avail. I'd only been in Manila for three hours, with most of that time spent in traffic. My arrival garnered more attention than I wanted. It was hard to stay incognito when I towered over almost everyone around me. Thankfully, Tala had been busy with back-to-back dance classes since this morning. If luck was on my side, the news wouldn't have reached her yet.

It only took a few seconds for one of the dancers to spot me in the wall of mirrors. The girl stopped mid-step, causing the person to her left to bump into her.

The guy snapped in Filipino, "*Ano ba!*"

From my self-study, I translated that to the effect of, "What the hell."

"*Si* Jason Meyer!" the girl said to the annoyed guy.

Heads instantly turned in my direction. I paid no attention to them, my eyes fixed on Tala's startled face in the mirror.

I grinned at her, even though I worried she'd be upset by my surprise visit. Maybe I shouldn't have snuck in, but I couldn't resist the opportunity to watch her in action without her knowing.

When she first started teaching at the local dance studio, people attended her classes only to get her autograph and see if she could hook them up with me. I'd asked if it bothered her, and she admitted that it initially did. Then she realized it didn't matter why they came as long as they stayed because they loved to dance.

Many of them did. The buzz became less about Tala being my girlfriend and more about the energy she brought to the dance scene. She still created videos and worked with various brands. On top of that, she posted dance tutorials for those who wanted to learn from the comfort of their own homes.

To say that I was proud of her was an understatement. She was a fucking superstar.

My superstar.

"Okay, okay," Tala raised her voice over the excited chatter. "Let's take a ten-minute break."

A guy called out, "Can you ask your boyfriend to give us autographs?"

"And photos," the girl who'd first seen me added.

Tala laughed. "Let me talk to him, and we'll see."

The fact that they did what she said showed she'd gained their respect. Some lingered, outright staring, but they left me alone.

It didn't escape my notice that a couple of those eyes were trained on Tala instead of me. Not that I blamed them. She radiated joy that came from doing what she loved. And maybe I was assuming too much, but I liked to think part of that was from me being there too.

As Tala drew closer to me, I straightened and shoved my

hands in my pockets to keep from reaching out for her. She tilted her head, indicating I should follow her to the hallway on the right, and led me to a small door marked 'Staff Only.' Opening it, she let me in.

I hardly had a moment to close the door before she was wrapped around me, her lips pressing against mine.

It had been two weeks since I last brought her to the airport, and it had been way too long. I wasn't supposed to fly in for another week, but I had the best motivation to wrap up everything I needed to finish in record time.

I met her kisses with equal fervor, supporting her weight with one hand while the other tangled in her bun. Fuck, did I miss her.

As abruptly as the kiss started, it gentled into sweet, lingering brushes.

"Did we use up the whole ten minutes already?" Tala murmured, her eyelids fluttering open.

"You should have said thirty."

She laughed. "Our class is only an hour long. Ten minutes was pushing it."

"I'll make up for it with autographs and selfies."

"Someone thinks highly of himself," she said, curling her lip.

"I got the girl, didn't I?"

Her response came in the form of an exaggerated eye roll.

We smiled at each other for a few quiet minutes, enjoying the comfort of finally being together. Tala was heaven and home wrapped up in one person. I never wanted to be apart from her again.

She moved one hand up my neck to stroke along my jaw. "You didn't tell me you moved your flight. I would have picked you up at the airport."

"It was supposed to be a surprise."

"You liked to spy on me dancing from the start."

I laughed as I realized the meaning behind her words. "You were the one trespassing in my garden."

"It wasn't yours then."

Technically, it wasn't mine now either. I'd donated it to Home of Hope, the nonprofit that Miles and I co-founded. We had converted the property into a place where kids could explore their interests in a safe and fun way, whether it was sports, sciences, or the arts. Of course, the garden lived on, and we'd expanded it to include an area where kids could learn about growing fruits and vegetables and composting.

We dedicated the center to my dad, the first person who encouraged me to dream.

"Next time we're in Sterling, you need to teach dance lessons there," I told her.

"Only if you do the waggle dance with me." Grinning, she wiggled her eyebrows. Then they pulled together. "What do you mean we? You'll be back there in September."

I shook my head and gave her my second surprise. "Guess who qualified for distance learning?"

She gasped. "Seriously?"

"I need to come in a few times, including the first two weeks of class. But for the most part..."

"You're moving here?" She bounced on her tiptoes.

I chuckled. "As long as my girlfriend is here. I have to convince her to stick it out with me for good."

"Ahh." Her cheeks flushed as they did whenever I said something particularly sappy. "Is that part of your agenda here?"

"You know it. What do you say to that, dance girl?" I ran my palms up her sides.

"I say bring it on, science guy." She paused. "Did you get to see Luna before you left?"

"Of course. I visited her after I wrapped up my meetings with Rob and closed down the house. Left her a copy of the keys just in case."

"Good idea."

"Why'd you ask?"

"I just realized now that you're staying here, Gabe's the only one who can look after her." The notch between her eyebrows deepened.

I bent my head to soothe it with my lips. "They seemed to be on better terms the last time we saw them together."

"Yeah, but you know she's always had a thing for him. I just wonder..."

"Tal. Stay out of it," I warned her. "Whatever happens between the two of them is their business."

"I know. But—"

"Nope. No buts. Go finish your class. The sooner you do, the sooner we can get through the autographs. And then I can get you alone."

"Someone's impatient." She grinned up at me, and I saw my entire future in her eyes.

"I'd say I've been more than patient. So if you want to finish your class, you better get moving before I lock you down."

"I'm going, I'm going!"

It took us an hour to leave the studio. Another one to get to her house.

I didn't mind, and I was sure she didn't either. We'd survived longer periods of waiting on our own. Now that we were together? No sweat.

As we walked hand in hand to her front door, Tala chuckled.

I glanced down at her and asked, "What's going on in that head of yours?"

"Just wondering how we ended up here. Freshman me

would never have imagined introducing you to my parents. In my home too. What are the chances?"

"Probably close to nil," I agreed, raising her hand for a kiss. "But hey. I've always lucked out with those odds."

The End.

Thank You

Thank you for reading *The Off-Chance of Me and You*! I hope you enjoyed Tala and Jason's story and that you'll stick around for book two in the Reyes Siblings series.

If you liked this novel, please consider leaving a review on Amazon or Goodreads—and share the word with your friends. This will help other readers discover this book too.

For access to bonus content, book updates, and more, subscribe to my mailing list at anjmiranda.com/newsletter/.

Acknowledgments

This book has been a long time coming. It's taken the form of different stories over the years, and I'm so blessed to have had my family's love and support to lean on through it all. I couldn't be more grateful to them.

To my parents, who introduced me to the joys of reading. Thank you for encouraging me to be my own person and to pursue my own path. More than that, thank you for teaching me the meaning of *home* and *family*.

To my siblings, who helped me through various parts of this process. Thank you for cheering me on and for partially inspiring the sibling dynamics in this series. Special thanks to Kuya for making my cover shine.

To my husband, the science geek and NBA lover who inspired Jason. Thank you for believing in me, talking me down numerous cliffs, and backing me up every step of the way. You are my go-to person and my safe space, and I'm so lucky to do life with you.

To my friends, who were patient with me while I locked myself in my writing cave. Thanks for being there and rooting for me.

Thank you also to everyone who helped me turn my draft into a real book—

My editor Jennia, for going over and beyond. Your edits, insights, and advice made this publishing journey a little less daunting;

My cover artist Aya, for accommodating my requests and bringing my dream Tala and Jason to the page;

My beta reader Jen, for your valuable feedback and suggestions—thanks to you, there's no *undulating* here;

And the folks on Reddit, for the treasure trove of tips on self-publishing and writing romance novels.

Lastly, thank YOU for taking a chance on this debut author. You've helped make this girl's dreams come true.

About the Author

Anj Miranda writes contemporary romance novels with heartwarming relationships and a dose of heat. Her books explore the journeys of flawed but strong characters striving for their happily ever afters.

Even more than writing, Anj loves to read and travel. Since she can't just beam herself to a new destination, she counts on stories to give her that thrill.

Anj lives in Metro Manila, Philippines, where you'll find her tucked away with her laptop and a signature iced coffee.

For more information, visit www.anjmiranda.com or follow Anj on Instagram (@authoranjmiranda).

Made in the USA
Las Vegas, NV
26 October 2023

79738160R00225